"It is hard to say how much I loved t[...]
short blurb. Fascinating... The wor[...]
coasts, monasteries, gardens, and the cou[...]
as are the people from monarchs to serving maids."
—Stephanie Cowell, author of *Claude & Camille*

"Out of the shadows of history, Sandra Worth has crafted a fascinating, vivid tale of a woman whose courageous love for her husband plunged her into the tumult and deception of early Tudor England."
—C. W. Gortner, author of *The Confessions of Catherine de Medici*

PRAISE FOR

The King's Daughter

Romantic Times *Reviewer's Choice Award*
for Best Historical Biography of the Year

"Meticulously researched, exquisitely written; here is a rich, magnificent novel of the Tudor court evoking a once forgotten queen, now impossible to forget." —Michelle Moran, author of *Nefertiti*

"A sumptuously detailed picture of royal life."
—*Knoxville News Sentinel*

"Worth vividly brings one of England's lesser-known queens to life in this luminous portrait of 'Elizabeth the Good'... An impressive feat." —*Publishers Weekly*

"A banquet of simply luscious and delicious history."
—*Romantic Times* (4½ stars, Top Pick)

continued . . .

BERKLEY TITLES BY SANDRA WORTH

Lady of the Roses
The King's Daughter
Pale Rose of England

Pale Rose
of England

SANDRA WORTH

BERKLEY BOOKS, NEW YORK

THE BERKLEY PUBLISHING GROUP
Published by the Penguin Group
Penguin Group (USA) Inc.
375 Hudson Street, New York, New York 10014, USA
Penguin Group (Canada), 90 Eglinton Avenue East, Suite 700, Toronto, Ontario M4P 2Y3, Canada
(a division of Pearson Penguin Canada Inc.)
Penguin Books Ltd., 80 Strand, London WC2R 0RL, England
Penguin Group Ireland, 25 St. Stephen's Green, Dublin 2, Ireland (a division of Penguin Books Ltd.)
Penguin Group (Australia), 250 Camberwell Road, Camberwell, Victoria 3124, Australia
(a division of Pearson Australia Group Pty. Ltd.)
Penguin Books India Pvt. Ltd., 11 Community Centre, Panchsheel Park, New Delhi—110 017, India
Penguin Group (NZ), 67 Apollo Drive, Rosedale, North Shore 0632, New Zealand
(a division of Pearson New Zealand Ltd.)
Penguin Books (South Africa) (Pty.) Ltd., 24 Sturdee Avenue, Rosebank, Johannesburg 2196,
South Africa

Penguin Books Ltd., Registered Offices: 80 Strand, London WC2R 0RL, England

This book is an original publication of The Berkley Publishing Group.

This is a work of fiction. Names, characters, places, and incidents either are the product of the author's imagination or are used fictitiously, and any resemblance to actual persons, living or dead, business establishments, events, or locales is entirely coincidental. The publisher does not have any control over and does not assume any responsibility for author or third-party websites or their content.

FIRST EDITION: February 2011

Library of Congress Cataloging-in-Publication Data

Worth, Sandra.
    Pale rose of England / Sandra Worth. — 1st ed.
        p. cm.
    ISBN 978-0-425-23877-6
    1. Warbeck, Perkin, 1474–1499—Fiction. 2. Gordon, Catherine, Lady, d. 1537—Fiction.
3. Henry VIII, King of England, 1491–1547—Fiction. 4. Pretenders to the throne—Fiction.
5. Impostors and imposture—Fiction. 6. Triangles (Interpersonal relations)—Fiction. 7. Great
Britain—History—Henry VII, 1485–1509—Fiction. I. Title.
    PS3623.O775P35   2011
    813'.6—dc22

                                                                                2010038252

PRINTED IN THE UNITED STATES OF AMERICA

10   9   8   7   6   5   4   3   2   1

For Bridget and Alexander

Acknowledgments

I wish to thank medievalist Jean Truax, Ph.D., for her invaluable comments, guidance, and support throughout the writing of this book and for contributing freely of her time not only to read the full manuscript, but to provide generous assistance with research, all while under deadline for an academic book of her own. My thanks also go to the owners of Lady Catherine Gordon's manor house, who very kindly permitted me to view their lovely private estate. At their own request, they remain anonymous. To Kay Chandler, owner of the historic White Hart Pub in Fyfield that was in Lady Catherine's time the chantry referred to in this novel, I extend my sincere appreciation for her instrumental role in providing access to St. Nicholas Church, where Lady Catherine is buried. No acknowledgment would be complete without mention of the contribution of my good friend Mary Tilley, who accompanied me on my research trip to Cornwall, and helped get me back to the United States when I broke my ankle in Southampton. To scholar Wendy Moorhen, I owe a special indebtedness. Not only did Ms. Moorhen arrange my visit to Lady Catherine's house and pick me up and drop me off at Heathrow, making a twenty-four-hour turnaround in a tight schedule possible, but it is on her research that I relied in main. Previous to Anne Wroe's book on Lady Catherine's husband, the so-called "Perkin Warbeck," Ms. Moorhen's four in-depth articles on Lady Catherine's life constituted the sole comprehensive study available on this fascinating medieval princess. Her affection for Lady Catherine was contagious, and in her knowledge I found inspiration.

At dusk the hunter took his prey,
The lark his freedom never.
All birds and men are sure to die
But songs may live forever.

—KEN FOLLETT, *THE PILLARS OF THE EARTH*

THE ROYAL HOUSES OF ENGLAND AND SCOTLAND

(Broken lines denote missing generations. For simplification, Catherine is shown as firstborn and Edward IV's children are not in birth order.)

EDWARD III

Edward, The Black Prince

RICHARD II

Lionel, Duke of Clarence

John, Duke of Lancaster   *m.*   Katherine Swynford (3)

Richard Plantagenet, Duke of York, *d. 1460*

Margaret Beaufort *m.* Edmund Tudor

HENRY VII

EDWARD IV   *m.*   Elizabeth Woodville

Margaret, Duchess of Burgundy

RICHARD III *d. 1485*

ELIZABETH   *m.*

Cecily *m.* Roger Scrope (1); John, Viscount Welles (2); Thomas Kymbe (3)
Ann *m.* Thomas Howard, Duke of Norfolk
Katherine *m.* William Courtenay, Earl of Devon
Bridget
EDWARD V, Prince in the Tower
Richard, Duke of York (1), Prince in the Tower

Catherine Gordon   *m.*

Richard Plantagenet *a. k. a. Richard Perkin*

James Strangeways (2)
Sir Matthew Craddock (3)
Christopher Ashton (4)

Robert Bruce, Lord of Annandale

ROBERT THE BRUCE *d. 1329*   —   Mary Bruce

Elizabeth Dunbar (1)
Annabella Stewart (2)   *m.*   George Gordon, Earl of Huntly
Elizabeth Hay (3)

JAMES IV

Alexander, Earl of Huntly

William of Shivas

James of Letterfoire, Admiral of the Fleet

Margaret   (and others)   *m.*   Patrick Hepburn, Earl of Bothwell

Prologue

CORNWALL, ENGLAND, SEPTEMBER 25, 1497

Pain washed over Catherine in waves of unrelenting agony. She heard herself moan. Where was she, and where was she going, she wanted to ask, but only dull cries issued from her lips. She tried to open her eyes, but her lids felt like stones.

"Bury—" voices whispered. "Bury—make haste to bury—make haste—"

Was she dead? Would they bury her while she still breathed, or did she merely imagine that she lived? *Help me—save me—Almighty Lord of Heaven! Forgive me my transgressions—*

Muffled sobbing came to her, then faded away. She grew aware of the soft chanting of monks. Their song lent her solace, for she knew that wherever she was, it could not be Hell.

"She is full of beauty, even now, even like this," someone said.

"She has the beauty o' an angel, though her hair be black as raven's feathers." Another voice. "God have mercy on her."

"Of late, 'tis of a pale rose that she makes me think," a man said sadly. "A pale rose, in a bitter winter's wind . . ."

The murmurs died away, and the chanting grew louder. Catherine felt raindrops caress her brow. The spasms in her belly faded. Blissful oblivion engulfed her, and she drifted away into the darkness.

When she opened her eyes, a blur of shadows, flames, and arches filled her vision. Church bells chimed the quarter hour, and somewhere a shutter creaked on a hinge as it banged in the wind. A sudden pain made her cry out. She tried to rise and fell back on a rough mattress. A gentle hand settled on her shoulder.

"Nay, child, do not exert yourself," a voice said. "You are very weak. What you need is rest." A white wimple framed the wrinkled face, and a large wooden crucifix hung across her black robes.

A nun, thought Catherine. "Where am I?" she whispered. Words required effort, and the nun had to lean close to hear.

"St. Buryan Church, my child. You are safe, for it has the privilege of sanctuary that the Mount does not."

"Sanctuary?" Catherine managed. Why did she need sanctuary? She grasped the nun's hand when another spasm seized her, and tried to lift her head.

"You must not strain yourself. 'Tis too early for the babe to come."

The babe. How could she have forgotten? She dropped back heavily. Church bells began to toll for compline, stirring a vague memory. All at once her mind cleared. "Where is my son?" she cried in a panic, clutching the nun's sleeve. "Where is my bairn—my Dickon—"

"Fret not, he is safe. Your ladies keep watch over him."

"I want to see him—I need to see him!"

"He shall be brought to you."

"What of my lord husband? Has he sent tidings?"

The nun averted her gaze. "All in good time, my child." She smoothed the girl's hair back from her brow.

"Is he—did he—" She couldn't finish the dread thought.

"We know nothing. Nothing for sure. Yet."

"Why am I here, Sister?" Catherine gasped.

"Your lord husband requested that you—" The nun broke off. "He requested that you be transferred here from St. Michael's

Mount—" Again that hesitation. Softly, she added, "In case matters do not go as hoped."

Even in her condition, Catherine knew that she was not hearing the full truth. She turned her mind back to St. Michael's Mount.

St. Michael's Mount.

She closed her eyes.

PART I

September 7th, 1495–
November 23rd, 1499

Chapter 1

Twilight on the Mount

"St. Michael's Mount," Richard said in awe, his arm around Catherine's shoulders as they stood together on the deck of his ship, the *Cuckoo,* huddled beneath his cloak. The wind blew in their faces, whipping his golden curls and her black hair. Above their heads, the banner of the White Rose of York beat wildly.

Catherine followed his gaze to the silhouette of the monastery-fortress rising up from the silvery sea, dark against a narrow crack of gold left by the setting sun. Behind the rocky outcrop curved a strip of land, as if in a protective embrace. The salt taste of the ocean on her lips seemed like wine to her, for Richard's joy at returning to his fatherland banished her unease. She looked up at her husband's shining face and laid her hand over his as it rested on her shoulder. Across the distance, the faint chime of abbey bells reached her ears.

"St. Michael's Mount is a-bidding us welcome," she said in the lilting Scottish brogue of her native land.

Richard brushed her brow with his lips.

She threw him a loving glance, nestling in his warmth. "Our babe shall be born here. In England. Your land. The land of your fathers."

The sun had sunk beneath the horizon and St. Michael's Mount was bathed in shades of purple when they drew into the harbor. The families that lived at the foot of the hill had gathered to give them warm welcome with cheering and applause. As soon as they dropped anchor, the men leapt to help them disembark. Richard assisted Catherine from the ship while his men-at-arms sorted out their weapons on the dock and her ladies supervised the arrangement of their belongings on the mules. A groom brought a donkey, and Richard gently helped Catherine onto its back. Catherine's kinswoman and lady-in-waiting, Alice Hay, took their babe and walked beside them. Little Dickon had already been fed his supper and, thickly swaddled against the wind, had fallen into a sound sleep in his nurse's arms. Catherine's lips lifted tenderly as her gaze touched on her child's sweet form.

Ponderously, by torchlight, they ascended the hundreds of steps hewn into the rock that led to the fortress on the Mount, Richard on foot leading Catherine's mule. Behind them trudged their men, their breastplates and pikes glinting in the fading light of day. They had arrived at vespers and the chant of monks floated down from above, bathing them with comfort in the gathering gloom. Massive stones and uneven rocks made the steep climb long and arduous, and the higher they moved, the more ferocious the wind became, but Catherine was oblivious to the hardship. Her gaze was riveted on the view of the sea that unfurled around them, reminding her of an expanse of beautiful silver taffeta waving in welcome. Slowly, she became aware that the monk-song had died away and silence had descended over the fortress. The summit was within reach.

With his silver crucifix gleaming on his chest, the prior waited to receive them by the church steps, much joy in his heart. Beside him stood his little group of four black-clad Benedictines, for the Mount had suffered many setbacks under the House of Lancaster and these few were all it could support. But the abbot was not thinking of his troubles with the Lancastrian King Henry VII now, or even of God; he was thinking that never in his life had he beheld two such beautiful young people with such grace of deportment, one golden as the fields of wheat in summertime; the other with hair that shone like moonlight around large, black-fringed azure eyes.

Richard lifted Catherine from her mount, and they came before him. "In the name of Christ our Lord, we welcome Your Grace, Catherine, Duchess of York, and Your Grace, Richard, Duke of York, true King of England . . ."

The young couple bowed their heads to receive his blessing, and he made the sign of the cross over them. Accompanied by a novice, he led them across the courtyard, up the steps past the Lady Chapel, and through an arched entry into a distant wing of the abbey where stone steps led down again. The novice pulled open a heavy nail-studded door and they passed through a vestibule into a curved tower. Three lovely chambers fanned out before them. Each was crowned with wood beams on the ceiling and had windows to the darkening sea with seats carved into the walls for viewing. Coffers serving as bedside tables were set with ewers and basins, and candles that flickered in welcome.

"These will be your quarters while you are our guests," the prior said, unable to take his eyes from Catherine's face. Wondrous fair with chiseled features, milky smooth skin, and a rose blush along the cheekbones, she had a beautiful smile and teeth as perfect as a set of lustrous pearls. He forced himself to look away. "Your men are lodged farther down the hill, my lord, but there is room here for the royal princeling and the duchess's attendants, Your Grace." He turned to Catherine again, welcoming the chance to gaze at her once more.

"Thank you, Prior John," Catherine replied. "After the cramped quarters aboard ship, this space is most welcome."

"Ah, indeed, indeed . . ." Prior John collected his thoughts and addressed Richard. "We observe the vow of silence at the Mount, and our dinner hour is past, but this being a special occasion, I would be gladdened to partake a cup of wine with you as you sup, Your Grace."

"We shall be delighted, Prior John," Richard said.

The rooms filled with bustle and commotion as Catherine's two ladies went to work settling in. Agatha picked up a ewer and poured water into a basin, and Catherine proceeded to wash, cringing with each icy dab. All the while, her gaze barely left Alice, who carried Dickon into the next room and laid him in his cot. She stood patiently as Agatha freshened the folds and embroidered hem of her tawny sea gown, straightened the flared sleeves of her square-cut bodice, and adjusted her low belt over her hips, but as soon as Agatha had secured her velvet headband and veil over her bound hair, Catherine tiptoed to her babe's side and laid a kiss on his cheek. She arranged his blanket over him with a tender touch, careful not to awaken him before she left for dinner.

Outside, night was enfolding the world and the wind howled. Giant torches burned in the stone sconces set atop the walkways and their flames danced in the gusty wind. They filed into the chapel, their footsteps whispering reverently against the stone floor, and knelt before the gray marble of the reliquary of the Virgin's milk. Catherine prayed for Richard's success in winning back his father's throne, but even more fervently she begged the Virgin for his safety, and the safety of her wee son, and her babe yet to be born, now five months in the womb. She lit a candle for her mother's soul and murmured prayers for her father, her four brothers and six sisters, and a special one for her favorite siblings, William and Margaret, left behind in Scotland. She concluded her prayers and made the sign of the cross. Taking Richard's hand, she left for the refectory, passing Agatha, who remained at her devotions.

The monks' dining room was a beautiful chamber with windows along two walls. Though sparsely furnished with a long table, benches, and a few chairs, Catherine thought it radiated warmth and welcome. A great fire burned in the small hearth at one end, and from a large copper cook pot emanated the delicious aroma of vegetables and spices that sent her stomach growling with appetite. Beyond the glass, the sea was drenched in the blackness of night, yet the candles that were reflected in the panes cast a warm glow over the darkness outside.

They gave their cloaks over to the novice and took a seat at the rough-hewn table that was already spread out with thick crusty bread and pewter dishes. A monk stirred the soup, and the novice brought them wine from an earthen flask before moving about the room to complete the final preparations for dinner.

"I pray your journey was not overly strenuous, my lord," Prior John said when he joined them.

"I fear it was difficult, Father," Richard said, toying with his mug. "Almost as soon as we left Scotland, we encountered a storm and were forced to take shelter in Ireland. We expected to meet Sir James Ormond while in Cork. As you may know, he is—was—one of our staunchest supporters. But on our arrival there, we learned that he had been murdered."

A silence fell. The prior leaned close and said, "Murder, terror, Byzantine torture—'tis all we've known since the bastard Tudor seized the throne." He kept his voice low, by force of habit. "He has spies everywhere. One cannot be too careful, even here, in this bastion of the House of York."

Richard nodded. "King James and I always spoke in whispers, yet it seemed to us that Henry knew our plans even before we knew them ourselves."

"How was your reception in Ireland?"

"Waterford was hostile, but the people of Cork welcomed us— some for affection, others because they desired change. Tell me about England. How do they feel about us here in the south?"

"Without exception, the Tudor is hated. All he has brought us is fear and taxes. We pray daily for the restoration of your royal father's line. When you leave here to march against the Tudor, you'll see the truth of what I say. All Cornwall will rise up to join you."

"The Cornishmen were cruelly punished for their revolt in June. Dare they rebel again?"

"Their defeat at Black Heath came at heavy cost, aye, but we are a stubborn lot. And you are made in your royal father's image, God assoil his noble soul. They will flock to your banner."

"In the north, they ran from me." Richard's tone was soft, almost a confession, and his gaze was averted. Catherine's heart ached for him. She reached beneath the table and placed a gentle hand on his knee.

"If the Tudor is so hated, why did they not join me against him, Father?" he asked, voicing the question that had tormented him since the failure of his northern invasion.

"You came with Scotsmen. We hate the Scots more than we hate even Tudor, but King James did not consider that."

"James was angry that my people spurned me. He punished them for it. I could not stop him—"

Catherine bit her lip, remembering Richard as he had looked when he'd returned from the invasion. From her high bower she'd seen him gallop up the steep slope of Stirling Castle in the rain with his few men. Flinging himself from the saddle, he'd disappeared into the tower and, moments later, burst into her chamber, disheveled, a look of such anguish on his face that her ladies fled as she and Richard stood and gazed on one another. Someone shut the door and Richard threw himself into a chair. He covered his face with his hands.

"What has happened?" she cried. "Dear God, why are you back so soon? Where is my cousin? Where is the king—tell me James is not dead!"

Richard did not reply. She knelt before him. He dropped his hands and met her eyes. "James is in England, butchering my people."

"I don't understand."

"The invasion failed. They did not rise up for me. He grew angry and gave the order to slay the men and rape the women—he cut them down like animals. He burned their homes. I could not stop him—it was terrible—terrible, Catherine—"

When she finally learned the full narrative of what had happened on that fearful day, she knew Richard was no longer welcome in Scotland. He had to leave, and there was nowhere left to go, except to England to win back his throne. But Richard had been consumed with doubts after the invasion, and it was left to Catherine to persuade him otherwise.

"Never mind what happened! You have the makings of a great

king, Richard, for you have a good heart and know what it is to suffer," she said. "And make no mistake about it—your people are suffering under that tyrant. Only you can save them—England needs you, Richard!"

The thud of boots broke into Catherine's thoughts and the memories fled. She composed herself and lifted her gaze to Richard's retinue filing into the refectory. They were led by the old mayor of Cork, silver-haired John O'Water, who had been loyal to King Richard III and the House of York through its many battles for the throne. Almost at the same moment, Agatha and Alice, relieved of her babysitting duty by a monk, entered from the opposite passageway. Amid a crosscurrent of greetings, everyone distributed themselves around the table. Catherine gazed at them, their wee group from the *Cuckoo*, and the thought struck her hard that their band of supporters had thinned woefully.

They had been left with only a single ship after their little fleet was scattered by the storm off the coast of Ireland, and they did not know where the others had gone, or if they had even survived. Richard had hoped for good tidings, but so far they'd had no word, not even at Land's End, where he had briefly disembarked to inquire about the rest of his party and set up his standard. He had been welcomed by the Cornishmen, and promises had been made, but his only true hope lay in the men of southern England rising up for him in great numbers to provide him with the army he so desperately needed.

Catherine had not worried about his prospects until recently. So certain had she been all along that the righteousness of his purpose would bring triumph in the end that nothing had shaken her faith until the storm at sea had nearly claimed their lives—and even more important, the life of her precious son. So far she'd managed to keep her thoughts to herself. Richard had enough doubts of his own and needed all the reassurance she could offer, for much had gone against them since they'd set sail from the Scottish port of Ayr.

He will prevail, Catherine told herself. She had to believe that as strongly as she ever did—for everything in the world depended on it now. Around the table, the small party bowed their heads and the prior said grace. Then they spread their napkins, broke bread, and smiled at one another.

*   *   *

Catherine closed her eyes. Though she was weary from the day's hard journey, she had trouble falling asleep. Waves pounded the rocks and the wind howled, reminding her of the tempest that almost sank their ship. The water had not been calm and silver then, but an angry white and frothing like milk. Memory carried her aboard the *Cuckoo*, and once more she stood peering through the open hatch. Drenched to the skin, his hair matted to his head, Richard shouted to her through the heavy rain, the thunderous roar of the surging sea almost drowning his words, "Go back, go back! Go—'tis not safe here—" In the cabin belowdecks, lashed to her bunk, she clung to her babe and gritted her teeth so that she would not cry out in terror as the vessel groaned, shuddered, and lurched, sending the bow headlong into the depth of the ocean in one breath, and lifting it up to the sky in the next. Men ran hither and thither overhead, and the creaking of boards and the clamor of their voices mingled together as if in a chorus drawn from Hell. She felt nauseous and dizzy; her stomach churned and she wanted to vomit. Coffers skidded back and forth across the plank floor and horn lanterns suspended from a beam in the ceiling swung wildly. Candles sputtered and went out, plunging the cabin into darkness. She heard Alice and Agatha weeping and moaning in prayer. *Holy Mother of God, take not my babe this night—save us, dear Virgin!* she pleaded silently as Dickon screamed in her arms. *Let my babe live! Let him not die—*

A hideous groan rumbled through the vessel and the ship shuddered violently. From above came the pounding of feet and the frantic shouts of men, "Save yourself! All is lost!" A fierce growling sound ripped through the cabin, then a hissing sound. The lumber was splintering, giving way—dear God, water was crashing through the hull! Water was everywhere; blackness was everywhere! She couldn't breathe, couldn't see—and Dickon was gone—

Catherine bolted upright in bed, panting in terror.

Richard was asleep at her side. The monks were chanting their matins and the waves were crashing against the rocks. She had been dreaming. Relief swept her. Dimly, she wondered why the ship had broken apart in her dream, for if it had, they would not be here now. One thing for certain: it was a miracle they had survived. She sent a prayer of thanks heavenward.

A cold, fresh breeze wafted through the window cracked open for air.

She glanced at Richard. She could just make out his face in the shadows: the thick golden locks, smooth brow, and square jaw with its cleft chin. She let her gaze caress his mouth, bowed with humor even at rest, and linger on the cleft chin she so loved. If he had a physical flaw at all, it was in the dullness of his left eye, which was set lower than the right and had a droop in the crease of the upper lid. But this was the stamp of Plantagenet royalty. Two of his forefathers, Henry III and Edward I, had both borne the same mark.

Richard's breathing was deep and even. That was good, for too often he slept fitfully and was awakened by evil dreams. She laid her hand lightly on his heart and its steady rhythm brought her as much comfort as the matins being sung to heaven in St. Michael's Church across the court. She raised up on her elbow and gazed outside. The moon hung like a silver ball in the sky and the sea stretched to the horizon with the uncanny radiance that only moonlight could lend. She thought of Loch Lomond, where she and Richard had spent the honey-sweet early days of their marriage, enfolded by ineffable joy and untouched by the cares that were soon to descend on them. Even then she had known enough to see time as her enemy, and to resent each grain of sand that seeped through their precious hourglass.

Her husband's peaceful form brought a smile to her face. She had loved Richard from the moment she first beheld him, and later she learned he'd done the same with her. So much had happened to them since that blessed day that she could scarcely believe it was a mere twenty-two months ago. In this short space they had met and married; she had borne one child, and now she carried another. She had shared with her husband the hope of success in claiming the throne rightly his, and had drunk with him the bitter cup of disappointment. Convinced that failure in the north would be erased by victory in the south, she had urged him onward when he'd wished to give up his dream. Then, abandoning kith and kin, she had sailed away with him through storms and disasters until they reached England.

Whenever she looked back, it almost seemed that time had altered its nature at the instant they met on that blessed day, the twenty-third of November in the year 1495, two days before her eighteenth birthday on the Feast of Saint Catherine. Striking from heaven like a bolt of lightning, it had borne her up and rushed her along on a glittering beam of light. With a clarity she knew time would never erase, she saw herself again in the courtyard at Stirling Castle, pearls in her dark hair, the king's rich gift of a gown of crimson velvet, silk, and brocade adorning her tall figure. Once again she heard the blaring trumpets announce the royal arrival of King James IV of Scotland and Prince Richard of England . . .

*   *   *

The skies were blue as thistle, and the birds were atwitter at their first taste of sun in many days. Excitement pulsed through her as she awaited King Edward's son, thought to have perished in the Tower of London at the hands of his uncle, King Richard III. Since her mother had been Annabella Stewart, sister to James II, and her father, George Gordon, Earl of Huntly, the most powerful magnate besides the king himself, she stood in the preeminent place of honor on the crenellated parapet overlooking the castle entrance, her heart pounding with anticipation as she craned her neck for a better view.

Ever since the news had blazed and thundered across Europe that King Edward's younger son still lived, she had listened with rapture to the tidings about the handsome Yorkist prince. The stories of his life resembled an Arthurian legend and never failed to touch her heart, so filled were they with romance, danger, and melancholy. Taken from his native land as a child and hidden among strangers, the lost little prince had wandered from one land to the next as he grew into manhood. At the age of eighteen he had cast off his disguise and come before his aunt, Margaret of York, Duchess of Burgundy. She had acknowledged him to all the world as her nephew, the younger of the two princes in the Tower, and hailed him as King Richard IV of England.

From Margaret's court the prince had gone to France, seeking King Charles's support against the Tudor, Henry VII, who had usurped his father's throne. But the Tudor mounted an invasion of France at a most inopportune time for Charles, and the French king was forced to make peace with England. As a condition of the treaty, Charles banished Prince Richard from his realm and withdrew his pledge of support.

From there the prince went with Maximilian, King of the Romans, to meet the pope while his Aunt Margaret tried to obtain the support of Spain for his invasion. But the Tudor had paid the pope to refuse his blessing, and Isabella and Ferdinand of Spain had just betrothed their daughter, Katarina, to Tudor's son, Prince Arthur. While they, too, secretly acknowledged the wandering prince as the true King of England, they would not commit to helping him regain his throne. It was then that Margaret wrote Catherine's cousin James, pleading for his assistance. James, taken with the inequity of Prince Richard's predicament, agreed to make the prince's cause his own.

And so it was that Catherine found herself in this shining castle drawn from the pages of Camelot with its pointed turrets and walls brightly painted with "King's Gold" awaiting the arrival of the fabled prince. Bugles blew, and music flooded the air. Minstrels appeared, clad in brightly colored hose, their pipes trailing ribbons of crimson, scarlet, and gold, and cheers erupted in a deafening roar, for King James and Prince Richard had ridden into view in the castle gateway.

Her glance touched on her cousin, King James. Though he was as handsome as any chivalrous knight from the tales of Camelot, he could not compete with the golden splendor of the young prince beside him. Clad in a white silk doublet, a furred cape around his shoulders, and a beaver hat on his sunny hair, Richard, Duke of York, cantered in on a pale war-horse, a hand resting on his hip, a smile on his lips. She gasped; he was the handsomest man she had ever seen.

Over the heads of the leaping musicians and dancers waving ribbons in the air, the prince lifted his head and their eyes met. In that instant, she heard no sound, took no breath, made no movement; she stood rooted to the parapet, and her heart, like a wild bird suddenly freed from captivity, took wing and flew to him.

During the ensuing weeks, day and night lost their measure and it seemed to Catherine that time had fractured into a thousand splinters of rainbow hues as it bore her along on its beam of light. An aura of mystery and romance clung to Prince Richard. He'd been to faraway places, and had met kings, doges, and popes, and the tales of his adventures mesmerized her.

At the dances that followed and the joust where Prince Richard asked to wear her colors, she lived in an enchantment not of this world. But when he told her that he loved her, and when her father blessed their match and King James bestowed his consent, she realized the full meaning of joy. Her only disappointment was that their wedding had to be postponed to the month of January, after Advent, for the season of Yuletide was upon them.

"I cannot wait—" Richard had whispered in her ear between hot, feverish kisses stolen one December night in a dark corner of the private royal garden.

"Neither can I!" she whispered back, burning with fire and faint with passion. "Tonight—meet me tonight—I'll get away—somehow!"

While guests and guards were downing malmsey and bellowing drunken songs of love in the great hall, Richard and Catherine escaped to the seclusion of the royal garden. There, protected by a battlement overlooking the torch-lit village below, whipped by the wind and shielded by the sighing yew, with his kisses singing through her veins, she surrendered her virginity to the man she loved.

Christmas brought more ecstasy and a blessed discovery—she was *enceinte*! She prepared for her marriage in a state of bliss, floating over the world, barely aware that she moved among the living, so glowing and ethereal did the earth seem to her. King James spared no expense for their wedding. Sweet was the music and the feasting, handsome was her beloved, and delicately did morning mist give way to glittering sun and twilight fade into moonbeams. Her wedding day seemed as if it were a gift wrapped in veils, for the hours unfolded like scenes in some exquisite pageant, each layer lifting to reveal a sight more dazzling than the one that went before. The next morning, beneath silvery clouds, they took their leave of family and guests in the castle court.

"May the best day ye hae ivver seen be the warst day ye'll ivver see, my bonnie, bonnie princess," her father said tenderly as he placed his strong arms around her and held her tight in a long embrace. Bidding her a silent farewell in his heart, he kissed the top of her head as he had done a thousand times when she was a lass. Then he clasped Richard's shoulders fiercely, and boomed, "May the moose ne'er lea' yer girnal wi a tear-drop in its ee!"

"And the same to you, my Earl of Huntly," Richard replied respectfully, with a slight bow. Leaning close as he lifted Catherine on her palfrey, he asked in a low tone, "What did your father say?"

"That he hopes the mouse never leaves your grain store with a tear drop in its eye—'tis an old Scots blessing." She grinned, unable to suppress her amusement at his expression.

Richard leapt on his mount. "And the very same to you!" he called to her father across the court, restraining his horse with a practiced hand as he waved farewell. "The very same!"

Laughing merrily, they rode out the castle gateway.

* * *

Catherine came back to the present with a smile on her lips. Dawn was breaking, and the silence of the monastery was lifting. A cock crowed in the distance and sea birds mewed as they flew past her window. From across the court drifted the voices of the monk praising lauds, and on the horizon, orange fire was bursting over the sky, drenching the water in shades of persimmon and ochre. *How beautiful the world is!* she thought. She cast a glance at her husband, who was stirring with the rest of the castle, and her smile faltered. Richard's quest for the throne of England was upon them and each day that passed would bring them closer to parting. She lifted her eyes to heaven's shining abode. *Blessed Virgin, ye who once walked this earth and knew what it meant to love, keep my beloved safe, protect him from harm, I beg thee, Holy Mother—*

"What are you doing?" Richard's voice.

She dropped down into the arms that reached for her. "I'd be admiring your land of England, my love."

"But you haven't seen England yet—the sea is the same everywhere," he murmured sleepily.

She nestled against his shoulder. "Nay—in Scotland 'tis an angry tyrant. Here it embraces you like a beautiful mistress." She shifted in his arms and looked at him.

"Be that as it may," he said, rolling over on his side to look at her, the sleepy unfocused expression fading from his eyes, "'tis nothing compared to your charms, my Celtic princess. Scotland has no sun now without your radiant smile to brighten its gloomy days, and no aquamarine eyes to sparkle like stars over its nights. No black hair to shine like moonlight over the land—no roses either, for you've gathered them all to stain your lips—"

She gave a chuckle. "Your words are not your own, Sire—you've taken them quite freely from the Gaelic love song I taught you." The song was dear to her heart despite its melancholy quality, for once he'd memorized the words, Richard sang it to her every night at Loch Lomond. She hummed the lament softly under her breath, and he lifted his rich voice in song:

My true love's the bonniest lass in a' the warld,
Black is the color of her hair.
She has roses for lips, an' milk for skin,
Her neck is lang like a swan's,
An' gleamin' as moonlight is her black hair.

He was about to sing the next stanza, but she placed a finger on his lips. "Nay, my love—not now—"

He fell silent and kissed her fingers. The next stanza was about parting. She lay back with a sigh. Richard spoke again, and she knew it was to dispel their thoughts. "Whoever wrote that love song had you in mind, for he even mentioned your long swan neck. Yet for all your beautiful parts, you will not guess what feature I love best. Your little mole."

"This?" She fingered the little brown spot on the side of her cheek that she had always regarded as a flaw.

"Aye, for I have long believed that God is an artist, and here is proof. Your beauty is so perfect that you seem drawn from another realm. Therefore, He added this touch. The mark serves not only as God's signature on one of His loveliest works, but also as His assurance to mankind that you are indeed mortal."

His gaze sent the familiar ache of desire coursing through her. She felt the movement of his breath quicken. Untying the ribbon of her nightgown, he eased her from its folds and flung the gown away. Her senses spun at his touch and her heart hammered in her breast. Locked in his embrace, intoxicated by the strength and power of his flesh, Catherine felt as if she were caught in a summer storm as their bodies found the tempo that bound them together. She clung to him, riding waves of delight on a perfumed sea that swept her in, and bore her out, submerged her under, and lifted her up again . . .

They lay still at last. She opened her eyes and gazed into his blue depths. "Here in the joys of the flesh is yet one more proof that I am mortal indeed."

He laid his hand tenderly on the swell of her stomach. "I love you—love you more than life itself, *Catryn*," he said, his melodious voice giving her name the Flemish pronunciation of his adopted land.

"I will always love you, Richard, to the end of my days, forever and ever." She snuggled close. Richard wrapped his arms around her. The babe in her womb gave a sudden kick that they both felt, and they laughed.

"Another boy, judging from the strength of that kick," Richard murmured into her hair.

"Aye, and what a strong bairn he is at only five months. Imagine what he can do when he's fully formed." Catherine smiled. She could have lain in Richard's arms till the end of time, savoring his warmth, his scent, his love. Too soon, however, came a rap at the door.

"Who is it?" Richard called.

"John O'Water, me lord," Richard's faithful retainer announced in his Irish lilt, his voice bursting with excitement. "I bring news—good news! A delegation has arrived from Penzance in support o' the Yorkist cause!"

"I shall be there at once!" Richard leapt from the bed and threw on his pleated shirt, embroidered blue-velvet doublet and belt, and leggings. He grabbed his heavy mantle and set his black feathered cap on his head. "'Tis what we have been waiting for, Catryn!" He bent down and gave her a swift peck on the lips. At the door, he turned back, a hand on the latch. "And what shall ye be doin' on this fine morn?" He grinned, imitating her broad Scots accent.

She propped herself up on a pillow. "I shall be takin' your son for a wee stroll on the bonnie, bonnie mudflats of St. Michael's Mount," she smiled, "and teachin' him his native Gaelic."

With a merry chuckle, Richard shut the door.

Chapter 2

Mist on the Mount

Catherine had not long to frolic in the sun with her child. By terce, at the first sign of a storm, they hurried back to the Mount, and 'tis good they did, for a fearsome sight it made. The entire world descended quickly into darkness and the frothing sea pounded the rocks and roared with fury, reminding her of the storm that had almost sunk their ship. Below, in the sheltered harbor of the Mount, the *Cuckoo* tossed and heaved at anchor. Catherine watched from the refectory as the great lantern was lit that served as a beacon to approaching ships to warn them away from the rocks, but its giant flame careened wildly in the wind that lashed the monastery. Inside, monks rushed about closing shutters, lest the glass break in the force of the gale.

Over the next few hours, the worst of the storm passed, but for several days they knew only blustery winds and chilling rain. Undeterred by the inclement weather, however, delegations continued to arrive from over the entire south, keeping Richard busy from dawn to dark. The monastery fortress became a hive of activity that echoed with men's voices and the thud of boots as they hurried up to the castle, eager to pledge their support to the House of York.

Unseen from behind windows blurred with raindrops, Catherine played with her babe and watched them pass. Some had tears in their eyes as they departed, so moved had they been to behold King Edward's son alive. As for Richard, he became again the prince she'd known in the days before the Scots invasion. Now he believed in the success of his enterprise as utterly as she had done when she'd urged him onward at Ayr. Bursting with dreams, buoyed anew with energy and enthusiasm, assured of victory, he plunged ahead with plans for his campaign against the usurper.

As much as she welcomed this change in him, Catherine still couldn't shake the misgivings that had come to her since the storm at sea had nearly claimed their lives. She had not known till then how much she'd wanted to live—and how much she had to live for. She could not speak of her doubts to Richard, however, for she had no basis for her fears. Nothing except that familiar and deepening distress at the thought of parting. It was why she had insisted on accompanying him to England, though he had begged her to remain in the safety of Scotland until he had matters in hand. She found parting such anathema that nothing would persuade her to let him go without her—not all his pleas, nor her father's anger. "Ye always were a stug lassie," her father had said, finally giving in, "and nane can say nae to thee."

As the days passed, she buried herself in her devotions in the Lady Chapel. When not at prayer, she delighted in her child. His golden curls and his eyes that were as bright blue as Scottish this-tle reminded her of Richard—but also of how much they risked by coming to England to battle for a throne. A single toss of the dice— one spin of Fortune's Wheel—and the world they knew, the hopes they cherished, could shatter and spin into night. She tried to dis-pel her fears by reminding herself of her words to Richard when he had wavered in Scotland. "Only you can save your people—England needs you, Richard!" There had been something exciting about not knowing where they were going and exactly what might happen next, and there was romance in helping Richard fight the righteous cause of regaining his father's throne. Anxious to be off, she had hugged her father farewell at Ayr and, with barely a backward glance, had run up the gangplank of the ship that would take them to Ireland and the start of their great adventure. Young, in love, tempestuous, they saw the world as a magnificent bauble; they had merely to stretch out a hand, and it would be theirs.

So she had thought.

Now she realized how precious life was. How mortal they were. How gossamer-thin the thread by which they hung. While she cooed to Dickon on the slopes of St. Michael's Mount, or supped silently in the refectory, her gaze would steal to their single ship, the *Cuckoo*, swaying at anchor in the protected harbor of the Mount. If Richard's bid for the throne failed, could they flee to safety? And where was safety in this troubled world—not in France, not in Ireland or Spain, nor in Scotland any longer. Only Burgundy could offer refuge. Aye—only Richard's aunt, the Duchess of Burgundy, could save her little Dickon, as she had once saved her husband, Richard—

"See, my Lady Cate," cried Alice, "our wee prince walks!"

Catherine turned her gaze from the rain-splattered window where she sat mulling over her thoughts to the delightful sight of her golden-haired child, a proud grin on his face, taking his first steps unaided. As she led her ladies in a chorus of praise, he made his way to her, one careful, wobbly step at a time. "Mama!" he shrieked when he stood within her reach. "Mama!" He fell into her arms and smiled up at her, beaming with pride.

"My sweet little angel," she laughed. "How clever you are—what you can do! You walk just like your father." She nuzzled his silken head against her breast, and drowned him in kisses. Soon he would be a year old, for he was born on Michaelmas, the Feast of Saint Michael the Archangel, on the twenty-ninth of September. "Shall we play peek-a-boo?" He giggled happily, for it was his favorite game. When he had tired of it, he grew fussy and rubbed his eyes. "Shall I sing to you, my sweet one?" she cooed, for music always soothed him. He clapped his hands in assent, and Catherine smiled. Young as he was, he already knew his own mind, and they had all learned quickly that Dickon meant what he said. Agatha brought her lute, and Alice set him down at her feet, where she could watch him smile and clap.

> *"Summertime*
> *And birds they're a'wheeling*
> *High in the branches they sing for thee.*
> *Hush thee my bairn, thy sire's a prince,*
> *And thy mother's a royal lady.*
> *The woods and the dales from the castle ye see,*
> *They are all belonging dear baby to thee."*

"And now, my bonnie little prince, 'tis time for a nap. It's been a long morning for you. You must rest and grow strong so you can celebrate your birthday. Is that not right, Alice?" She picked up her child, and went to hand him over to her cousin, but he clung to her, crying. Gently, Alice helped Catherine pry the protesting child loose from his mother's arms. "Princes need naps so they can take even longer steps one day," she murmured to her charge.

"Aye, Dickon. Sleep and grow strong, my tiny one," Catherine said. She watched Alice leave. Dickon squirmed in her arms and made his objections more strenuously the closer she drew to the door. They disappeared from view. His wailing ceased, and Catherine's heaviness returned. *What is wrong with me?* Restlessly, she rose from her window seat and stood uncertainly for a moment. Agatha, sewing a baby gown, paused her needle to regard her.

"The rain has stopped," Catherine announced. "I shall take the air—Agatha, would you fetch my lute?"

Descending the wet stone steps carefully, she made her way to a rocky outcrop midway down the slope. The bad weather must be to blame for her mood, she thought. She had been confined too long and needed solitude. Maybe here, alone with the sea and the sky, she'd be able to sort herself out and regain her compass. She looked around. It was a solitary spot, shielded in all directions from prying eyes, even from above, for clouds shrouded the tip of the castle in mist.

Gathering her skirts around her, she took a seat on a ledge covered with a patch of dying grass that was still damp from the morning rain. The thin green remnants brought to mind her days of summer in Scotland. What joy had been hers since Richard had come into her life! Reaching deep into her bodice, she gently moved past the gold and diamond locket that Richard had placed around her neck on their wedding day and pulled out his love letter from the leather pouch attached to a chain around her neck. She unfolded it carefully. Inside, she kept his tiny silver coin, one of many minted for him in Flanders that bore the profile of a crowned head encircled by the words *King Richard IV.* She removed the groat and held it in her palm as she bent her head to the letter. Many times had she read it, and she knew the words by heart, yet the need to feel them between her fingers never left her. The days at the Mount were sweeping by too quickly, crammed with incessant noise and commotion, and she barely saw Richard anymore. The words of this missive, and the touch of his silver coin, brought him close.

"Love makes me your slave," he'd written. "Whether waking or sleeping, I cannot find rest or happiness except in your affection. All my hopes rest in you, and in you alone. Most noble lady, look mercifully down upon me your slave, who has ever been devoted to you from the first hour he saw you." He had signed it, "Farewell, my soul and my consolation! You, the brightest ornament of Scotland, farewell, farewell."

Richard's letter always brought a smile to her lips, for it was his earliest declaration of love to her and his words touched her like a caress. She placed the groat back into the heart of the letter and refolded the parchment along its worn creases. She slid the missive back in its pouch and dropped it deep into her bodice. She felt such a need for him at this moment, yet with each passing day she saw him less and less. Only after vespers, when darkness fell and the castle settled down to rest, did they have a few moments together. Oh, how she wished it were night! It could not come swiftly enough for her—the magnificent night—sometimes tender with lovemaking, sometimes delirious with passion. Yet entwined with their ecstasy ran a desperation they both felt. She clutched Richard, and he clutched her back, as if each night were their last. If only she could capture time and slow it down! If only she could bid the future gone, and keep the present!

Below, waves dashed the rocks with the loud, steady roaring of thunder to which she'd become almost accustomed. Sometimes she feared the sound when it became too wild, but in the main she loved it, for it spoke to her of incredible power and freedom. She lifted her face to the wind and closed her eyes. *Such*, she thought, *is the breath of Heaven—fierce, all-powerful, everlasting.* She felt its strength beat at her, loosening her bound hair and bathing her lips with salt spray. She took a deep gulp of the frigid air and picked up her lute. Bending her head to the instrument, she strummed the chords of the lament she had taught Richard on the banks of Loch Lomond, the song she had cut short on her first morning at the Mount. For some inexplicable reason, she needed to hear all the words now—needed to remember the unclouded joy that had been hers in the early days of her wedded bliss:

> *—Her neck is lang like a swan's,*
> *An' gleamin' as moonlight is her black hair.*
> *For the bonniest lass in a' the warld is she.*
> *But the winter's passed and the leaves are green,*
> *The time is passed that we have seen.*
>
> *If you no more on earth I see,*
> *An' I be in Heaven afore ye,*
> *I'll be waitin' there for thee, my black-haired love,*
> *Look for me there, my black-haired love,*
> *For the bonniest lass in a' the warld an' in Heaven*
> *Be ye.*

The wind carried back the memory of Richard's voice in her ear. "That is so sad, Catryn," he had said the first time he ever heard it. "Who would write something so sad?"

"'Tis believed it was a Scots soldier awaiting death in English captivity. In his last letter he wrote this song, telling of his love and how much he missed her."

"Everything is mournful in Scotland, even the love songs. Why is that, Catryn?"

"We have a sad history, Richard. Suffering is what we know best. We have endured much grief at the hands of the English."

"Is there anything happy here in Scotland?"

"There is a blessing we give one another."

Richard laughed. "The one about the mouse in the granary?"

"Nay, another. It goes like this—" She put down her lute. "May the hill rise behind you, may the mountain be always over the crest." Taking his hand, she closed a finger over his palm one by one as she spoke the words, until all five were folded over. "And until we meet again, May God hold you in the hollow of His hand."

"Now, that pleases me." He echoed the refrain in his resonant voice. "May the hill rise behind you, may the mountain be always over the crest—"

"And until we meet again, May God hold you in the hollow of His hand," she prompted.

Richard had risen to his feet and drawn her up. He had smoothed her hair with a tender touch. "When I am King of England, Scotland shall be a favored nation, for her queen will be the fairest rose of all England. And when I am king, the queen will be forbidden to sing a lament. By law, laments will be banished and only gay ditties sung all over the land."

*   *   *

Catherine put down her lute. A white-haired monk in the brown habit of the lay brothers was appearing over the rocks below, leading four black-and-white cows. Her glance followed the direction of his gaze, and for the first time she noticed the weathered old shed behind her. She rose to her feet.

"Brother, I greet thee well. Forgive me for claiming your domain." She turned to go.

"Nay, m'lady," he called out breathlessly, drawing near. "Do not leave on my account—I couldn't help but catch the strains o' the melody you sang, and I must say it lightened m'hard climb back with my charges!" He came to a halt before her. He had a pleasant rosy face, deeply lined by the years, and gray eyes as silver as the sea that surrounded them. "Indeed, even the cows mooed approval. Bessie, in particular."

The monk fixed his eyes on Catherine. A fairer creature he had never seen. A perfect oval face, lips like berries, coloring that combined the best of night with the finest summer's day.

Catherine blushed beneath his gaze. "Which one is Bessie?" she asked, for want of something to say.

"This one, with the big brown eyes, m'lady."

"But they all have big brown eyes, do they not?"

"Not like Bessie's," grinned the monk. "Her markings are more distinct than theirs, an' a richer velvet. She's a blue-blood, that one. Once you've seen her, you know."

"Indeed. You know." Catherine fell thoughtfully silent, thinking of Richard. Those who had seen him "knew." Indisputably royal, he had been acknowledged as the true King of England by all the crowned heads of Europe.

"May I?" The monk pointed to a large wooden water barrel near the cow shed.

She nodded. "Do the others have names, or only Bessie?" she asked, watching as he filled a large pail and set it out for the cows.

He smiled broadly. "Allow me to introduce you. This is Jessie, and Molly—and here is Michelle."

"Michelle?"

"Her name is French, for Saint Michael."

She found Michelle's face surprisingly sweet up close. "And you, Father?" she asked, rubbing Michelle's silky black ear.

"I am Brother Nicholas, m'lady. I see that Michelle's taken a liking to you."

"Too bad that her destiny is to end on a platter," Catherine said sadly.

He threw his head back and laughed. "Her destiny is milk, m'lady. We don't eat flesh, lucky for Michelle and her friends—" He gave her a pat. "Should she fall sick, I'll nurse her, and when she dies, I'll grieve. I daresay she knows it, too. Animals are a good bit smarter than most o' us give them credit for."

There was something endearing about this monk. "Have you been here long, Brother Nicholas?"

"Aye, a long time. Came as a young 'un in the fifties, during the time of the she-wolf, Margaret of Anjou, queen to poor saintly Henry VI. Now there's a Frenchwoman to put the fear of Satan into a man! Many a candle was lit for Edward IV all o'er the land when he finally vanquished Lancaster and set things to right." His gray eyes soft, he added, "As his son, our bonnie Prince Richard, has come to do now."

A raindrop fell on Catherine's face and she looked up at the sky. Clouds shrouded the castle and no part was visible now, making her feel empty and alone. For some reason, she thought of her father and how much she missed him at this moment. He'd always been able to fix whatever was wrong, like the time she'd been skipping through tall grasses and come face to face with a serpent. She could still remember her terror vividly and the ugly hooded eyes that stared at her, and she could still hear in her ears the swish of her father's sword as it came crashing down on its terrible head. But her father was not here to save her anymore, and soon Richard would be gone as well. She tore her gaze away.

Brother Nicholas caught her distress and grew solicitous. "I beg your forgiveness, m'lady—here you are, with child, and I've been ramblin' on about nothing. May I help you back up the slope? Or fetch you a cup o' wine?"

She shook her head. "I am fine. 'Tis nothing—"

"My dear lady, you are ashen pale," the old monk said. He took her by the elbow and brought her back to the rocky ledge where she had sat. "Something is troublin' you. Do not deny it. I have been around a long time, and I know when someone is afflicted in their soul. Do you wish to speak of it? Mayhap I can help."

Catherine swallowed the lump in her throat. "I know not why I feel as I do, Brother Nicholas," she said in a small voice. "But of late a heaviness has taken hold of me. I cannot dispel it, no matter how much I pray."

"This heaviness you speak of, what is its source?"

She stared at him, unable to form the words.

"May I sit?" He gestured to the ledge. She inclined her head, and he took a seat beside her. "You may confide in me, m'lady. I do not seek to judge. If the course be righteous, I can grant a blessing. Or advise, if advice can be given." He took her hand into his own, and she thought of her father. She had not known she would miss him so much. Tears stung her eyes.

"I have doubts—and fears, for my husband—my child—" She averted her gaze from his searing gray eyes and twisted a pleat of her sea-gown between her fingers. "Once I was so sure about my lord husband's enterprise—so certain that justice was on his side—that he would prevail. I was confident that he was God's chosen, that his quest was righteous and he was meant to purge the evil that has beset England. But now—now—I fear—Brother Nicholas, fear is always with me—"

The old monk threw her a penetrating glance, the wind whipping his white hair as he looked at her. He turned away and they sat together side by side, staring out to the gray sea.

"Aye," he sighed at length. "You are both too young to have such burden placed on you. Much as I wish to, I cannot give you the assurance you seek. Scripture says the battle is not to the brave, nor the race to the swift, nor bread to the wise, nor riches to the learned, but time and chance happeneth to them all." He brought his gaze back to her. "Right is on your side, but the outcome of your lord's enterprise depends on time and chance. God's ways are not ours, and remain beyond our understanding. One day all shall be revealed, so it is promised. Meanwhile—" He broke off and turned soft eyes on her. "We must endure."

"But there has to be a reason for the way I feel!" she cried in desperation. "Why this sudden change in me? I used to be carefree, confident—nay, 'tis not the child in my womb—I have been with child before, and not felt as I do now. Surely God sends me this heaviness for a purpose! Is it—is it—could it be to deter my husband from his path?"

"The burden you bear may be sent by the angels as a warning to you. Or it could be from the Devil, who takes many guises and has an arsenal of tools to use against us. We cannot know." After a long pause, he said, "Pray for guidance, child."

She blinked back her misery and attempted a smile. "I am glad for Bessie, and her friends, that you eat no flesh, and that they are safe," she said to change the subject, for she was suddenly drained and weary to exhaustion, though it was not yet nones. "For I am only now realizing what an uncertain world it is, Father."

The old monk dragged himself to his feet. Strangely, she felt the weight of his years on her own shoulders as she watched him.

"There is one thing I can do for you, my child. I can pray for God to bless you. That He see fit to reward thee and thy husband of the noble House of York."

She fixed her eyes on his wooden crucifix hanging from the rope chain around his neck. His robe billowing around him, he placed a hand on her bowed head. On the wind, she heard his words: "Child of God, may Richard, Duke of York, save England. And may England save King Richard."

*　*　*

Their fifth day at the Mount, like their first, dawned bright and glorious. Catherine decided to take Dickon across the causeway for a stroll on the beach. The sun shone on the glittering water, and white sea birds squawked noisily as she made her way across the old causeway to the little village of Marazion with her ladies, her babe held close in her arms. She kissed his soft cheek.

"Mama!" he said.

She rubbed noses with him and pretended to bite his chubby cheek. He giggled.

"Aye, my sweetin', you love me, too, don't you—you love your mama." She gazed into his clear blue eyes. Never could she have guessed before he was born the delight that would be hers each time her little one reached out his arms to her. Never could she have fathomed the joy of what it meant to have a child until she'd had her own. It was as if she had stepped into a new world, a glittering world of daily discovery and wonderment.

She squeezed his precious body to hers, but he protested and wiggled in her grasp, for they had reached the beach and he wished to be free to taste the sand. "Nay, nay," she laughed. She set him down for a moment, and pried loose his grasp on a fistful of mud that he was taking to his mouth. "You canna eat that, 'tis not good for ye!"

Dickon bawled. "Look what I have here," she said, picking up a shiny seashell and holding it up so that it sparkled in the sun. "If ye are good, maybe Mama will give it to you—"

He set his eyes on it and reached out a hand. Intently he examined his new toy as she led the way to a dark outcrop of rock where she could regard the Mount in all its grandeur.

The ladies who accompanied her gathered their skirts and settled themselves on the rocks. They were good lasses, Catherine thought, and so pleasant, they made you forget they were not great beauties. Dear, plump Agatha was always jolly and good-natured, with a kind word for everyone and a warm smile that lit up gloomy days. And any man would be fortunate to get Alice. Her fair-haired cousin was a poor relative of her father's third wife, Elizabeth Hay, and at sixteen, she was the youngest of the group, yet she was wiser than them all. Being kin, she had been entrusted with the responsibility of caring for Catherine's babe. In this she had never failed her. Her sea green eyes remained ever vigilant when watching wee Dickon, as now, while he studied his seashell.

"'Tis lovely here, is it not?" Catherine sighed on the wind.

"Near as bonnie as Scotland," Alice replied softly.

Catherine caught the wistfulness in her voice. Aye, they could all use some cheer. She asked Agatha for her lute, and bending her head to it, she broke into the merriest song she knew and raised her voice in song. Even Dickon paused his scrutiny of his shell to listen. But as the ditty drew to a close, Catherine realized the music had made them all melancholy instead of lightening their spirits. 'Tis the homesickness, Catherine realized, making a promise to herself. If Richard won his throne back from the Tudor, she would send these girls back to Scotland, where they belonged. Without love and a family of their own, England would always be exile for them.

The sea birds overhead mewed feverishly. Shielding her eyes from the glare, she glanced up as they careened above her. In that instant, a cloud passed over the sun and a stabbing pain came and went in her belly, yet it was Richard who filled her mind. *Dear God,* Catherine thought, *if he loses to the Tudor—what then?* She staggered to her feet. Her lute fell from her hands.

"Mama!" Dickon cried, reaching for her, dropping his shell.

She looked at him in horror. *What of my bairn? What of us?*

Dickon screamed. She covered her ears. Faces pressed around her. A voice rose above the others, "M'lady—dear lady—what canna the matter be? Is it the child in your womb—"

Her hand went to her belly. A spasm of nausea seized her, and she bent over and retched. Alice held her gently, while Agatha ran to moisten a cloth with seawater and returned to wipe her face. She closed her lids until the sick feeling passed. When she had recovered, she grew aware of her child's piercing cries. Alice was bouncing Dickon in her arms, but he would not be comforted, and his own were outstretched to her.

"Naught—'tis naught but a wee pain," she said, embarrassed to have frightened her ladies for no reason. "'Tis gone now—all is well." She put out her arms to her little one, wailing as if his heart would break. "Come, my sweetin'." Forcing a smile, she tossed him lightly into the air and caught him again. He giggled with delight. Somehow, she thought, gazing at her child, she must fight the fear that had taken hold of her heart, and focus on hope.

*   *   *

There was a swarm of activity at the Mount when they returned. Men lined the steps halfway down to the harbor, and the waiting rooms were crowded to overflowing. Catherine's heart flew to her throat. Something had happened.

She found Richard in his council chamber poring over documents, surrounded by his advisors. He broke into a broad smile when he caught sight of her, and his face shone as he came and took her hands. "I have an army, Catryn! Ten thousand men stand ready to follow where I lead! The time has come to oust the bastard from my throne!"

Something had happened indeed. The day of parting had arrived. She swallowed hard, and glanced around uncertainly. "When—"

"When?" He turned to his men crowding the council table behind him. "Why, as soon as possible, of course! We leave tomorrow."

A roaring cheer went up as pandemonium broke out. The room seemed to shake with the gleeful shouts of men, the stamping of feet, and the calling out of messages. Slaps were given on the back, bear hugs received, and people rushed to and fro to pass on the news. But Catherine could not breathe. Her heart pounded so wildly, she thought it must surely leap from her breast. She heard Richard's voice only dimly though she stood but half an arm's length from him.

"You look pale, my love. Here, have a seat—someone fetch wine for my lady!"

She stared at his face as he bent down to her. "Send them away," she whispered.

He knelt before her and took her hand in his. "I cannot do that, Catryn," he said, his tone evincing puzzlement at her request. "It would be unseemly, but they shall be gone soon enough, my beloved."

"I must speak to you!"

"Whatever it is, surely it can keep till the night, my sweet?" he asked gently. "'Tis but a few hours from now."

She regarded him. He was alight with excitement and anticipation, and now, for her own sake, she needed to speak of her doubts and perhaps deter him from his chosen path at the moment when victory seemed most within his grasp. She felt suddenly weary. Realizing she needed a chance to compose herself for the task, she gave a nod. This was too important to blurt out, and she had not the words for it now, nor the heart. The timing was wrong. Perhaps the night would be better.

* * *

Catherine retired to the solitude of her chamber. She had to think, to prepare for the vital moment when she would present her case to Richard. She could not bear to let him go without him knowing her thoughts. But by voicing her dread, would she be blunting his confidence in his enterprise, and sowing in his heart seeds of doubt that could lead to failure? She had to tread warily.

She thought of Brother Nicholas. Were her fears sent by the angels or by the Devil? No one could answer that. All she knew was that the time had come to bare her heart, for there might never be another chance.

After dinner that evening, she stood with Richard in the high courtyard by the church, where the prior had met them, hidden from view in the curve of a turret screened by a stone wall. Stars glittered in the silken sky. All below them flamed torches in their stone sconces, and these were reflected in the water, bathing the night in ethereal beauty.

"God has blessed us," Richard murmured.

"He has, Richard. With a love I never dreamed to find." She drew away from his arms and looked at him. His hair stirred in the breeze, and in the low light of the flickering torches, his eyes had darkened like the ocean. She raised a finger and traced the line of his mouth and chin.

"I know I should be grateful to the men of Cornwall, but"—she braced herself and struggled for the words she had prepared—"but I don't want to give up what we have found together. Pray, let us return to Burgundy, Richard. Let us not go against Tudor. Not yet—not now. I am not ready."

Richard took both her hands tenderly into his own. "But we cannot turn back now, my love. I thought you wanted this as much as I did—nay, maybe even more, my Celtic princess."

"I thought I did, too—at Ayr."

"Remember the words of the wise-woman . . . 'You shall be queen one day.'"

"I remember. But I no longer wish to be queen. I wish only to be with you and our wee ones—together—safe."

"We must believe in God, Catryn—that He will help the virtuous against the tyrant. We must have faith in Him to set things right. For God knows my heart, as He knows Tudor's. How could He turn away?"

"But we do not know God's heart, Richard. His ways are a mystery and few things in this world happen as they should. I had persuaded myself that I wanted this for you—as much as you did. But I don't, and I can't let you go without speaking of it. I want you to see your new babe born, and be at my side to watch our Dickon grow into manhood. I want so much more than these twenty-two months we've had together. Let us board your ship and return to Burgundy, my dearest love. We would be happy there. One day we can come back to England to strike the Tudor from your throne with greater assurance of success."

"Catryn, there is no better time to strike than now! I have no doubt that I would be happy anywhere if you are with me, but however much I want to—and I do want to—I cannot leave now. You know that. The longer Tudor sits on the throne, the better he can cement his power and destroy those who would support us. Time is his friend, and our enemy."

"That time is our enemy is something I have always known, Richard. But I feel that never was time more our enemy than now, on the eve of your departure to fight the usurper."

"You've seen the Cornishmen who have come here. They have placed all their hopes in me. These people have been taxed into starvation by the usurper. They are desperate. How can I abandon them now, when we stand on the verge of victory? So much depends on me, Catryn! Aunt Margaret has seen a tyrant usurp the throne of England and kill every male of her blood royal. How can I give up and return to her in Burgundy without ever striking a blow? What would I say to her?"

"You would say that the time is not right. That the Tudor has murdered everyone who was in a position to help you. That you have no knights, no money, and no true army—and that the time will come when England will revolt against the blood and torture this beast has unleashed on her, and you must be there to save her when she does."

Richard sighed. "What you speak is truth. Yet it is impossible."

"I know you believe it your duty to see this enterprise through to the end. But Richard—all who would have helped you are dead!" She couldn't stop the rush of words that fell now that her lips had been unsealed. "Tudor found them and beheaded them—even his own close kin Sir William Stanley—the one who won him the crown! You have no one to vouch for you—no one to speak for you among the nobility. And it is only the nobility that count, not the poor. This much I have learned from my father! Ten thousand men with pikes are scarcely a match for the thousands of knights in armor that will be brought against you. Without the nobles, there can be no victory. If you lose, God forfend, the Tudor would send you to the Tower—"

She broke into a shudder that sent her trembling visibly from head to toe. Richard drew her to him. "Hush, hush, my love, speak no more of such dread things, lest you break my heart. You wouldn't wish to send your husband to battle with a broken heart, would you?"

She shook her head as he wiped her tears with his handkerchief. She had failed. He was not to be dissuaded from his course. She had to accept what she could not change. Her father had told her that hope was stronger than fear, and now was the time to remember his words.

"I wish to send my husband to victory," she said, laying her cheek against his strong chest.

"Victory," he echoed, his lips seeking hers.

* * *

Mist lay so thick around Catherine that she could not see her way forward. She heard Dickon cry, but she couldn't find him. Richard spoke, but his voice came to her vaguely. She could not see him. Blinded by whiteness, she groped her way through the fog. "Richard!" she cried in panic. "Richard—"

"Hush, my love, hush," he said. "I'm here. All is well.

"'Tis but a bad dream," he murmured, kissing her brow.

Nestling against him, she sighed with relief and fell asleep again. When next she opened her eyes, mist covered the darkness of the world, but this time she was not dreaming and she could not turn over and go back to sleep, for the monastery-fortress was awakening from its deep slumber. Soon the rooster would crow, the sun would rise, and Richard would leave for his enterprise against Henry Tudor. With iron control, she prepared herself for the inevitable.

Richard wished to bid her farewell at the Mount, but she insisted on walking with him to Marazion on the mainland. Too soon they were crossing the causeway with their entourage, Richard's men-at-arms leading the way with torches, for the sun was only beginning to stir in the east. Wisps of mist drifted across the fortress and the sea, but inland it was dissipating. The ocean sighed in the chilly morning air, and birds shrieked loudly as they flew low over the water, seeking breakfast.

On the beach at Marazion, they came to a halt. Richard's men-at-arms huddled together near a rising slope covered with heather that led to the high road going northeast, stomping their feet and rubbing their hands against the cold. Richard and Catherine stood a distance away on the silver sand where puddles of water caught the reflection of the sunrise and glittered at their feet like scattered jewels. With the sky as his backdrop, and bands of crimson and purple hailing the ascent of the sun that was now an immense orange ball on the horizon, Richard took Catherine's hand in his. His hair glowed rose-gold and his eyes were blue as the sea would soon be. How she hated to see this sunrise! Beautiful though it was, it was hideous to her. Not trusting herself to speak, she stared at the sunburned hands that held hers.

Richard's resonant voice broke the silence. "If something should happen to me and I don't come back, I want you to—"

She waited, the constriction in her throat tightening. Tears blurred her vision. She lifted her eyes to him but she could barely see his face.

"Take the *Cuckoo,* and go to Burgundy."

"If something—something should happen—" Catherine said, forcing the dire thought away even as she spoke it, "I will leave here, but only for Dickon's sake—and for the sake of our bairn yet to be born."

"And, Catryn—" Richard braced himself to say what he must, for her sake. "If I do not return, I do not wish you to mourn me forever. I want you to leave your heart open to love."

She looked at him, stunned. "I cannot promise that! How can you ask such a thing? I can never be happy without you."

"You must promise me, Catryn."

"Never!"

"Catherine, I beg you—grant me the peace of knowing I do not leave you bereft forever. I could not bear that."

Catherine swallowed on the terrible choking sensation that constricted her throat. Closing her eyes, she cast about for strength. Richard's hands tightened their hold on hers with urgency. "Do it for me—live life for me—remember me in happiness, not in tears; smile for me, Catryn; laugh for me. 'Tis how I want to see you remember me. I want to look down from Heaven and see you smiling, not weeping."

"I promise," she said at last. A tear splashed her wedding ring.

He bent down and brushed her lips with his own. She longed to fall into his arms and clutch him to her, to scream, and sob, and beat at his breast. But she did not. She held herself rigidly erect with the decorum of the princess that she was. She had to be strong, for his sake. She lifted her eyes and met his gaze. Resolute, determined, he would do what he had to do, though he did not wish it. For her, it was the same. They had no choice. This was their destiny.

"God willing, victory will be yours," she said, in a voice she did not recognize as her own.

He managed a smile.

"May the hill rise behind you," she said, taking his hand into both of her own and closing a finger over his palm.

"May the mountain be always over the crest," he replied softly.

"And until we meet again, may God hold you in the hollow of His hand." She folded his last finger as she spoke.

Drawing her close, he held her tenderly for a long moment. He kissed her one last time, and strode to his war-horse.

Her fingers strayed to her face and the imprint of his kiss. He mounted his stallion and sat for a long moment, looking at her. He turned his destrier. His men fell behind him, and the rhythmic beat of horses' hooves filled her being as he faded away into the mist.

Chapter 3

Darkness on the Mount

Such panic seized Catherine on the beach as Richard faded from view that she fled back to the Mount as if chased by a torrent of fire. Snatching her babe from Alice's arms, she did not give him up even for his changing and feeding. Seated by the cow shed, she tended his needs herself, and rocked him to sleep in her arms, thinking every moment of Richard—not of the future, for that seemed suddenly filled with nameless terrors—but of the past. All the while, she clutched her son fiercely. He was her flesh and blood link to his father. She could not let him go, not for a moment. He was, suddenly, all she had.

Even with Dickon close, the day felt unbearable and without end, but as the ocean lashed the shore and monks chanted their songs of praise, Richard came to her again in remembrance as he'd looked the first time she'd ever seen him, riding through the castle gate at Stirling. Like a favorite melody, the memory ceased abruptly, and reverted to the beginning to echo its refrain. It restored to her the glorious moment when Richard had entered her life, and she clung to it, knowing she'd not forget a detail, however long she lived.

That evening she sought the curve of the stone wall where she had stood with Richard the previous night. Shielded from the eyes of monks passing for prayer, and seated with her child in a turret, she savored the day's end. Birds screeched louder than they had ever done before. The arms of Marazion that hugged the Mount turned black around her, and darkness gathered the world into her folds until the moon came out. In her mind she saw Richard on the shore of Loch Lomond, pointing up to the stars. Her hand strayed to where his had rested on her shoulder that night, and she heard his words again. "See those three stars in a straight line down?"

She followed the direction in which he pointed.

"What does it remind you of?"

"I think I see the outline of a man—kneeling, perhaps—because of the fourth star that juts out—"

"Aye, they say that is Orion, son of Poseidon, stung to death by a scorpion." Richard brushed her brow with a kiss. "At his father's request, Zeus placed Orion in the sky, at the opposite side from Scorpio, so they could never meet again. One legend has Orion chasing the scorpion to finally kill it, and another has him forever fleeing away. But never can they be seen together. Orion only rises when Scorpio falls, and Scorpio rises when Orion falls."

She looked hard at Richard. The significance of the legend was not lost on her. "And you are Orion."

"I hunt my prize, as Orion did, to lay it at the feet of the one I love." Richard took both her hands into his and gazed into her eyes. "Whenever I am gone, look up at that third star in Orion—the one with the bright blue light—and remember me. Then I will always be with you, my Celtic princess."

Catherine came back to the present abruptly and kissed the sleeping babe at her breast. Richard's blue star glittered over them both, and the thought comforted her. She lifted her eyes to its steady gaze. "My beloved, may God be with thee tonight, and keep thee safe—"

Dickon let out a wail and squirmed in distress. "Hush, hush, my wee one—ye be hungry, I know. I'll get ye something to eat—"

"My Lady Cate—there ye be!" It was Alice. Catherine turned to find her appearing inside the wall, a thick blanket thrown around her shoulders, her hair whipping in the wind. "We have been so worried! We searched everywhere! Ye disappeared from the cow ledge, and no one knew where ye had gone."

"You need have no concern. Surely you know I would come when I was ready?" Catherine said, tangling with Dickon.

"But, my Lady Cate, ye've not eaten and neither has the lord master."

"He is hungry now, and you may take him." She had to shout for Alice to hear her over Dickon's cries. She kissed her sweetheart on his tender cheek and surrendered him, but Dickon was not happy with the arrangement. Yelling louder than before, he put out his hands to grab a strand of his mother's hair, and struggled to pull himself back into her arms. "Nay, 'tis time for you to go inside, poppet. 'Tis time for bed." She untangled her hair from his grasp.

Alice tucked him firmly beneath her blanket but made no move to depart as he squirmed to free himself. "Will ye not come in, my lady?"

"Not yet. I am not ready."

"But the wind is picking up. 'Tis chill." She shivered visibly as she bounced Dickon in her arms. "Ye may catch cold if you stay."

"Nay, I do not feel the cold. This is where I need to be. Go, Alice. I'll come soon."

Alice was about to protest again, but changed her mind. Much as she loved her cousin, and as grateful as she was for her employment, she didn't care for the stubborn streak that sometimes made Catherine so willful. She decided to enlist the prior's help. Maybe he would have better luck.

Catherine gazed up at the sky. Sometimes she thought she'd fallen in love with Richard even before she ever met him. In the darkness, Richard's twinkling star seemed to wink at her from its black velvet bed.

Velvet. That's where it had all begun. With a king's gift of fifteen ells of crimson velvet for her eighteenth birthday, and an invitation to a royal feast. Her thoughts filtered back to that day . . .

* * *

"By sweet Saint Marie, yer beauty lights up this gloomy day like a torch, Cate."

She'd turned at the unexpected sound of her father's melodious voice, thick with the accent of the Highlands. He stood watching her from the threshold of her chamber and in his blue eyes danced the special look he reserved only for her.

"Father!" she cried, running to him so suddenly that she almost knocked her nurse from the low perch where she sat adjusting the hem of her new velvet gown. "Do you like my dress?" She twirled for him.

"Very rich," he smiled. "The color becomes you well."

"King James sent me the fabric! He said the same—that crimson is my color. And he—" She broke off, suddenly realizing how weary her father was. She decided to wait for her brother, William, to arrive before giving him the most exciting news to come to Strathbogie in years. "Father, I am so glad you are back. I worried about you and William."

"He'll join us in a wee bit when he's done with some other matters that need tendin', me bonnie princess." He held her out at arm's length to gaze at her. He seemed to brighten until his glance drifted to the bleak, rolling hills beyond the window. "We are back, aye, but not for long." He heaved an audible sigh.

The feuds with the Earl of Ross have claimed their toll, Catherine thought. As one of the king's chief advisors, her father, the Earl of Huntly, had the responsibility for maintaining the king's peace. "Never mind the Rosses and those other quarrelsome Highland families. They're always fighting, Father; I doubt they'll ever stop." Linking her arm in his, she led him to the settle by the hearth, where a fire blazed to warm the cold, dreary November day, and assumed an imperious tone. "Now—as your princess—I command you to forget them. Cease all talk of trouble in the realm until I grant permission to resume the tiresome subject." She sat down and draped her rich velvet gown across the silk cushion. "Ye are commanded to have a joyous time here at Gordon Castle in beautiful Strathbogie for as long as I shall decree. Which might be forever, Father."

Clutching her hand tightly in his own, her father threw his head back and roared with laughter. "I see nothing has changed though I be away many months, Flora," he said, directing himself to Nurse. "My youngest daughter still rules the roost, just as she has since the day she was born!"

Nurse shook her head helplessly. "'Tis the wise-woman's prophecy that did it, m'lord. Said she'd be loved by a king, an' she's never forgotten it. Went to her head, it did, and ever since, our Cate's been nigh on impossible."

They both threw Catherine a glance overflowing with affection.

"Then you'd best remember that I require the utmost deference, or I might send you to the chopping block when I am queen," she replied.

Her father and Flora laughed, and that was how her brother, William, found them. Catherine rose from the settle, and kissed him, breathless with excitement.

"Father, William—I have an announcement to make! While you were galavantering around Scotland, our royal cousin sent me the velvet for this dress"—she gave a pirouette—"and an invitation to Stirling Castle!" She picked up the document from the desk and held it up for them to see. "Our presence is commanded by King James! Richard of York is coming to Scotland and James states that he cannot receive the prince until all the Huntlys are at his side! Is that not splendid?"

"Do you mean King Edward's son, Richard, Duke of York? The boy-prince who disappeared in the Tower?" her father inquired, rising.

"The very one. All this time, he's been sheltered by his aunt, the Duchess of Burgundy. Now that he's grown, he's coming to fight the usurper Henry VII for his throne! Is that not exciting?"

The anxious look was back on her father's face. "I said I'd not be back for long, but this is indeed much shorter than I expected. I wonder what James wants from us."

"O Father, you are so accustomed to trouble that you expect it even when there is none." She drew to his side. "It shall be interesting to meet the prince, don't you think? They say he's very pleasing to look at—and what a romantic story he has to tell us."

"Romantic it may be, but is it true? And if it's true, what is James going to do about it?"

"'Tis what we go to learn, Father."

"Pray he is a false lad," my father said, patting her hand. "Pray he doesn't persuade James to take us to war with England. I canna lose more men."

* * *

Catherine jolted back to the present and stirred in her seat on the turret. She had learned later that her father knew far more about Richard's visit than he had allowed her to guess. He had, in fact, been privy to the negotiations with Burgundy but had reluctantly signed the agreement that was reached, for it had touched him personally. If the Scots council found merit in Richard's claim that he was the true Prince of England, they had pledged to support him with men and arms, and her father had agreed to give him the hand of his favorite daughter, Catherine.

Footsteps intruded into her thoughts. All at once the prior appeared from behind the curved wall. *Alice must have sent him*, Catherine thought with annoyance. He tried to entice her inside with plaintive entreaties, but she dismissed him. Then, at compline, as monk-song filled the night air, Alice returned with John O'Water, whom Richard had left in charge of the crew of the *Cuckoo* in case Catherine should need the ship. He pleaded with Catherine as Alice stood shivering in the night air.

"My lady, will ye not be comin' to bed now? The wind is blustery and we fear ye may be catchin' cold if you stay. My lord duke would not be pleased, and that's the half of it—I'm fearin' for my head, my lady, for he'll be wantin' that—should harm come to ye."

Catherine could never be angry with the dear man who was one of Richard's staunchest supporters. His old face was etched with concern, and his wispy gray hair, like his black cloak, blew around him. "John O'Water, I appreciate your concern, but sleep eludes me this night and I must stay until I know it can find me again. Fear not for your head. You are too beloved a servant to fret about such a thing."

After a hesitation, he gave her a bow and retreated. Alice, however, would not be deterred.

"I pray ye, my Lady Cate—forgive me for speaking bluntly, but I do it for the duke's sake—come with me to bed. 'Tis not wise to remain outdoors on such a night. Your condition is delicate. God forfend that ye catch yer death of cold. It would break Prince Richard's heart should anything happen to ye—"

"By the rood, let me be!" Alice had never known love, so how could she understand the emptiness Catherine had to endure now that Richard was gone? But her cousin's hurt expression fanned remorse for her harshness, and she added, more gently, "Alice, I cannot heed your plea. Not tonight—tomorrow, for certain. Now go to bed, and may your dreams be kind. I shall come soon. 'Tis all I can promise."

"May I have a chair sent ye?" Alice asked in a small voice. "The turret does not foster confidence in such a wind."

Catherine gave her assent and soon a man arrived to set a chair against the curving wall. She took the seat and inhaled deep of the salt air. Why toss and turn in bed when she could be here, with the sea, and the stars? She loved the tolling church bells that marked the hours and the pounding of the surf against the rocks. She loved even the beating wind. Neither its bite nor its fury could pry her loose and blow her inside. All night she listened, praying fervently for Richard, but though she tried to banish fear and focus on the good memories, there was one that kept intruding—Richard's address to the Scots council that had moved everyone to tears. She closed her eyes. Again the great hall at Stirling rose up before her and she saw the faces of the nobles assembled to hear about Richard's escape from the Tower.

King James had lounged on his throne in the newly completed hall, painted pink to dispel the winter gloom, as Richard took up a position on the dais steps. On the wall behind them, dominating the chamber, glittered the jewel-colored tapestry of "The Unicorn Found" that Margaret of Burgundy had sent James in gratitude for his support of her nephew. Richard's fair hair and princely attire of green cloth of gold shimmered in the light of candles and torches so that he seemed to have stepped out of the forest depicted in his aunt's tapestry. The thought struck Catherine that he had been, like the unicorn, reborn. He was the lost prince, now miraculously found.

"Most high and excellent Prince, my gracious and noble cousin, I commend myself to your majesty, and to the honorable barons of the Scots—" Richard fell silent for a moment. Everything depended on this address, for the men in this room were his last hope. In order to secure Scotland's aid, he had to set his case before them, and that meant stirring up his painful memories of the past.

He found his voice. "Pray listen, I beg you, to the tragedy of a young man that by right ought to hold in his hand the ball of a kingdom, but by fortune is made himself a ball, tossed from misery to misery and from place to place.

"I died a manner of death when I was taken from England at the age of nine, for in order to preserve my life, I was made to swear that I would never reveal my name, my lineage, or my family until the time was right to do so. To save myself, I had to forget who I was— Prince Richard was dead, and not till I was grown could I live again. From the moment I left England, my life was one of constant peril and flight. I had the face of my father, King Edward IV, and I lived in fear that someone, somewhere, should recognize me and turn me in to the usurper Henry Tudor for the bounty he had set on my head. I was tossed from misery to misery, and from place to place, without country or kingdom, home or mother or father, family or friends. In this manner I wandered desperately for many years, an empty child, ever a stranger among strangers. I wept and suffered much affliction for my loss, and many times I wished I had died like my brother."

Already a tear had risen to Catherine's eye, listening.

"As you know, my royal brother, King Edward V, and I were

declared bastards and set aside from the throne by my uncle, King Richard III—" An angry murmur arose in the hall. "Nay, King Richard had his faults—as any Scotsman will attest—but unlike the usurper, he was a benign ruler to his people. He had not intended our deaths, but as a consequence of his taking the throne, my royal brother, King Edward V, died in the Tower most pitifully.

"I remember when I first arrived there to join him. He was a melancholy child while I was merry and liked to sing. To cheer him one day, I put on my Garter of gold and silk, and said, 'My brother, learn to dance.' And my brother replied, 'It would be better if we learned to die.'"

No one moved in the hall; there was no rustle of fabric, no sound of breath. If a pearl had loosened from a brooch, all would have heard it fall.

"How I survived is little less than a miracle. While my brother still lived, a certain lord came to take us from the Tower. My royal brother could not travel, for he had caught a sickness and suffered from fever, so he stayed behind. I left with the lord on a long journey to a remote castle in the north of England, and there I was concealed. Not long afterwards I was given the sore tidings that my brother was dead."

Richard bowed his head, overcome with emotion. His hair shone in the low light, and the jewel in his collar flashed so that even the silk and gold unicorn shimmering in the tapestry above seemed to blink down at him in pity. Catherine's heart overflowed.

"I never left the castle," Richard said, "except once, when I was taken to Westminster Abbey to see my mother, who had thought me dead. Now she knew I lived. She came out of sanctuary with my sisters and wrote her brother, who was with Tudor in France, that all was well and to come home. Then she gave up plotting King Richard's downfall. But the Tudor did not abandon his evil designs. The Battle of Bosworth was the result.

"I didn't see the lord again who had removed me from the Tower until the night before the battle when I was taken to King Richard's tent. My royal uncle informed me that if he lost, I had to go into hiding beyond the seas until I was grown and could fight the usurper for my throne. Till then it was death to be a Plantagenet, he said. He commanded me to forget who I was and gave me the name *Wezbecque*—'orphan,' in the Flemish tongue. He said that my aunt, the Duchess of Burgundy, would know me by it, and that the lord who had taken me from the Tower would be there to aid me when the time came. But I never again beheld his face."

Richard turned to look at Catherine for encouragement. She managed a smile, though her heart was weighed down with sorrow.

"And so I lived my life for about eight years with the two men who had been charged as my guardians, until one of them died and the other returned to his own land. We traveled through many countries together, and I spent nearly three years in Portugal. But at last I was reunited with my Aunt Margaret, and for the first time in a long while, I was embraced with love and tears. She prepared me to regain my throne from the evil grasper of the kingdom of England. The rest you know."

Richard's glance moved over the barons, and fixed on James. "If you, my kind benefactors, can do nothing else for me, perhaps you can give me a home so I will not have to wander anymore."

That night in the castle garden, Catherine and Richard stole a few minutes of solitude together and she wept in his arms for the sufferings he had endured. He dried her tears with kisses, and said, "The road God gave me was blessed, Catryn, because my misfortunes have led me to you. Had all gone smoothly for me as a prince of England, I might never have met you, and look what I would have missed. Nay, Catryn, love is worth everything we have to pay."

Catherine came back to the present and swallowed the lump in her throat. The sea murmured softly around her. She raised her eyes to Orion, but the stars were gone. Gray light filtered over the earth, and church bells were tolling the hour of five. *This is lauds the monks are singing*, she thought in amazement. She tried to get up, but her back was stiff and her feet unwilling. She looked down at her skirts. Puddles of water stood everywhere; it had rained heavily and she hadn't felt a drop! She rose on unsteady legs and was immediately seized by a violent fit of sneezing. Making her way around the circular wall, she encountered her ladies emerging from her privy chambers, holding blankets over their heads to shield themselves from the drizzle.

"Lady Cate—have ye been here all night?" exclaimed Alice, throwing a cloak around her. "Your—" She bit her lip. She was about to say that Catherine's obstinacy would be the death of her. Instead, she said, "Your unborn child—God forfend, 'tis as I feared—ye have caught an ague!"

The girls hurried Catherine into her bedchamber. They changed her wet clothes for dry, and brought her a tray of steaming soup and hot mulled wine, but Catherine found herself without appetite. Outside, the wind howled about the windows and rattled the shutters. She thought of Richard, marching to battle, unprotected from the elements.

"Prayer is what I need," she mumbled, with frozen lips. Pushing herself to her feet, she let Alice and her ladies help her up the steps to the courtyard and into the church. Catherine found she could move only slowly, for she seemed made of ice. Monk-song flowed from the Virgin's Chapel nearby, cut into spurts by the blustery wind: *Andeamus omnes in Domino* . . . May we always go with the Lord. Their chanting filled her heart, but not with peace. Peace was something she would not know again until her beloved was safe again at her side.

She dropped to her knees at the back of the empty church before the silver-gilt statue of Saint Michael, protector in battles and trampler of dragons, where the most urgent pleas for intercession were made. Clad in cloth of gold, he looked a prince, much like her own Richard. She clasped her hands to her heart and, from the depth of her being, beseeched Heaven to grant victory to the man she loved.

* * *

Catherine could not have guessed with what heaviness of heart and depth of reluctance Richard had taken his leave of her. Nor could he afford to let anyone know. He trotted his white mount, leading his men to Bodmin, thankful for the mist that hid his face and his thoughts.

He had left behind the two most precious things he possessed in the world—and for what? A throw of the dice for the crown of England. Had he a choice, he would never have gambled such high stakes. Ever since his failed northern invasion, he had wanted to give up his quest and return to Burgundy with his family, for now he knew what it meant to love, and what it meant to war; and war revolted him to the pit of his stomach. Never would he be free of the memory that had become his nightmare—helpless people flee-ing for their lives; the world filled with screams, weeping, terror. The invading Scots army had brandished their swords in Northumber-land and cut down unarmed men as they ran. With lust in their eyes, they had chased the women who retreated before them, and raped them as their menfolk lay dying, their hovels burned and their ani-mals screamed in their death-throes. He had galloped up to James.

"James—end this carnage—I beseech you!" he begged with tears in his eyes.

"They're not rising up for you!" James shouted over the din of battle."They must be punished!"

"They are my people! This is my country! Lordship means noth-ing to me if it must be obtained by spilling the blood and destroying with flames the land of my fathers!"

"But they are not your people!" James had retorted. "Far from recognizing you as their king, they don't even know you as an Englishman!"

Richard had stared at him in stunned disbelief, unable to com-prehend this other face of his good friend and benefactor to whom he owed the shirt on his back. "I cannot abide it! I'll have no part in it!"

"Then leave!" James had cried.

Richard had turned his horse and galloped off.

When they met again at Stirling Castle, King James no longer regarded Richard's cause as his own. He was a warrior who gloried in fighting and killing, and had no use for a man of feeling; a man who felt the commoner's pain as his own. He saw Richard as a coward.

"'Tis clear I have misjudged you," he said. "'Tis best if you leave. The English are rebelling in the south. Mayhap you should go there and see if they'll give you a hand getting back your throne."

Richard rubbed his eyes, and the memory faded. Catherine had agreed that they had to leave Scotland—not for Burgundy, but for England. She could be persuasive when she wished, and he had given in against his better judgment. "When I was ten years old," she had said, "a wise-woman prophesied that I would be queen. This is what she meant, Richard. Don't you see—this is our destiny. You must fulfill the prophecy—the crown is yours for the taking!"

Far more than anything in the world, he wanted to win her admiration and respect and bring her the laurels owed her rank. She had married him for love, but if he could not give her the throne of England, what could he offer? Naught but an uncertain future, and the heartbreak of wandering and beggary. There was also James. Richard had been unable to forget his face as he'd shouted at him to leave. Dishonor clung to his name now. The only way to redeem himself was to win back his father's throne.

If these reasons were not enough, there was yet one more—in the guise of his Aunt Margaret, Duchess of Burgundy, the poorest widow in the world, as she called herself. Richard owed her everything. She was his rescuer, and his only kin, and she was depending on him to restore to her the properties that were hers in England. More important, she was expecting him to avenge the wrongs done by the usurper to the House of York.

No, there was no turning back from this road he was on. He had to win back England. For love; for honor; for duty's sake. He had no choice.

A voice came at his shoulder. It was Nicholas Astley, a scrivener and one of the three members of his council. "My lord, we are approaching Camborne. Shall we read the proclamation?"

He realized that the fog had lifted. The outcome of his righteous quarrel with the tyrant would not be put off any longer. Now Divine Providence would decide his fate. Twelve years ago she had made a king of a French-Welsh adventurer with naught to his name but bastard blood. If she wished, she could spin her Wheel of Fortune once more and set him in the tyrant's place. If she did, he would give thanks to her and to God with deeds of royal magnanimity and kindness to the end of his days. He bowed his head and sent a last prayer heavenward. Then he gave a nod to Astley.

His councilor unfurled the proclamation as a group of tin miners put down their oil lamps to gather around and listen. A few ran into the hovels that housed the winches in order to spread the word into the mining holes. From these enclosures streamed out blackened creatures who seemed scarcely human, some bent double by years of toiling in tiny, cramped spaces. Many were wracked with coughing fits and, being accustomed only to the dark, blinked at the gloomy light of the rainy day. Astley began to read, "Richard, by grace of God King of England—To all who hear this, greeting . . ."

Richard watched the villagers, deeply moved by their plight. In Bohemia, where he had traveled with the Holy Roman Emperor, laws had already been enacted to improve working conditions and to protect women and children from laboring in mines. When he was king, he would see to it that his people received the same rights. He listened quietly to the proclamation that he knew by heart, hoping it would convince the people of his sincerity.

"We will end the manifold treasons of the tyrant, his Byzantine tortures, abominable murders, robberies, extortions, and the daily pillaging of the people by taxation and illegal means," Astley read. "According to law and conscience, we shall right the wrongs committed, and we promise pardon to all those who accepted the reign of our foresaid enemy, unless they have attempted murder against us—"

Richard waited with rapt attention. This was the moment of reckoning. In the north they had turned their backs. Would they turn away from him in the south?

Members of the crowd threw down their shovels, and with one voice shouted, "Out with the dirty hound Teudar! He has no right to rule us!" Richard beamed; he felt as if the sun had burst through the clouds to drown him in golden light. He murmured a prayer of thanks to the Lord for blessing him so mercifully.

In Redruth, Truro, and St. Austell, he was greeted the same way. As word spread, men flocked to his banner. By the time he approached the edges of Bodmin, he had twelve thousand peasants at his side, brandishing weapons. And when they reached Canyk Castle, to his delight, the gates were thrown open wide to him.

He sent a messenger to take the news to Catherine.

"Tell her how it pleases my heart to send these joyous tidings!" Richard beamed. "Forget not to tell her every detail! Ensure she knows that, on the news of my arrival at Castle Canyk, the usurper ordered the sheriff of Cornwall to muster the county against me, and though he came at me with twenty thousand men, they defied his orders to charge, and instead, they turned and fled!" He grinned, remembering the glorious sight of the sheriff's men tripping over themselves as they scrambled to get away over the purple moors.

Wasting no time, Richard rode into town to proclaim his victory to the folk of Bodmin. A jubilant multitude had already assembled to greet him. Men from forty guilds waited to do him homage, and so many people had come from the surrounding villages to celebrate his victory that the hilly streets of Bodmin could take no more. With blaring trumpets and bonfires, he was pronounced Richard IV, second son of the late king Edward IV, undoubted heir to the crown of England.

How good it felt! Richard had feared this homecoming would never arrive, and now, at last, it had. He was home again in the land of his birth. He gave thanks in each of Bodmin's three churches for God's great bounty, and sent Catherine a missive in his own hand.

"I cannot stay long in Bodmin, for I must subdue the rest of the kingdom. But O, Catryn, how I hate to leave this beautiful place, and these good people—my people! It is such unbearable joy to be here with them at last," he wrote. "Pray God that I may soon send you more such glorious tidings!"

*   *   *

The day after Catherine's all-night vigil outdoors, her throat pained her so terribly that she could scarcely swallow, nor could she hold her child for fear of transmitting her sickness to him. How she regretted refusing the wise counsel of all who had tried to lure her inside! At least the Almighty had seen fit to answer her prayers, for the tidings that Richard had sent her could not have been happier. She received his messengers in her chamber, and their smiling faces lit up the room like bright tapers as they recounted news of Richard's stunning successes in Cornwall and Devon.

"The duke's boon grace and affable deportment is winning the hearts of all who set eyes upon him," messengers reported. "In this short time, he has grown so popular and formidable, that no force dares oppose him."

Catherine's heart was finally at ease. How foolish she had been to let fear overtake her. To her great happiness, she was being proven wrong—and the unknown terrors that had plagued her were proving hollow. With gratitude for Heaven's benefices, she read and reread Richard's missive during the hours when her weak and feverish body did not force her to sleep:

Beloved Catryn,

As you have been informed by my messengers, my quest is blessed by Divine Providence and matters are proceeding better than I could have hoped when I, with bitter reluctance, bid you farewell at Marazion. By now you know that men have flocked to my standard from the first moment, and that I entered Bodmin as king by right of battle. How joyous it is, Catryn!

I was proclaimed king in Bodmin's large and beautiful hall of the church of the Franciscans, as fine as any at Westminster. 'Tis not so poor a place to begin being King of England, my dear love.

I have been making certain my troops pay for the wine and food they are given in the villages they pass, so that my people have proof of my goodwill and the manner of king I plan to make to them. I must admit to finding the landscape here strange with its moors and red-earth hills, as I have never seen anything like them before

*in all my travels on the Continent. I marvel at all my discoveries,
and thank God for each moment.*

*Tomorrow we reach Exeter. My expectation of success is high.
Exeter supported the Cornish rebels against the usurper only a few
months ago, and they have no love for him there. Surely, they will
throw open their gates wide to me. I have heard that the usurper
is in a state of great agitation and distress over my victories. That
comforts me mightily and bolsters my resolve to oust the villain
from my father's throne.*

*My beautiful Celtic princess, you should know that wherever
I am, and whatever I do, you are foremost in my thoughts. Your
image floats before me like my banner of the White Rose. You are
queen of my heart today, and with God's blessing I shall see you
queen of my realm of England soon.*

May God have you and our babe in His safekeeping.

*Your adoring husband,
    Richard of England*

*By my own hand, this day Saturday, September 16th in the year of
our Lord one thousand four hundred and ninety-seven.*

For the next three nights, Catherine slept better than she had
since Richard left, and the dreams that came to her were sweet. At
long last, she felt strong enough to rise from bed and don her gown,
though she had been unable to shake the fever that caused her
ladies much concern. The improving weather helped her spirits, for
the tempestuous sea had calmed, and the rain had eased. Soon she
would be strong enough to venture outside. She longed to smell the
freshness of the wind.

She was seated in a window seat dangling a bauble before Dickon
when she heard the messenger arrive. Catherine knew something
was wrong as soon as he came into view, joining her and her ladies in
the refectory. Richard had sent none other than Nicholas Astley, one

of his most senior advisors and the head of his council. The expression Astley wore could not have been more sober. He fell to a knee before her.

"My lady duchess, fain that I had better tidings to relate. Alas, matters have changed most fearfully since Bodmin." He lifted pained eyes to Catherine. "On Saint Lambert's Day, King Richard IV arrived at the gates of Exeter. His herald shouted his proclamation at the city walls, commanding surrender by duty of its allegiance. In reply, the Earl of Devon locked the gates against him."

A shocked murmur ran through the little group, and Catherine caught her breath. Alice put out her arm to sustain her, and Astley half rose with concern. "My lady—"

"'Tis nothing. Pray, continue," she managed.

He swallowed visibly. "King Richard tried to besiege them, but they had guns, and all we had were rocks, fire, and battering rams. For two days, he tried to get our men over the walls by ladder, but was repelled. Eventually, we broke through the east gate, but we were driven back and lost many men. At the news of Lord Daubeney's impending arrival with ten thousand of the royal army, King Richard made a truce with the Earl of Devon and left Exeter. He is marching to Taunton as we speak."

"Lord Daubeney—is he not engaged in fighting my royal cousin James on the northern border?" Catherine exclaimed in surprise, for the invasion was always meant to be a coordinated two-pronged attack, from north as well as south.

"Word has it that the fighting on the Scottish border ended last month. King James attacked in August, as he and King Richard had planned, but King James had no way of knowing that we had been blown to Ireland by weather. The storm has cost us much."

Catherine's head swam. Here was her great fear, taking shape before her. And there was more. She could see it on Astley's face. "Pray, continue—" she whispered.

"King Richard's forces are badly outmatched by the army royal. The usurper has nobles and guns, cavalry and armor, my lady. King Richard has naught but men in leather jackets with pitchforks and a few swords. The usurper has many lords experienced in warfare, but King Richard is his own commander and has no experience of military matters. Discouraging numbers have been killed. Further, he has run out of money, and his men are weary and hungry. Many are sick, dying not only from wounds, but also from sickness. The Cornishmen who have eaten grain harvested since the rebellion, or drunk beer brewed with this year's barley, have died as quickly as if they had taken poison. 'Tis said they are felled by the pope's excommunication, but His Grace believes that it is by Tudor's poison. There is nothing the tyrant would not do to keep his crown, and murdering his own people is as good a way as honorable battle to him."

Nicholas Astley hung his head, as exhausted by the telling of these dread tidings as the little group on the Mount was to hear them. Catherine felt nauseous and faint. The ocean roared so loudly, it made her head ache. She knew she would not be able to endure much longer. "I—" A sudden pain pierced her stomach. She doubled up in agony and would have fallen but for the quick action of those around her. She heard John O'Water's voice as her ladies helped her to her chamber. "Whatever else your tidings," he said, "give them to me in private. The duchess can bear no more this day."

The prior, his monks, O'Water, and the crew of the *Cuckoo* watched Catherine disappear through the passageway. Astley dropped into a chair and ran a hand through his hair. John O'Water kicked a chair away from the table and took a seat beside him. "That bad?"

Astley gave an anguished sigh. "Worse than anything you can imagine. The situation is hopeless. Tudor has kept us harried, sleepless, and hungry. We cannot eat because there is no money for food, and even if we could pay, we know it's tainted with Tudor's poison. There are wholesale desertions, but you can't blame the men. Given the situation, they have no choice but to accept Tudor's pardon." With stricken eyes, he said, "His Grace wishes you to take the duchess and the lord master to Burgundy posthaste."

Silence.

O'Water looked at the Barton brothers, both sea captains who had brought them safely through the Irish storm. To their skill, they owed their lives. Andrew Barton was the first to speak. "You saw Her Grace's condition; there's no way she can survive a rough sea voyage." His brother, Robert, echoed the sentiment. "She'll lose the babe for sure, and likely her life, too. In any case, we don't even know if the *Cuckoo* can survive such a storm." All heads turned to Guy Foulcart, the previous owner of the vessel. He was the only one who could answer that question.

Foulcart didn't respond for a long moment but stood at the window, assessing the raging sea below, where the *Cuckoo* tossed violently at anchor even in the sheltered harbor. The storm had worsened in the last hour and now the ferocious wind howled around the Mount, lashing the windows with rain, loosening shutters, and tearing away pieces of roof tile. He shook his head. "We'd be dashed to splinters on the rocks before we could even get out to sea. We must await better conditions."

"What's to be done with the duchess if she can't be comin' with us?" O'Water demanded.

"She'll have to stay here," Nicholas Astley said.

"But the Mount has no right of sanctuary," the prior interjected.

"Then she must be taken where there is," Astley replied. "What is the closest place?"

"St. Buryan. 'Tis not far from here, but in this weather it will take at least two days to get there."

Nicholas Astley drummed his fingers on the table. "We have not much time then. Tudor's man, Lord Giles Daubeney, is expected to reach Taunton within the week. The duchess can rest four days at most, Prior. I have to apprise Prince Richard of the situation and see what he wants to do. If he decides to send the duchess to St. Buryan, can you manage the journey alone?"

The prior was a figure of misery as he stood rubbing the edge of his crucifix between his fingers. He was thinking of the beautiful young woman in the tawny sea gown who had stood before him little more than a week earlier, her babe asleep in his nurse's arms, her handsome husband at her side. They had come with such high hopes, such noble designs for the kingdom, and now here they were, their doom fast approaching. Though he was a man of faith who would never question God's plan, sometimes the uncertainty of human destiny and its tragic consequences brought him to the edge of grief.

He gave a nod.

*　*　*

Alone in his tent, Richard contemplated what lay ahead. The blood and terror that he had seen in the north nauseated him even now, months later. With an anguish of soul as desperate as it was hopeless, he called out to Catherine in the dark. The candle in the sand bowl flickered, almost as if she had heard him and had tried to respond. He rubbed his eyes. His army was crumbling around him, and of the men that remained, many were sick, others hollow-eyed from sleeplessness and hunger. He blinked to banish the images of the poor wretches who would meet their doom on the morrow—thanks to him and his bid for the crown of England. None would last an hour against Daubeney's forces.

And what of him? He had never been taught to fight—certainly not the way a knight was expected to fight. The art could only be learned in a baron's household, and that had been too dangerous for a child who looked so much like his father, King Edward of England. He passed a hand over his face. Of what use was he to his men? He had brought no army with him to England's shores because he had believed in his countrymen. When they saw him, they would know him, so he had thought. They would rise up for him and cast out the usurper with one voice. So he had thought. But it had not happened. Tomorrow he would die, or worse.

If his limbs weren't cut to pieces on the field, he'd be taken to the Tower, where untold horrors awaited a man. Such was the usurper's dedication to destroying his enemies that he had spent the ten years of his kingship refining its methods and making a fine art of torture. At considerable expense, the miser who avoided spending a groat had imported expensive instruments and machines from France to inflict unendurable pain. One that he knew about tore the skin from a living man but left him still living, each breath an agony as he cried out for a death that took its time. He, Richard, had promised to restore justice and law to England and to cleanse the land of such cruel terrors, if only England would help him rid the land of the tyrant. But the people had not heard. They had turned away from him.

Rain pounded the tent he had pitched near one of the roofless chambers of Taunton Castle. The castle was owned by Bishop Thomas Langdon, an avid Yorkist. Richard had sent him a missive pleading for support, but the bishop had not replied. He knew, as did Richard, that the cause of York was lost. Richard's eye fell on the beautiful gateway that the bishop had crenellated two years before. It was decorated with an escutcheon, a cross and five roses, symbolizing the five wounds of Christ. The date was carved underneath: 1495. A curious coincidence: that was the year Tudor had discovered the plot against Richard and destroyed all who would have helped him—from Tudor's own powerful uncle, Lord William Stanley, down to the humblest bowmaker. Richard thought of Catherine as she'd looked on their last night at the Mount, begging him to abandon his invasion. "Too late, too late, my love!" he whispered to the memory. Too many promises had been made, too many princely clothes, jewels, and attendants had been accepted. He had taken on a king's cares, and a king's enemies; the necessity of fighting, and the risk of failing. He had gambled all; and he had lost. Never would he see Catherine again. He swallowed hard. At least she was safe, God be thanked. She and Dickon would sail to Burgundy. They would receive loving welcome from Aunt Meg.

"My lord—"

Richard looked up. It was Nicholas Astley, whom he had sent to Catherine. He rose from his stool.

"My lord," Astley said, "the duchess is very ill. She cannot make a sea voyage in her condition. They await your instructions at the Mount."

Richard felt himself pale. He loosened his collar and leaned a hand against the wall for support. "I must go to her—" He pushed away from the wall, headed for the door. Astley blocked his path.

"My lord, forgive me, but the troops await," he said.

"I have no time for them! I must get to the Mount!"

"My lord, think what you are doing. Do not act in haste."

"How can I think of anything when the lives of my family are in peril? They come first—aye, before my men, Astley, before my country, before the crown—before anything else in this world!"

"My lord, I understand. After you have addressed the troops, let us discuss matters with the full council. All I beg is that you do not act in haste. An hour or two won't make a difference. 'Tis all I ask. Surely your country is worth that much?"

Barely able to concentrate, Richard issued his orders and watched the muster call. His captains noted carefully who was there, and who was not, and wrote their names down on parchment that was then secured in a coffer. Dutifully he went up and down the muddy lines of his ragged army, feigning confidence. In the pouring rain, his hair and clothes drenched and sodden, Richard encouraged his men.

"I am in close touch with certain lords of the realm, who will soon help," he lied. "If the bridges ahead are cut, we will track to the right and find another way through Somerset. Do not give up—do not go home—do not believe Tudor. You know his word is writ on water. March with me to London and see me crowned."

Some had stayed with him, but more had left. In Taunton's ruined castle, Richard sat in his tent, awaiting his council, his head in his hands, a man comfortless. Henry VII, through his lord, Daubeney, had issued him a challenge to fight, but he had also tendered another offer. "If the war does not end in a battle, it can end by agreement. 'Tis your choice." Richard had not sent back a reply. He couldn't surrender, not until Catherine and Dickon were safe.

He knew that Henry referred to him as "the boatman's son, Perkin Warbeck." Still, he must know that Richard was who he claimed to be. Challenges were issued to equals, not to rebels or those of inferior rank. But that scarcely mattered anymore. Taunton Castle was little more than a fortified house. The place had no roof, nor a wall around it or the town. It was entirely indefensible. If he was killed tomorrow—as he surely would be—what would become of Catherine?

"My lord," said a scout.

Richard glanced up. He could barely make out the man with his bleary eyes, for he hadn't slept in twenty hours, or eaten all day, except for a single crust of dry bread.

"Lord Daubeney has left London with the royal army and is nineteen miles away. The Tudor king is also on the march from Woodstock with ten thousand troops equipped with knights and many guns. We estimate Daubeney will arrive to give battle early tomorrow morning."

Tomorrow morning—Saint Matthew's Day; the twenty-first of September. Next week would be Dickon's first birthday. Richard gave the man a nod, and he withdrew. When Richard looked up again, Astley stood before him. "How can God have turned His face against us so, Astley?" Richard demanded in a voice hoarse with emotion.

Astley made no reply. His councilors filed into the miserable chamber. Richard stood to address them.

Chapter 4

Eye of the Storm

Catherine heard herself moaning, but the sound came to her dimly, as if from someone else across a far distance. Where was she, and where was she going, she wanted to ask, but only dull cries issued from her lips. She tried to open her eyes, but she could not lift her lids; they felt like stones.

"Bury—" voices whispered. "Bury—hurry to bury—hurry—"

Perhaps she was dead. Would they bury her while she still breathed, or did she merely imagine that she lived?

With a scream of terror, she awoke to find herself in the monastery infirmary. She had been dreaming of her journey to St. Buryan again. She blinked and looked around her at the stone wall and the single high-barred window that afforded a view of a patch of sky. Across from her straw pallet hung a crucifix with an image of the suffering Christ, and below the crucifix sat a nun, murmuring over her rosary. "I'm in sanctuary," she whispered aloud. "I had forgotten."

"Aye, my lady." Agatha rose from a stool and came to her side. "You are safe."

Catherine tried to sit up, but Agatha restrained her with a gentle touch. "Not yet, my lady. There has been bleeding. You must lay still."

Catherine grabbed her hand in panic. "Is my babe all right?"

"'Tis too soon to know, my lady. The monks are preparing a potion for you. Meanwhile you must rest."

"But where is my wee one, Dickon—and what of my Lord Richard? Has news come yet?"

Agatha exchanged a look with the nun and lowered her lids. "The lord master is with Alice, and he is well. He is sleeping—" How could she tell her the rest? It was too terrible. Outmanned and out-provisioned, the duke had no chance. No doubt he was already dead.

"Where is everyone—where is John O'Water? Why did we leave the Mount—I've forgotten..." Catherine managed to rise on an elbow. Pain exploded in her belly, and she dropped back down on the pallet, gasping for breath.

"There, there, my lady—try not to move—" Agatha was grateful that these questions were ones she could answer. "The lord duke wanted you taken to Burgundy, but since you were too ill to travel, they brought you here, to St. Buryan's. Alice is at mass, and John O'Water—he's away right now. We know not when he will be back." It was not a lie. He had sailed to Burgundy with the crew of the *Cuckoo* as soon as weather had permitted. And who knew? He might return one day. "Now rest, m'lady. I will fetch you something to eat. Sister will watch over you until I get back."

Catherine grabbed her hand. "Dickon—pray, bring me Dickon. I need to see him."

So Richard had been preparing to give battle to Daubeney. She had lost count of the days, but surely news of Richard's battle at Taunton would arrive soon. Until then, she would pray for his victory.

Finally the door flew open and little Dickon toddled forward on his unsteady little legs. Catherine stretched out her arms to him.

"Mama, Mama!" he beamed. "Mama."

Oh, what a wondrous sight he was! How piercing sweet was his voice after so long an absence! Only he could make her smile in darkness. "Come to me, my precious..."

Laughing, Dickon took her hand and snuggled down at her side. Catherine kissed his brow and silken hair, taking care not to brush his lips with her own, in case it should pass on her sickness. "Have you been well?"

He nodded his golden curls. "Pay."

Catherine chuckled. "That is good. 'Tis always good to play, my sweet." She devoured him with her eyes and traced his face tenderly with her finger. She never wanted to forget his feel, his smell, the way he looked at this moment. She wanted to remember it for all eternity, even when he was grown.

A knock came at the door. The sister bowed reverently when she saw who it was.

"Lady Catherine," said the abbot, looking with great pity on the figure of mother and child nestling together on the pallet. "The king's messengers have arrived with news of great import to relate. Will you receive them here?"

Catherine's smile vanished. Fear stopped her heart for an instant, and then it took on a frenzied beating. *Why the king's men? Why not Richard's messenger? Dear God—*

She passed Dickon to Alice. News of this import could not be brought here; she had to stand. She had to dress. "By your leave, I will receive them in the Chapter House shortly."

The abbot gave a nod.

* * *

After leaving Taunton, Richard and his men tore through the black night, the flaming torches they carried casting fearsome shadows around them. Daubeney's army was miles away, but though Richard could not hear or see it, he felt it with every beat of his pounding heart and every sore sinew of his body. No part of the landscape could be trusted in the darkness. The hedges he flew past might harbor enemies, and the thistles in the field might be men lying low, bristling with weapons. In a flash, they could loom up and cut his troops down. He did not pause, even for a moment. He had to get to St. Michael's Mount before Henry Tudor's men. That meant riding back by the shortest possible route.

His council did not offer opposition once they realized his

decision was made. The battle was as good as lost and he had chosen family over country. Through moors, misty forests, and rolling chalk terrain they sped, often with no track to guide them. As day broke over the land, Richard and his small band of men, exhausted and out of breath, halted in Exmoor Forest and regrouped.

A scout, who'd been sent into Tiverton, galloped back within an hour with grim news he'd picked up in an inn. "We cannot go south by road or sea!" he cried. "King Henry's sent ships from Lyme Regis to Exeter to Barnstable. His men guard the roads. We're cut off in all directions."

Richard had no intention of accepting defeat. "There has to be a way! There's always a way." He spread his worn map on the rough ground. Southampton had water and ships, and it offered the sanctuary of Beaulieu, in case—God forfend!—of desperate need. "If we can't go south or north, we'll fool Tudor and go west. To Southampton. He can't be guarding every port in England! From Southampton, we'll take ship to St. Michael's Mount."

"We are too many," Nicholas Astley said, gazing around at the weary party of sixty men, drooping in their saddles and leaning against the trees. "We can't all fit in one small ship, and we don't have enough money for a large one."

"You're right," said Richard. "We'll attract attention in the towns. We have no choice—we must split up and try to make our own way."

As rain pelted them and thunder rolled, Richard's chaplain, William Lounde, prayed over the men. Then, in a secluded corner where they would not be overheard, he took Richard's confession.

"What I did—leaving those men at Taunton—can God ever forgive me, Father?" Richard demanded with tortured eyes.

"God understands and forgives all sins, if penance is done."

"What kind of penance will absolve me, Father?"

"God will send it to you. You will recognize it when it comes."

"I will embrace it," Richard said, his voice choked by emotion.

It took Richard and his men less than two days to reach Southampton in a journey that should have taken a well-horsed man at least three. Weary, hungry, and cold, they arrived in the early morning as church bells rang for prime, but their spirits fell at the sight that met their eyes. They had not known a city wall protected the harbor, and now the water gate was shut against all traffic and the docks were all but deserted. With their hats pulled low over their eyes, they made careful inquiries about passage aboard ship and learned that King Henry had ordered no ships to dock until further notice.

"There's naught to be done. We must go to Beaulieu and seek sanctuary," Nicholas Astley said as they huddled near an inn. "It'll buy us time to devise a plan."

"Time we don't have!" Richard exclaimed. "Soon Henry Tudor's men will be at the Mount."

"There is naught that can be done about it, my lord," said Astley.

"You're wrong. There is something—" Richard turned to the one man who was not a member of his council. "Roger, take a message to the prior of St. Michael's Mount. Tell him I want my lady wife and child moved to St. Buryan." He pulled off his gold ring from his finger. "Give him this and he'll know it's from me that you come."

"Aye, my lord," Roger whispered. He mounted and spurred his horse to the west road. They watched him gallop away.

John Heron, a mercer and the second member of Richard's three-man council, turned to his fellow Yorkists. "Poor Roger, he'll get no food this day either," he sighed. "But mayhap we can buy bread and ale to eat on the way to Beaulieu? If only one of us went in, we wouldn't attract much attention."

"As long as it's not the duke. Forgive me, my lord, but you don't look much like a peasant," Edward Skelton said. He was a mercer and the third member of Richard's council.

"What's wrong with me?" Richard smiled wanly.

"There's naught we can do about your hair—though the rain's helped darken it a bit—but the larger problem is that you carry yourself like a prince, my lord," Nicholas Astley said. "A peasant has not such erect shoulders and regal deportment. You need to sag your back as though you've been carrying sacks of potatoes all your life."

Richard did as Astley suggested.

"Good—but not enough. Here, let us show you . . ." The miller, the mercer, and the scrivener all helped to round his neck and shoulders. "Better."

"Let us not forget they're going to be on the lookout for strangers." Skelton stole a glance at the inn.

"Can't be helped," Astley replied. "We need food. We haven't eaten in two days."

"Starving I am, and a round of sausage would be as welcome right now as salvation itself," John Heron agreed.

"Then you go in, John. I'll see to the horses. Sire, how much money have we?" Astley asked when Richard made no reply.

Richard opened his velvet pouch and checked his coins. "The royal sum of twelve crowns."

Astley's face paled.

"What?" demanded Richard. "Surely that'll buy us a bit of sausage? Prices can't be that high merely because we're near London."

"The velvet—'tis a dead giveaway," Astley said in a hoarse whisper.

Richard stilled his hands as if he touched fire. He emptied the purse and slipped the coins to Astley. Casting a furtive glance around and seeing no one, he bent down and scooped up some horse manure with the pouch. At a nearby rubbish heap, he took a few moments to bury it from sight before returning to his band of riders. "There, that should take care of it."

"Best we not stop here," Astley said abruptly. "I don't have a good feeling about this place. Let's look for an inn closer to Beaulieu."

No one gave him argument. They mounted, and turned their horses north.

Astley didn't realize that his sudden discomfort had sound cause. A face had been watching them from an upstairs window across the street. The band of four horsemen looked out of place to the man, though his town was used to rowdy foreign types. And what was it they scrutinized in their hands?

When the horsemen left, he went downstairs and into the street. He had to know what was important enough to bury so deep in a rubbish heap.

* * *

Dusk had fallen when Richard and his three councilors reached New Forest. In the gathering gloom, they rode hard for Beaulieu Abbey, home to the monks of the Cistercian order. Founded by King John, it was one of the few abbeys in England that offered permanent sanctuary, not merely within the church but over the entire perimeter of the land inside the walls. The abbot didn't answer to any bishop or king, only to the pope himself, and the laws of sanctuary were strongly enforced. Beaulieu also had a water gate that afforded access to ships in the river, for the monks had the right to trade in wool.

"Once we're there, we'll await our chance to escape by ship. With God's help, you'll see Flanders soon," Astley said to Richard as they galloped up to the twelve-foot walls that protected the abbey. Drawing rein before the outer gatehouse, they pounded on the doors.

"Open up, in God's name!"

A head popped out of the gatehouse. "Who's there?"

"We want sanctuary!"

After a silence, the heavy door creaked open. Ahead stood another gatehouse, even larger and more fortified.

"Sanctuary seekers!" the porter called out to the monk manning the Great Gatehouse. That gate swung open, this time with a loud grating sound of metal.

They galloped inside. Richard exhaled with relief. Safe at last! He had not realized until this moment how tense he was. He dismounted and waited in the open courtyard for a monk, for they had arrived at vespers and the community was at prayers. Listening to the monk-song helped soothe Richard's troubled heart, though the smell of the dangerous world outside still enfolded his nostrils. At last, a lay brother appeared, clad in black. He led them inside, where a white-robed monk sat at a desk in a vestibule, with pen, paper, and a small chest set neatly before him.

"In seeking sanctuary, you must first give up your weapons," the monk said. He waited until the four men had unbuckled their swords and set them on the table. "There is also a fee of two shillings for each of you."

Astley removed his soiled leather pouch from inside his shirt, and counted out the coins. "There's another four pence for recording your name in the register."

As Astley, John Heron, and Edward Skelton complied, Richard felt himself turn pale. He bit his lip.

"Your name?" demanded the clerk.

Richard swallowed hard. "Piers . . . Osbeck," he managed. He wondered if the clerk who regarded him so strangely knew that he lied. He glanced at Astley, and was relieved to see approval on his face. He had done the right thing. "Perkin Warbeck," a version of his childhood identity, had been widely circulated by Henry Tudor and was closely associated with the Pretender.

"Piers . . . Osbeck," the monk repeated, recording the name. He scattered sand to dry the ink and gathered his papers. "First you will be taken to the lavatorium. After you have washed, you will be shown your quarters in the lay area of the abbey, where you will don the black habit of the lay community. You will not mingle with the fully ordained monks, those in white, either for eating or sleeping. You have separate facilities for prayer also, and will use separate doors to enter the church. Brother Roger will take you to your dormitory." He nodded to the black-clad lay brother who waited by the door.

Later, at mass, Richard was relieved to have his face hidden by his hood, for his misery was acute. Now that he felt safe and had time to think, it was Taunton that filled him with torment. Torchlight flickered in the passageways of the beautiful abbey, but in their shadows he saw the faces of those he had deserted, and of Catherine, whom he had dishonored by his flight, and of his babe, whom he loved and could not kiss, and now might never know. He knelt in the chapel and pressed his palms together.

That night, Richard tossed and turned on his straw pallet, too tortured by memories of the past and by the uncertainties of the future to find rest. He wondered how his companions could sleep. *Because they have courage, and I have none,* he thought, overcome with shame.

The next morning, after services, Richard walked the grounds with his small party, telling his beads and hiding his thoughts as they looked for ways they might escape. The sight of ships passing on the river heartened them, but it was autumn, and no tall wheat fields weaved in the wind to hide a fugitive making for the riverbank. His heart lightened somewhat to see the river come almost to the abbey walls at high tide, leaving behind seaweed when it receded.

"We shall have to leave in the dark of night," whispered Astley under his breath, "so take note of the rise and fall of the land." Richard nodded. Since monasteries never truly slept, eyes would be watching. They fell silent as a laborer passed them, and again when a lay brother approached.

When it was safe to speak, Richard asked, "How much money do we have left?"

"Ten crowns," replied Astley.

"Barely enough to buy ship's passage, or a bribe," murmured Edward Skelton. "We'll have to devise how we can stow away."

"We can help load the ships," offered John Heron.

"No, we're sanctuary seekers," Astley replied thoughtfully. "We'd be watched too carefully to slip past that way, even if they let us help, which I doubt."

They took their meals, sang their hymns, and chanted their prayers while around them servants toiled at their chores, sweeping floors, picking fruit, carrying sacks of flour and goods to the kitchen, feeding the animals and weeding the flower beds. After vespers, they went to their dormitory. They had not yet devised a plan that might work. "Maybe something will come to us in the morning," John sighed.

It seemed as if it were the middle of the night when Richard felt the sudden jab that woke him. It was Edward, and he was ashen-faced.

"What?" whispered Richard, seized with fear.

Edward threw a glance over his shoulder to make sure the door was closed, put a finger to his lips, and pointed to the window. Richard rose. What he saw sent him sagging against the wall, weak-kneed. His friends stood staring beside him, their faces drenched of color. The monastery was surrounded by armed men.

"How?" Richard uttered, feeling faint. He loosened his collar.

"They must have picked us up in Southampton," Astley whispered.

"What do we do?" Richard's throat was parched and he had trouble forming the words. "I must escape—" He flung himself past Edward to get to the door, but his friend held him back. "You cannot escape. There is no escape."

"I can see the inlet—the water comes up to the abbey—there is a ship—I see it—"

"It's the king's ship, my lord. It bears the banner of the dragon! It's here to guard you."

"*Jesu—*"

"Can they do that? I thought the abbey grounds were out of bounds to the king's men!" Edward's voice seemed strangely hoarse in Richard's ears.

"I heard the monks talking—Henry had the laws of sanctuary changed to permit him to surround an abbey if there's a traitor inside," Astley replied.

"I'm not a traitor to that tyrant!" Richard cried.

Astley put his finger over his lips to quieten him. "But we are. He's always a step ahead of us, no matter how careful we are—but heed me. They can surround us, but they cannot violate sanctuary. The usurper has extracted many men by force, 'tis true, but Beaulieu is different. The pope would excommunicate him if he dared such a thing. Let us go down and break fast. We can assess matters more clearly on a full stomach."

Richard nodded miserably. "The Tudor thinks of everything."

"That he does," John Heron grumbled under his breath. "He has been preparing for this day from the moment Richard III's crown tumbled into the thornbush at Bosworth field and William Stanley set it on his head."

With heads lowered, they filed into the lay refectory and went up to a sparsely occupied table set with cutlery. Richard and Nicholas took seats facing the window, their backs to the room, while John and Edward sat across from them. A server poured them wine. Richard downed his cup in one swallow, for he was in sore need of courage. The wine was good, and so was the food: boiled beans steaming on a wood trencher served with salted herring, a piece of cheese, and a slice of crusty bread. They ate in silence, as mandated by the rule of the Cistercians, and kept their heads low, but each time they looked up, they made sure to take in their surroundings. The river stood at high tide, gleaming in the morning sun, its banks full and almost up to the abbey walls.

When Astley jabbed his side, Richard stole a glance over his shoulder in the direction of Edward's gaze. Three hard-faced men stood in the doorway, surveying the refectory. They might have been guests but for the fact that they didn't act like weary travelers and made no effort to hide their scrutiny of those breaking fast.

Richard felt himself pale. He hunched his shoulders and buried his head deeper into his bowl as he ate. The men's footsteps crunched in his ears as they strode slowly past the tables, examining each man present. When they reached him, they halted. Swinging their legs over the bench, they took a seat at the end. One of the men picked at his teeth with a piece of wood as he stared at Richard.

Richard swallowed hard and tried to gather his rampaging thoughts. As Astley and the others rose from the table, he followed, taking care to hunch his shoulders and retreat deep into his hood. His body trembled as he passed the three newcomers and he felt their eyes bore into his back. Footsteps sounded behind him. Sweet Jesus—were they following him out? Richard could barely focus as he and his men took the path to chapel. To his horror, the three men appeared on the bench behind him.

After the service, Richard and his group left for the orchard. There was no doubt now. These were Tudor's men. They trailed him as he strolled, and kept pace with him all day, watching him eat and wash and pray; following everywhere he went, even to the privy. By vespers, Richard's nerves were shredded, his every sense on alert. "I must escape—" he whispered again to his friends.

"We've been over this—there is no escape—he has the place surrounded by land and sea!" Astley whispered back.

"We must pray for deliverance," John said under his breath. "There's naught else to be done!"

Richard murmured his prayers with even more frenzied desperation in Beaulieu's magnificent house of God. With bowed head, he offered many sacrifices and made endless promises to God, and while these words spilled from his lips, the church door creaked open, and a dark-eyed late-comer entered and joined the group of three at the end of his row.

Richard barely knew what words he sang to the last hymn of vespers. Such panic assailed him that he shook. When hymns were over, the lay members filed out, and Richard and his party had no choice but to fall in with them. They were approaching the west door that led to their dormitory when the stout man stepped out to block their way. "We have a message for you. You'd best come with me, all of you," he said.

A cold sweat broke out on Richard's brow and he saw his own dread reflected on the faces of his councilors. More than anything in the world, he wanted to turn and run. But to where? This was sanctuary! The safest place in England, protected by the pope! How could this be happening?

The stout man led them to the chapter house, where the abbot awaited them on the dais. Richard froze at the entry. Someone gave him a shove and he stumbled inside. The door slammed shut and the bolt slid into place with a thud. Somehow Richard found his voice and his courage. He turned to the stout man. "We are in sanctuary! You have no right to be here. Abbot Humphrey, tell them!"

The abbot clasped his hands together at his breast, and a look of pity came over him. "I fear, my son, that Mayor Godfrey and his men have every right. The laws of sanctuary have been amended to permit the king's men entry, so they may keep vigilance over traitors who enter."

"I am not a traitor!" Richard exclaimed. "I am the son of my father, King Edward IV, and the true king of England!"

"You be a boatman's son!" retorted the mayor. "Perkin Warbeck, that's who you be!" He cleared his throat and spat out his phlegm on the inlaid tile floor.

"Mayor Godfrey, there is no spitting in God's house."

"Forgive me, Abbot. His lyin' words drove me to it."

"State your business with these men," the abbot replied.

The stout man turned to Richard. "As you may have surmised, we came here from Southampton to watch you and make certes you didn't escape. That is, till Richmond Herald gets here. He's on his way now, and he carries an offer from King Henry—and that be mighty generous and merciful of His Grace for it be better than you deserve! Plunge us into another war, would yeh? I'd kill you me-self if it wasn't for King Henry's merciful heart. He demands you be brought to him alive, and that's the only reason you stand here breathing, you no-good cur! Welladay, 'tis the end for you now!"

There was a commotion at the door and the bolt was withdrawn. A group of men marched in. Richard's eyes flew to the tallest among them, clad in a rich velvet tabard embroidered with red roses and a golden dragon, a plumed cap on his head.

"Richmond Herald here, on the king's business," one of the group announced.

"Abbot Humphrey . . . Mayor Godfrey of Southampton, I presume?" said the tall man. "You have done well."

The mayor bowed, and the abbot inclined his head. Richmond Herald turned his attention to Richard. "And this, no doubt, is the lad who would be king? You've given us all much trouble, young man. What do you have to say for yourself?"

"That this is no way to talk to your king," Richard replied with a bravado he didn't feel.

Richmond Herald said nothing for a moment. Despite his casual disdain, he had been unsettled by the sight that had met his eyes. Even in his rough homespun dark robe, the young man's startling good looks, his graceful stance, golden hair, and regal bearing bore a remarkable resemblance to Edward IV, whom he himself had known. There was no denying the power of his presence. He might well have been a prince.

Richmond Herald recovered his composure. "We are—" he said at last, "empowered by His Grace King Henry VII to offer you an arrangement. If you leave by your own free will."

"My councilors and I are quite comfortable here, Sir Herald," Richard managed, assuming a royal tone. "Why do you think we should wish to leave? We are not fools. We know King Henry's word is writ on water." He spat the word "King," so that it sounded like an epithet.

"King Henry—" Richmond Herald said reverently, "urges you to consider your situation. We can extract you by force—"

"You wouldn't dare!" Nicholas Astley cried.

"You may put me to the test, if you wish. Or you can hear me out." Richmond Herald waited.

Richard felt himself grow pale. "Pray continue."

"As I was saying, we can extract you by force, or we can negotiate. King Henry is adamant that you, Perkin, be apprehended alive. If you leave of your own accord, he will grant you pardon of life, and full pardon to those who are with you, heinous though their crimes be. If you refuse, not only will you die, but consider what will happen to your wife and son."

Richard stared at him aghast. "My wife—"

"And son."

"My son—"

"We have them both."

Richard felt a hammering in his head. For a moment, the man's face wavered in his sight. He clenched his jaw and steeled himself to stand firm. This was no time to be faint of heart.

"How do I know you speak true?" Richard demanded.

"You only know what I tell you, but I doubt you will wish to test us. They are at St. Buryan. Lord Daubeney is on his way there from Taunton."

Richard drew a long breath to relieve the aching tightness in his chest. If they knew that, they had them, just as they had him. "My wife and child must be kept safe," Richard uttered in a voice he scarcely recognized as his own.

"They shall not be harmed. You have King Henry's word on that."

"And my men? I will accept nothing less than a full pardon for them."

"That is what I am charged to offer."

Richmond Herald hesitated before he replied, "Before you refuse, I am urged to remind you of Humphrey Stafford, Robert Chamberlain, Richard White, Thomas Bagnall—" He rattled off the names of a multitude who were forcibly extracted from sanctuary on the usurper's order and butchered at Tyburn. Richard suppressed the shudder that ran through him.

"And you would permit that, Abbot Humphrey?" Richard demanded, turning to the old man on the dais.

"The king has an army, and we have but two hundred men," Abbot Humphrey said kindly. "There is not much we at Beaulieu can do to protect your person should King Henry decide to seize you now, and negotiate for his soul later."

"I merely ask you to consider your options," urged Richmond Herald.

"Our options. That we have none, you mean?"

"Precisely."

For a long moment, Richard hung his head. He was remembering his uncle, King Richard III, in his tent on the eve of battle, passing him the papers that would prove his identity to his royal sister, Margaret, Duchess of Burgundy, and the crowned heads of Europe. A vision of his aunt rose before him and he saw her weeping with joy over him in her private chamber, where the walls were hung in purple, and green velvet cloth covered the table. He thought of his mother, kneeling in sanctuary at Westminster, as she gave him the password known only to her—the password that would marshal troops to his side and win back his throne.

Now she was dead. No doubt, Tudor had seen to that, too. In this game of Fortune, he had thought of everything. From the moment he had seized the throne, he had set to work to keep it, unleashing spies over all the continent, bribing the pope, securing treaties with those who would be Richard's friends, and murdering any who stood against him. Always he was a step ahead. Now Richard stood truly alone. Everything he loved, everyone he trusted, had been wrenched from his side. So much had been lost in this hopeless quest for the crown of England!

He lifted his head and brought his gaze to his friends. He could not undo his terrible sin at Taunton, but he could help these three hapless men and save them by his surrender. And he could save the two great treasures of his life—Catherine, and the child who would soon celebrate his first birthday.

"I shall give you my answer in the morning," he said, although he knew it already.

* * *

Leaning heavily on the abbot's arm, Catherine slowly made her way into the Chapter House at St. Buryan and took up a stance in the center of the dais. Her ladies had coiled and bound her hair, and for the first time in England, pinned her mother's garnet brooch to the black velvet headband and veil that covered her hair. Now they draped the folds of the short gauzy veil that fell to her shoulders and arranged her skirt around her. They stepped back. The abbot took up his position on the dais.

"Are you certain you can stand without help, my lady?" asked Agatha.

"Aye," Catherine managed in a hoarse whisper. *I must stand*, she thought. This moment would decide the entire course of the rest of her life. She had to meet it with dignity.

The abbot, who had a vague knowledge of the content of the messengers' report, tried to persuade her differently. "My lady, mayhap a chair can be placed—"

"Dear abbot, I fear I am not as strong as I would wish, but a chair would appear to be a crutch. That is not seemly under the circumstances. I must stand without assistance before the king's men."

From the corner of her eye, Catherine saw Alice appear with Dickon in her arms. In spite of her anxiety, her mouth lifted at the corners. "Alice—pray, give me my bairn."

"My Lady Cate, are ye strong enough to carry him? 'Tis the first time you have stood in weeks—"

"For that reason you may remain here on the dais—but behind me, by the wall—in case we should need you." Though she spoke firmly, in truth Catherine felt weak. Her legs were unsteady and she feared to move lest she lose her balance and fall. Rigidly, she accepted her sleeping child from Alice's arms and placed the lightest of kisses on Dickon's angelic face so as not to awaken him. But Dickon, his slumber disturbed by the sudden jolting movement, stretched out his hands and splayed his fingers wide. Catherine's smile widened into one of such sweetness as she gazed upon her child, that it pierced the abbot to the heart and he whispered a prayer for her under his breath.

Catherine braced herself, and gave the abbot a nod. "They may enter now."

The abbot, in turn, passed the signal along to the monk at the door, and the man undid the latch. Across the octagonal room, Catherine watched a group of nobles and knights approach, their boots clattering against the tile floor, their swords clanging at their sides. At their head strode a well-made man in silver and red velvet. Catherine knew immediately that this was the seasoned warrior and king's chamberlain, Lord Giles Daubeney, who had suppressed the Cornishmen's rebellion a month earlier at Black Heath. With him came the Earl of Shrewsbury, master of the household to Henry VII, and Lord William Courtenay, son of the Earl of Devon. Courtenay had recently wed Richard's sister, the Yorkist Princess Katherine Plantagenet, but she knew better than to expect help from that quarter, for he and his father had expelled Richard from Exeter.

Lord Daubeney swept his plumed cap from his head with a low

bow. Catherine noted absently the touch of gray at his temples and the creases around his eyes and mouth. His was a good face, not unduly fierce. She took in these things without being aware, for her mind was focused on Richard, and this man brought news of him.

"My lady, we are here to inform you of the outcome of your husband's efforts to seize the crown of England." Daubeney tried not to stare at the singularly beautiful girl with eyes like gems and hair of gleaming ebony who stood so gracefully before him in a stained tawny sea gown, her flaxen-haired babe asleep at her shoulder. The Scottish princess aroused his Yorkist sympathies, reminding him of the oath of fealty he'd once taken to York. Knighted by King Edward IV, he had espoused the Lancastrian cause only because he believed that Richard III had killed his royal brother's sons and usurped the throne. Now her husband claimed to be the younger prince, to have survived the Tower, to be the rightful King of England. He could not know the truth of the matter, but he hated with all his being the distress he was about to cause this fair damsel. He disliked the Tudor's harsh ways, and mitigated them when it was possible to do so without harm to himself, but recently he had fallen into disfavor for taking too long to get to London to quell the Cornish rebellion against Henry's high taxes. By his delay, he had secretly hoped to give the Cornishmen a chance to prevail, but they had failed, and he had been obliged to crush them, the poor bastards. Even now, at great personal risk to himself, he had managed to destroy the names in the coffer that the Pretender had abandoned in his haste to flee Taunton and save himself. Daubeney's mouth curved in distaste. At least the coward could have burned the coffer before he so foully deserted his men.

Daubeney did what he could, when he could, but he was a pragmatist. The Pretender had failed—and miserably so—to wrench the scepter from the iron grip of the Tudor who held it. Whether he was the true son of Edward IV made no difference any longer. The House of York had been led to destruction by a coward and a fool, and there was absolutely naught to be done for this young woman, no matter how it shredded the heart to deliver such cruel tidings.

"Lady Catherine Gordon, I am here to inform you of the events that have transpired in these two weeks since Taunton. No doubt you know much of what has happened, do you not?"

"I have been apprised of events at Exeter, Lord Daubeney, but nothing more. I know not the outcome of the battle at Taunton. I pray you to impart it to me now."

So it fell to him to deliver the sorry tidings. Daubeney inhaled a long breath. "My lady, there was no battle at Taunton."

"No battle?" Catherine echoed in stunned amazement. "I don't understand—"

"We did not fight, my lady. When I arrived, the battlefield was empty. Your husband, the one who calls himself Richard, Duke of York, son of King Edward IV, deserted his troops in the night and fled to Beaulieu Abbey to seek sanctuary with a small band of followers."

An audible gasp resounded from the abbot, who had not known this detail, and Catherine's ladies cried out in shock. But Catherine took no breath, for the air seemed to have gone out of the room. She stared at Daubeney, not knowing what to think, casting about in her mind to make sense of the jumble of words she had just heard. Desertion of his troops? Flight in the middle of the night? She could not believe such a thing—it was too dreadful—it was not possible! They could tell her whatever they pleased now, and she would not know what was true, and what was false, but of one thing she was sure—Richard would never abandon his troops this way. *Never.* She found her voice. "You are a liar, sir!"

"I regret deeply, my lady, that I speak truth. Your husband deserted his men in the dead of night. They waited for him to return, but he did not. Many of them remained steadfastly loyal and did not leave until I was almost upon them. In the end, sorely disheartened, they were forced to abandon his cause and take flight themselves."

Catherine felt the pang of doubt, for Daubeney's grave expression suggested that he did not prevaricate, nor did he relish the tidings he brought her. But she refused to believe such an appalling thing. She tightened her hold of her babe and lifted her chin. "Where is my lord husband now? Is he at Beaulieu?"

"He has left sanctuary and is on his way to meet King Henry at Taunton."

"Left?" Catherine echoed in horror. "Left—" She felt her blood drain to her feet. Dear God—the room was tilting around her. A burning pain ripped through her body and she closed her eyes to steady herself. *No—no—Richard, Richard—* All knew how this usurper violated the laws of sanctuary! He had sent sixty men to snatch Sir Humphrey Stafford, and a hundred and twenty to take Sir Robert Chamberlain. He did not fret about his soul when his crown stood in jeopardy. She braced herself to ask what she had to know. "Left—or extracted by force?" She had no idea where her courage came from, but the Scots were never supple at the knees, and the adversity of climate, geography, and history had made them fiercely independent. The Gordon Highlanders were made of even sterner stuff, her father had always told her, and it seemed she was her father's daughter, as defiant as the rest of them, even in the face of doom.

"He left of his own accord, by arrangement with King Henry," Daubeney replied. "He has confessed to being Perkin Warbeck, a boatman's son, and has written his mother in Flanders asking for money to buy luxuries that might ease his imprisonment."

"That is absurd! I am well aware how confessions are obtained—and the Tower stands to remind those who forget. If he wrote such a letter, he wrote it under duress. I know him. He is Richard, second son of King Edward IV, and a prince of England—"

Daubeney made no reply, but he looked at her with compassion. Gently, he said, "My lady, my instructions are to take you to King Henry."

"I am in sanctuary, in case you have not noticed. Would you extract a helpless woman by force, as you extracted my husband?"

"My lady, I assure you he left of his own free will. In any case, he is now in the king's custody, and I urge you to consider how much more harshly matters will go for him if you do not comply with King Henry's request."

Full realization dawned. A shudder tingled along Catherine's spine. No doubt they had used her and Dickon against Richard, and he had complied for their sake, as she would comply for his. For a moment, it seemed to her that she stood outside herself, looking down on this dread scene from somewhere high above, that it was not real, not happening to her but to someone else. She blinked. She was indeed here, and Daubeney awaited her answer.

"Very well," she said softly, her strength ebbing away. "We shall be ready for you in the morning. Pray excuse us now. My son needs his rest—"

Hastily, Daubeney cut in, "Your ladies may come with you, if you so choose." He hesitated again. He had no wish to deliver the rest of his message, but Henry VII was watching him, carefully assessing his performance, and this involved his own survival, and that of his family. He braced himself and rushed on, "But not your son."

Clutching her child tightly to her, Catherine backed away in horror. "Not—my—son?"

"King Henry has other plans for the babe."

"What—other—plans—" Her voice trembled violently.

"I am not at liberty to say, my lady," Lord Daubeney replied through ashen lips. "But the child has no need of sanctuary and must be taken now." He turned and nodded to Courtenay to seize the babe, but Courtenay made no move. The young man stood staring at him as if he were rooted to the ground, his eyes full of desolate entreaty. *Do not ask this of me,* they pleaded. *I cannot do it.*

Daubeney swung on the lord chamberlain, and the older man knew that if he valued his life, liberty, or goods, he must obey. Daubeney would not be gainsaid twice before his men. His heels clicking on the tile, the doddery old Earl of Shrewsbury approached the dais and mounted the steps. As he did so, in Catherine's consciousness, each step he took struck the solid stone of the walls and pillars, resounded against the vaulted ceiling, and was cast down with the force of a thousand shards of glass exploding to earth. She felt her blood surging through her body as she turned to flee with her child wailing in her arms, but her legs were leaden and she had no power of movement. She doubled up in agony; her grip loosened on her child. And from far behind her, deep in the darkness, a faint, distant voice sang a lament that she heard but dimly, for the voice was falling away; fading along echoing passageways, as if into deepest night. *"Dic-kon-on-on-on—"* it whispered and, like a wind, was gone.

Chapter 5

Quo Es Tu, Deus?

Disembodied voices mumbled around her. Catherine strained to make out what they said, but she could not. It was a gloomy place where she stood, dimmed by floating vapors. When the vapors cleared, she saw that the place was a cemetery, one choked with weeds and crowded with crooked tombstones. Backing away, she lost her footing and fell to ground of burned earth, broken by fissures that emitted foul sulphurous fumes. She struggled to her feet. Men on horses galloped to and fro, bearing pale banners that fluttered vaguely above their heads like torn veils. *I know this place*, she thought. *'Tis the kingdom of the shadowy dead.*

She continued forward on the grim terrain. A hissing came to her and she looked up. The wind was making an arc above her head. Caught in its circling currents were vile black things with birdlike forms resembling dragons. They had scaly wings and coiled tails, and one, more hideous than the rest, bore the face of a man. The creature gnawed on the carcass of a child he carried by his tail as he whirled about in the dark wind. Terror found her then, and she screamed for Richard. All at once he beamed at her and she forgot about the birds.

She smiled at him, so handsome in his white damask robe and short furred cape of taffeta, his wedding crown on his golden hair. "Dance, my Celtic princess, dance—" he said, not moving his lips. She took his hand. Music played, a ferocious Highland melody. Its wild pace kept quickening, forcing them to leap and twirl ever faster, but who was that crowned figure who watched them? She turned to ask Richard but he was gone and there was naught but silence now; a silence more dreadful than the shattering music that went before.

She kept walking, and looking, but the landscape was strange and she saw no one she knew. All at once there appeared a hemisphere of light ahead that lit the darkness. Someone stood against the light, and she saw it was the crowned figure that had watched her dance with Richard. *I want to go there*, she thought, and she was there, and she saw that the figure, tall and stately, was neither male nor female. It was stained with blood and crowned with a horned serpent, its waist bound in cords of spotted snakes. Behind the dread figure, in the radiant light, a beautiful hillside sloped down gently, covered with exquisite lilies and horses grazing, and a creek, and she saw her mother sewing a silken embroidery in a field.

"I want to come to you," Catherine said to the figure, recognizing it as Death.

"You may not enter here. It is not your time," said Death.

As Catherine watched, a soft mist floated across the idyllic scene and closed it off from view, and Death vanished into its floating whiteness, leaving her friendless again in the hellish landscape. "Father, help me!" she cried, and instantly her father stood before her, laughing, and merry with wine. He toasted her with a golden goblet while her younger brother William looked on. She was at Huntly Castle on the banks of the River Deveron, a child skipping with other children around the ancient circle of stones in the village. She moved past the circle of stones and halted. The terrain had changed back to burned earth beneath her feet, and the fearsome birds had returned. They formed a black cloud over her head and emitted a cacophony of evil sounds. She turned to flee, but each marker in the ancient stone circle that she had passed now leapt up before her to block her way and they were all spotted, writhing serpents. She screamed, and awoke to find herself in a creaking wagon, lying on a pallet.

"M'lady, my Lady Cate—" Alice's eyes were moist as she gazed at her and mopped her brow with a damp cloth. "What ails ye? Do ye have pain?"

"Nightmare," she managed. "Where are we?"

"We are passing the Merry Maidens near St. Buryan."

Catherine turned her head. In the distant fields a stone circle marked the bleak terrain, but otherwise it was devoid of life, and thankfully, there were no birds. "The Merry Maidens," she echoed.

"'Tis what the natives call them. They remind me of the ancient circle of stone in Strathbogie where we used to play as children. Remember, M'lady Cate?"

"Aye," said Catherine, closing her eyes, "I remember . . ."

"How is she?" demanded Lord Daubeney, riding up to Alice's side.

"Asleep for now," Alice replied softly, her voice trembling. "Her fever still rages and her heart beats too rapidly—" She bit her lip. "She has lost much blood with the dead child she birthed, m'lord. I fear she will not survive the journey to London."

Daubeney turned his eyes on Catherine. His heart ached for this still, nearly lifeless figure who only two days ago had displayed such courage in the face of cruel Fortune. *God help her,* he thought, *and God forgive me for what I must do next.* "I shall send to King Henry and inform him that the Lady Catherine is in dole and needs time to mourn. Meanwhile we shall take her to the Mount instead of London. I will join you there after I have discharged a pressing duty."

Alice's eyes filled with tears, and one by one they rolled down her cheeks for she knew too well what that duty was. He was taking Dickon away to where no one would ever find him again.

*   *   *

Richard dismounted, an oppressive tightness in his chest. In the last few days, his fear for Catherine and Dickon had reached frenzied proportions. The Tudor would get them, and there was nothing in this world that he could do for them. He might as well be dead, and now he wished he was. His horror of capture had worn itself out and an onerous burden of shame had descended in its place. The last time he had been at Taunton, he had an army at his back, and honor. Now the captain had returned as captive. Worse, men called him a coward, the vilest epithet in the English language. Whatever Fate held in store for him, he had to meet it with fortitude. Maybe then some shred of honor would be restored to him. Maybe then Catherine would not be repelled by the thought of him, as she surely must be now. That was the greatest shame of all—that she would learn of what he had done, and despise him for evermore.

He looked up at the elegant Augustinian Priory where the usurper waited. The building could not be more different from the roofless, dilapidated so-called castle where he had made his last stand. But to the victor go the spoils, not the least of which was comfort.

"This way, my—" Richmond Herald bit his tongue, and not a moment too soon. Once again he was about to say "my lord." The young man not only looked every inch a prince of the blood, but had deported himself with dignity throughout the journey. Richmond Herald remembered with near-blinding clarity the moment the young man had surrendered himself from sanctuary at Beaulieu, and never would he forget, such a shock had it been.

The Pretender had discarded his homespun cowl and emerged from sanctuary arrayed in cloth of gold, looking every inch the prince he claimed to be. He had charm and wit; he had the manners, grace, parlance, and bearing of a Plantagenet, and it was impossible to believe that he was a boatman's son in disguise—a *garçon*—a "feigned boy"—as King Henry liked to call him. During their long journey together, Richmond Herald had stolen many a surreptitious glance at him and received the curious sensation of time flown backward. As if the tears rent in its fabric by the Wars of the Roses had never happened and at his side rode the new king, son of the late Edward IV, as it should have been.

But Richmond Herald quickly quelled his treasonous thoughts. This young man was a coward, and not fit to lead England, even if he were the true son of the beloved King Edward. Passing through the arched entrance of the abbey and ascending the marble steps of an elegant double staircase, Herald led the would-be king to meet the king-who-was, a couplet spoken by a dead Yorkist friend chiming in his head: "Treason doth never prosper—what's the reason? For if it prosper, none dare call it treason." Aye indeed, such were the rules in the game of kings, and best he never forget. He took his leave of Richard at the door of the chamber.

Richard surveyed the room as he entered. It was as grand and impressive as any he had seen in France, Flanders, Venice, Rome, or Bohemia. His eye fell on a desk in the corner, set with a candelabra such as he had admired in Vienna when he'd attended the funeral of the Holy Roman Emperor, Ferdinand III, and was proclaimed Richard IV.

A commotion in the hall announced the king, and the door was thrown open to reveal a lanky man in his early forties, wearing a crimson and gold velvet robe studded with jewels. He was about Richard's height, with a bony face, pale hooded eyes, and limp brown-gray hair. A sudden, overwhelming impression of coldness struck Richard with full force. The man stood perfectly still, taking Richard's measure in one long, unwavering gaze as servants shut the door behind him. Richard could see from his flushed cheeks that he was as nervous as he was excited and that he was much taken by surprise, and trying to recover his composure.

In truth, King Henry VII was astonished into speechlessness. What he saw before him—and not without a pang of envy—was a weary, fair-haired, muscular young man in the full bloom of youth who discontented him both with his good looks and his graceful princely stance. No one could have mistaken him, Henry, for a king in the days before Bosworth. Arrayed in cloth of gold and unadorned by jewels, the young man exuded as much royal presence as he himself did in circlet, furs, gems, and rich velvet robes after eleven years of kingship. The only physical imperfection Henry could see was the young man's dull left eye. He thought, uncomfortably, that this had been a mark of the Plantagenets, borne by the two kings Henry III and Edward I. Abruptly his thoughts took a more pleasing turn. In one important aspect—and the only one that counted—he bested the fellow. Of what use were his princely attributes and pretensions when he stood here a captive, no better than a slave? Richard's fate rested entirely in Henry's hands and no one could help him now. The thought brought a smile to his lips.

"So . . . you have bedecked yourself in the apparel of a king," he said, closing the distance between them.

Because I am a king, Richard wanted to reply, but he said nothing.

"Yet you claim to be—" Henry strode to the desk. He turned the papers toward him, and glanced down. "Piers Osbeck. At least, such is the name you gave at Beaulieu."

"You have promised me fair treatment and that you will not harm my wife and child. For this reason, I am willing to say I am whoever you wish."

Henry slammed his fist on the desk. "I want to know from your own lips who you really are!"

Richard's heart thumped wildly. He knew this man could tear him from limb to limb as he'd done to many others, but he would rely on Henry's royal word, transmitted to him by Richmond Herald, that he would be treated honorably. More bravely than he felt, he said, "You already know that. It is what the world is given to know that matters, is it not?"

"Do not delude yourself—you are no prince of the blood, you coward!" Henry spat.

"You, too, ran away the night before Bosworth," Richard reminded him. He could have also reminded him—had he dared—of Henry's terror at St. Malo, when Duke Francis of Brittany had delivered him up to an English embassy about to take ship to England. Henry, in a frenzy of fear, convinced he was going to his death, fell desperately ill with an ague, and Duke Francis, taking pity, changed his mind and did not send him back to England.

Instantly, Richard regretted his words. A vein twitched in Henry's forehead, and his eyes took on a wolfish glare. He closed the gap between them until they stood almost nose to nose.

"You'll pay for that, mark my words—" he hissed. "I won Bosworth.

You lost Taunton. You are my captive now, and no more to me than dog flesh—"

Henry recovered his cool demeanor, and drew himself up to his full height. "I am a patient man. Unlike you, I do nothing rashly and always calculate the consequences of my action. Every battle is won before it is ever fought. And I won Exeter in 1495."

"When you executed William Stanley."

They locked eyes. Henry VII smiled coldly. "Exactly."

And Bosworth when you had King Richard's son poisoned. Richard dropped his gaze to hide his thoughts. More than anything in the world, he wanted to live.

"I tell you this because I have not yet decided what to do with you," Henry resumed. He strode back to the desk and rubbed his jaw thoughtfully as he regarded Richard. "However, one thing is certain. It can go hard for you, or it can go easy. Which is your preference?"

"When you put it that way—" Richard gave Henry a wan smile, but if he thought to soften Henry's stern expression, he failed. More gravely, he added, "I pray you remember that regicide is a loathsome sin in God's eyes, and that He will send the devils of Hell to tear out the throat of the sinner."

"Brave words from a coward and you shall vomit them when I have done with you! I shall show you as a fool before all the world. You shall be known to the ages as the false prince who would be king."

Richard swallowed hard. Henry was a superstitious man, and Richard had thought to help himself by using his fear of God against him, but it had instead fired his anger. "I am what I am, and I will do anything you wish of me. I beseech only one boon."

Henry waited.

"I beg you to send my wife back to Scotland. She has no part in our quarrel."

"Perhaps not," replied Henry, "but as I explained, I do nothing rashly. Therefore I promise nothing. Meanwhile, to get back to the matter at hand, I hold the crown, and you are who I say you are. Whatever you call yourself, you are naught but a boatman's son."

Richard lifted his chin in reply, but said nothing.

"You are going into that room across the hall and you will tell the lords assembled there that you lied," Henry resumed. "You will tell them that you are an imposter. That you have not an ounce of royal blood in your veins. Is that understood?"

"Clearly," Richard replied.

"But first," said Henry. "You'll need a change of clothes. Cloth of gold does not become you."

*   *   *

Henry strode into the council chamber, and Richard followed behind. Even though he was now attired in a humble tunic devoid of the trappings of nobility, he thought he heard a soft gasp as he entered, one hastily suppressed. They, like their master, were taken aback by his likeness to his father, King Edward, and he wondered absently if that bode him well, or ill.

"We present to you the imposter prince—the boatman's son, Piers Osbeck from Flanders," said Henry.

Richard gave King Henry a stiff bow, and asked for mercy, as he had been instructed to do. At least he didn't have to prostrate himself on the floor, as traitors normally did. Henry had not demanded that, perhaps because Richard was not supposed to have been born an English subject, or perhaps because Henry knew it was not something to which Richard would have readily submitted, even in his circumstances.

"We have heard," said Henry, "that you call yourself Richard, son of King Edward. In this room are some who were companions of that lord. Look around and see if you recognize them."

Richard didn't bother to glance at the faces. "I do not know any of these men," he said without hesitation. But among those in the crowd that he had glimpsed as he'd entered was John Rodon, the servant who had turned down his sheets and brought him his nightly cup of watery wine when he'd been a child. Rodon had not joined the conspirators of 1495 because he had received several royal appointments from Henry and enjoyed a good life that he had no desire to relinquish. Richard had also seen his half-brother, Thomas Grey, Marquess of Dorset. Though Dorset had changed much in the intervening years—as Richard had—neither could say they knew one another. Dorset had not joined the conspiracy because Henry held his son hostage, and he was also in financial bondage to Henry, his lands and titles forfeit until such time he proved his loyalty to Henry's satisfaction. Every man here knew—as Richard knew—that he had to be the imposter now.

"I do not know these men," Richard went on, as Henry had instructed him. "I have never been to England. I have been induced by the English and the Irish to learn the English language and commit this fraud. For two years I have longed to escape these troubles, but Fortune did not permit me to."

At least the last sentence was true, Richard thought, remembering with an ache the night at the Mount when Catherine had begged him to abandon his quest. With all his being, he'd wanted to turn back, but to do so would have meant letting down those who depended on him. Yet, in the end, he had betrayed them all in the most faithless and despicable fashion possible, from his royal Aunt Meg down to the poorest tin miner. He let his head drop, depleted by the effort and strain of surrendering his hopes, his dreams, his freedom, and everything he held dear to his bitterest foe on earth.

"Guards, remove him," said Henry. "You, my lords, have heard what this feigned boy has to say. He didn't recognize any of you and"—he turned to Richard's boyhood servant—"for certes, he should have known you, Rodon, shouldn't he, my man?"

"Aye, Sire," replied Rodon. "He should have."

Rodon kept seeing in his mind's eye the beautiful fair-haired boy he had once served, and loved. The young man who had come into the room was that child grown: the same dull left eye, the same little scar beneath the eye. Maybe even the same mole high on his thigh, if anyone had cared to look.

What would become of his prince? Rodon heaved a long sigh.

Best he not think on it, he told himself. There was nothing to be done about it now, was there? Nothing at all, and in this world every man had to look out for himself.

*   *   *

Lord Daubeney finished reading King Henry's missive, and turned thoughtfully to the window, assailed by a gamut of tangled emotions. The winds were roaring around the Mount and lashing the waves, as if to whip them into submission, and for some reason, he thought of King Henry and the young Pretender, and the road he himself had taken long ago that had brought him here, to this point in his life and the distasteful task that awaited.

Mayhap, Daubeney thought, he'd made the wrong decision in 1484, but what good was regret when the shit could not be put back into the horse? Would he change anything even if he could? Henry had been grateful to him. He'd done well under the Tudor. Though he was low born, he enjoyed a high position as Tudor's foremost military commander, for Tudor had a distrust of those better born than himself. Daubeney had even been created lord, one of the few times that tight-fisted Tudor had given away a barony.

He glanced back at the letter in his hand. Henry had instructed him to deliver Lady Catherine to him as soon as he'd taken her from sanctuary, but he had delayed. His sovereign had accepted his reason for keeping her back, but his letter also held warning. Daubeney had explained Catherine's delirium following the birth of her dead child, and last week, he'd followed up that missive with another advising the king that Catherine would likely survive, but her health remained delicate and she needed to build up her strength for the journey to Shene.

"We trust she shall shortly come unto us," Henry had written back, "as she is in dole." The "dole" meant she could have time to mourn; the "shortly" meant she couldn't have much. King Henry had looked forward to this moment for two years, and he wanted to see his prize. He had an eye for women, and Lady Catherine was a beauty of legendary fame across Britain. *Aye*, Daubeney thought with an audible sigh, Henry wanted his prize, and he didn't want to wait a moment longer than he had to.

Daubeney had seen much on the battlefield, both of suffering and of valor. But this was different. Catherine was not simply in fragile health physically; she was in deep emotional distress from the capture of her husband and the implosion of her world. In a single blow, Fate had stripped her of husband, children, kith and kin, and surrendered her up to the mercy of her enemies. Yet in the face of cruel Fortune, she had held her head high at St. Buryan with a courage he had found deeply touching. He simply didn't have the heart to surrender her to the Tudor, who had taken so much from her already, and might yet take more. He turned to his scrivener.

"Write this in answer to the king . . . To His Most High Grace and Savior of England, Henry VII, by God's Grace King of England—et cetera . . ." he dictated. "The Lady Catherine has but one gown, and that gown is torn and stained, and shows evidence of her travails. Should you wish to have her displayed in more suitable attire—since that would reflect on your great mercy—I most humbly request your royal permission to order a new gown for her. If you could advise me yea or nay as to this matter, and if yea, how much I should spend, I would be most grateful to your Majesty."

That should buy her a few more days, he thought. With a wave of his hand, he dismissed the scrivener.

Daubeney leaned his weight on the windowsill and gazed out at the gloomy clouds passing swiftly overhead. Never would he have had to trouble King Edward IV or Richard III on such a trivial matter, for both had been generous men. Tudor's parsimony had raised eyebrows across the land from the first, but now, with his spies well launched in the kingdom and the Tower generously supplied with horrific instruments of torture, men no longer dared take anything for granted, even the expenditure of such a small sum from the royal purse. Henry had a long memory, was tight-fisted and vengeful, and Daubeney knew he had to be careful where he trod.

There were, however, some things a man of conscience could not do. One was to deliver this poor young beauty to the dragon before she had the strength to stand and meet her fate with dignity.

* * *

At the Mount, oblivious to the murmur of voices in the court and the chanting of the monks in the chapel, Catherine stood quietly as her ladies dressed her in the new attire King Henry had sent for her journey to London: black hose and shoes, black kirtle and satin gown with a braid of black ribbon decorating the high square collar and running down the front and along the hem. They adjusted the braided belt low on her hips, and helped her into a black velvet riding cloak and a matching velvet hat. She found it ironic that what had been set in motion by a king's gift of fifteen ells of crimson satin on her eighteenth birthday and an invitation to a royal feast should end two years later in a king's gift of black satin for a mourning gown, and a summons to appear at his court.

She remembered little of these past weeks, for she had been fading in and out of consciousness, and her ladies had feared for her life—so they had told her. But one day, she had opened her eyes and not drifted back into deep sleep. "Agatha?" she'd asked, gazing at her lady-in-waiting with an unusually bright and steady look. Agatha had laid down her rosary beads and run to summon Alice, crying, "The Virgin has answered our prayers—our lady lives!"

So they told her.

The sick giddiness Catherine remembered was gone, though her head still pounded. Alice set her riding cloak carefully over her shoulders, and handed her the black gloves the king had sent. As Catherine pulled them on, she lifted her gaze to Alice's empty arms. A thought from Scripture froze in her mind: *He giveth, and he taketh away.* She turned her face to the window; the panes were glazed with ice, and she could see nothing. Now she heard the words the monks chanted in the church, *Quo es Tu, Deus? Quare me repulisti . . . quare tristis incedo, dum affligit me inimicus?* Where are You, God? Why do You reject me? Why must I go about in mourning, with the enemy oppressing me?

Catherine joined her voice softly to theirs. "Why are you so downcast, O my soul?" she sang. "Why do you sigh within me? Send forth Your light and Your fidelity, O my God. Then I will give thanks to You upon my harp, O God, my God—" She broke off. The words felt hollow to her and gave no comfort. She noticed tears glistening in the eyes of her companions, and wondered why they were touched when she felt nothing.

"You are ready," Agatha said.

Catherine took the arm Alice offered, for she still had difficulty walking. Today they would leave the Mount, and on the way she wished to stop at the cow shed to bid Brother Nicholas farewell. Slowly she maneuvered the steep stone steps that wound down to the ledge, trailed by a flock of Lord Daubeney's men who had been set to guard her. She was nearly upon the old monk before he noticed her approach.

"Lady Catherine—" He broke off, his eyes misting at the sight of her. Beneath her black hood her face was even paler than he remembered. The last time he'd seen her, she was stretched out on a litter, prostrate and near death as they'd carried her to St. Buryan. Even so, she had brought to mind a pale rose that shines bright against the gloom of downcast skies. Even time might not be able to erase beauty that deep, he thought, yet what good did it do her? He averted his gaze lest his eyes betray his thoughts. Taking Bessie and Michelle by their halters, he led them to the barn, their bells tinkling loudly in the wind, and deposited them by a bale of hay where the others already stood lazily munching the cud.

Catherine watched as he came toward her. She, too, was thinking of the last time she had seen Brother Nicholas. It was before Richard had left for—no, she must not dwell on what was, and what can never be again. She attempted a smile as she threw a glance behind him at the cow shed. "How are they doing?" she asked.

"They are well, my dear lady, and Michelle is blessed to have a healthy new calf born to her last month."

Tears sprang to Catherine's eyes. She blinked them gone. "Forgive me—"

"There is nothing to forgive, my child." He stretched out his hand to her, penitent to have inflicted grief with his careless words. "Here, let us sit together, as we did long ago."

Of course, it was not long ago, only a few weeks past, but so much had happened that it might as well have been another lifetime. Of Richard, and wee Dickon, and her dead babe, she dared not think, but thoughts of her father did not need quelling. Despite the monk's gentleness and her father's stoicism, this dear man reminded her of him so very much. A vision of her father bidding her farewell at Ayr rose up before her . . . Ayr, where she might have stopped Richard. "If only we could turn time back, how much could be set right," she whispered.

He patted her hand, but didn't trust himself to speak.

Catherine found her voice again. "I could not leave here 'ere I spoke to you. They tell me that my lord—my lord—" She could barely get out the words, so terrible were they. "That he—he deserted his men at Taunton. Is it true?"

The old monk bowed his head and didn't reply for a long moment. Some of those men had returned to the Mount from Taunton, weeping, still disbelieving and asking the monks for answers that none could give. "I was willing to die for him," one cried, "and he abandoned us—" He had looked at the poor man on whose head the tyrant's fearful wrath would soon fall. "Remember, my son, the flesh is weak," he had replied, "and tender are the petals of youth."

"Aye, 'tis true," Brother Nicholas murmured.

In the silence that fell between them, Catherine heard the deafening force of the howling winds, the mewing of the birds, and the angry roar of the ocean dashing the rocks below. She closed her eyes against the tumult in her mind. To have this dreadful knowledge confirmed—it was too terrible to be true! And yet—and yet—

She couldn't believe it of Richard. He would never desert his troops to save himself. Compassion was his most compelling trait, and compassion alone would not have permitted him to abandon his men so heedlessly. The suffering of others had always affected him deeply, and over their twenty-two months together she'd borne witness to a multitude of little acts of pity and largess. He once encountered a blind dove slamming into walls and slew it for mercy's sake as he wept for what he had to do. But his greatest act of pity was his vain effort to turn James back from the pain of war. That such a kind heart should shrink from killing others—even his enemies— must surely come as no surprise?

No, she would not accept cowardice, but she did accept partial blame. Mindless, oblivious, giddy with excitement and the promise of adventure, had she not recklessly urged him on at Ayr? But for her, Richard would not have gone into battle unprepared the way he did, alone and facing terrors unimaginable.

If she had only allowed herself to see matters more clearly, she might have anticipated this outcome. Without the knight's training to harden him to killing and warfare, and with no military commander to advise him, how could Richard not shrink from what lay ahead? Nor did his soft heart help him in war.

She closed her eyes. She would not be so quick to condemn him. His defeat had already condemned him. That was the cruelest tragedy—for Richard, and for England. He would have made a fine king, could he have but won back his throne.

She said, "I had a fearful dream, Brother Nicholas. I dreamt of Death."

The monk looked at her, but said nothing.

"He—it—wore a terrible guise—and still, I wished to go with him. Have you ever heard of such a thing?"

"Indeed I have, my dear. Those who have returned from the threshold of death tell us of such things."

"I wanted to go with it—with him—I begged to go. But he wouldn't have me. He said it wasn't my time. God has rejected me, and so, too, has Death. What do I do, Brother Nicholas? How do I go on? What do I live for? You have to tell me. I know not how to go on—"

"Nay, nay, my child! God has not rejected you. In all your woe, He is ever with thee, but you must believe—you must have faith. The Devil sends us trials to turn us away from God. You must cling to

Him with all your strength, and I am thinking that you are stronger than you know. Your husband lives, and somewhere your child also lives. They need you, my dear. You must be strong and carry on—for them."

Catherine closed her eyes to better feel the soothing salt spray of the sea against her cheeks, and to better hear the steady rhythm of the waves, ebbing to and fro as if nothing of great import had happened to alter their direction since Creation. How wonderful it would be to turn into a droplet of water and become part of the sea; to be safe in the serene, unfathomable depths that mortal man can never touch. Safe from winds and storms that ruffle the surface but never reach deep enough to break the heart.

She opened her eyes and lifted her gaze to the Mount. Armed men stood on the ledge above, looking down on her. How she wished she could believe that God cared, that her life mattered, but inside she felt scraped hollow, emptied of all emotion. Her wandering gaze settled on the sky, seat of the heavens. Hope in the world beyond held no luster for her and seemed more a waning point of light than even hope in this earthly world. More for Brother Nicholas than for her own sake, she made the request she knew he expected.

"Brother Nicholas, will you bless me?"

The old monk rose to his feet, and Catherine went to her knees before him.

"Thank you," she said, rising wearily. "I will not say farewell, for there have been too many of those of late. But know that I will never forget you."

They embraced one last time. As she turned away, her glance fell on the Mount looming dark against the sky. There, in that corner jutting out over the sea and lashed by the winds, stood the chamber where she had lain with Richard and held her child against her heart. This stone fortress had borne witness to her dreams, and to the destruction of her world.

She leaned heavily on Alice's arm as she mounted the mule that was brought for her. Her heart a leaden weight in her breast, she picked her way down the steep stone steps, the men who trailed her following closely behind.

As he watched her leave for the vessel that would take her to London, memories swirled in Brother Nicholas's mind: the arrival of the *Cuckoo*, which had borne the tiny royal family to England; Catherine, with child, riding up to the Mount, her husband leading her mule; the nurse carrying their babe in the twilight. He remembered the hope with which they had come, a bleak contrast to the despair in which she left. And it touched him to the quick that she had not asked for his prayers.

Chapter 6

Red Rose, White Rose

The palace of Shene rose up before Catherine, splendid and festive, for the Feast of Saints Simon and Jude was fast approaching. The sea voyage from the Mount to London had been taxing and she was glad to have it behind her, yet she could scarcely say she was pleased to have arrived here, in this dread place. Imposing it was, and set like a jewel on the south bank of the Thames with a lovely view along the river, but it boded her no good, this lair of the monster that had usurped Richard's throne and torn her babe from her arms. Her roving eye caught on Tudor's shield, carved into the stone of the gatehouse looming ahead. Emblazoned with leopards and fleurs-de-lis, the shield displayed a dragon on one side and a lion on the other, all standing on a scroll of roses. She felt a vague tremor and cast down her eyes as they trotted over the moat and into the great court.

Behind her and her small party strode more guards. To ensure she would not turn and flee, she supposed. But where was she to flee? The Tudor must be an overly cautious man if he did not know she had no friends in this alien land that hated the Scots and had rejected her husband.

Richard . . . Would she see him here? She both yearned—and

feared—such a possibility. To see him captive, in the hands of his arch-enemy, could not be a blessing—

And what of Dickon—

Somewhere my babe cries for me, she thought, and stumbled in her steps.

"My Lady Cate!" Alice exclaimed.

Daubeney's arm went around her shoulders, and she sagged against him gratefully. "We may rest a moment, if you wish, my lady," he said. "The path is steep."

Catherine's broken heart felt like a heavy black rock within her chest. *Nay, I must not think on him now, not yet.* She swallowed her torment and looked at Daubeney in bleak despair. She shook her head.

All she knew for certain was that she would meet the Tudor—and Richard's sister, Elizabeth of York, his queen. She wondered if Elizabeth ever thought about her brother. Surely she would not let her husband harm Richard, for how could she live with herself if she did? Ah, but they said Elizabeth had no influence on the Tudor. She had loved her uncle, Richard III, who had been slain at Bosworth by the Tudor. Scandalized by the rumors of Elizabeth's torrid affair, the Tudor had spurned to wed her when he took the throne, but Elizabeth's mother, an ambitious and determined woman, contrived to prove to him that Elizabeth was a virgin, and arranged a liaison in the month of Yule. From this encounter Elizabeth emerged *enceinte.* Henry and Elizabeth wed in January, after Epiphany, and their child, a son, was born eight months later, in September.

The tale bore an uncanny resemblance to her own circumstances. Dickon, too, had been conceived out of wedlock and was born a month early, in September. Uncertain hope flared in Catherine's breast. *Maybe Elizabeth will get me back my child.*

She and her sister-in-law seemed bound by destiny in many ways. Had Richard's bid for the throne proved successful, she would have been queen and Elizabeth would be walking up to this palace in her stead. Then her wee Dickon would have been the heir to the throne instead of Elizabeth's son, Arthur. A stab of pain came and went, but this time she did not falter. She merely closed her eyes.

If she could trade places with Elizabeth and be queen, never having known a day of wedded joy, would she do it? And if Elizabeth had been offered the same choice, would she keep what she had—or trade it all for love? Sometimes Catherine thought Fate played the Jester. In her mind, she could almost see Fate hiding in the shadows, laughing at them behind her jingling sleeve.

Daubeney escorted her to her chamber and left her with a small bow. If she had hoped to rest for a short while, she was disappointed. Three ladies waited to receive her.

"Lady Catherine," said a handsome, dark-haired, older woman coming forward. "King Henry has put us at your service. My name is Lady Elizabeth Daubeney. You have already met my husband, Lord Giles—" She gave Catherine a smile. "I am lady-in-waiting to Her Grace, Queen Elizabeth. There is water in the basin for washing, and wine in the pitcher. Here you see we have fruit on the tray, cheese, and cake. Is there anything else you would like that we can bring you?"

"I thank you for what you have provided me." Catherine spoke in a tremulous whisper.

A soft look came into Lady Daubeney's hazel eyes. "Perhaps you would like to be attended by your own ladies?" she asked gently.

"If it is permitted," Catherine replied, startled by kindness where she expected malice.

Catherine and her ladies were left alone to tend their needs, and soon Alice and Agatha were adding the final touches to her toilette and dressing her hair, securing it neatly at the nape of her neck. They tied her embroidered velvet belt low on her hips and adjusted the black undersleeves beneath the flared outer ones of her heavy black satin gown. As always, they freshened the folds of her skirt so that the ribbon trim was seen to advantage.

She didn't have to wait long for the knock at the door. It was Lord Daubeney. He had two men with him, one of whom kept something hidden behind his back. Catherine felt sudden alarm. Daubeney had been naught but gallant throughout her journey to London, and seemed unable to do enough for her. Now he avoided her eyes and looked utterly miserable. She drew to her feet.

"My lady, I—" Daubeney cleared his throat nervously. He glanced briefly at her hair. "My lady, King Henry wishes you to wear your hair loose about you—"

There was a gasp from her ladies. Catherine raised her hand haltingly to the coiled braids beneath her veil. No self-respecting woman wore her hair loose at court, unless she was to be wedded or crowned. Her voice was faint when she spoke. "Lord Daubeney, I did not know it was the fashion for ladies in England to appear thus at court."

Daubeney looked down at the floor. "It is not, my lady. But it is the king's wish that you wear your hair unbound—and that your hands be bound instead."

Catherine reached out to support herself on the table. Even so, she faltered. Her ladies rushed to her side and turned their horrified eyes on Daubeney.

"Forgive me, my lady," he said.

His voice held such a tremor that Catherine forgot her own misery. Here stood a valiant knight, trained in the Age of Chivalry that lay dead with Richard III on the field of Bosworth. Now was the Age of Tudor, and this king had cast out all the old rules. Instead of protecting a helpless damsel, a knight was required, at the bidding of his king, to cast dishonor on her. Brother Nicholas's words came to her: "Be strong and carry on—for them." Drawing herself up to her full height, she lifted her chin. "Lord Daubeney, here are my hands. Fault yourself not, for one must do as one must do, and I forgive you."

He managed a nod, as his men came forward to bind her hands. "I fear, my dear lady, that there is one more thing—" He lifted his head and looked at her, misery naked in his eyes. "The king has asked that you appear barefoot before him."

Gasps went around the room. *Like a bondswoman,* Catherine thought, *he brings me as low as he can—I, who the wise-woman said would be a queen.* Her vision blurred as she gazed at him, and the room tilted around her. Only by imposing a rigid control over herself did she keep erect. With a nod of her head, she acknowledged Daubeney's words.

*　*　*

The doors were thrown open to the Presence Chamber at Shene. Catherine heard a sound that might have been the shock of a hundred throats catching their breath at the same moment, but she barely made out the faces in the crowd that stared at her from the sides of the room, or the figures straight ahead on the dais where a man and a woman sat on their ornate thrones, draped in furs and glittering with gold and jewels. She saw only the blindingly bright candles of the candelabras and the sun's rays that poured through the windows. The air of the room was close and still. She turned from the hurtful light and her glance caught on a mural on the wall that depicted colorful birds in gorgeous plumage grouped around the feet of a dragon. Lowering her lids, she shuffled forward in her bare feet, drawn along by the man who jerked the rope that bound her wrists. Animals moved thus; bears who had been blinded and were about to be set upon by dogs for sport, and slaves who had lost every human right and breathed at the will of their captors. When there were no more tugs, she knew she had reached the dais. Only then did she look up. She saw that Elizabeth the Queen wore an expression of sorrow, and that a tear glistened in the corner of her eye. Her glance took in the gaunt king, the fat bishop at his side, and the stern matron who stood beside the queen.

King Henry leaned forward in his throne. "Who is responsible for this outrage?" he roared, looking at everyone and no one before riveting his eyes on Catherine. "Untie the Lady Catherine at once! Dear lady, forgive our ignorant servants. They mean to please us, and do not know their sin." His voice was grave, filled with concern. Beside him, his queen threw him a confused look, for she had heard her husband remark to the bishop standing by his throne, "Here is a prize suitable for a king!" Now he sat as if mesmerized by the captive princess who lit up the hall with all the tender brightness of youth, beauty, and innocence.

Catherine watched as her jailor drew a knife and slashed her ropes, which fell to the floor in jagged pieces. She rubbed her sore wrists, already reddened by the rough hemp, but said nothing. She was not about to thank this gap-toothed king for the indignities and griefs he had heaped on her. She averted her gaze and stood blushing with eyes downcast, humiliated by her bare feet and the unbound hair falling over her shoulders.

"Noble lady," the king said, "we see that you are weary from your travail and in sore need of rest. We shall speak to you in private, *illustris domina.*" He rose to his feet.

There was a rustle of silk and flash of gems as the lords and ladies curtsied and bowed. The king and queen descended from the dais. "Allow me, Lady Catherine," the king said gently, taking her hand as he escorted her out.

* * *

The private chamber where Catherine sat on a settle beside the king was comfortably furnished with silk cushions embroidered with colorful flowers: no dragons, serpents, or evil-eyed birds adorned these walls, and the single tapestry displayed only angels. The queen had sent Catherine slippers and a net caul so that her hair was caught neatly at the nape of her neck once more. Though her dignity was restored to her, Catherine didn't look at the king but sat stiffly erect, her hands tightly clasped together in her lap. Yet she knew that he gazed at her intently, for his stare burned her face.

The king took her hand into his own. "Noble lady, you have been through much, and all reports have informed us of your dignity and grace throughout your ordeals. Tell us what we can do to make you feel at home here in our realm of England, for we know you must sorely miss your family. Your father, the Earl of Huntly, is a great man of high fame, and I wish to honor his daughter."

Catherine swallowed the lump in her throat. Her father, and Scotland, and all that had been familiar and was now lost to her, formed an iron weight across her heart. Catherine lifted her eyes to the king's face for the first time. Though he was about the same age as her father, he looked nothing like him with his blackened, gapped teeth and lanky build. Still, he seemed kind, this man she had thought a monster. "Aye, my lord, I do miss him—so very much—" With effort, she choked back her emotion. "My lord, I see you are good and merciful, and that gives me courage to beg from you a boon—a great boon—"

It was the first time King Henry had heard her voice. For two years he had studied her from afar, fascinated by the reports of his spies that spoke of her alluring beauty. Finally, here she was before him, and he could say with full authority that their reports had been vastly understated. Even the lilt of her Scots accent was enchanting.

When the king did not reply, Catherine rushed onward. "My babe has been rent from my breast. You cannot know the sorrow of a mother who has lost her only child. Pray, my lord, for pity's sake, return my babe to my empty arms!"

"My Lady Catherine, this child is fathered by a boatman's son and an adventurer who tried to murder me and steal my crown from my brow. I cannot restore him to you."

"My lord, my child is innocent of any crime against you! He is of my blood, and therefore of the royal lineage of Scotland! Give him back to me! Send us both home where we belong."

The king did not reply, and Catherine choked back the sobs that came to her throat, not daring to speak further lest she dissolve into a fit of weeping that might never cease. Breathlessly, she awaited his reply, but when he spoke, he did not address her plea.

"Now, now," the king said, patting the hand he held in his. "Most noble lady, I grieve, too, and it pains me very much, second only to the slaughter of so many of my subjects, that you have been deceived by such a sorry fellow. You shall be a lady-in-waiting to my queen and enjoy every advantage we can bestow upon you. You shall lack for nothing. We are ordering that you be given a generous allowance and more gowns of your choosing, and that sober matrons be given to escort you, for you are but a young woman."

Catherine stared at him, disbelieving. Was he a monster after all? She stiffened. "I should like to have my own ladies in attendance."

Barely conscious of her words, Henry murmured, "If that is what you wish, my dear . . ." He was staring at her, thinking that she must surely be God's own masterpiece, for she was in truth the most heavenly creature he had ever seen in his life. A swan neck, lustrous black hair, a milky complexion tipped with delicate rose along the cheekbones, all this crowned by an exquisite little mole near her luscious mouth and a set of teeth as tiny and perfect as daisies.

"You must feel so alone, dear lady. But rest easy, *illustris domina*, for we intend to do you every reverence."

"There is kindness and generosity in you or you would not do me reverence," Catherine replied. "But more than reverence, I pray, Sire, give me back my child!" To her horror, emotion broke her composure and she erupted in sudden sobs. Henry gathered her to him, clucking softly. She let her head fall against his shoulder and wept in his arms, aware only that here was a refuge against the pain that swept her being.

Henry held her patiently as her grief poured out from her. Yet it was not with a father's tenderness that he held her, but with a lover's heat. Her hair was silken soft against his cheek and his lips. He had not felt such powerful swirling emotion in all his forty years—care, concern, and a need to protect, aye, but far more urgent than all these was the need to possess. He let her drench his gem-encrusted robes with her luscious tears that tasted so delicious on his lips, and now and again he dabbed at her eyes with his handkerchief and murmured soothingly.

At last, her sobs eased and she drew away. "Forgive me, my lord," she sniffled, taking his handkerchief and wiping her own cheeks as she attempted a wan smile.

"You have been through much, my dear, but have no fear. I am prepared to set everything right again for you."

Catherine looked at him, a ray of hope lighting her heart. Had he relented? Was he going to give her back her babe and send her home to Scotland after all? And Richard—what of Richard, would he treat him with honor as his brother by marriage—or better still, let him go? Surely, he would let him go, for now that Richard had disgraced himself by deserting his troops, he no longer posed any threat to this king. No man would ever follow him into battle again.

"I am prepared to obtain—as soon as it can be managed—at whatever cost the pope demands—a divorce for you from that wastrel you married."

"Nay, my lord!" Catherine recoiled at the words. "I do not wish a divorce! Never—I love my husband!"

Henry leapt from the settle and looked at her. "You know not what you say! How can you love him? He has deceived you! He is nothing—worse than nothing—a despicable coward—a knave, a liar, a feigned boy! You have been reduced to this miserable condition by the perfidy and wickedness of this lying scoundrel, and you deserve far better—your royal birth, your grace and dignity all cry out for a far superior man! And I can make everything possible for you if you but divorce him. Think about your . . ."

Catherine stared at him in dismay as he went on, a terrifying realization washing over her. The "far superior man" he had in mind for her was himself! He coveted her person! It was for his own sake that he wished her to divorce Richard! She fought to control the panic that assailed her. This was a horror she had never anticipated and for which she was totally unprepared. Without realizing that she moved, she rose from the settle and inched away from him until she stood with her back against the wall. Unable to master her revulsion long enough to answer his demand, she remained frozen in wide-eyed silence.

The king, too, seemed to need time to recover his composure now that he had finished his diatribe. He assumed a stiff posture and stood immobile. *As still as a snake eying his prey,* thought Catherine, for the gaze he fixed on her was far from gentle; he was ashen-faced with anger, and a muscle worked at his jaw as he studied her. But when he spoke again, his tone was calm. "You still believe he is who he says he is, don't you?"

"I do, my lord," Catherine replied. "But I am willing to agree he is not, if you give me back my child."

"There is only one thing to be done then. You shall hear it from his own lips," Henry replied, as if she had not spoken about her child. "This wastrel shall confess to you how miserably he has deceived you. Perhaps that will persuade you." He strode to the door and yanked it open. "Bring in Piers Osbeck!"

The king took a seat on a tapestried chair, knees wide. With a wave of the hand, he indicated Catherine should also sit, and she almost fell onto the window seat nearby. The room went silent but for the distant twitter of a few birds and the soft hiss of the sand seeping through an hour glass on the mantel.

She was going to see Richard. She would see him, though she could not embrace him nor let him know her thoughts, nor touch his hand, nor kiss his lips. And what must he feel after what he had been through, and how could she give him comfort when she could do none of these things? And what of her dismay at what he had done? Could she forgive him—or would that forever color the way she saw him? She swallowed hard and riveted her eyes on the door, for she caught the sound of footsteps in the hall.

It was thrust open and Richard stood before her. He hung his head and did not look at her, as if he dreaded what he would see in her eyes. He had lost so much weight and looked so weary—yet seeing him again, even this way, seemed to her a gift from heaven. Aye, he had disappointed her, but now she knew it didn't matter to her what he had done, or what they said about him. She loved him. *I have seen you in your humiliation,* she wanted to tell Richard, *and it makes no difference to me.*

She rose to her feet. *Richard—look at me—look . . .* But he didn't bring his gaze to hers and she could tell him nothing. Catherine stole a quick glance at Henry. The king was watching them. Now he stood with his hands clasped behind his back, feet apart, a thin smile of satisfaction on his lips and his nose held high, as if he might foul himself by breathing in the same air as filled Richard's lungs.

"Get down on your knees and confess to this noble lady, whom you have so shamefully and dishonorably abducted and disgraced, who you really are!" he demanded.

Richard did as he was commanded, and the awkwardness of his

movements conveyed to Catherine more eloquently than words his abject shame. Catherine could only think that the last time he had been on his knees to her, it was to propose marriage. How graceful he had been then, how happy he had looked, how hopeful—how different it had been!

Staring at the floor, Richard recited his other identity. "I was born in Tournai," he said. "My father was a boatman ..."

It was the tale he had rehearsed with her in Scotland on many occasions. Fashioned of both truth and fiction, it had served to disguise him after he fled England as a child of nine and was deposited for a few years in the care of a family named Werbecque in Tournai, a town on the border between Flanders and France. The choice of a bourgeois family and of Tournai were both deliberate. The fugitive prince would be less likely to be noticed in a family that did not cross paths with the nobility, and the border town conferred an additional measure of security by confusing the usurper's spies who were scouring Europe searching for him, for he could be whisked from Burgundy to France and back again at a moment's notice, confounding them further. At the time of his arrival, Tournai belonged to Burgundy, making it possible for his Aunt Margaret to control matters and provide any forged documents he might need. Ultimately, however, the tale had another chilling purpose: to protect him and his royal mentors in the finality of capture.

"My father's name is Jehan Wezbecq and he lives at St. Jean de Schedlt ..."

This was the history he was to fall back upon under duress. Catherine had seen it a jest as she'd corrected him during the course of his recitals, for he would forget names and confuse dates and details. "No, your father's name is *Werbecque,* not Wezbecq, and he lives at St. Jean des *Caufours*—not Scheldt. And your mother is not *Cateryn*— she is *Nicaise*—you dunce!" Then she'd laugh, "Cateryn is me—your wife."

Sometimes Richard would gather her into his arms and murmur between kisses, "The only beloved name that ever comes into my mind is Cateryn." But sometimes he'd chastise her: "I'd like to see you remember the names of a hundred people you met and places you lived when you were ten!" And each time when he was done, she had laughed and said, "'Tis all so foolish! One would have to be an idiot to think you could be a boatman's son. Who came up with that tripe?"

Richard's voice broke into her thoughts, scattering the memories. "My mother's name is Cateryn . . ."

Catherine looked at his bowed head, thinking how he had knelt to her, just so, beneath a starry sky, in a secluded corner of the royal garden overlooking the torch-lit village of Stirling, barely a week after his arrival in Scotland, to ask for her hand. The words he had spoken filled her mind: "You were not born as humans are, but fell from Heaven. Your face, so bright and serene, gives splendor to the sky. Your eyes, brilliant as stars, make all pain forgotten and turn despair into delight. In looking, they can only praise you; in praising, they can only love you; in loving, they cannot but reverence you. Love makes me your slave. Waking or sleeping, I can find no rest. Turn your eyes upon me, for you are my only consolation. I do not deserve you, but I can hope you might notice me among your crowd of admirers—"

"Pierart Flan was my grandfather . . ." said Richard's voice, cutting into her reverie.

In her mind, Catherine heard herself prompt, "No, Pierart Flan was your *godfather*, not your grandfather!" Then memory, like the sweep of the ocean's tide, bore her back once again to the garden at Stirling Castle, where Richard had knelt at her feet.

"To accept my love would be a burden for you, and I can offer you nothing until I have won the throne and made you the queen God intended you to be. Most noble lady, my soul belongs to you. Have pity on me for I have been your servant from the first hour I saw you. I beseech, therefore, O most beautiful ornament of Scotland, that you might consider cleaving to me in marriage—though I know I deserve it not, I, who am willing to do your will in all things as long as life remains in me . . ."

Richard's voice jarred her back into the present, scattering her precious memories. His confession was at an end, and the words on his lips now were ones Catherine had never thought to hear: "I beseech therefore your forgiveness—though I know I deserve it not, I, who will never forgive myself for the dishonor I have cast on you as long as life remains in me."

The silence that fell was shattered by Henry.

"There is your proof," he announced, smiling coldly. "He is a fraud. A lowborn boatman's son. What do you think of him now, noble lady?"

Catherine did not trust herself to look at the king. Instead she stared at Richard, who was so close to her—within arm's reach—but lost to her forever. Her mouth was dry as parchment.

"What do you think of him now, *illustris domina*?" Henry repeated more gently, taking a step nearer to her. "Surely you can no longer care for this pathetic scoundrel who claimed to be born a royal?"

On her answer hung her child's life, and Richard's fate. She knew it; and Henry's face told her what he expected. If her darling child still breathed, if Richard was to somehow survive, she could not afford to offend this man. Yet she could not give him what he wanted, which was to deny her husband.

"*Illustris domina*—" prompted Henry.

Catherine barely heard him. All her energy was riveted on Richard's golden head. *Look at me, my dearest love,* her heart cried out. *Look—look—*

As if by a miracle, Richard lifted his head. Their eyes met. With her gaze riveted to his, in a deliberate tone that was yet tender with emotion, Catherine said, "It is the man and not the king I love."

Catherine cast no glance at Henry, though her words were meant equally for him as for her husband. Richard's face lit with tremulous, disbelieving joy. Catherine felt his joy herself, knowing that by her forgiveness she had helped him shoulder a portion of the guilt he carried. But she also nursed another hope. That when Richard realized the full extent of the horror into which they were plunged, her words would continue to offer solace as their double meaning became clear. This king might stand between them; he might wield the power of a

god over them; he might be his captive's rival in both love and war—
but it made no difference. Her heart belonged to Richard, and this
other man, king though he be, could never touch it.

Catherine smiled at Richard, and with her lips, silently, she
mouthed to him the shadow of the words she knew he needed to
hear: *Richard, I love you . . .*

Chapter 7

In the Dragon's Court

"I've sent the boy who calls himself Plantagenet back to London," Henry said forlornly as he lounged in the private solar at Shene that he shared with his mother. "But I know not what to do with him."

"How can you not know? The outcome was always decided," said his mother, Lady Margaret Beaufort, enunciating each syllable with exaggerated clarity, for she was given to precision in all things. "That is why France and Scotland refused to give him up to you. They knew he would be put to death. Is that not so, Morton?" She turned to the trusted cleric who sat in with them on important policy decisions.

Cardinal John Morton spread his bejeweled fingers across his ample belly as he relaxed in a velvet chair and pondered the matter. At seventy-seven years of age, he had witnessed both the start and the finish of the Wars of the Roses. During those years of strife and inflamed passions, he'd managed to serve three out of the four kings who had ruled England. Only once did he have to put aside his Lancastrian sympathies, and that was for Edward IV. With Edward's brother, Richard III, he had never got along, and Richard's idealism had provoked his disgust. He had worked—successfully—to bring him down, for it was Morton's contention, born of his considerable experience, that bleeding hearts belonged in a nunnery. Soft rulers invariably lost their thrones to those better suited to wield the scepter and keep the peace. Thus had Henry VI given way to Edward IV, and Richard III to Henry VII.

In Tudor, Morton felt he had been matched ounce for ounce with the right mettle. He and Henry saw eye to eye on all things, and he was the king's most revered senior statesman. That he was also the people's most hated royal councilor troubled him not a whit. As far as he was concerned, they existed to serve their king as worker bees served their queen—by pouring golden honey into the royal collection coffers. This he made sure they did through repressive policies of fear and taxation. It was thanks to Morton's wits that Henry Tudor had gained, and kept, his throne, and amassed enormous riches in the process. And Morton was satisfied that the king knew it.

"By the law of nature, opposites do not spare one another, my Liege," he said at length. "Water does not pardon fire, nor the predator the prey. Nor the powerful victor his helpless captive. But"—he held up a finger to restrain Margaret Beaufort's approval—"there are several reasons you should not execute your captive."

Morton saw that he had the king's rapt attention. "One is this. You can use him as a bargaining chip to secure a treaty with Scotland and bring peace to the border regions. James is fond of him, and does not wish for his death. He is certain to oblige us. There is also Burgundy to consider. He could prove valuable to us—alive." Morton closed his eyes to better remember his other reasons, for it was after supper and he felt sleepy. "Additionally, this young man claims to be your queen's brother—of course, we *know* he's not—" Morton opened his eyes again as he said this, though he knew no such thing and was aware of Henry's own grave doubts on the matter. "But that may not seem as clear to her. Therefore, you must tread carefully in such a delicate matter. Time would be a benefit and, likely as not, show us the way to proceed."

"Very good," said the king. When Morton did not continue but fell into deep thought again, he prompted, "Any other reasons?" Unfortunately, Morton was growing old and sometimes he dozed off.

Morton snapped back to attention. "Ah—yes. This lad was removed from sanctuary by the promise of life. It behooves a king to show mercy, for in so doing he honors God's law. You did this with Lambert Simnell, and all praised your clemency."

"Aye, but that boy was eleven years old," interjected Margaret Beaufort. "This false prince is a man. He led troops against my son. To put him in the kitchen would make light of his fearful offense and give heart to others who wish to bring down King Henry."

"You are not suggesting we keep him alive and place him in the kitchen as a scullery boy, are you?" Henry inquired.

"Nay, my lord. For one, *Perkin* would not make a suitable scullery boy." He smiled to himself at the ridiculous image of a young man with the hauteur of a prince peeling potatoes. "Nor can you treat *Perkin* kindly. It would only raise questions about who he really is. You were a captive yourself for many years, and you know that esteem and status determine how a prisoner is kept. As a child in Brittany, out of regard for blood, you were treated *très doucement, n'est-ce pas?*"

"Very gently indeed, Morton," Henry smiled. "But I do not feel inclined to treat this lad gently. He has cost me sleep for far too long."

"Exacly. What I suggest is something a little different. Remember, my Liege, how many times we have said that the people have short memories? You placed Lambert Simnell in the kitchen as a scullery boy, and it proved a brilliant move. Ten years later, no one has forgotten the lesson you taught them and he remains a jest to this day. If you execute this 'Perkin' now, you risk the people forgetting their lesson. By keeping him alive at court, crushed and beaten, you are indicating your utter confidence that no one would take him for Prince Richard and adhere to him. And 'gently' has its interpretations, does it not?" He looked pointedly at the king, and waited. One of the reasons for his long and spectacular career was that he always placed the thought into his superior's head and never demanded the credit. He led the fox to the hole, but let him ferret the mouse out for himself.

Margaret Beaufort raised an eyebrow as realization dawned. "Morton, you are a clever devil."

Henry's lips curled with a satisfied smile. "Indeed you are, Morton.

In this manner I may lay claim to being the most magnanimous king in Christendom, while at the same time disbursing the threat to my dynasty for as long as history lives. It is a revenge I shall delight in. I will return to London forthwith to set plans in motion."

He rose and went to stand by a tall gilt chair. "There is one other matter. Lady Catherine wants her babe restored to her. She would like to be returned to Scotland with the child."

"You are not seriously entertaining such a move?" demanded Margaret Beaufort, rising to her feet with shock. "Why, it's preposterous! What reason does Lady Catherine give for her demand?"

Henry was a man in love. He wasn't entertaining the idea at all, but not for the political reason he was sure his mother would give him. He felt guilty and needed affirmation for what he planned to do. "And why is it preposterous, Mother?"

"Because the child is a threat to your throne!"

"Lady Catherine states, not unreasonably, that if her husband is not the prince, as we believe, but a boatman's son, as we say, then his child has no claim to the English throne. It cannot be denied that the royal blood of Scotland flows in the child's veins, and that he is innocent of any crime. He is indeed a prince of Scotland. Therefore, he should be returned to Scotland."

"Not a good idea," said Morton.

Henry and Margaret Beaufort waited for him to continue.

"He must not be returned to Scotland. The simple reason is that all of Scotland, all of Europe, and far too many Englishmen believe the father to be the true prince. Therefore, give this babe twenty years and he will be back to claim your crown for himself. And he will come not only armed with royal blood, like his father, but with a real army. He is, indeed, a threat to your throne."

"Well said, Morton," said Margaret Beaufort.

As Henry had hoped, the discussion had allayed his guilt. Relieved, he stood and placed a hand on Morton's shoulder. "My friend, I admit now to having been most reluctant to pay the exorbitant price the pope set on your cardinal's hat. But I see it was worth every pence."

* * *

Well guarded by a troop of men, Richard rode through the city streets, his feet bound to the stirrups of a mangy horse that was led by a groom. For the first three weeks of his detention, he had been kept in seclusion. In the last fortnight, however, he'd been taken out daily after mass to be paraded before the people. Whatever the weather—rain, wind, or sunshine—multitudes turned out, eager to see him as he rode past unshaven, in shabby clothes, on his shambling horse. Amid their spitting uproar, he endured the curses, venom, and threats of those who pelted him with rotten food and dung as he rode from Westminster to Saint Paul's and back again through Cheapside. They stared at him as they stood on walls and balconies. Some even climbed rooftops for a better view—and perhaps a better aim, Richard thought wryly, dodging a rotted apple.

Even at court, people stared at him thus—boldly and with amazement. To that he had become accustomed. Here and there among the crowd he caught a face that gazed without malice, sometimes impassively, sometimes with pity. Some were scholars, clerics, physicians and men of God; and some wore the garb of other lands he had visited. These foreign merchants and travelers from distant lands would carry the tale of his humiliation across the seas. He was, he realized, a spectacle for the world.

On this occasion the Tudor had thoughtfully provided further amusement for the rabble by tying a poor Cornishman to a mule with his head in the ass's tail, bringing the mob to side-splitting laughter as he passed ahead of Richard. But Richard's hurtful injuries came not from the stones thrown by the gleeful little boys who ran after him with their slingshots; it came from the people. "There goes the brave Duke o' Runaways," scorned a bystander, throwing a rotted egg in his direction. Riotous laughter erupted as the egg scored its mark on Richard's cheek. Burning shame ripped through him. He wiped at the splatter with his sleeve, inducing more laughter. "Here's one more gift for the Prince o' Cowards!" jeered another, smacking him in the chest with a rotten piece of meat.

He pretended not to hear the epithets, focusing instead on his memories and pretending the magnificent gold and silver shops of Cheapside were the shops he had viewed in Venice, Rome, Milan, and Florence. The wares they displayed glittered brightly in the sunshine. He thought of his mother, whose hair still glinted in his memory, and of Catherine, whose birthday it was in two days. In his game of pretense he perused their wares as if to purchase a gift for her, and it came to him suddenly that this day marked the second anniversary of when they'd met at Stirling. His heart twisted in his breast. He looked away. *This is my penance*, thought Richard. *'Tis just that I do penance.*

* * *

Henry Tudor's man, Sir Charles Somerset, was waiting in the great hall when Richard returned, exhausted by his ordeal. Somerset threw a nod to Richard's two guards. With a bow, they stepped back.

"How was your outing today, Perkin?" Somerset asked pleasantly.

Richard regarded the captain of the king's guard. He came from a line of fervent Lancastrians who had died fighting against York, and his deceased father, Henry Beaufort, Duke of Somerset, was the last of the legitimate line related to the king's mother, Margaret Beaufort. Charles Somerset was a bastard, born out of wedlock to Somerset and his mistress, Joan Hill, and this further ingratiated him to the king, who feared the nobility. Richard had met him for the first time at Brabant, when he came on a mission to the Holy Roman Emperor Maximilian. He had refused to bow to Richard, who stood on the dais with the Emperor, his son Philip, and Margaret, Duchess of Burgundy. When Margaret angrily demanded why Somerset didn't reverence her nephew Richard of York, Somerset had declared that her nephew Richard of York was long dead, and if she would loan him one of her people, he would take him straight to the chapel where the little prince was buried. Richard had stepped forward then and called him a base-born liar. He had said that when he was back on his throne, he would make him painfully regret his words.

And here they were.

To Charles Somerset, Tudor entrusted all his most important business, large and small. It was Somerset who first set up Richard's forays into the public streets. Now Richard wondered what cruel new jest had been devised for him.

"Do you remember the old sergeant-farrier, William, who was the keeper of King Henry's mares and foals until he fled to you in 1493?" Somerset asked.

A jolt of pain came and went in Richard's breast. He doubted that Somerset had come to impart to him merely that William was dead. Death was too simple for this Tudor king and his clever mother. No, he was beginning to see that nothing was simple in the Tudor court, and nothing was as one expected.

"You may recall that he donned a hermit's outfit when he fled after your capture."

Richard held his breath.

"Tomorrow you shall have his company on your sojourn through Cheapside," Somerset said. "Only you shall be the one leading the horse this time, and William shall be the one riding. King Henry has commanded that you deliver William to the Tower yourself, as reward for his faithful service to you."

Richard bit his trembling lip and averted his face. Poor William; poor dear, faithful old man! That night Richard lay awake as he had done since Taunton. But this time he prayed for forgiveness not only for men he had led to slaughter by the sins of his past, but for what he must do come the morrow.

*　*　*

Everyone in the queen's chamber at Shene watched the silent newcomer who sat with her eyes downcast over her embroidery, including the queen's eldest sister, Cecily Plantagenet, though she did so more discreetly than the others. She had heard from her sister the queen that the Scottish princess had infuriated Henry by declining his offer to secure her a divorce. Her refusal was the talk of court. Cecily found something admirable in it, though she herself was made of a more pragmatic nature and had managed well enough through two marriages forced on her without love.

Cecily didn't know what to think about the matter of Perkin Warbeck. She had not seen the young man who had been sent back to London almost as soon as he'd arrived at Shene, but she doubted he was Richard. Her brother was dead, if not on their uncle's order, then by the hand of their cousin, Harry of Buckingham, who wanted the crown for himself. King Richard had quarreled with Buckingham around the time her brothers vanished, and she'd always felt that her brothers' disappearance had something to do with their argument. Harry of Buckingham had been so angered with King Richard that he'd raised a rebellion against him soon afterward. The revolt failed and Buckingham was captured and executed, but her brothers, Edward and Richard, were never seen again. All this took place while she and her sisters were confined with their mother in sanctuary at Westminster Abbey.

She gave an inward sigh at the memory of that time. Strange to admit, but sanctuary had not been without its charms. Often at night when her aged husband snored at her side after claiming his marital rights, she'd lay thinking of those starry nights when she'd been a maiden with dreams in her heart. But that was long ago, and one soon realizes that dreams are naught but fantasies of youth and have no place in the real world.

It was said that the Scottish princess would not divorce her husband because she loved him, and that King Henry was in love with his rival's wife and had commissioned a love sonnet from his blind poet, Bernard Andre, to win her affection. If so, what developed next should be very interesting, Cecily thought, not without a touch of pity for Lady Catherine. A captive princess wooed by the king who held the man she loved at his mercy—who wouldn't have sympathy?

Cecily shifted her gaze away from the forlorn figure in black. Of love, she knew little; and what she knew, time had dimmed into a distant memory. It was better that way. Maybe it would be so for this princess one day—if the fates proved kind.

Catherine had felt Cecily's eyes on her as she guided her

embroidery needle through the heavy cloth, and had caught a soft look on Lady Cecily's face before the queen's sister had looked away. *Here is someone who could be a friend*, Catherine thought. Then a small voice came at the back of her mind: *You are in the land of enemies and no one is your friend.*

There was a rap at the door and the queen looked up. "I come from Westminster, Your Grace, with a missive from King Henry." The messenger handed it to her as he knelt.

"Very curious," murmured Queen Elizabeth. She passed the missive to Lady Daubeney.

In her corner of the room, Catherine halted her stitch. She knew it had to do with her, for the queen and Lady Daubeney had glanced her way as they spoke, and she was not surprised to be summoned. Nervously, she rose and made her way across the room.

"My lord king requests that you be sent to Westminster Palace immediately," the queen said. Noting that the girl had gone pale, she added gently, "He does not say what it is about, my dear, but I do not believe there is cause for concern."

Within the hour, Catherine and her ladies were bouncing along in a litter, hanging on to her coffer. No one spoke, for now Catherine was accompanied by two ladies from the Tudor court who had been assigned to her by the king. She knew, as Alice and Agatha knew, that these women were Tudor spies.

Catherine barely saw the winter landscape they passed through: the rolling meadows lightly dusted with snow, the sudden rushing waterfalls around the bend of an old bridge, the winding expanse of the Thames, where white swans glided on dark waters. Her mind was focused on what lay ahead. Richard was at Westminster. She wondered if she would see him.

* * *

Through the torch-lit corridors Catherine followed the king's messenger. No one had told her what this was about, but it was clear from the whisperings and the glances that had come her way at Westminster that something was afoot. At an arched door studded with nails and crossed with a heavy iron bar, the messenger paused. "Lady Catherine Gordon to see Perkin," he said to the two armed guards who stood on either side.

If Catherine disbelieved her ears, there was no denying the burst of ecstasy in her heart as the iron bar was lifted and the door thrust open, for there stood Richard. Clad in hose, soft leather shoes, and a plain brown doublet with long hanging sleeves that she had never seen before, he wore a simple leather belt and a small hat with a single feather. He had been seated and now he rose to meet her, a dazed look on his face, as if the world had stood still for him at the sight of her. By his side were two men who bore no arms except daggers at their belts. *As if they are courtiers, not guards,* Catherine thought contemptuously. Her gaze returned to Richard. Propelled forward by the joy in her heart, she fell into his arms. For the first time in two long months since Marazion, she felt her husband's flesh against her own and her joy was so great that she broke into sobs.

Richard held her as she wept, and kissed her tears. His soul had been filled with lament, and now boundless happiness poured into him. "Is it really you, my love?" they both said to one another at the same moment, breaking apart to look into one another's eyes. Then they laughed.

They were aware of the guards watching them, and Catherine realized that they had not been prevented from embracing, or commanded to refrain from speaking to one another. She took Richard's hand and led him to the window. The guards made no complaint, so this, too, was permitted.

She leaned her head toward Richard's. "Do you know what this is about, my love?"

"The Scots ambassador is presenting his credentials to Henry. It seems that he, as well as the Milanese and the Venetian ambassadors, desire to meet us and know that we are well," Richard said in a low tone. "However, I have been told that we are not to speak or mingle with them, merely greet them as they leave."

"How strange," Catherine whispered, gripped by unease once again.

"Everything is strange here, Catryn—but I take my sweets gratefully. This day that began so cruelly is ending most marvelously."

"What happened today?" she demanded, anxious to know everything at once. But Richard shook his head. "Nay, not now—now I just want to look at you, feel you, be with you."

He could not tell her what happened. It was too terrible.

That very morning he had delivered his friend, William, the old sergeant-farrier, to the Tower. At the gate he'd helped the old man dismount, and they had stood for a moment looking silently into one another's anguished eyes before William's handlers seized him and drew him into the tower of doom. Farewell was left unspoken, and no words passed between them, for no words could ease such cruel calamity. When he'd returned from his grueling ordeal, Somerset had the grace not to gloat on Richard's misery, for he referred not at all to his outing to the Tower. Instead, he'd said, "You are invited to attend a gathering of nobles this evening. The Milanese ambassador, Raimondo Soncino, and the Venetian ambassador, Andrea Trevisiano, wish to meet you. New clothes have been laid out for you in your chamber. You are expected to be well groomed. I'd advise a shave." He paused, and added, "Lady Catherine will be at your side."

Richard pushed a stray tendril of Catherine's hair behind her ear, not taking his eyes from her, for fear she was a mirage and would vanish if he did. "Catryn, I know not when next we shall meet, and there is something I must say—" He broke off and gazed at her. "Catryn, I did not desert my troops because I was afraid to die. It is because I didn't want to die without making sure you and Dickon were safe."

Tears sprang into Catherine's eyes. She had been right. Richard was no coward. She imparted a kiss on the back of his hand and met his eyes. "The king wants me to divorce you. I have refused. I have asked him to give me Dickon, and to let us go to Scotland. That, too, he has refused."

Richard's eyes darkened with pain. "I am so sorry, Catryn. I wish—"

She placed a finger over his lips. "Richard, I love you, and I will never abandon you, not to the end of my life. But there is one thing..."

He waited.

"If he offers me Dickon in return for divorcing you, it is an offer I cannot refuse, my love." Her throat ached. She felt Richard tense. Then he gave a nod.

"I shall pray he does so," Richard said.

Catherine bit her lip and cast around for something to say, something that would take their minds off their pain. "They call you Perkin now, not Piers. Why is that?"

" 'Piers' is an English name. Henry doesn't wish to suggest I am English—for if I'm English, I could be the one I say I am. But 'Perkin' is foreign and evokes suspicion. It is also a diminutive, used for children, so it has insult for a grown man."

"Where do you sleep?"

"In the king's wardrobe. With them." Richard indicated his guards with his chin.

"That's an odd place to keep you."

"Henry thinks it a jest. He says that in his wardrobe I am as easy to find as a fresh shirt or pair of gloves." He grinned.

She returned his grin. "I wish I could say the same. It would be helpful to have you as easy to find as my hose and kirtle."

They both laughed. Then they fell silent and looked at one another. For each the thought was the same. It had been a lifetime since they had laughed.

"Why do your guards not have weapons, and why are they dressed like courtiers?" Catherine demanded.

"So they look like my servants, and give out the impression that I am not guarded. But they guard me well. I even sleep between them in the same bed at night."

"Oh, Richard—"

The sound of the bolt being lifted drew their attention to the door. Sir Charles Somerset entered.

"Lady Catherine," he said with a bow in her direction, "and Perkin. 'Tis time. The ambassadors await."

Hand in hand, Richard and Catherine followed Somerset into a small chamber where a crowd of nobles mingled in close conversation.

Richard put his arm around Catherine's waist and they stood quietly together, unnoticed in a shadowy corner by the door. Fire crackled in a massive fireplace that was decorated with stone roses entwined with ivy and lions. Banks of candles threw twinkling light over the faces of the men and the silver goblets they raised to their lips; silk robes rustled and gems flashed with their movements. Servers passed, offering trays laden with wine and delectables, but none approached Richard and Catherine.

"Do you know any of these people?" Catherine whispered to Richard.

"I do, and so do you—there's your cousin, the Scots ambassador, Sir Alexander Stewart of Garlies."

Catherine spotted the burly noble who was a maternal relative. For a moment her heart lifted.

"No doubt James has sent him to find out about you, and it is at his request that we are here."

"That may be. But I feel there's more to it—" She broke off, leaving her doubts unsaid. She was together with her husband, and she could not spoil this precious occasion with uneasy thoughts. She relaxed against Richard, but as her glance moved over the room, it touched on a French-style cap: a flat affair with a peak in the front.

"*He's* here—" She had not expected King Henry to be present, but there he was in the midst of the crowd, talking to the Venetian ambassador, close enough for her to hear his conversation. "We have heard reports that the French are planning another Italian expedition," he was saying. A man wearing a golden collar of curling snakes leaned forward then and whispered something to Henry, who glanced over his shoulder at the French ambassador standing behind him. Henry gave the man a rueful smile and lifted his shoulders in a barely noticeable shrug. His comment had not been meant for French ears.

So he is human and makes mistakes, too, Catherine thought with surprise. At that moment, Henry's glance moved to her, and their eyes met and locked.

Catherine felt herself in the grip of a powerful force. She couldn't look away, but she stared at him defiantly until he did. Beneath her brave front, however, she trembled. He had dared to look at her in this bold fashion though she stood at her husband's side—as if Richard didn't exist. As if Richard were nothing, and meant nothing. The realization struck her more forcefully than ever that he could make Richard disappear with a wave of his hand. An old memory stirred uncomfortably in the dark reaches of her mind. She had been newly married at Stirling Castle, and was seated in King James's privy chamber with her father, playing with a pup. Her father and the king had been chatting pleasantly when James suddenly grew serious and turned the subject to Richard.

"Henry Tudor wants to assassinate Richard," he said.

Catherine's laughter had died on her lips.

"How do ye know?" the Earl of Huntly had demanded.

"Henry is not the only one with spies," James had replied. "What you should know as Lady Catherine's father is that there is no doubt this young man Henry Tudor calls a 'feigned boy' is Richard of York. An imposter could never engender such hate and fear. If Scotland can win back a lost throne, my fair cousin, one day your daughter will be Queen of England. And this I vow to you before Heaven—I shall do all I can to serve this cause of justice and make it so."

Catherine returned to the present abruptly. Now Henry had the power to act on his hate and fear. Feeling her agitation, Richard whispered, "What's the matter, my love?"

"Nothing, dearest—nothing at all except that the evening draws to a close and when I shall see you again, I know not."

"But being close to you like this, Catherine—it shall sustain me till, God willing, we meet again." He planted a kiss on her brow.

The envoys began to leave. The Scots ambassador was the first to head to the door and see them. He acknowledged them with delight and a measure of perturbation, for he was about to address Richard as "Prince." He caught himself and gave Richard a bow instead.

"I swear to gawd ye are still the bonniest lass I ever did see," he said, "tho' I hav to sae, ye've lost a bit o' weight—both of ye." In truth he was taken aback. The two young people looked gaunt and about them hung a heaviness that had not been there when he'd known them. *But there be nae wonder in that, would there naw?* he thought to himself.

"Kindly give my regards to King James and to—my father," Catherine said, her voice almost breaking at the mention of him.

The ambassador regarded her silently a moment, and then gave another bow and kissed her hand. "I will, my bonnie lady. Sure it is that I will."

Chapter 8

This World, My Prison

The day after the reception, the entire court returned to Westminster from Shene. The wind blew bitter cold, but Catherine went for a morning stroll, accompanied by her two minders and Alice. The garden was deserted and she was surprised to find herself crossing paths with the Scottish ambassador between the hedgerows.

"Me lovely Lady Catherine!" Sir Alexander Stewart exclaimed, his blue eyes twinkling beneath his white grizzly eyebrows. "An unexpected pleasure, indeed! The Scots blood leaps in m'veins at the sight o' ye, dear lady. Ye make me smile, for seeing ye be like hearin' an auld Scottish sang." He gave her a deep bow.

"An' ye, gracious kinsman, gladden me and make me to smile as well," Catherine replied, reverting to her old Scots brogue. "My heart goes back to auld Scotland to hear ye, and I bless the Scottish tongue that speaks to me." Though her words were light, Catherine felt the sting of tears.

"Lady Catherine, if it be no intrusion, may we walk together for a short spell? I am only recently back from Edinburgh, where I spent Yule, and to talk o' Scotland lightens the winter clouds around me."

"The honor is mine, dear kinsman."

Alice retreated with a curtsy, and Catherine knew she was preparing to distract the minders, in case there was news to be had.

"Have you tidings of my gracious father, the earl?" Catherine asked as they strolled along the path, which was lightly dusted with snow.

"Indeed I do! He has been appointed Chancellor of Scotland by our noble sire, King James."

A wide smile curved Catherine's generous mouth.

"It brings a tear drap to me eye to see ye smile, Lady Catherine," the old man said softly under his breath.

Catherine blinked back the emotion that his kindness stirred in her. "Pray, tell my royal cousin James that I cherish him for what he has done for us, and for not abandoning us. He is a beloved, honorable, and noble king—" Catherine's mouth trembled. "And pray tell my dear father when ye next see him how much I love him, and that I miss him more than he can ever know—" There was a quaver in her voice, and she fell silent to recover her composure. For it had become clear to Catherine that Henry would never let her go, and never would she see her native land again. Nor could she leave England as long as her stolen babe was somewhere on these isles.

Sir Alexander nodded sadly, as if following her thoughts.

"And my brothers, William and Alexander?" she managed. "How do they fare, do you know, Sir Alexander?"

"They spoke to me of you before I left bonnie Scotland. They wished ye to know that yer charm lingers around their hearts an' sometimes they think they hear the voice of their lang-lost sister in their ears."

The silence that fell was suddenly broken by a medley of laughter. Sir Alexander stole a hasty glance behind him. Alice was playing with a group of children who had skipped into the hedgerow, and Catherine's two minders, not wishing to seem rude, had stopped to join hands and sing "Ring-Around-the-Rosie." He lowered his voice to a hushed whisper, said quickly, "Can ye not write them?"

"I have done so—clearly my letter was not passed on to you!"

"Give it to me directly—I'll take it when I go back."

"I cannot—'tis too dangerous—I must do naught to displease the—" She spoke in a rush, but she caught herself before she said "tyrant."

"I understand. I have something for you. Smile and give me your hand."

She did as he instructed. Sir Alexander took it and bowed low. In a loud tone, he said, "Dear Lady Catherine, thank ye for yer glad company. Ye have made the Scots heather bloom for me this day." He kissed her hand, and left.

She gazed after him, her hand tightening over the note he had slid into her palm. Their meeting had been no accident after all.

Catherine read the ambassador's note in the privy and was buoyed by its tidings. "Offer made by Burgundy and Holy Roman Emperor to Tudor. If prince released into their custody, they will abdicate all rights to the English throne for him, and themselves, and all their heirs in perpetuity."

That evening, she found an opportunity to ask Richard whether he'd be able to read a note, if she slipped him one.

"Little chance. My minders are always with me. One even comes to the privy."

"Then," Catherine whispered, "you shall have to force him out."

"How do I do that?"

"With milk pudding," she replied, a smile dancing on her lips. Milk always upset Richard's stomach, and in addition to the flux, he farted for days.

Richard laughed until his sides hurt.

She passed him a note. "A test—let me know how it works," she grinned.

Late that night, clutching his belly, Richard headed for the privy in an antechamber at the end of the hall, accompanied by his two minders, Robert Jones and William Smith, Henry's trusted royal servants.

"'Tis your turn," said Smith to Jones as they neared the room.

"Nay, 'tis yours," said Jones.

Jones won the argument and dropped back to lean against a

pillar and make eyes at a servant girl sweeping up the ashes from the hearth while Smith followed Richard into the privy.

Hastily, Richard pulled down his hose and sat. "You won't like this one," Richard said with a smile as his bowels loosened.

"Caw!" exclaimed Smith, covering his nose and mouth and turning away.

"There's more—" said Richard, "coming . . . Ah . . ."

Smith ran out of the privy, gasping for air.

With a chuckle, Richard removed his note, and read.

"I love you," it said.

The next afternoon, his eyes twinkling, he sauntered to Catherine's side and took her arm. "It worked, my Celtic princess," he whispered merrily.

She gave him a smile and slipped him the note from the Scottish ambassador.

The days passed but no word came about Henry's decision.

* * *

Catherine's duties as lady-in-waiting to Queen Elizabeth resumed with embroidery work on the large tapestry in the queen's solar. She had been disappointed to the depths of her being that the queen had made no overtures to speak to her personally in the weeks she'd been at court. She had hoped secretly—and had fervently expected— that Elizabeth, her sister-in-law, would help her get back her child. After all, she and Elizabeth were not only related, but their situation bore uncanny similarities. They were both captives, no matter how free they seemed, and how well treated they were. Even if Elizabeth believed that Richard was not her brother, Elizabeth was royal and Henry was not, just like Catherine. Elizabeth's son, Arthur, was half-royal, just like Dickon.

And they were both mothers. Surely Elizabeth could understand a mother's pain. Yet she did nothing. How could she not wish to help? She avoided all personal contact and made no allusion to Catherine's heart-wrenching situation—as if nothing had happened, Catherine thought, when the world had been turned upside down.

I hate her! Catherine cried inwardly.

She felt everyone's eyes on her, but kept her own downcast. After a while, she glanced up and encountered the soft gaze of the queen's sister, Cecily Plantagenet. She was indeed the fairest of the five York-ist princesses with her bright blond hair, sparkling blue eyes, and fine features. At twenty-six years of age, Cecily was three years older than Richard, and five years younger than her sister the queen. Before her father's death, she had been betrothed to James IV, but those marriage plans were discarded when Richard III took the throne and wed her to his friend Ralph Scrope of Upsall. Clearly, Fate had ordained them to be kinswomen, for here they were, sisters by marriage, sitting around the same table—but in England, instead of Scotland. Catherine forced her thoughts back to the tapestry.

When a messenger entered the chamber, Elizabeth accepted the missive he brought from her mother-in-law, and read it. "The king wishes to throw a masque for Yuletide," she said. "Lady Margaret has decided the theme will be Camelot. We are commanded to begin preparing our costumes."

Catherine could scarcely believe what she heard. In Scotland, no one commanded the queen except the king.

"Is it not the king's mother who plans royal events in Scotland?" asked Kate, the queen's youngest sister, noting Catherine's expression.

"That falls within the purview of King James's queen, when he marries," replied Catherine, dropping her gaze back to the tapestry she was stitching and hoping Kate would move on to a different subject. She knew that spies were among the queen's thirty attendants, who were, in the main, widows and daughters of slain Yorkists. In reality, the queen's court served as a prison. Being a captive herself, the queen was closely monitored and wielded no power, and access to her was almost impossible to obtain. Margaret Beaufort, the king's mother, was the true queen of England. "The imposter queen," the people called her. The subject was fraught with danger, and Catherine's position was precarious enough already.

"Elizabeth never decides anything," Kate announced wistfully.

Catherine's eyes flew to the queen, who worked the tapestry with them. "Because I don't want to," smiled the queen, unperturbed at her favorite sister's careless remark. "I prefer Lady Margaret to manage matters that involve a great deal of work. That way I can devote myself to doing what I most enjoy."

"Prayer," said Kate knowingly, tipping her head close to Catherine, but not lowering her voice. "And charitable acts, and music," she amended.

Catherine decided she liked this girl, who was about her age and seemed incapable of artifice. The second youngest female of King Edward's large brood, she was wed to Sir William Courtenay, who had shut the gates of Exeter against Richard. He had been one of the three nobles that Tudor had sent to bring Catherine out of sanctuary at St. Buryan, but to his credit, he had refused to snatch Dickon from her arms. Her eyes softened as she looked at the Yorkist princess. Katherine of York's marriage to Courtenay had been a love match, like her own, and Kate was an incurable romantic. Naive, too, though—and in this nest of vipers, innocence could be dangerous.

"What do you think if I altered the design of the tree so the fruit hangs thus . . ." Catherine asked in an effort to change the subject. "Then we could use red silk on this side, and pink on the other, as if it were lit by sunlight from above. It seems to me more lush."

The queen studied her sketch on the fabric. "Indeed, you are right. It adds dimension. You have a gift with things artistic, Lady Catherine. From now on I wish you to be in charge of laying out the design of our tapestries."

Catherine blushed at the compliment and murmured her thanks. The noon bell sounded. Elizabeth rose with a rustle of her black silk gown. "Ah, 'tis time for luncheon."

Catherine fell into line behind the queen while her sisters and other ladies took up their positions behind her in the procession to the great hall for luncheon. As a princess of Scotland, King Henry had accorded Catherine high rank at the Tudor court, and she stood fifth after the queen, the king's mother, and the king's two small princesses. When they arrived in the great hall, the queen's ladies peeled away and the royals went to the dais to take their seats at the dining table. Catherine was often seated next to the king's mother unless high-ranking visitors of other lands were present. This made mealtimes difficult. Beside Margaret Beaufort, she felt like a bird pecking its food under the watchful eye of a cat.

While the nobles still milled about seeking their places, a clarion fanfare rang out, announcing King Henry's imminent arrival. Those who had taken seats rose to greet him, the men to bow, and the ladies to dip into their curtsies. But the one who entered on the heels of the trumpet-blower was not King Henry. It was Richard. Everyone burst into riotous, side-splitting laughter at the jest. Catherine felt herself blush with shame for Richard and sank into her chair, her misery a steel weight.

*   *   *

In the month of December 1497, as the court prepared to leave for Shene to celebrate Yule, Henry, Morton, and Margaret Beaufort closeted themselves in their private solar at Westminster.

Henry opened the discussion. "As you know, we held a reception for the Scottish ambassador. Afterwards, the envoys were permitted to see the one who calls himself Plantagenet and speak to him briefly. Welladay, our spies have reported back to us. It appears the Milanese ambassador, Andrea Trevisiano, who had called him 'Perkin' previously now refers to him as the Duke of York." Henry's voice held a peculiar listless quality that was not lost on the others.

"Perhaps he should read Perkin's confession?" Margaret Beaufort retorted coldly.

"He has read it, and he's witnessed the boy's humiliation," Henry replied.

"That tells us a great deal," Morton said. "So we know what he believes."

"The same applies to Soucino, the Venetian ambassador," Henry added.

"If he is the real prince, he cannot be allowed to live," Margaret Beaufort announced abruptly.

"For if he lives, I am a usurper," Henry said miserably. "Aye, Mother, I am well aware of that." He drew an audible breath and turned to gaze out the window. He had no wish to kill the young man . . . no wish to hurt Catherine. He had no wish to love her, either, but he did. He could not deny he hoped for her love one day, but if he killed the one she cared for, would she ever forgive him?

Gazing at her son, Margaret understood the unspoken reason for his anguish. Princess Catherine. But Henry did not speak again. "I assume this concludes our meeting then?"

Henry stirred himself. "No," he said. "There is more."

He hesitated. The issue at hand was painful, but he had to bring it to their attention. "You may not be surprised, Morton, to find that you are proved correct yet again regarding Perkin's value to us."

"Since he has already secured us a truce with Scotland, that leaves Burgundy," Morton said, mulling his thoughts aloud. "You've received an envoy?"

"Not exactly from Burgundy," said Henry. "I have received an envoy on behalf of the Holy Roman Emperor Maximilian and Margaret, Duchess of Burgundy. He is sent to us by Maximilian's son, Philip the Handsome, the one who took Juana of Castile as bride last year. Philip is acting as mediator in this matter."

"Ah, the Spanish connection. Juana is Katarina of Aragon's sister," said Morton.

"The choice of Philip and the Spanish connection is deliberate, since our Arthur is betrothed to Katarina. It is meant to pressure us to do as they wish."

"And what is that?"

"To send the one who calls himself Plantagenet back to Burgundy."

Margaret Beaufort laughed; Morton gave a snort.

"And what do they offer for such a gift?" inquired Morton, in an amused tone. "Or should I say, what can they possibly offer?"

"To us—or to our councilors?"

"Both. As a councilor, I may be interested." Morton's lips parted in the crooked sneer he considered a smile.

"You, Morton, stand to gain ten thousand gold florins if you can persuade me not to kill the one who calls himself Plantagenet."

"Ah, I can always use gold, though I daresay I have enough," Morton replied, remembering how he had once stuffed his pouches with France's gold for persuading King Edward IV to abandon his war against Louis XI back in '76. "Am I the only one who is offered these riches?"

"No. Anyone who has a hand in persuading me is paid the same. Maximilian is being exceptionally generous despite his financial difficulties. As to what is in it for me—Maximilian has made a remarkable offer." Henry bowed his head and put a hand to his brow. "One that defies and confounds me, Morton."

The old cleric edged forward in his chair expectantly.

"If we do not put our captive to death," said Henry in a soft voice that was barely audible, "and do no injury to his person, and we send him back to Burgundy safe and sound, he has offered—" Henry looked up with anguished eyes, and swallowed visibly.

Margaret Beaufort moved to her son's side and laid a hand on his shoulder in comfort. She could not fathom what had agitated him so terribly.

"The Holy Roman Emperor has offered to renounce—*in perpetuity*—for himself and for his cousin of York, and all their heirs and successors, all rights in our kingdom of England. It is a grand offer."

The king's mother let herself down heavily into a chair. Morton, who suffered from gout, was agitated enough to rise from his seat. He went to the window and stared out.

They all understood the full import of this missive. Though Maximilian's interests were no longer remotely served by this young man, the Holy Roman Emperor loved and honored him to the point of abandoning all his own claims, and York's, too, merely to have him back safely. They would not do that for a false prince.

We should have expected it, Morton thought. There was simply no explanation for how a so-called boatman's son could become what this young man was.

Margaret Beaufort looked at Henry, sitting miserably in his chair. To secure the throne for her only child, she had done things in her life that she preferred not to remember—things even her son did not know. But it had been worth it in the end; now he sat on the throne of England. Nothing was going to change that. "He is doing all this for a self-confessed boatman's son?" she said, ripping out the words. "Then Maximilian is a fool! No ruler in his right mind relinquishes power."

"Maximilian says he does it because York is a kinsman and an ally, and because he holds him in great affection and is saddened by his evil fate. For these reasons, he is obliged for the sake of his conscience, and his honor, to do all that he can to secure his release." Henry had recovered his composure. "He stands ready to provide us his letters patent of assurance, stating whatever we wish, so we can be satisfied and completely assured, and rest easy forever." He drew a heavy breath, and added, "If there was ever any doubt, now we know the truth from all directions. The one who calls himself Plantagenet is who he claims. Prince Richard of York."

Margaret Beaufort slammed a fist down on the table. "It means no such thing! All it means is that Maximilian—and these other foreigners—believe the boy is who he says—and it makes no difference to us what they believe. The only thing that matters is what the people of England believe, and they will believe what we demand they believe! He is a feigned boy, and he shall remain such! Where is your iron, Henry?"

"Mother, there is more. Maximilian entrusted a secret verbal message to the envoy. He said I should bear in mind that even if I say he's a false prince, all of Christianity knows he is the true son of King Edward IV. Therefore, if I put him to death, I will be putting to death my own brother-in-law, to my eternal shame, dishonor, and reproach. Because York is unable to do me any more harm, alive or dead."

"You put your uncle to death, and there was no question about who he was. Why do you shrink from this?"

"He is my queen's brother, for God's sake!" Henry said.

Margaret Beaufort came to him and rested a hand on his arm. "She cannot be certain of that. Keep Elizabeth away from him—as you have done—and she will never know."

"Sooner or later the truth had to come out," Morton said, "at least to you, Sire, if not to the people. Lady Margaret is right—the people are a beast to be led wherever you deem. They have a short memory and are easy to manage. Twisting the truth may require twisting their bodies, but that is why we have the Tower. Nevertheless, it must be managed with utmost care—to ensure not only that the people never know, but that no harm is done to your fledgling dynasty, Sire. That is what matters, is it not?"

Henry ran a hand over his face, and sighed.

"You don't have to decide this minute, my son," said Margaret Beaufort gently. "Put this aside for now. Do not accede to Maximilian in your present state. See how matters develop. Give yourself time to think. And remember, time is on our side."

"Sound advice, my Liege," Morton said.

*   *   *

Queen Elizabeth proved thoughtful, gracious, and considerate. She did not demand much of Catherine in the way of duties and left her free to seek out Richard. Mornings were taken up with his procession through the streets and Catherine's needlework, but they spent the afternoons together, parting only at night. Though Catherine couldn't help despising Elizabeth for never standing up to her husband, she was grateful for her kindness.

When the court journeyed back to King Henry's favorite palace of Shene to celebrate Yule, Catherine rode at the front of the procession with the other princesses, while Richard was placed in a cart at the back with the kitchen help, surrounded by guards. The Tudors had much to celebrate: Richard's capture; the proxy marriage of Henry's son, Prince Arthur, that now bound Spain and England to one another; and the truce with Scotland that Henry had made with James in exchange for the promise of treating his young captives honorably. At these banquets there was much feasting, dancing, and merriment, but Catherine's relief in having Richard back at her side was blighted by Dickon's absence. She ached for her child and he was ever on her mind. Nights were especially hard. She dreaded to sleep in case her evil dream of Death and tombstones recurred, as it often did, and she lived in terror that one day it might reveal Dickon as the headless child the bird-creature held in his coiled tail. She decided to confront her nightmare head-on in order to put a stop to it. With the small monthly allowance Henry allotted her, she bought yard-age of black silk, and some embroidery thread in shades of olive, gray, brown, and white. When the dream awoke her, she sat through the night and embroidered the terrible images, stitch by stitch. The dream never returned, but she continued with the tapestry of her nightmare, for stabbing at the fabric with her needle brought great comfort.

At the Yuletide banquets for Twelfth Night, Richard and Catherine attended the lavish feasts and entertainment provided by mummers, troubadours, tumblers, wrestlers, and leapers. For Richard's sake, in an effort to make the most of the few good moments that came their way, Catherine pretended to be merry, though Dickon's absence left her with no heart for merriment. She pretended, too, to be oblivious to the lustful glances King Henry threw at her. Courtiers followed the king's every move, wondering how this tale of spurned royal love might unfold, and taking the measure of every sigh, frown, and smile. That it would end with Richard's death was certain—but when? Some put their money on Candlemas, but most favored May Day, the day of the pageant of love.

As Twelfth Night approached, Richard and Catherine realized that nothing could compete with what King Henry personally offered his court this Yuletide. On the day of the mask, he gave his nobles more to whisper about by introducing an unusual addition to the royal household: a monkey named Prince with a white-whiskered face, who wore a jacket of golden cloth. Henry led him around by a gilt chain attached to a golden collar. "I am fond of the creature, he amuses me," he liked to announce, turning in Richard's direction. "Especially when he drinks." His courtiers would burst into knowing laughter.

Catherine was appalled at the king's new cruelty. Gossip, back-biting, and false flattery prevailed, as it did at courts everywhere, but Tudor took malice to new heights. That the masque was themed after Camelot, the most chivalrous court in Christendom, and the king had come dressed as King Arthur was to Catherine more of a farce than the monkey. She set her jaw and tightened her hold of Richard's arm as they moved through the great hall, her head held high.

If she had doubted it before, she no longer did: the old days were gone, and with them the old ways and every dream she and Richard had dreamt together. No one knew how she longed for the life they had lost and for what had been, not even Richard—but she was fighting a different kind of war now, and she had to keep walking erect in the black gown King Henry had given her, so no one would suspect how vanquished she felt inside. She hoped by this to give Richard hope, for he belonged to her, and it fell to her to protect him now that they had lost the war they'd come to wage. The old monk's words came rushing back often in these days. *Naught is ended*, he had said. *Your husband lives, and somewhere your child also lives. You must be strong and carry on—for them.*

Richard took a cup of wine from a passing server. Catherine eyed him; he was rarely without a drink these days. After dinner, she took his wine from him and gave it over to a server. "Let us dance, my love," she whispered. Though her misery was acute, and Richard's spirits were no better than hers, they launched into their game of pretense, clapping to the merry tune of the minstrels, twirling each other as the king watched Catherine for a glimpse of the tawny kirtle she wore beneath her gown.

When the minstrels in the gallery set aside their instruments, Richard grabbed another drink. Catherine took him by the elbow, bit her tongue, and smiled at him. She turned her attention back to the hall. The hubbub of conversation was dying down and King Henry's jester, "Dick the Fool," was taking the floor. She noted inwardly that Richard wasn't the only one to be the butt of Henry's malice, for the Fool was named after Tudor's predecessor, King Richard III—another whom Henry loathed, and feared even now, when he was dead.

"Tonight, we have the eminent Poet Laureate Merlin to entertain us with a new composition," the jester announced. "Most noble majesties, princes and princesses, lords and ladies, I present to you the incomparable 'Merlin'!"

Wild applause rang out, and a small man wearing the green and white that were the colors of the king, sprang into the center of the hall.

Richard gave a groan.

"What is it?" Catherine whispered.

"That's John Skelton—the man's a beast and a bully. He has hounded me from the first and loathes to find me playing the lute. His new composition is no doubt about me."

Skelton began to strut. Catherine listened with increasing concern.

"My hair busheth so pleasantly—" he sang in a high voice, flipping his hair. "My robe rusheth so dashingly—" He made an elegant twirl. "Meseem I fly, I am so light—"Skelton skipped up to Richard. "For I am a butterfly with wind in my belly and no guts to weigh me down! I dance to delight—" Pursing his lips, he blew a kiss along the palm of his hand to Richard's lips. "Let me sing for you." He raised his voice to a high, quaky treble and squeaked about a groom who bragged of his base birth and thought himself talented: "He thinks he can play the lute. He thinks he can sing—" Skelton warbled off-key to Richard, "but he knows not he sobs like an old sow—" Skelton made an ugly sucking noise and the hall burst into derisive laughter. "A sow that sobs and stinks—la-de-rah-de-la—"

Pirouetting around the floor, he paused to insert his nose into a woman's bosom and exhaled an audible sigh of pleasure when he emerged. He skipped up to Richard once again. "This proud page looks comely as he plays the clavichord, whistling so sweetly, he maketh me to sweat—" He pretended to swoon, and moved away to work the crowd. "What is this person who was born in a cart—is he a master, a minstrel, a fiddler—" He pointed to Richard. "Nay, he's a fart!"

Everyone roared with laughter. To Catherine the applause seemed to go on forever. She stood rigidly beside her husband, unsmiling. Richard placed an arm around her shoulders. Skelton's voice rang out again over the thunderous ovation, "Lord, how proud Perkin is of his pea-hen! Jack hath his Jill!" He was met with more snorts of laughter. Tears stung Catherine's eyes but she lifted her chin. Never would she give her enemies the satisfaction of letting them see her weep. Hand in hand, they left the hall, followed by their Tudor spies.

"Oh my love, I am so sorry!" Catherine cried when they were out of earshot of the revelers. They turned into a small vaulted chamber and went to the window while their minders watched.

"It is my penance, Catryn."

"If it's any consolation, I heard the Venetian ambassador tell the ambassador who has only one arm—"

"The Spanish ambassador, Doctor de Puebla," Richard offered.

"Aye, him—that you bear your fortune with spirit and courage."

A wan smile lifted Richard's mouth. Catherine embraced him, squeezing herself tightly against him. "'Tis done, and nothing can change it. We must go on as best we can."

"Catryn, I cannot help but think how it used to be for us, what joy it was when Dickon was with us. Now there is only torment. My family is torn asunder. I cannot love you as a husband and I cannot protect my child. We do not even know if he still lives."

Black panic choked off her breath to hear her child's name spoken thus. In keeping them from their marriage bed and taking Dickon from them, this king had shown how greatly he feared Richard. He knew—he had to know—that Richard was the true prince. Otherwise, he wouldn't be so afraid of a second generation.

"I live on hope, Catryn," Richard went on. He glanced at their jailors conversing with one another a short distance away. "Hope"— he bent down as if to give her a kiss, but instead he whispered in her ear—"of rescue."

In reply to Catherine's stunned surprise, he bent down as if to nibble her other ear. "My aunt—soon—"

Catherine's eyes widened. She was seized with mingled hope

and dread. It was dangerous; she didn't want him to take the chance. But could they abide this terrible fate forever? If Richard escaped, he might be able to find Dickon. Yet Henry was clever. He had spies everywhere. She dared not pursue the subject, for an alertness had come to their guards and now they listened intently. In as casual a tone as she could manage, she said, "I love you, too." To throw them off the scent, she forced back her unease and went on. "In my mind, I keep seeing you ride through the castle gate at Stirling on your white stallion. The pipers are playing and the girls are dancing and twirling their ribbons before you. Our eyes meet . . . It is a memory without end that is etched into my soul. How I wish we could turn time back the way I do in my mind."

"You want to know what I see when I think of you?"

Catherine smiled. "Tell me."

"Gold pouring from the sea. Rose petals in the sky. The sun staring down at me like the Eye of God."

Catherine's smile vanished at the mention of God. "There was a time when I thought there was no wrong we could not right, no fight we could not win, for God was on our side. Why did God not help us, Richard?"

"He has His reasons for everything, but I don't blame Him for my loss, Catryn. I blame myself. I did not have the training to lead men into battle. Nor did I have the stomach for bloodshed. I knew that in Scotland, but I didn't want to believe it. I wanted to make you proud of me, and make Aunt Meg happy. She has had little happiness in life. And look where it led us—" He averted his face. "I cannot forgive myself, Catryn. I should have done as you wished, and turned back at St. Michael's Mount."

Catherine placed her hand on his. "St. Michael's Mount was too late, Richard. The time to have turned back was Ayr. I should not have urged you on. I am the one who bears the blame."

"Even Ayr was too late. Even Scotland was too late. Henry told me that every battle is won before it is ever fought. He uncovered the identity of my supporters across the realm in 1495. My fate was sealed when William Stanley's head was put on a pike on London

Bridge months before we met, but I was too fool to know it. Too filled with dreams—" His voice broke. "Fortune can be so wicked."

Catherine felt his words like the touch of an icy finger running along her spine. They never had a chance! God must have hated them to do this! She shuddered. She had to force back her newfound and terrible knowledge or she might not be able to go on. She turned her face to the dark sky. "Where is your star, Richard?" she cried in a panic. "I cannot see it!"

Richard glanced at her in bafflement, but his tone was soothing when he spoke. "All is well—it's there, Catryn. Clouds obscure it tonight, but we'll see it on the morrow." Richard looked at her meaningfully. "On the morrow," he said squeezing her hand on "morrow."

Morrow. Realization struck with the force of a lightning strike. The rescue he expected was imminent! The plans had already been set in motion. Her heart hammered violently in her breast and she sagged against him. The knowledge seemed suddenly oppressive.

The next evening—December twenty-first—a fire started in the king's wardrobe. Walls collapsed in the conflagration, and flames spewed from the windows amid the cries of children and shouts of men trying to douse the blaze. Catherine stood on the frozen ground with a thousand noble lords and ladies, servants, men in armor, and men of the cloth, all of them shivering in night shirts and blankets and watching the palace flame. Her thoughts were all of Richard, if he had made good his escape. Her eyes sought his star in the sky, shining bright. Though she had not prayed since St. Michael's Mount, she found words to send to heaven this night.

Chapter 9

The Horns of Fate

1498

The court moved back to Windsor from the charred remnants of Shene as January blustered toward its close. To Catherine's anguished thoughts of Dickon were added new worries about Richard. She hadn't seen him since the night of the fire and spent her days in desperate and growing despair.

At the threshold of the queen's privy chamber, she heard her name spoken and halted. "All she is guilty of is love," the queen said. Such sadness clung to her words that Catherine no longer had any doubt that Elizabeth had drunk deeply of both love and loss. When a hush came over the room, she realized she had been noticed.

"I have brought your illuminated manuscript of Boethius's *De Consolatione*, as you requested, my lady." She gave a curtsy.

"Thank you, Lady Catherine," the queen said in her gentle way. "You may place the Boethius there. Was the bookmaker able to repair the tear in the cover?"

"He was, Your Grace. You can no longer tell where it was damaged." Catherine set the queen's treasured volume carefully on a coffer.

"That is good. I shall have to ensure the book is well hidden the next time my lord visits with his monkey, so his creature has no chance to try to eat it again." She smiled at the memory of Prince tearing up Henry's precious memorandum book, then realized how Catherine must feel about the king's pet, and rushed on. "The Boethius is a source of great comfort to me. You should read it, Lady Catherine. I think you would find much solace in its pages."

"Thank you, my lady," Catherine said. But Elizabeth was a fool if she thought Catherine's troubles could be healed by a dead old man.

"You are pale, my dear. Did you not sleep well?" the queen inquired.

"No, my lady." Catherine thought, *I never sleep well*. And not knowing how Richard fared made it worse.

"Then why do you not take the rest of the day off? There is nothing pressing here. Rest and regain your strength. 'Tis the king's forty-first birthday on the twenty-eighth of January, and you would not wish to fall ill and miss the wonderful feast that is planned."

Catherine bobbed a curtsy. "Thank you, my lady."

She left the queen's quarters and headed to the great hall, her pace matched by the two spies Tudor had set on her. Sarra was an older woman with round cheeks, and though she was brusque with her words, she was pleasant enough. There was nothing pleasant, however, about her companion, Meryell, whose pale eyes and color-less lips set in a bony face gave her the appearance of an angry vul-ture. Often, when Catherine felt the urge to stroll in the rain, or sit for long hours on a bitter cold day watching birds wheel in the sky, Meryell would press her thin lips together in disapproval at being so inconvenienced. But of what use was it to explain to this tight, hard-faced woman the emotions that tossed her like a rudderless ship on a stormy sea? She was a mother who had lost her only child. She was a caged bird that had once been wild and dreamed of freedom still. Who could understand that who did not walk in her shoes?

Oblivious of the heads she turned along the way and the admir-ers who bowed and vied for her attention, Catherine continued along the passageways, searching each room for Richard. If there had been an escape planned, Catherine knew he had not made good his attempt on the night of the fire, for the talk at court centered on the loss of jewels, treasured tapestries, hangings, beds, cloths, plates, and furniture. Not a word had been uttered about any escape, nor did King Henry seem unduly troubled. She had overheard him telling the Venetian ambassador that he would rebuild the palace all in stone and much finer than before, and that the fire was not due to malice. Palace whispers, however, suggested otherwise. They took note that the blaze was suspicious because it started where Richard slept—in the king's wardrobe. Based on what Catherine had overheard as she passed the Venetian ambassador's chamber while he was dictating a letter to his Doge, Trevisiano felt the same way. "The fire began in the king's wardrobe where the Duke of York sleeps . . . And by accident a blaze was set by a candle tilting into a curtain, or a glowing brand dropped onto the dry rushes on the floor—"

Welladay, envoys had to be obtuse; they never said what they meant. Trevisiano's Doge would decipher the meaning of "by accident," and know it was no accident.

If Richard's escape attempt had been foiled by Henry VII, either he didn't recognize it as such, or it had been a conspiracy he had manufactured himself to lure Richard into an escape. Otherwise, why would he let the matter drop? A dread thought struck Catherine. Had he truly let the matter drop? Or did he merely pretend to do so in order to spring a trap later? There was no telling, for this king was nothing like her cousin James. Cold and secretive, he had a devious mind and no one could fathom how it worked behind those hooded eyes. She grew anxious as she neared the great hall. Richard was nowhere to be found. *What had this terrible man done with her husband?*

As she turned the last corner, a flock of children ran past her, almost knocking her down. Prince Harry was among them. He had his arms out like a butterfly and was running along on tiptoe, yelling, "What's pretty and golden and flies from battle?" "Perkin!" screeched his little friends. "For he has no guts to weigh him down!" Squealing with delight, they disappeared into the tower staircase.

Catherine closed her eyes and took a moment to recover her composure before she entered the hall. She found it bustling with activity, but Richard was not there either. She made her way to a far-off corner window that was clear of people, passing as she did so Edmund de la Pole, Earl of Suffolk, and his brother, Richard. Both young men bowed low to her. Edward IV and Richard III had been their uncles, and their oldest brother, John, had died leading the Lambert Simnell rebellion against Henry back in '87. If royal blood had counted for anything, Edmund should be king. He stood highest in the line of succession after Edward, Earl of Warwick, who was kept in the Tower. All three de la Pole brothers—Edmund, Richard, and William—had been pardoned by Henry and were received at court, and Catherine favored them, for they were always respectful of Richard.

"My lords, have you seen my husband?" Catherine inquired.

"Regretfully, we have not, my lady," they replied.

A multitude of nobles, ladies, knight, squires, and servants milled around, leaning against walls, sitting in window seats, jabbering and laughing while servants wiped spills and offered them silver trays of mincemeats. No one took much notice of her except a group of the king's squires, who always made a pantomime of bowing and scraping to her in admiration whenever they saw her, as they did now. Their leader was a well-built, dark-eyed man who had once been a seafarer. She acknowledged them with a distracted nod and headed to the window, where she could be alone. At least as alone as possible, she thought, with a glance at Sarra and Meryell. Across on the opposite wall, children ran to and fro, trying to get away from their nurses, and squealed with delight when they were caught. Sudden pain shot through her. She turned away from the sight, but the children's gleeful laughter and tearful protests twisted her heart. She should have two babies of her own now, and both were gone, vanished like phantoms.

The children's cries were drowned by the blast of a clarion fanfare. "'Tis no doubt Perkin, back from the kitchen," said someone nearby. Everyone exchanged snide laughter but Catherine tensed and held her breath. *Richard, my love, pray let it be you—*

King Henry appeared in the entry. The laughter in the hall was checked abruptly and all present scurried into their obeisance. An overwhelming dejection settled over Catherine. She bobbed a curtsy, dropping her gaze to hide her disappointment. When she looked again, the king stood before her.

"Lady Catherine, what a pleasure. I had not expected you to be here," Henry said, though in fact he had been advised by one of his spies that Catherine had been dismissed early by the queen and could be found in the great hall. She had dominated his thoughts to the exclusion of all else that morning—as she had done every morning since he had first met her.

Out of the corner of her eye, Catherine saw that her spies had moved away and she stood alone with the king in an isolated pocket in the crowded hall. He called for music, and all at once the clarion minstrels were joined by pipers and gittern-players.

"There," he said with a grin, "that should take care of the eavesdroppers."

Catherine managed a smile.

"What ails you, dear lady . . ." He tilted her chin up to him. "You look pale. Perhaps you are in need of sun? Perforce we should take a stroll together in the garden."

"It is not sun, I need, but my child, my lord," she replied.

He dropped his hand and was silent for a long moment, his eyes on her face. She met his gaze without flinching.

"I regret that your child is not with you—"

"Dickon. His name is Dickon."

The king was not accustomed to being interrupted and he looked stunned for a moment. "Yes. Well. I do regret that. I had no choice."

"We all have choices, even when we think we do not," Catherine said.

"And you made yours when you came here." His voice was hard as flint and the tenderness was gone from his eyes.

"Is my child still alive?" she demanded.

The king swallowed hard. Catherine realized he was not used to being challenged. His voice came again, so tender that it took Catherine by surprise.

"Lady Catherine, you think me cruel, do you not?"

"If you have killed my child, you are beyond cruel."

He blinked. For a long moment he didn't reply. Then, "He lives."

Catherine put out her hand to the mullioned windowsill for support and closed her eyes. When she opened them again, he was looking at her with heart-rending tenderness.

"Give me proof," she whispered.

He did not speak. She seized his hand. "My babe is a child! An innocent. If his father is a boatman's son, as you say, then he is no threat to you as King of England! I am of the ancient lineage of Scotland. My son is a royal son of Scotland. Show me you are merciful. Send my child back where he belongs!" She lifted her gaze to his face. He stood as if frozen, his eyes fixed on some point above her head far in the distance.

At last he stirred. "I cannot." He couldn't tell her that children grow up, that sons take up their father's fight. Her child would return to avenge his father one day, and he would not come armed only with royal blood, as his father had done. He would come with an army at his back.

Catherine realized she had not moved him one whit. She had only one play left. "If you allow me to see my child, and will send him back to Scotland, I will divorce my husband."

"I—I . . ." Henry found himself at a loss for words. It had not happened since he was a king, not since he was a boy of fourteen in mortal fear of his life on the dockyard at St. Malo, trembling to be sent back to England. Desperately, he wanted Catherine to divorce her husband. It would shame the Pretender before all the world; it would give his kingship legitimacy. It would free the woman he loved to be more to him one day. He cast around for words to deny her offer, yet give her a reason not to believe him a monster, but he found none.

"Have I not given your husband honorable captivity?" he said at last.

"Honorable?"

"Better than he deserves, certainly. He came to us bringing war. More than anything, I wish peace for my land. I abhor bloodshed, Catherine."

"There is bloodshed in the land, and it is not because of Richard."

"Ah, Catherine . . ." He took her face into both his hands. "You mean the Tower? That is a necessary evil. Before there can be peace, there must be obedience. Surely you understand that?"

Catherine knew the talk had turned dangerous. If she offended him, he would take it out on Richard, and there was nothing to be gained for Dickon; at least, not now. "My lord, I have not seen my husband in weeks. Can you tell me if he is well?" She averted her gaze from his and he dropped his hands from her face.

"He can tell you himself. We shall have him brought to you," he said, his expression tight. With a curt nod, he turned on his heel and strode from the room, people dipping and bowing as he passed. The clarions left with him and the minstrels dispersed. Conversations resumed, though they seemed more muted now. Catherine gazed after Henry in stunned surprise. Though it displeased him to know she longed for Richard's company, he was willing to unite her with him in order to gratify her, however begrudgingly. Never would she understand this king. He was ruthless, but not without scruples, and a touch of kindness.

Richard appeared soon afterward, trailed by his minders. Catherine stroked his hair and gazed up into his eyes. "'Tis as if the sun comes with you when you enter a room, Richard." She reached out a finger and traced the lines of the face she loved, from the cleft in his chin to the brow that was as smooth as marble. Richard pressed his lips into the palm of her hand. "The summer is gone, but in your eyes I see it still."

"'Tis not for nothing they called you the most chivalrous prince in Christendom," she smiled. More than anything she wanted to speak the thoughts on her mind and ask Richard so many things— why she hadn't seen him all these weeks, where he'd been, if anyone suspected him—but she could not ask such questions with their minders listening. *Someone must have given them a tongue-lashing,* she thought, for now they were as watchful as they had once been lax. Indicating their guards with a flicker of her lashes, she said, "I am grateful you escaped the fire at Shene. Thanks be to heaven you managed to get out."

"But not till it was almost too late—" Richard said, pressing her hand on the words "too late."

So there had been a delay of some kind; something had gone wrong and only the fire was set successfully.

She decided to venture another question. "Why have you been absent all week?"

"They did not let me out. I know not why."

A squeeze on "I know" and "why." She understood. It was punishment for the fire. They suspected that Richard had set it. She glanced at the minders. All four had fallen silent and were listening intently. Richard took a cup of wine from a passing server with a silver tray.

"Welladay, you are with me now," said Catherine.

That evening, they watched King Henry unwrap the gifts he received for his forty-first birthday, among them two bright feathered popinjays. As soon as the velvet was thrown back from their gilded cage, they squawked out bits of French and Flemish that sent the hall into tides of laughter. Many in the crowd turned to look at Richard while Catherine, seated at the dais, averted her gaze from the king and his offending birds. As soon as dinner was over and the trestle tables cleared, she fled the dais for Richard's side. Launching their game of pretense, they chattered and smiled as they moved about the hall, Catherine leaning on Richard's arm, Richard with a happy look on his face and his eyes only for her.

"They're like two love birds," the queen said sadly to no one in particular.

From his throne, King Henry watched them. *If she would smile at me like that,* he thought, *what I wouldn't do for her . . .*

The minstrels broke into a lilting tune. Henry's gaze followed Catherine as she took the dance floor with her husband. Then his eyes went to Richard. Handsome. Young. Golden—all that he was not. Jealousy burned his breast and the hand he rested on the arm of his throne balled into a fist.

* * *

They celebrated the queen's thirty-second birthday on the eleventh day of February. That snowy month gave way to stormy March, and Windsor Castle bustled with preparations for Easter. Servants dusted windows, swept rooms, beat carpets, and moved furniture to make more space for guests arriving for the sacred observance. Richard and Catherine, seeking relief from the noise and commotion, took refuge on a bench by the Thames, watched as always by their spies, Smith and Jones, Sarra and Meryell, who conversed among themselves, flirting and laughing with one another.

The day was cold, and heavy mist rose from the river. Nestled in their woolens, Richard and Catherine huddled together, admiring the swans that glided past.

"I hear the king calls you his black swan," Richard said sullenly.

Catherine cast Richard a quick look. His breath reeked of wine. "It distresses me to know that. I am naught but his captive, and never will I be more to him. Do not let it disturb you, my love."

Richard dropped his voice to a whisper so their guards wouldn't overhear. "It is disconcerting to have him always follow you with lustful glances. I want to punch him in the nose . . . and cannot."

"It is as it is, my love. We must endure."

Richard shut his eyes against the despair that swept him. They were impaled on the horns of Fate, left to blow in the wind, and help-less to help themselves. "When it touches you and Dickon, I find my penance hard to bear. I wish you had not insisted on coming with me, Catryn."

Insisted. Aye, Catherine thought; she had insisted. The words she'd spoken were etched in her mind and now she recalled the scene as vividly if it were yesterday, and not a lifetime ago . . .

"'Tis too dangerous," Richard had said. "You must stay with your father. You'll be safe in Scotland."

"I don't want to be safe!" she'd cried. "I want to be with you!"

"God knows what lies ahead for me, Catryn. I cannot put you in harm's way—pray, don't ask me to. If I win against Tudor, I'll send for you, and you'll come to me as queen, my Celtic princess."

"Nay—I'll not be parted! I'll share with you whatever lies ahead, be it joy or sorrow." She'd put her arms around his neck and pressed her body to his. "For joy is doubled when shared, and sorrow halved, my love."

She came out of her reverie. She knew now that sorrow is not halved, but doubled, when it descends on those we love. Softly, she said, "You never could deny me anything, Richard."

"I never could. Only now I wish I had." Richard sighed and stared at the water. "What have I done by coming here?"

Catherine put her arm around his shoulders. What had they done indeed? She was tired of being afraid, of going without. The ache for Dickon and for home was always with her, eating at her like a cankerous sore. But she had to be strong, for Richard, and for Dickon. She was all they had. They both depended on her, though neither of them knew it.

"You are all Aunt Meg has left of her own blood. She will not give up her efforts to rescue you." She kissed him on the cheek and took his hand into her own. "Let us dwell on that hope, my dearest love. Such sweet hope."

When Richard made no answer, Catherine said, "'Tis strange. I have never met your aunt, or exchanged many letters with her, yet I love her as if she were my own mother." Margaret had written her when she'd wed Richard, and again when Dickon had been born. An ache for the past came to her and she shut her eyes. She removed Richard's love letter from inside her bodice. "Remember this?" She withdrew the silver groat from its folds. It was one of many minted for him in Flanders and bore the profile of a crowned head, encircled by the words *King Richard IV.*

"I remember," Richard murmured.

"Minted for you by Aunt Meg."

Catherine put the coin away. They sat quietly for a while. Catherine broke the silence. "In your confession, you gave your father's name as *Wezbecque.* Did no one notice?"

Richard grinned. "That it means 'orphan,' you mean? No, no one did. It was my private jest. My uncle, King Richard, gave me the name of my foster family on the eve of Bosworth. Odd, isn't it, that their name can be made to read 'orphan' by changing a single letter? It's so apt. I keep thinking about my uncle, Catryn. If he'd won, all would be different now."

"Aye, my love. *Right to the wrang did yield on that heartless day.* 'Tis from a Scottish poem." After a pause, she said, "Why does good keep losing to evil? Why do many die that should have lived?"

"We cannot fathom God's will."

Another silence.

"Sometimes I wonder if I'll be able to remember who I am by the time Henry is through with me, Catryn."

"Look at me Richard—I have no doubt who you are. You are the son of your father, Edward IV and the true king of England. Never forget that. As I never will." Catherine realized that waiting for Henry's decision on Maximilian's offer weighed heavily on Richard. She searched for a way to get his mind off his worry. "Tell me about your first marriage," she said, keeping her voice to a bare whisper, as always.

Richard gave a little laugh. "If you can call it that, my Celtic princess . . . I was four years old, and my little bride, Anne Mowbray, Duchess of Norfolk, was eight and the richest heiress in England. I remember sitting with her under a canopy of shining silk at our wedding jousts. My bridegroom's crown pressed down hard on my brow and I was most uncomfortable—" He grinned, then his smile faded. "She died in 1481, when she was eight years old, poor child."

They listened to the gentle lapping of the water and watched the swans glide past. Occasional bursts of laughter came from their minders nearby. On the river, a barge passed, in defiance of the weather, its oars splashing and the men aboard singing a merry tune, making welcome noise. Otherwise few people were out this day. Everyone was preparing for the observance that would begin with the morrow. Catherine had no guests to receive, and no new gown to supervise, for she would wear one of the two black ones she owned, and Richard would don the outfit that had been tailored for his appearance at the ambassadors' reception.

Catherine threw a glance behind her. Through the floating mist she saw that there were only two minders now; one of hers, and one of Richard's. The others must have gone for a stroll of their own. The two who remained watched them from the side of a small building where they had found shelter. She relaxed. They were too far away to hear what was said.

"Richard, would it help if I spoke to Elizabeth about you?"

"I doubt it. Sometimes I see her looking at me across the room as if she is trying to decide if I am her brother, but she has never cared enough to try to ascertain for herself by speaking to me. Aunt Meg hates her. She says Elizabeth sold her soul to the devil for a throne."

"Nay, this much I know. She thought you dead, and wished to bring peace to her land by uniting York and Lancaster. I despise her, too, for she is a little mouse before Henry's will, yet she is not completely to blame. Henry does not wish there to be contact between the two of you, and she obeys his will in this and everything else, because she knows he can do away with her and her sisters, as easily as he has done with others who have displeased him—" She broke off. Her train of thought was too terrible to dwell on. "But if she knew for certain that you are who you are, it has to change things."

"How can I prove my identity to her? Anything I know is known to others as well. We were never alone."

"You had to be, at least once in your life. Talk to me about your memories, Richard—tell me anything. It doesn't have to do with Elizabeth."

"That is not difficult, Catryn. I live in my memories these days . . . I remember the names of our favorite hounds and the horses we used to ride, but that scarcely helps, for others know them, too. With my brother Edward I was not close, since he was kept in Wales and we were raised apart. I remember little except for the time we spent together in the Tower—" Richard shuddered visibly. "It was always cold and damp in those chambers. We looked forward to playing in the garden, shooting arrows and cavorting with one another. Then, one day, someone came to tell us we would not be allowed outside, for it was raining. This had never happened before, and we were sad. We loved the outdoors. After that day, come rain or shine, we were not let out to play."

Catherine tightened her hold of his hand.

"Edward began to mope. His toothache grew worse, and he cried out more in his sleep. I tried to cheer him, for I truly believed all would be well in the end, but he remained unconvinced. I spent my days looking out the window and watching people pass, hoping to catch sight of someone I knew. It was good to smell the grass and feel the breeze on my face—" He paused; Catherine waited for him to resume. "Then Edward caught a fever. I wasn't allowed near the window anymore. They said it was too dangerous for me to be seen at all."

"How could King Richard have been so wicked?" she said angrily.

"It seemed that way to me at the time, but looking back, I realize he was protecting us. Tudor was trying to kill us even then, and he succeeded with my brother, Edward."

Richard fell into reverie. Behind them, their minders chatted about the forthcoming feast, wondering what would be served. A few people walked along the riverbank, throwing them glances.

"One night, a man came to us—a noble, judging by his dress," Richard resumed softly. "He didn't give his name. Our guard was sent away, and he sat and chatted with us for a spell. Edward was feverish, so he didn't say much. The man seemed kind. I liked him. While he was with us, there was a knock at the door, and a pageboy was let in. The noble took him by the hand and introduced him to Edward. Then the noble said I had to leave with him and the pageboy would stay in my place, but that he hoped we would return soon and see Edward again—"

Richard froze, a faraway look in his eyes, as if he were back in that moment again; that terrible moment in the Tower when he looked on his brother's face for the last time.

"I gave Edward an embrace, and we left."

"Where did you go?"

"To a castle somewhere in the north. I think it was Barnard." He exhaled audibly, giving Catherine a sense of what it had taken for him to relate these memories to her. "That was it. Until the time I was taken back to London to see my mother again."

"Your mother—" she cried, and then hastily lowered her voice. "You saw your mother again?"

"Only one time. They gave me a pail, grimed me up with stains on my cheek, and told me I was a stonemason's helper and took me to sanctuary. King Richard was in the room with Mother when I entered."

"Why didn't you tell the council any of this?"

"I did mention it. You have forgotten. What difference does it make?"

"What time of year was it?" Catherine asked, pondering an idea.

"I'm not sure. March perhaps, for there was snow on the ground when we left the north, and spring flowers were breaking through the frozen ground when we reached London."

She tensed. It was only with great effort that she kept her voice to a murmur. "March? Then all this makes perfect sense!" She met his eyes. "It was in March that your mother accepted King Richard's offer of pardon and moved from sanctuary into a country home. It was in March that she wrote her son Dorset that all was well and to escape Tudor and return to England. It was in March that she allowed your sister Elizabeth to join King Richard's court, and gave up plotting to wed her to Tudor."

Richard stared at Catherine. "That last time I saw her, she gave me a password." He spoke quickly, excitedly. "She told me that when the time came, I should send her a marguerite, and she would know that I lived. She said no one would suspect a Yorkist with a marguerite, for that was the emblem of the Lancastrian queen, Marguerite d'Anjou. She said she would wait for me forever." He dropped his head.

"If only your lady mother were alive," Catherine said, brushing a tear from his lashes, "she would know it was you, and all the land would rise up for you."

"She died as I was preparing to come to England. The timing was most convenient for Tudor."

Too convenient, Catherine thought, averting her eyes. Knowing the Tudors now, she could believe that they had poisoned Richard's mother over a period of months to make it look as if she had died of a slow illness. She had no wish to speak the thought aloud, preferring to bring up a matter of hope, not pain. "Richard, might your mother have given the password to Elizabeth?"

Richard looked at her, hope forming in his eyes.

"Who else was present when you last saw your mother?" she whispered, stealing a glance over Richard's shoulder at their minders. The other two had returned, and all four were both standing in the shelter of a nearby oak tree now, shivering together, but too distant to hear their words. "Surely you were not alone?"

"There was the man who took me to Westminster from the north, but I do not know his name. All others are dead who were there— King Richard, my mother, Lord Howard. My sisters are too young to remember . . . except for Elizabeth and Cecily."

"Elizabeth," Catherine echoed. "It keeps coming down to Elizabeth . . . She could verify this. She is kept a virtual prisoner, but if she knew—if she knew . . ."

* * *

As was his custom every evening before dinner, Henry closeted himself in his privy chamber to go over the account books his treasurer left him. Carefully, he scrutinized purchases and questioned those that seemed excessive. But on this cold March night, his mind kept straying to Catherine.

On the chair beside him, his monkey gulped wine from a cup, spilling more than he swallowed.

"No, Prince," Henry said, slapping his wrinkled hand as he reached for Henry's quill. "I do important work here, and you cannot eat my pen. Avoiding needless spending, you see, is the primary responsibility of a king . . . Not that you would understand."

The monkey jumped up and down on his chair beside Henry, as if objecting to an insult.

"Now, now, Prince, no need for that. You are a good fellow, and I am fond of you. Here ... have some more wine—" He refilled his cup and watched him drink. Then he scratched his ear. The monkey tilted his head with a sigh of pleasure. "Aye, we all need love, don't we?" Henry said, his tone wistful. Forcing his attention back to his account book, he signed the page and flipped to the next.

His mother and Morton had advised him to reject Maximilian's offer, tempting as it was. Even more might be wrung out of the Holy Roman Emperor in exchange for the safe delivery of the one who called himself Plantagenet, but the effect of returning the prince to Burgundy—even defanged this way—would be to stamp him as legitimate in the eyes of the English people. That would not do. Conspiracies were bound to form around him, with or without his consent, undermining Henry and the dynasty he hoped to establish. Soon he would have to inform "Juno," Margaret of Burgundy, of his decision—but not just yet. It gave him satisfaction to know he had her dangling in the wind. He bent his head back to his ledger and moved down the column, checking each expense.

"Two shillings for a man who scared away crows around Shene, is that not excessive, Prince?" he demanded. The monkey snickered and banged his hand on the table. "You're drunk, my friend," Henry said with a smile. He put a question mark beside the charge and turned the page.

But he wouldn't have sent the Pretender back, even if they had recommended he do so. If the Pretender returned to Burgundy, Catherine would go with him, and he couldn't bear that. As hard as it was to see her, knowing she cared nothing for him, it would be harder not to see her at all. She had to stay here, in England.

He put a hand to his brow and turned to gaze out the window at the snowy scene below. He didn't understand this thing called love. There was his queen, Elizabeth, of course. He supposed he loved her, but not in this way. She was beautiful, so much so that he'd been taken aback when he first saw her. In an arrangement with her mother, Elizabeth Woodville, who wished to prove that her daughter was a virgin and worthy to be queen, he'd bedded her a few weeks before they were married. In truth, he'd been reluctant to marry the girl because of the rumors that she'd loved his predecessor, Richard III, and had slept with him. Certainly he hadn't expected to enjoy their encounter as much as he had, but Elizabeth had turned out to be a virgin and a good match in every way. She had sweet breath, and was fruitful in bearing children, and—unlike her dreadful mother—gentle, and pleasantly submissive to his will. The people loved her. She had united York and Lancaster, and legitimatized his throne. She had served her purpose well, and he had to admit, he did enjoy his evenings in her private solar, for she had a gift for music and song. *Like her brother—*

The thought vanished even as it came, for Catherine's image immediately rose up before his eyes, banishing the Pretender.

There had been that girl in France who'd borne him a child, but she'd been dark-eyed and olive-complected and nothing whatsoever like Catherine. He had been young then—too young to know his mind—and desire had been easily aroused. The passion of his youth had been but a pale imitation of his need for Catherine. Even the child born of that liaison had not touched him unduly. But this—

He gave a sigh and passed a hand over his face. The monkey copied him. Henry looked up. "Have you ever been in love, Prince?"

The monkey beat his chest.

"Aye, you are right . . . It hurts." He fell silent for a moment. "What do you monkeys do to woo the one you love? Bring her bananas?" His mouth quirked into a smile. The monkey grinned, showing his teeth.

"Aye, I follow your meaning," Henry smiled. Then he gave a sigh. "She wants her son back, Prince. She says he's no threat to me, since I claim his father is base-born. But, Prince, you know my maternal ancestors, the Beauforts, were only half-royal, don't you? And illegitimate when they were born. They were barred from the throne by an act of Henry IV's parliament. Then there's my father. He was only half-royal, and he was also illegitimate. Yet here I am. King of England. If I return her son to Scotland, as she pleads with me to do, who is to say he will not take my throne one day?"

Prince shook his head. Henry put down his pen and closed his ledger; it was hopeless. He couldn't concentrate tonight. "Did you know you are my only true friend, Prince? The only one with whom I can discuss the affairs of the heart?"

The animal threw his apple core into the fire and grinned at Henry, bearing his teeth. "More to eat? Another treat, is that what you want?" Removing a small bundle from his breast pocket, Henry unfolded the handkerchief gently to reveal a square of marchpane. "I brought this especially for you." The monkey gave an excited yell when he saw what it was. Henry watched him pop it into his mouth, chew joyfully, and wipe his hands on his velvet jacket. Leaning forward in his chair, Henry dusted the marks he left. "Prince, I've told you before, you should take better care of your clothes. They cost me a hefty sum."

He turned to stare into the fire, drumming his fingers on the table. Morton's words echoed in his mind: Water does not pardon fire, nor the predator his prey. He looked over at the monkey. "I'll wager you didn't know that Ovid said love is a form of warfare, did you, Prince? That is because love's searing arrows wound as painfully as real ones, and in the end one side must vanquish the other and have them surrender . . . What would you do if you had a rival for the hand of the damsel you loved—what would you do?"

The monkey turned his attention to an itch. He scratched himself, caught the offending gnat, and ate it.

"I see." Henry gave him a small, tentative smile. With a sigh, he took out his black memorandum book in which he wrote his innermost thoughts and most important memoranda, such as the names of those who needed to be watched, and who stood in line for execution. He flipped through his notes until he came to a few loose leaflets inserted carefully midway. He withdrew the pages. Here, he could step into his dream, for it related the capture of Perkin—not as it had played out, but as he wished it had played out. It was written for him according to his instructions by his blind poet, Bernard Andre, and he always read it when he was at his lowest ebb, as now. For the man's labor, he, Henry, in a burst of generosity, had pressed a gold noble into his hand. At the time, Henry had thought he'd been too liberal, but now he knew he had been given full value for his money. Bernard Andre had written:

Perkin had confessed. King Henry, with great clemency and forbearance, merely chastised him. The two were alone, Perkin limp and dazzled with the king's mercy, when the door opened and Perkin's lady, with a modest and graceful look, and singularly beautiful, was brought into the king's presence in an untouched state, blushing and tearful. To her, this kind king offered his sympathy.

"Most noble lady, it pains me that you have been deceived by this lying scoundrel here. For the nobility of your blood, the excellence of your manners, your great beauty and dignity cry out for a man of far greater superiority. But take comfort. A new life lies ahead of you. No longer need you concern yourself with this idle liar that was your husband, for you will cast him off soon enough."

As the king spoke, Catherine lay on the ground, weeping and soaked through with a fountain of tears. Because she could not move for grief, Henry had to command her, though gently, to stand. When she had done so, Henry ordered her husband to repeat to her the same things he had said to the king.

At first there was silence. Partly out of shame, and partly for fear, Perkin could not bring himself to say anything. At last, he openly confessed he was not who he said he was, and asked for forgiveness. He had been poorly advised, he said, and he grieved for her abduction. He begged the king that she might be sent back to her family.

His wife broke out in fresh tears, convulsed with a storm of loathing for him. "After you seduced me with your false stories, and had what you wanted of me," she sobbed, "why did you carry

*me away from the hearth of my ancestors, from home and parents
and friends, into enemy hands? O wretched me! O that you had
never come to our shores! O misery! I see nothing before me but
death now, since my chastity is lost. Alas for me! Most wicked man,
are these the scepters you were promising we would have? Most
accursed man, is this the honor of a king of which you boasted
our glorious line would come? As for me, hopeless and destitute,
what can I hope for? Whom can I trust? With what can I ease my
pain? I see no hope except in the one who stands beside me. This
most powerful and merciful king has promised not to desert me. I
place all my faith, hope, and safety in him. I would say more," she
whispered, "but the force of pain and tears chokes off my words."*

With great tenderness, Henry caressed what Andre had written
for him.

Chapter 10

Perilous Shadows

The March day was blustery and wild; howling winds rattled the windows and seeped through the cracks in the castle wall, billowing the tapestry coverings. Catherine was reminded of the Mount and gave a shudder as she sought the path at Windsor that led to the hedgerows. The Scottish ambassador had sent her a missive. Nothing written—but she had understood nevertheless. A minstrel had come to her as she sat waiting for Richard in the great hall and sang "Ring-Around-the-Rosie."

"And whom may I thank for this?" she'd smiled.

The minstrel had handed her a single sprig of thistle. "'Tis with the compliments of Sir Alexander Stewart, my lady."

Catherine gave him a coin. Twirling the thistle around in her hand, she tried to decipher its message. He wanted to meet, aye, but when, and at what time? The clock tower chimed the quarter hour and realization dawned. *A single sprig meant one!* One o'clock. He wanted to meet *now!*

Her heart beating furiously, she'd returned to her room, donned her black mantle and velvet hat, and announced to her stunned ladies that she would seek some air. That she wished to go out at such short notice did not surprise them, for they had become accustomed to her changing moods. She gave Alice and Agatha a barely perceptible nod that told them she needed their presence to distract the Tudor spies so they would not suspect anything amiss.

With both dread and hope in her heart, and taking long breaths to steady herself, she turned the corner into the shrubbery where she had met Sir Alexander nearly a month earlier. The wind was fierce, and the path littered with half-melted snow and patches of ice.

As the clock tower tolled the hour of one, Catherine ambled forward, as casually as she could. Then, down the path, from around a bend, appeared Sir Alexander. She caught her breath.

"Why, my Lady Catherine, what be ye doin' out roamin' on a day like this?" he demanded in a shocked but solicitous tone. He gave her a bow.

"I could ask you the same question, dear kinsman," Catherine smiled.

He inhaled deep and threw a glance up at the moaning branches. "There be such a wind in the trees that this could be the forests of our native isle, I'm thinkin'." He gave her a broad smile. "Still an' all, I'm headin' back indoors as ye should be doin', dear lady. Pray come with me to the hearth. We can drink a warm cup o' sweet white wine together—" He offered Catherine his arm. She smiled as she took it, and slid his note into her sleeve.

She read it by the flickering light of the candle in the privy. "Maximilian's offer refused. Efforts underway to rescue prince and Warwick. Maximilian to lead army himself. Prince—do not give up hope."

Catherine crushed the note in her fist.

* * *

Catherine looked for an opportunity to speak to Elizabeth, but none presented itself. Though she was the queen's lady-in-waiting, she was one of thirty-five, many of them spies set on Elizabeth by the king. Their contact was minimal and kept formal, and they seldom conversed with one another except to exchange polities, for both knew spies were listening. On this sunny day in April, however, Elizabeth and her ladies enjoyed a walk through the garden that was budding with lilies, roses, and snapdragons. Catherine bent down and plucked a marguerite as she strolled beside the queen. She gave it to Elizabeth, watching her intently.

"Thank you, Lady Catherine. 'Tis a lovely flower."

Then she passed.

She did not know the password.

Catherine sank down on a bench, wretched with disappointment. Her two minders checked their steps to watch as they pretended to admire a bed of narcissus. To her surprise, Elizabeth's fool, Patch the Dwarf, left the queen's party as it disappeared along the garden path, and came to her. He climbed up beside her, his awkward movements jingling all the bells attached to his patchwork orange and green costume.

"My lady, may I sing for you? I am sure it would delight you entirely, for I vouch that never have you heard a sound so unforgettable." He grinned. It was the first time in all these months that he'd spoken to her directly, and Catherine was taken aback. No doubt he was a spy, but didn't he know he wasn't needed? She already had two women reporting on everything she said and did. She glanced at her minders. What she wanted more than anything else at this moment was to be left alone—by Tudor spies and everyone else. She threw him a hard look. "I have heard you sing before, but I don't remember when."

"My lady, you have a cutting wit." He looked up at her with sad brown eyes.

"Forgive me, Patch," she sighed, "I seem to have forgotten how to laugh." There was no need to punish this man for her ills.

Patch burst into laughter, parroting first the high-pitched giggle of a maiden, then one in the tenor of a man, then that of a gleeful child, and then the gurgle of a baby, followed by a mule, and finally a monkey. When he jumped up and down on the bench, flailing his arms and showing his broad white teeth, he looked exactly like Prince. She laughed, along with others who had gathered to listen, for now there was a large group around them, including Sarra and Meryell. But Patch was not done. He placed his hand under Catherine's nose and caught a needle that appeared to drop out of her nostrils. "My lady, you should embroider less, for you are veritably sneezing needles!" he exclaimed.

As Patch clambered down from the bench to give a deep bow, he whispered to her, "You must not forget how to laugh, my lady."

* * *

That afternoon, she went in search of Richard, followed by her ladies. Passing through the high-arched entrance of the great hall, she saw him in a far corner, standing by a mullioned window that had been opened to the breeze from the river. His lute had been laid aside and he was in conversation with the Spanish ambassador, Doctor Rodrigo de Puebla. Behind him, his two guards lounged against the wall as they listened with bored expressions. Now they straightened up and smiled to see Meryell and Sarra.

Spain's one-armed envoy had come to England to negotiate the marriage of Prince Arthur to Isabella and Ferdinand's daughter, Princess Katarina of Aragon. He had a round, kindly face and wore his empty sleeve neatly tucked into a leather belt with a silver buckle. He gave Catherine a bow and kissed her hand in the courtly fashion of his country.

"Ah, the beautiful Lady Catherine. Always a joy to behold," he said.

A warmth came to Catherine. Like the other foreign envoys, the Spanish ambassador was one of the few at court who treated Richard with respect and didn't address him as Perkin, which he hated. They were both outsiders: Richard for his princely blood, and de Puebla for his Jewish blood, if not his deformity. Catherine gave him a smile that conveyed her affection and gratitude. "'Tis good to see you also, Doctor de Puebla. My lord husband is very fond of you, as you must know."

"I enjoy our discussions immensely. His grace is most knowledgeable and well read."

They fell silent as a young man, who they knew to be a servant of the queen, bowed to them. "Pray, forgive this intrusion, Doctor de Puebla, but your company is requested by the queen."

They looked to the opposite end of the room, where the queen stood on her dais surrounded by a group of ladies. She gave them a nod.

A silence fell as de Puebla left them to attend to the queen. Catherine knew she had to tell Richard that Elizabeth didn't know the password, but when? Their guards were listening. She had thought of writing Richard a note, but pen and paper was difficult to procure unnoticed and the love note she'd written as a test had required much effort. She dared not risk it again for a while.

When a group of playful children appeared abruptly, screeching merrily, Catherine leaned close and whispered her news to Richard. He kissed her brow, and nodded. Disappointment was an inevitable part of their lives now, and they had learned to take it with a measure of equanimity.

Two of the children grabbed her skirts, while others hid behind Richard's legs to evade capture. He bent down and tickled one of them, and the child's delighted giggle sent a spasm of pain rushing through Catherine. Richard looked at her, then drew her to him. She knew they were both thinking of Dickon.

"How is your leg?" Catherine asked softly to banish the thought that dredged grief in its wake. They had not spoken about Prince Harry since he'd kicked Richard on the day of the Feast of Candlemas.

"Fine now."

"He may look like a cherub but he's not," said Catherine softly, thinking of the many times she had witnessed Harry spit on Richard as he passed.

"Skelton is his tutor, and Henry his father," whispered Richard under his breath.

"When I think of our darling—" She caught her breath.

"I know, my love. Sweet were the days when he was with us." He fell silent, gazing out the window.

Catherine leaned her head against his shoulder. "At least we have each other, my dearest."

"We have each other, and yet we do not."

Catherine looked up at him.

"I never knew it would be like this, Catryn. I never knew he'd take Dickon from us and keep us apart. He has me penned up here, dangling you before my eyes. It is a special form of torture he has devised for me. I am in my own Hell."

"He is good at devising Hell for others," Catherine whispered.

Richard lifted his hand and gently tucked a stray lock of hair away behind Catherine's ear. She smiled up at him sadly.

At that moment, John Skelton entered the hall. Catching sight of them, he swooped around and dived down on them, a dark look on his face. "How dare you teach young Courtenay the lute? Who do you think you are? I am the poet and the composer of this court, and the teaching of singing, and the performing of music, falls in my purview, not yours!"

He was so affronted that his face had blown up into a round red beet-root as he shouted at Richard. In his black robe and hose, with his darting eyes and sharp little movements, he reminded Catherine of a bat, despite the laurel wreath he wore to remind everyone of his degrees in music and rhetoric.

"I meant no offense," Richard said, standing before him like a prince, his head held high. "Courtenay asked me, and I obliged him. No harm was intended to you, or anyone else. In fact, I never gave you a thought."

"You intend harm merely by breathing!" Skelton fumed. "I look forward with pleasure to watching you die at Tyburn, you dirty river rat!"

The hall had fallen silent. The queen, far away on the dais, was listening, and Lady Daubeney was marching toward them. Catherine suddenly realized that Skelton did not know Queen Elizabeth was present.

"Master Skelton, Her Grace demands to know the meaning of this uproar," Lady Daubeney said.

Skelton gave her a deep bow, and offered his explanation.

"The Queen commands that you never again use such vile language in the presence of your betters, especially when noble ladies are present. Pray apologize to Lady Catherine."

Skelton's red color deepened and a vein twitched at his forehead. He murmured an apology, bowed to her, and turned to bow again in the direction of the queen. The hall watched, riveted by the spectacle.

Lady Daubeney turned to Catherine. "Lady Catherine, the queen will be taking dinner privately in her solar this evening and requests the pleasure of your company. It shall be a small group, only the princesses of the realm."

"I shall be delighted," Catherine said, curtsying gracefully in Elizabeth's direction.

"Skelton, you are dismissed," Lady Daubeney said sharply.

Lady Daubeney exchanged a look with Catherine as they watched the little man scurry away. The queen had interceded on Richard's behalf this time, whereas the king had evidently given him wide latitude to insult Richard with impunity. Few dared challenge Skelton— a favorite of the king's mother, Margaret Beaufort—but few liked him. For once, the miserable creature had been put in his place.

* * *

Catherine rejoiced in her good fortune. She had what amounted to a private audience with Richard's sisters—and without her minders. The queen had been clear on that point. She nervously made her way down the various hallways, nodding absently to the men who bowed to her as she passed.

At the threshold of the antechamber, her ladies departed to dine in the great hall and Lady Daubeney came forward to greet her. "All the princesses await, Lady Catherine," she said. "Her grace, Sister Bridget, has arrived from Dartmouth Priory. She is eager to see you again. This way, my lady . . ." Lady Daubeney led the way to the queen's private chamber, bobbed a curtsy, and left.

From window seats and settles around the room, the five York sisters turned to look at her. It was the first time she had seen them gathered together this way and not dispersed among a host of unrelated people. They were a markedly handsome family, with a strong resemblance to one another—and to Richard—all fair, with good bones, fine features, and large eyes that were either bright blue or sea green. Even the severe habit of a nun couldn't hide Bridget's charms, just as Elizabeth's black gowns and ugly gabled headdresses failed to dim her beauty. In the corner a minstrel played his gittern, and nearby, a table was set for dinner before a blazing fire, covered in white cloth and laden with silver trenchers and goblets. In the flickering light of candles and torches, the colored glass and tapestries in the vaulted chamber blinked with welcoming warmth.

Catherine was about to curtsy when all except the queen rose and bobbed to her. Although she was a captive, she outranked these English princesses by virtue of her royal Scots blood and nearness to her cousin James. Flustered for a moment, she stood blushing. Then she turned to the queen and gave her a gracious dip.

Elizabeth's sister Cecily, sparkling in yellow velvet embroidered with gold thread, her V-collar and flared sleeves cuffed with fur and wearing a golden headband over her fair hair, came forward to greet her. Of all the royal ladies, it was with Cecily that Catherine felt a close affinity.

"Dear Lady Catherine, we greet thee well," Cecily said, "and are pleased that you can dine with us this evening." She took her hand and gave her a kiss on her cheek.

Catherine wondered much why she had been invited to such an intimate group. Perhaps the queen was trying to make amends for Skelton's rudeness. Much as she resented Elizabeth for refusing to fight for Richard, not for naught did the people of England call her "Elizabeth the Good." Her kindness of heart was legendary.

They dined on roast pheasant, poached fowl and bacon, and meatballs made with currants, spices, and almond milk and decorated with tiny flowers. Catherine's glance touched only fleetingly on each member of the family, so she wouldn't be noticed observing them. King Edward's daughters ranged in age from sixteen to thirty-two. The youngest sister, Bridget, had been but three years old when Richard was removed from sanctuary, so she would not remember her brother. But Cecily would, Catherine thought, turning her glance on her. She had been fifteen at the time.

"I adore mushroom pasties!" exclaimed Anne of York, and she seized a handful from the server.

Catherine turned her attention to the striking figure in scarlet velvet, thinking how well it complemented her milk and roses complexion. Anne of York was a year younger than Richard. As a child, she'd been betrothed to Maximilian's son, Philip the Handsome. Those plans had been dropped when her father died. Now she was married to Thomas Howard's son, the Earl of Surrey, in a love match arranged by her sister the queen. Father and son were trusted military commanders who had helped to turn the tide against Richard and secure the tyrant's throne. She wondered if Anne's husband ever questioned his action, and if he would come to regret it. Even if he did, what good could it do Richard now?

Seventeen-year-old Kate looked as fresh as a rose in pink satin embroidered with silver. Richard's altercation with Skelton had involved her elder boy. She had married William Courtenay, the young lord who'd refused to snatch Dickon from her arms at St. Buryan. Her marriage was another love match arranged by the good-hearted queen.

The table was cleared and the desserts brought in: rose pudding, fried fig pastries, golden steamed custard. The evening was almost at an end and Catherine had not yet broached the subject that consumed her mind.

"What I would have given for such delights in sanctuary," she smiled, accepting a portion of rose pudding. "All I knew during that time was stale food and leaky roofs. One storm so damaged my cell that a stonemason had to be sent in to repair it." Elizabeth and Cecily were listening, their spoons halted midway to their mouths. *They remember,* she thought. She hurried on before she lost her courage. "The stonemason brought his young helper with him. I remember the child vividly . . . a sweet boy . . . so beautiful . . ."

Elizabeth and Cecily went pale. *They know—they know now!* The two sisters exchanged a look but said nothing. They put down their spoons. Kate was the one who spoke. "I was only four years old and I do not remember those days. I am glad for it. They sound dreadful."

Catherine nodded. "You are blessed."

Chapter 11

River of Flames

The next morning, in the queen's chamber, Catherine detected a tension in the room that had not been there before. The queen and Cecily greeted her with more warmth than usual, but they avoided one another and seemed distracted. Catherine knew—she *knew*—they had pondered her words. But what had they decided? Would they help Richard? *Could* they help Richard?

On a stroll through the garden, Catherine found herself alone with Cecily. Spring was in the air; flowers were in full bud; birds swooped and dived around them. Cecily picked a rosebud.

She held it to her face and passed it to Catherine. "Already it has a fragrance." As Catherine inhaled the perfume, Cecily said softly, "You are much admired by our people. Did you know they call you the Pale Rose of England?"

Catherine glanced up in surprise.

"But—and I pray you not misinterpret my words—"

Catherine nodded.

"You are a princess of the blood. Your beauty is much noted, but they look at you and think that, however wretched their own lives, it could always be worse for them." She gave Catherine a long look. "I hope you do not mind me asking, but do you ever regret marrying Rich—your husband—instead of the young man you might have wed instead of your sister?"

Catherine knew she was referring to Patrick Hepburn, Earl of Bothwell, who had been given his choice of either Catherine or her elder sister, Margaret, as his bride. He had chosen Margaret. She decided to answer honestly. "I cannot deny I have thought about that—about how different it would have been for me had I married the Earl of Bothwell. But Meg and Patrick were in love. I did not begrudge them their happiness then, or now. And I cannot regret knowing love myself . . . My time with my husband was brief, but the world had luster then—a beauty you cannot know unless you've known love, and the arms of the one you love." She fell silent, remembering.

Cecily took Catherine's hand. "You have lost much, Catherine, but I want you to know that you are not friendless."

"Thank you, Lady Cecily."

"How strange life is," Cecily sighed, linking arms with her. "I would have known you as a sister had I come to Scotland and married King James. Now here we are in England, and you are my—"

She broke off, glanced around, bit her lip. Catherine's heart missed a beat in that moment. Cecily had almost uttered *sister*.

"Friend," she said, and gave Catherine's hand a squeeze.

*   *   *

For Easter the court made a pilgrimage to Canterbury. As the royal procession arrived at the gates, a monk was being led into the cathedral precinct in chains. Henry drew rein.

"What is his crime?" he demanded, addressing himself to the guard.

"Heresy, Sire. He was found in possession of an English-language Bible and he denies the efficacy of relics. He is to burn."

"My man, 'tis a dread fate that awaits you, both on earth and in the world to come. Let us discourse together. Mayhap I can make you repent the errors of your way."

Henry took time to speak with him, and after a while, the man, in terror of his fate, renounced his heresy.

"You are now reconciled to God. Here is a blessing." At a nod from Henry, one of his men gave the monk some coins from his pouch.

The man fell to his knees, sobbing with gratitude.

"It contents me much that I have saved your soul," Henry said. Turning his horse, he cantered off, leaving the man staring after him.

Catherine looked back and saw her own horror and disbelief reflected on the man's face. On his open palm glittered the coins that Henry had given him. Of what use were they to him, a man about to be burned at the stake? He had thought to be spared his terrible fate; it was why he had recanted! All he received for denying his beliefs was a few alms that could do him no good.

The queen must have shared her dismay, for she said, "My lord, will you not save him from the fire?"

"I already have," Henry replied. "He will not burn in Hell."

*   *   *

"You may have noticed that my royal sister and I are not as close as we would wish," Cecily announced one morning in mid-April, when they found themselves walking together along an empty corridor. Catherine's minders were not with her in the morning hours, since Henry believed her to be well guarded by the queen's ladies.

Catherine didn't know what to say, so she made no reply.

"The roots of our discord go back to childhood. I act decisively once my mind is made up, whereas she considers every side of a matter. Then she does nothing—except to let matters take their course. God's will, she says. She seems unable to comprehend that God gave us the ability to think, and if He does that, then He means us to use our intellect to make reasoned choices—"

Catherine opened her mouth to object, but Cecily cut her short. "Nay, hear me out. The matter is of interest, have no doubt.

"My royal sister never takes a stand, perhaps because the one time she did it proved disastrous—" Cecily broke off. That was the most charitable light she could throw on Elizabeth's decision not to flee Tudor after the battle of Bosworth. The truth was that her sister had sold herself to the tyrant for the price of a throne. Had she fled, all would be different now, but she had remained, waiting to be captured. To unite the White Rose with the Red and save her land from bloodshed, she claimed. But Cecily believed otherwise. It was to be queen that Elizabeth had stayed. Her lips curled in distaste.

She turned her head and met Catherine's eyes. "My royal nephew Arthur is such a genial boy. The apple of my sister's eye. She loves him dearly."

Catherine understood now what Cecily was trying to say. The queen would not help Richard. *She had chosen her son over her brother.* She had loved King Richard, too, but when he was dead, she'd wed Henry Tudor—he, who had slain the man she loved! What was she made of? Catherine had thought her gentle, but she was as hard as flint. The thought disoriented her, and she stumbled in her steps.

"Let me help you—" Cecily said. "Though there is little anyone can do—against sickness," she added quickly, touching Catherine's brow.

Catherine knew she had found an ally, but Cecily's message filled her with woe. For Cecily believed no one could help Richard. Before she could digest the full import of this new knowledge, a party of the king's ushers approached in the hall, laughing. Catching sight of Catherine, they swept their hats from their heads and fell to their knees in a pantomime of swooning love, led by the tall, dark-eyed seafarer she had come to dislike. The man was always the instigator of the drama that in the beginning had seemed innocent enough. Lately, however, he had grown overbold. His eyes passed over her with none of the deference she was accustomed to, and when their paths crossed, after giving a little bow, he'd stand with his head held high, a mocking grin on his face, looking at her as if he saw straight through to her undergarments. The nerve of the man! Catherine lifted her chin and passed on without acknowledgment. She heard his mocking laughter follow her down the hall.

"Who is he?" she asked Cecily when they were out of earshot.

"James Strangeways? He has a terrible reputation. He's a drinker, a gambler, and the biggest rake at court, my dear."

"Indeed?" said Catherine, her interest piqued.

"No woman can resist him. He's always getting them with child. Once he got an earl's daughter *enceinte* and refused to wed her." She inclined her head to a group of clerics who greeted them.

"What?" Catherine replied fiercely. "Who does he think he is?"

"He's naught but a commoner, but you'd never know it the way he carries himself, would you? His family is from Yorkshire and he is related to Lord Giles Daubeney. His father was devoted to Warwick the Kingmaker, and died in his service."

"A Yorkist?" Catherine's brows lifted in surprise.

"He was connected with the Staffords—you know, Sir Humphrey Stafford, who led the Lambert Simnell rebellion against Henry after King Richard's death"—Cecily leaned her head close and whispered—"and was extracted by force from sanctuary?" She straightened and smiled at a group of noble ladies who bobbed curtsies. "Strangeways stood high in my father's favor. He used to command ships for him, and Papa said he was brave, but reckless, yet he never lost a vessel, or even a cargo. My father always said he was a good Yorkist. Now look at him. In loyal service to—" She broke off, but Catherine knew what she was thinking. Lancaster.

"Why didn't King Edward make him wed the earl's daughter?"

"Some say it was because he had little money and was not of noble birth, and the earl didn't want him in his family. But others claim Strangeways refused the earl point-blank. He that do get a wench with child and marry her afterwards, he said, is as if a man should shit in his hat and then clap it on his head."

In spite of herself, Catherine burst out laughing.

"The earl sent his daughter into a nunnery, and the child was given away. Since he and his kin were all loyal Yorkists, my father protected Strangeways, and he never paid for his misdeed."

"So he never wed?"

"Nay, and never will."

"Then he does womankind a great service," said Catherine.

* * *

The following week dealt another blow. The Scottish ambassador informed Catherine that Maximilian was forced to abandon his efforts to put together a fleet to invade England. There was a lack of money and serious troubles at home. But, Sir Alexander said kindly, Richard should not lose heart. His aunt remained fully committed to doing whatever it took to free him, and a plot was under way to secure his rescue. More would be known soon.

The string of disappointments depressed Catherine's spirits and made onerous her task of helping the queen prepare for the May Day revels.

"My Lady Cate," Alice said one morning, breathless with excitement, as Catherine left Elizabeth's quarters. "You must come with me—at once!"

"What is it?"

"The king has sent you a gift! A large gift—his gentleman usher brought it himself. He awaits in your chamber!"

Catherine was baffled. What could this mean? In April, the king had doubled the pay of her ladies and increased her own draw from seven to ten pounds for the month. Was he having a change of heart toward Richard? She turned the corner into the passageway that led into her chamber.

The king's man had been standing at the open window in the small vaulted chamber, staring out over the garden as he waited, a tall, powerfully built figure in topaz and fur. At her footsteps, he turned. She saw that it was detestable James Strangeways. Catherine's eyes went to the large parcel spread out over both his arms. A roguish smile lit his face as he gave her a bow.

"Dear Lady Catherine, the king sends greetings—and a gift—" He held out the mysterious package, his dark eyes dancing.

"You may place it on the bed," Catherine said, disliking the boldness of his gaze. Keeping her distance, she watched as he draped the long velvet package over the embroidered coverlet. "The king also sends you this note—"

"For our right dear and well-beloved Lady Catherine Gordon," Henry had written in his own hand, using terms of endearment reserved for lovers.

Alice, who'd been unwrapping the gift, gave a cry and leapt back as if she'd touched a hot iron. A sumptuous gown glimmered in the sunlight, of tawny satin edged with an embroidered hem of black velvet. Catherine gasped. Henry had copied every detail of the sea-gown she'd worn when she'd first come to England! Then, she'd had Richard and their darling child. With his gift, Henry was offering her his love and the riches his kingly power could place at her feet. With his gift, he was pretending that Richard had never been—that he counted for nothing—that Dickon had never been born and had never been stolen from her! He thought he could obliterate all that, and begin anew with her, as if he had never harmed her! Her hands balled themselves into fists.

"The king wishes you to wear it for the Love Day revels," Strange-ways grinned. "There is also a kirtle beneath." He turned the hem of the lovely gown to reveal a kirtle of black worsted and a selec-tion of ribbons for her girdle. "There is more," said Strangeways. "See here," he added when Catherine made no move to draw closer. "A set of hose spun of kersey and lined with soft white gauze—" His mouth lifted in a crooked smile that Catherine knew he considered irresistible to women. His gaze went to her feet, and Catherine read his thoughts. The rogue was imagining how it would feel to draw the hose up her legs himself!

Catherine felt herself redden. She wanted to wipe that smirk off his face. "Take it back."

Strangeways's grin vanished. "Back?" he echoed in disbelief.

"You heard me."

"To the king?"

"Who else?"

He swallowed visibly. "But he has made a matching riding cloak for himself—"

Catherine stared at him.

"M-May I give him a reason?" Strangeways was beginning to

realize the seriousness of her words. But who dared spurn a gift from a king? Never had he expected such a reaction. Already he could feel the royal wrath that would fall on his head.

"Tell the king that I thank him for his kindness, but I cannot accept his gift. I expect to be in mourning for the rest of my life."

"But—"

"Tell him." Her stomach lurched and bile flowed into her mouth as her fears for Richard mounted. But she saw no other way out of her impossible situation. What would Henry do to Richard in punishment for her refusal? Yet, if she accepted his loathsome gift, would that not hurt Richard more—and worse—give heart to the man she despised?

She spun on her heel and quitted the chamber abruptly, leaving Strangeways standing in the middle of the room. Alice fled after her. When Catherine turned the corner into the passageway, her sight blurred. She lifted a hand to her head and leaned against the wall to still her faint heart.

"My Lady Cate, my dear lady—" Alice said gently.

Catherine fell into Alice's arms and sobbed.

*   *   *

Despondent and preoccupied with her thoughts, Catherine was reluctant to go to her husband. She sought the garden instead, followed by Henry's two spies. She had no desire to impart any of her discouraging news to him, and for this reason, she'd commanded Alice and Agatha to remain behind and tend to their duties. Maybe then he would have no chance to ask questions. *I'll mention Aunt Meg's plot*, she thought, *and leave out all else.*

She threaded her way along the river and had not gone far when suddenly she heard her name called. Cecily was strolling past on a parallel path, arm in arm with the king's mother, clad in a sumptuous square-necked gown of green velvet and fur. Margaret Beaufort said something to her and Cecily dropped a curtsy. Cutting across the grass, she made her way to Catherine.

Catherine smiled. There was something attractive about Cecily, who seemed to have no fear of anything, not even of speaking her mind.

"Why aren't you with Richard?" Cecily demanded, dropping her voice to a bare whisper on his name. This was the time of day when Catherine was normally in his company.

Catherine bit her lip. Cecily turned to Henry's spies and made a sweeping gesture with her hand. They understood, and fell back.

"You haven't quarreled, have you?"

"No, nothing like that." Catherine decided to be frank. "I am the bearer of tidings I have no wish to give him."

Cecily linked her arm through Catherine's so that they walked closely together, as she had done a moment before with Margaret Beaufort.

"You count the king's mother as a good friend," Catherine said, by way of conversation. "You have courage. Everyone else is terrified of her."

Into Cecily's mind flashed the memory of her planned offensive against the king's mother that had rendered such handsome dividends. Flattery had been the tool she'd used to good effect, for Margaret was desperate to be admired. "I wish I had paid more attention to my studies, Lady Margaret," she had told her. "Like you, I would be able to read Latin now, and know things that most women have not the intellect to understand." She was pleased to find that her words were working. Like all vain and pompous people, Margaret Beaufort was exceptionally susceptible to flattery.

"I shall let you in on a confidence," Margaret Beaufort had replied. "I wish I had studied the ancient Greek more avidly for the same reason. I converse with the most learned men in the kingdom, and they respect me highly, but they know not how I yearn to translate the works of the great masters, which they can do, if they so choose, and I cannot."

"My Lady Margaret, it seems but a small regret. If you were translating the ancient scholars from their original tongue, who would have advised the king? You are the one most instrumental in securing the crown for Lancaster. Without you, the wars might never have ended."

"You evidence a wisdom far beyond your years, my dear," Margaret Beaufort had replied. "Clearly, God ordained it so. He wished me to be there to guide my son and the kingdom along His righteous path."

Cecily tried not to let her feelings show. The older woman barely came up to her chest, and the plunging V-collar of her gaudy, bejeweled crimson satin gown was scarcely becoming to her age. She made Cecily think of a thistle pretending to be a rose, and she felt sorry for her. She cast around for something generous to say. "When I look at you," she had replied, "your piety beckons me to prayer, for you remind us all that we are an instrument of His plan. God Himself has chosen you to preside over us, and I am blessed to know you, and to learn from you. Will you come with me to chapel, dear Lady Margaret, and guide me in my words to God? For you know the way that best pleases Him."

Much good had flowed from that beginning. Beautiful gowns, rich furs and gifts, a place of honor at court, young men to dance and laugh with, and what her heart desired above all else: the annulment of her first marriage to Ralph Scrope. Margaret Beaufort opened many doors for her. Unfortunately, one of them was to the viscountcy of Welles.

Following her own rules, she had flirted with Margaret Beaufort's maternal half-brother, John, Viscount Welles, as she did with every old man—not much, but enough to tickle their vanity and make them feel devilish and young. Experience had taught her that the old farts would then become her friends and do her favors, should she ever need one. But John, Viscount Welles, had taken her seriously and fallen in love with her. Next thing she knew, the good times were over, and she was wed to the old lecher—proving her sister Elizabeth right for one of the few times in her life. Cecily had always blamed Elizabeth for getting her married off to bumbling Scrope, and one day, she'd had it out with her. "It was your own fault!" Elizabeth had declared. "If you hadn't flirted with him and given him hope, you might not have had to marry him when his friend became king!" Cecily had forgotten Elizabeth's words and learned too late that it was risky to play around with the powerful, or those connected to the very powerful. She had, however, amended her rules. But that was like watering a plant after it was dead.

Now she glanced at Catherine, who was still waiting for a reaction to her observation. "Oh, that's not courage. Margaret is easy to get along with if you give her what she wants." Cecily threw a glance over her shoulder, leaned close, and whispered, "Approval and flattery." She put one foot gaily in front and added, "Everyone desires that, but I've never known anyone who needs it more desperately than she does. Despite her power—or maybe because of it—she is at heart a lonely old woman."

Like her son, thought Catherine. Two lonely, utterly miserable, and desperate people making everyone else pay for their emptiness. "Richard is probably wondering if I am coming today," she said sadly.

Cecily gave her hand a squeeze, and unlinked her arm.

*   *   *

At Westminster, Henry waited for his mother and Morton in the small private chamber that connected his lodgings to hers. Standing with his hands clasped behind his back, he looked forlornly at the Thames. Catherine had spurned his gift. The implication was as clear to him as if she had screamed the words aloud for all the world to hear. She would have none other than the captive who was her husband, though a king sought her heart. For seven months he'd wooed her with kindness; for seven months he'd shown her husband mercy, thinking it would sway her feelings. Each time, he'd met with rebuff. Again, in his mind's eye, he saw Strangeways bringing back his gift of the gown, and his misery gave vent to cold fury. He slammed a fist on the stone sill. No more—no more kindness! There would be no more mercy! Things would change now. How they would change—

A hand pressed his shoulder lovingly. "Mother—" He gave her a small smile and laid his hand over hers in gentle acknowledgment. She took a seat. A man-at-arms opened the door to let Morton enter.

Henry's smile widened at the sight of the familiar figure in black cassock, red cap, and sash. "Ah—here is good Morton. I thank thee for making the journey, my friend. I know you have been ailing."

Henry clasped his hands behind his back again and looked at the river in order to compose his thoughts. A silence fell, broken by the cawing of ravens and the tolling of church bells across the Thames. He turned around to find Morton settling into a gilt chair. Linking his ringed fingers across his ample girth, Morton gave him his full attention.

"I find myself in an untenable situation," Henry began. "The feigned boy is a thorn in my side that festers bitterly. Plot after plot is hatched to free him, and putting the plotters to the rack has no effect on infernal Margaret of Burgundy. She merely hatches another—" He strode to the desk, picked up a piece of paper, and waved it at them. "'Tis time to lance this boil. My question to you—how best can it be done?"

"There is always poison," said Margaret Beaufort with a thin smile.

"A secret death would give rise to rumors and not solve the problem, Mother."

She pondered this thought. "You are right, my son. The people do not expect a king's heir to the throne to be put to death in a public execution, for that would be regicide and a sin against God. Therefore, a public execution is exactly what is needed."

"Aye, Mother, but our hand must not be suspected in his death, except with the weight of the law behind us. I cannot be seen to be afraid to kill him. Yet my hands are tied by the agreement at Beaulieu, and my promise to him of life and honorable captivity. How I wish I could rescind that."

Margaret Beaufort looked lovingly at her son. She had been twelve when she'd given birth to him, and though she had wed four times, she had been unable to bear any more children. He was everything to her and she loathed with passion those who caused him a moment's distress. "Perhaps we should poison Margaret of Burgundy," she said. "That should not be difficult to arrange."

"No, Mother. It would bring Maximilian down on us with a

vengeance. Remember Ramsey's response when I inquired about murdering the boy in Scotland?" he demanded, referring to one of his high-ranking Scottish spies, Sir John Ramsey. "He said it would enrage James, who would use it as a pretext to wage war between our two nations. We must find another way. We don't want Maximilian and his allies to invade us. We cannot afford the cost of war, nor to put weapons in the hands of our enemies and give them the chance to rise up against us." Henry regarded Morton thoughtfully. "You are quiet, my friend, but if I guess rightly, you have a solution, do you not?"

"Aye, my Leige. A good one, if I say so myself. Your problem is that you gave the boy your royal word. But if he were allowed to escape and were caught again—then the original agreement would be rendered null and void, would it not?"

"I have considered that, but there is a measure of risk in allowing a plot to go to fruition, however."

"Not if it is *your* plot," replied Morton.

"Control the plot?" said Henry. "Ah, good Morton, I see. We merely need the nectar to lure the butterfly into an escape—"

Margaret Beaufort rose excitedly and began to pace. "Do you remember how we moved to the Tower for Yuletide in '95 when we discovered Stanley's plot? It was most convenient. We moved the conspirators directly from the feasting hall into the Tower prison, and from there to the place of execution. We can do the same now." She halted in her steps and looked at Henry and Morton.

"Take the young prince back to the Tower. Back into his very nightmare—very clever, Lady Margaret . . . very clever indeed. That may be the only impetus he needs—short of an unlocked door, of course. But may I advise caution?"

"Speak, Morton," said Henry.

"His escape must be arranged carefully. Few can know. People must see it as the Hand of God—or the Devil—but no one should see your hand in it, Sire."

Henry nodded thoughtfully. "I knew that if I could gather the three of us in one place, we would arrive at a solution. I hope you find yourself in better health soon, Morton. I know not what I'd do without you, my friend."

* * *

Following the revels of May Day in the year 1498, court moved downriver to the Tower and Richard found himself back where he had been imprisoned with his brother as a nine-year-old boy. There, in that damp, hemmed-in place, the dread memories of his childhood awakened in the shadows on the walls and the darkness in the stairwells. By what quirk of fortune had Fate allowed him to escape, only to deliver him back into his old nightmare? He had escaped Hell, found Heaven in Catherine's arms, and now he was back in the Hell he had fled.

Richard slept more fitfully than ever in the Tower. Pursued by evil dreams, he bolted upright drenched in sweat and crying out in terror, but this time Catherine was not there to soothe him with loving words. His minders cursed him for their lost sleep and threatened to knock him unconscious the next time he roused them from slumber.

Catherine, too, hated the Tower. Richard shrank into himself in this place that harbored such frightening memories for him, and he drank more heavily. His breath reeked of wine these days, even before breakfast. To soothe herself, she pursued her needlework with feverish intensity. Each morning before daybreak, she secured the silken panel beneath her skirts where no one would find it. After four months of application, the embroidery was emerging as vividly as her evil dream. Now she had a lower strip completed, showing the gasses of Hell pouring forth from the cracked earth. One day she thought, she would reach the part where Death stood before Paradise, and she could embroider her mother in a field as lush and green as emeralds. Until then, she had to labor through the dread landscape. She was not sure why she felt compelled to resurrect her evil dream, but doing so brought release from the turmoil of her nights.

Since the joyless Festival of Love, however, her hands shook as she stitched her silken tableau, for reality had grown nigh impossible.

Henry had asked her again to divorce Richard, and again, she had refused, unless he returned Dickon to Scotland. Sometimes she felt as if Fate had horns and that she and Richard were impaled on them, unable to move or to flee. Skelton had performed yet another of his vitriolic mummeries, showering the drunken court's ridicule on Richard's golden head, and Prince Harry and his friends tormented Richard with increasing frequency. Even the palace servants pelted him with rotted food as he passed along the passageways.

And worse than this, Richard had informed her that he wanted no more efforts made to free him.

So this was to be their life forever. Dear God, it was too terrible! How would Richard bear it? He was losing strength as he was losing hope, and no wonder. At least she had Alice and Agatha. He had no one; none to show him kindness; none to confide in when she wasn't with him. What would become of them?

And what of Dickon? Where was he? Did he still live?

Her breath caught in her throat. Taking Dickon's little coif that Alice had saved for her, she brushed it tenderly against her cheek and inhaled the baby smell that still clung to his little hat. *Oh, Dickon, my child! One day I will find you, my sweeting! Whatever it takes, I will find you, and I will see you again, and I will kiss your dear face. O my beloved little one . . .*

* * *

The delicate green leaflets of springtime gave way to the dense green of summer but the merry month of May lacked joy, for court remained at the Tower, where the raucous cawing of ugly ravens drowned out the notes of the songbirds. There were no surrounding parklands to disport in or verdant gardens to stroll in, only a small tuft of green, and the views were of walls and stone buildings. Where flowers had perfumed the walks of Windsor, the stench of privies and clogged drains poisoned the air here. From below the ground, like a growling from Hell, came the roar of lions penned up in their cages, but from the cages of suffering men there was only silence, for the thick stone walls of the dungeons muffled their cries.

Trailed by Henry's two spies, Catherine passed the Beaufort Tower. A chill always went down her spine as she neared the place. There was only one window, and like a malevolent eye, it looked on the scaffold set in the green tuft of lawn in the inner court. Edward, Earl of Warwick, had been imprisoned at the Beaufort Tower since he was eleven, and now he was twenty-three. This poor lad, also a nephew of King Richard III by his older brother, the Duke of Clarence, had been orphaned as a child, and abandoned by his guardian. He was said to have a slow mind that couldn't tell a goose from a capon. King Richard had adopted him, and for two years the child had enjoyed a normal childhood with his aunt and uncle. Then came Bosworth, and Henry Tudor. And everything changed.

She took the muddy path that dead-ended into Traitor's Gate and forced the poor young man from her mind. The skies of London were covered this day with heavy, dark clouds, and a steady drizzle fell. The ravens she had come to loathe were everywhere, reminding her of Death and depressing her spirits further. She dropped her gaze to her feet so she wouldn't have to look at them, these monstrous birds that fed on human flesh. When she looked up again, Patch the Dwarf's colorful green-and-orange-clad figure was making its way to her.

Patch threw her an elaborate bow, and pulled a needle from her nose. "Ah, still at your embroidery, I see—" He handed it to her with a flourish.

A smile curved her mouth as she took it from him. God had given him precious little, yet he was always cheerful. "How do you do it, Patch?"

"The needle?"

"No, your good humor."

"Laughter is the best potion for illness of body and soul, my lady." After a pause he added, "We all need something."

Her gaze went to the church. "Do you pray much?"

"I pray."

"Does God answer your prayers?"

"Not that I recall." He grinned.

His reply confirmed what she had come to believe. God only answered the prayers of His favorites. He was deaf to all others. "I fear Heaven is too comfortable," she said. "And God sleeps too much."

Patch laughed.

"Have you seen my lord husband, by any chance?" She had searched everywhere and not found Richard. His mood all month had been depressed, but she had encouragement to offer. Henry disliked the Tower and wished to return to Westminster as soon as possible.

"I think he may be there, by the Salt Tower, m'lady."

She nodded her thanks and made her way up to the wall walk that overlooked the river. Richard stood gazing at the River Thames, the wind stirring his bright hair. A short distance away, his two guards leaned against the wall.

"Richard!" Catherine called, running to him. He turned and gazed at her, but there was no answering smile. "Dearest," she murmured, giving him a kiss. "Are you not happy to see me?"

"You are the sun and the stars to me, my Celtic princess." He fell silent.

"But?"

But—

He had a beautiful wife he could neither embrace nor provide for. He couldn't be a father to his son, nor protect his child as a father should. For as long as he lived, no matter how courageously he bore his fate, this accursed Tudor court would proclaim him a coward for what had happened at Taunton, while forgetting that Henry ran away from Bosworth. For Richard was the vanquished, and Henry the victor.

He had been born a prince, and now he was ridiculed as the son of a boatman of Tournai and spat on by the children of bastards. The low one had risen, and the high one had fallen, and no one, it seemed, had noticed the aberration in the order of things, or cared enough to right it.

"But I've been wrestling with a decision." He lowered his voice and glanced behind him to his guards, and to her ladies who had gone over to join them. "And now I've made it." He embraced her tenderly.

"What decision?"

He held her tight and kissed her ear. "Escape."

Catherine willed herself not to move lest the horror of his words attract the attention of their guards. Her gaze fixed on the rotted heads of traitors on London Bridge in the distance and the ravens that flocked around them. "But I thought you had abandoned the idea—" She kissed his mouth.

"Not the escape . . . only the help."

She looked at him aghast. "Are you mad? You must not give up hope of rescue. We have"— Catherine lowered her voice—"friends."

"Who cannot help us," Richard said. "Is that not so?"

Catherine raised her eyes to his face. So he knew. Somehow he had found out. "One failure is not the end. There can be other—" She glanced around. Their guards were busy chattering. "Efforts," she whispered.

"No," he said firmly. "I will not have any more men die for me."

"But—"

"No more. 'Tis finished."

"The dream doesn't die with the dreamer," Catherine whispered desperately. "If not today, then tomorrow. If not this year, then next—" Urgently, desperately, she tightened her hand around the back of his neck, and drew him close. "There is nothing you can do, not a move you can make, not a thought you can have that he doesn't know about!" she cried against his ear. "You can't do it alone!"

"No more men will die for me," he said between kisses. "I do this alone . . . because I must . . . if only to prove to myself . . . that I can succeed at something."

She hugged him tightly to her and kissed first one ear, then the other. "Listen to me . . . do not risk it . . . we are leaving soon for Windsor—"

He pulled Catherine away and held her from him. She stared

at him in bewilderment. She had never seen him with such a look. His eyes were glazed, his jaw set with determination, and his breath stank of wine. "Then there's no time to be lost!"

"Nay!" she breathed. "I beg you—if you love me—do not do this!"

"This is my decision, and mine alone." There was no emotion in his voice. He dropped his hands.

"You have not considered what you stand to lose."

"Only a life not worth living."

"But we have each other!"

"We do not have each other."

"I will not help you destroy yourself."

"Then you will not help me save myself."

"If they catch you, it will be the Tower—" The river tilted around her. She closed her eyes and put a hand to her head.

Richard watched her tremble but he did not take her into his arms. He wanted nothing and no one to dissuade him from his course. All he knew was that he could no longer live this way. "I have always done as you wished. But not this time."

That Richard had not drawn her back into his arms cut through Catherine like a blade. Whatever the fates brought them, they'd meet it together. Or so she had thought.

"I am right about this, and you are wrong," she said coldly. "You will rue your decision, have no doubt."

"Once before, you persuaded me to take a course I had no wish to take. You were wrong then, and you are wrong now."

Catherine stared at him, stunned. He blamed her for everything that had happened, and she had not known it until this moment! She twisted her hand to her mouth and gave a cry. "You are responsible for everything that happens to you from now. I no longer care!" She flung the words at him too loudly, for the guards and the workmen fell silent to watch them.

Sick at heart, she turned and fled down the staircase.

Chapter 12
Fortune's Dance

That night, Catherine sat at the window in an agony of mind, pondering Richard's words. She'd thought he blamed only himself for the disaster that had befallen them, and she had offered to share culpability with him in order to lighten his guilt. He'd wanted to turn back at Ayr, aye; he'd gone on because of her, aye. But that he saw her as pushing him into the venture against his will and better judgment? He'd barely objected—it hadn't taken much to persuade him at all—merely a few kisses and choice words. Hadn't she tried to dissuade him at St. Michael's Mount? He didn't give in to her then. Had he forgotten? She hadn't raised her doubts until it was too late, and she knew even as she did so that turning back would be difficult, but she had tried nevertheless.

Yet now he saw her as the driving force of their calamity. Why had he not objected more vehemently if he'd been against the enterprise? Why had he given in so readily, without a fight?

Was she a shrew? Had she dominated him so completely that—desperate to be free—he was willing to throw himself to the hounds? Or was the fault in him? Was Richard too compliant a husband willing to gamble his own life and everything he held dear to please the whim of a domineering wife? Or had she been blinded by her own ambition, planted there by a soothsayer who once said she'd be a queen?

Catherine searched her memory for the words the wise-woman had spoken. "You shall be loved by a king, me wee beautie," the old woman had said.

Not queen—but *loved by a king!* The difference had escaped her childish mind and guided her life, bringing them to this place where she stood. *Fool!* Catherine heard Fortune laugh from the darkness, 'twas *merely a jest, me wee beautie.* Covering her ears, she closed her eyes and bit down on her lip until it throbbed, longing for her home and her father as she'd never longed for anything in her life.

If Richard had spoken up when he'd wished to turn back, a small voice demanded at the back of her mind, *would you have listened? Would you not have fought him until you changed his mind?*

In the black night, her words at Ayr returned to mock her: *There is no wrong we cannot right; no fight we cannot win. For God is on our side, Richard!* The person she used to be had spoken those words, and now they had the bitter taste of gall.

* * *

The sleeping castle stirred at daybreak. It had turned suddenly cold, and ice formed in the ewer overnight. Catherine sent Meryell to fetch a bucket of water, then stood patiently as her ladies helped her wash and dress.

"You are pale this morning," Alice said as she braided her hair, aware that Catherine hadn't slept. The entire fortress knew about the fight her mistress had had with her lord husband, and no doubt it gladdened King Henry's cruel heart to hear of it. "May I see if Countess Cecily's maid has a few drops of pomegranate juice for your cheeks?" she asked. She wished there was something she could do to take away the distress in Catherine's eyes.

"Nay, Alice," Catherine said softly. "I am late to the queen's chambers as it is."

Alice was about to pin the garnet to her headband when Catherine stopped her. "I shall not wear it this day, but I wish to take it with me," she said.

Alice gazed at her in bafflement.

"Pray find me a pouch to carry it in."

Alice knew that the goldsmiths were coming to the castle after luncheon. So Catherine was planning to sell her mother's brooch, but why? Stiffly, she moved to Catherine's small casket that stood on a rough-hewn chest. She riffled through the bits of ribbons, tin brooches, and pins until she found a pouch with a string. She slipped the garnet inside and handed it to her mistress.

Catherine tucked the garnet into her bosom beside Richard's love letter. It was all she had left of her dead mother. She adjusted the locket around her neck, avoiding Alice's inquiring gaze before heading toward the arched passageway to the queen's privy quarters.

Music drifted along the hall. Elizabeth's golden head was bent over her lute and her sweet voice was raised in a lament that Catherine recognized too well. It was the old Gaelic love song Richard used to sing to her a lifetime ago. In her mind she returned to Loch Lomond, and it was Richard she saw there, strumming his lute, lost in the music:

My true love's the bonniest lass in a' the warld,

Black is the color of her hair.

She forced the memory away, and made her way forward into the chamber. The queen was singing the last words of the lament as she entered:

But the winter's passed and the leaves are green,

The time is passed that we have seen . . .

Catherine could scarcely keep her mind on her tapestry duties. She moved about the table blindly like a wooden figure. Richard hadn't said when he would attempt his escape, and she feared he might have already fled in the night, for he had missed breakfast. Why had she said those things to him? What if she never saw him again? How would she live with herself?

All morning the minutes dragged intolerably. She found herself throwing constant glances at the Tower clock, but it seemed painfully silent, and it took an eternity for the periodic quarter hour chimes to sound.

At long last, church bells pealed for sext. With curtsies around the room, the ladies let the queen pass, and Catherine fell in behind her. Henry had accorded her precedence over all the royal women except the king's mother and his two daughters, nine-year-old Margaret and five-year-old Mary.

Luncheon was another interminable affair. She scanned the hall for Richard, to no avail.

As soon as the meal was over, she went in vain to search for him, followed by three of her ladies. Admitting defeat, she made her way unsteadily to the merchants' chamber. Many goldsmiths had come to offer their wares, and it bustled with activity. Robed in elegant dark gowns edged with fur around the collar, and each wearing on the right hand the gold and ruby ring that was the emblem of their guild, they stood in front of the tapestries and tall iron candelabras that were set around the room. Ladies and noblemen milled about the tables, inspecting crosses in gold, silver, and bronze; reliquaries, chalices, goblets, engraved platters, candlesticks, and jeweled book covers. Even a few clerics were present.

Catherine scanned the chamber and her gaze settled on an earnest-looking man who held up a rolled parchment that displayed a variety of rings. He removed a sapphire and handed it to an admiring noble. When their transaction was completed, Catherine approached the goldsmith.

"My lady," he said with a courtly bow. In one sweep, his glance took in the heavy black of her mourning gown, headband, and veil, and settled on the necklace with the fleur-de-lis design that only royalty was allowed to wear. "For you, there is this cross, or perhaps a locket for a miniature portr—"

Catherine held up her hand. "Sir Goldsmith, I am not here to buy, but to sell."

The goldsmith lifted his eyebrows. He had never known royalty to part with any jewel. Then he saw the tears that sparkled at the tip of her lashes.

Catherine removed the pouch from her bosom, and hesitated. Resolutely, she thrust it out to him, before she could change her mind again.

The man wore a pair of spectacles as he studied her stone. "'Tis a fine piece . . . flawless . . . well-cut . . . the silver heavy." He looked up. "Most likely from Bohemia, where the best garnets are mined. Are you certain you wish to sell this jewel?" His tone was surprisingly gentle, and for some reason his kindness cut her to the quick. She averted her eyes and nodded.

"I can offer you seven pounds. But 'tis the highest I can go."

Seven pounds! It was a full month's allowance from Henry— enough to buy passage aboard ship. She hadn't expected that much. He was being generous. She looked at him gratefully.

The jeweler counted out the coins.

* * *

The next morning, Richard appeared at breakfast, and Catherine's heart took up a glad pounding. As soon as the king and queen had filed out, she fled to Richard's side. For a long moment, they stood silent, then both spoke at the same moment:

"Pray for—"

They laughed together.

"Celtic princesses first," Richard grinned.

"Pray forgive me, Richard. I regret my words to you and want you to know I didn't mean what I said."

"Pray forgive me, my love. Neither did I mean what I said."

She moved into his embrace. He held her tenderly and brushed her cheeks with his lips.

"Shall we go for a stroll in the garden?" Catherine asked at length, conscious of the eyes on them. The hall seemed suddenly stifling hot. "'Tis a lovely day, is it not?"

"A splendid day," said Richard, offering her his elbow with aplomb.

Outside, ravens flew around them as they strolled, cawing vigorously. Catherine leaned into Richard with a shiver. "I hate this place," she whispered.

Richard slipped his arm around her shoulders. "I know. You can almost smell the evil." They passed the Beaufort Tower. "Poor Edward of Warwick has never left the Tower." His eyes sought the window of his chamber.

Catherine shuddered.

"Being here has made me think of him lately. I find myself so very fortunate in comparison. I have known what it is to love. To be happy. To father a child—"

Catherine closed her eyes at the thought of Dickon and swallowed hard on the sudden constriction in her throat. Her hand tightened on Richard's arm.

"We must speak of him, my love. To remember," he said gently. "Our blood is mingled in his veins, and when he has children, we shall pass on into them. And on. Forevermore. 'Tis a good thought, is it not?"

Catherine's mouth had gone dry. She gave him a plaintive look.

"Aye, I know. If he lives. But Catryn, we must believe that he lives. We cannot allow ourselves to think otherwise. Everything we do rests on that premise. *He lives*—" He halted his steps, and took her by the arms. "Catryn, will you make me a promise?"

She nodded.

"Promise me to find him. Promise you will not rest until you find him—or what happened to him."

She closed her eyes. "I promise."

They resumed their pace. He threw a careful glance behind him. His guards lagged a distance away, strolling with her ladies and chattering merrily, as if they truly were servants and not spies. They had grown lax lately. "Forgive me, Catryn, but I must say these things now. If it is forever that we part, I bid you know what is in my heart, my dearest love."

She felt his arm tighten around her waist. Her eyes flew open in panic. She willed herself to be strong.

"When I look back, I see my life as water, flowing here, flowing there, belonging nowhere. Until I found you. You have been my oak, Catryn, giving me strength and succor, and helping me stand tall in the fiercest wind. How I love you! If you could only see yourself with my eyes. Your peerless beauty. Your courage and loyalty. Never have I loved you more than I do now."

"You know what my father liked to say," Catherine replied, fighting to suppress the emotion that threatened her composure. "Today's mighty oak is merely yesterday's nut that held its ground. So I suppose I am a nut."

He laughed. Then he grew serious. "Skelton is right about one thing. I am proud of you, Catryn, and I hate myself even more for the disaster I have wrought on your lovely head. I know not how you forgive me, or how you bear it."

"We are alone, Richard, and cannot look anywhere for strength except within ourselves. For me, you will always be riding through the castle gate at Stirling. You will always be with me at Loch Lomond. You will always be at my side as I hold our newborn babe in my arms and look up to see you smile. When life is at its lowest, I come to you in my mind, Richard, and remember. That is what sustains me. That, and Dickon. One day I shall find him. One day I will know what became of our sweet child." More than the beautiful past, it was the hopeful future that she looked to in the darkness of night. It was her son who gave her will to carry on.

They had reached the staircase to the wall-walk overlooking the river, where they had parted in anger two days before. They fell silent as they mounted the steps. The wind, so fierce on the parapet, blew from the west, carrying their words to the river and away from their guards who followed them. Richard bent down and covered her face with light, tender kisses.

"You see, Catryn," he said gently, "I no longer know who I am. I always saw myself as English but everyone else sees me as a foreigner. I am not Flemish, nor Scots. I am worse than that monkey Henry carries around. At least he knows where he once belonged. I have no country. No mother. No father. No brother. A wife, yet no wife. A son somewhere—God willing—but a son who knows me not and who I cannot protect. Another man pays for your dresses and sends you hose."

Voices came to them from the circle of green below. The queen was passing with her ladies. "I have a sister, yet no sister—" Elizabeth looked up at them and inclined her head in greeting. Catherine curtsied, and Richard threw her a bow. They watched as the royal party disappeared around the building.

"Do you understand, Catryn? I need you to understand." He looked at her with eyes as blue as the thistle that covered the Scottish spring, but such a depth of misery swam in them that she could no longer stem the tears that sprang to her own eyes.

"When?" she asked.

He threw a glance at his guards at the other end of the wall-walk. "I know not. When the time is right. When I can. As soon as I can."

She covered her mouth to choke off her cry. If it was not now, it would soon come. Like a dangling sword, the blade was waiting to fall. One morning, she would awake to find him gone.

He took her chin. "One thing you must promise me, as you did at St. Michael's Mount."

She lifted her eyes to his.

"If I do not succeed, you must promise me not to mourn forever. You are not meant to be alone."

Anger edged through her grief. "I will never love again—how can you ask such a thing?"

Richard took her hand. "Catryn, there are many kinds of death. If I should fail and find my life forfeit, I must know I do not take yours as well. That would be a burden I could not bear. If matters should not go . . . as we wish . . . you must not remain alone forever. You are made to love—to dance. If our parting is—forever, I want to know—nay, I *need* to know—that you remember me in happiness, and not in tears.

"Treasure the happiness, Catryn. 'Tis only when darkness falls that the stars come out. Honor our love with your smiles. Look for me in the stars, and wherever I am, I will live in your happiness."

She turned to the river. For thousands of years, through the time of dragons and unicorns, through storms and mist, in darkness and in light, it had flowed relentlessly, inexorably to its destiny. *As we must flow to ours, bearing what we must bear.* Her time with Richard had reached an end. If the Fates were kind, it was a promise she would not need to heed. But if they were not, could she send him away without this comfort?

"'Tis curious, Richard, that what brought us together is what tears us apart." She looked at him through her tears. "The English throne."

"Fortune's dance, Catryn."

"Will I ever see you again, my love?"

"That is in the hand of God."

Catherine bit her lip until it throbbed with pain like her heart. Then she removed the velvet pouch with the coins from her mother's garnet, and put it into his hand. "For you—to help you. And this is for good luck—" She gave him the little groat with his image and *King Richard IV* stamped on the silver.

"May the wind be always at your back," she murmured in a choked voice she scarcely recognized as her own. She folded a finger over his palm with each wish. "May the sun shine warm on your face—"

"May the rain fall soft on your field," Richard murmured, picking up the prayer. "And until we meet again, may God hold you in the palm of His hand."

* * *

On Trinity Sunday, June ninth, one of the great feast days of the year, Richard bided his time and waited for his chance. There was much music and carousing all day; wine flowed and folk celebrated with merrymaking and the lighting of bonfires. Richard lay in bed between his two jailors, waiting for the fires to die out and the drunken revelers to fall asleep.

At last the only sound that broke the silence of the night was the chirping of insects. Stealing over his sleeping guards, he tiptoed to the window they'd left unlocked and crept out to the ladder the workmen had forgotten to move in their rush to begin the festivities of Trinity Sunday. His heart pounded so loudly in his chest that he thought his captors would surely hear. The climb down was tense; he had to move slowly and with utmost caution to avoid making a sound. Beads of perspiration blurred his vision and his palms were so slick with sweat that he feared losing his grip. Finally he reached the ground. So far, so good, God be thanked! He glanced up at the sky. There was no moon this night, only layer upon layer of magnificent stars. Enough to guide him to the Salt Tower, where workmen had left a coil of rope. From there it was but a short distance across the garden to the Cradle Tower. The outside wall overlooked the moat near the river. He hoped the rope would be long enough to get him down on the other side. Then he'd steal a boat, row out to a fishing village, and buy passage across the sea with the money Catherine had given him.

Here and there a guard snored at the foot of a tower. Hidden in the shadows, Richard stayed close to the walls and moved to the Salt Tower, keeping an eye out for the foot patrols. As their rhythmic footsteps approached, he flattened himself against a wall, not breathing until the sound of their march had faded away. With rope in hand, he stole along to the staircase of the Cradle Tower near Traitor's Gate. His heart hammered in his breast as he took the steps two by two and neared the entrance to the rooftop. What would he do if the gate were locked? It would take time to pry it open with the dagger they'd allowed him to keep, for the blade was barely long enough to cut his meat. Let it be open—let it not be—

God be praised—his prayer was answered! He crossed himself. The gate was open. Removing the coil of rope from his shoulders, he tied one end securely to the bracket that held the flagpole for the pennant and threw a glance over the side of the wall. Nothing but silence.

The work of escape was strenuous; by midway of scaling the wall, he was panting. He hung helplessly in the darkness until he had caught his breath again. The rope was only a few feet short of the ground, and he marveled at how well matters had gone. His escape—logistically so difficult—had proven incredibly easy to accomplish.

He dropped to the ground, scrambled to his feet, and made for the river. He had gone only a few feet when out of the darkness, at a distance of about five hundred feet, voices drifted to him and a group of men with torches appeared, striding purposefully toward him along the wharf. He couldn't hear what they said, but they were looking around, as if searching for something—or someone.

God Almighty—had this been a trap? If he was going to escape, he needed to take his chances—*now!* He ran to the edge of the river and quickly lowered himself into the icy water. The river was shallow and he found himself knee-deep in the boggy marsh on the edge. He staggered forward a few steps before he realized there wasn't enough time to reach the reed beds or the deeper water that would offer full cover. Inhaling deeply, he flattened himself into the mud, holding his breath while he shivered with cold.

The voices came closer. They stopped and grew faint again. They were going back the opposite way! He caught a snippet of their words, and it sent him quivering where he lay.

"—four boats are looking for—"

He opened his eyes. They had to be talking about him. If they were already searching for him, there was no time to lose! To get away, he had to outwit them somehow—go where they didn't expect him to—west, not east—

Aye, he had to change his plans—that was the only hope! But where could he go? And how? He couldn't swim upstream, or walk along the river. Unless—maybe on the south side? He'd have to swim across, make his way through marshland. That would not be easy. The reeds would help give him some cover, but their growth had been stunted by the drought and heat, and they were not tall enough to hide a man. Cautiously, he lifted himself up and peered into the shadows. The men's flaming torches were disappearing from view. He scanned the river. There was nothing but the gentle lapping of water. *Now!* he told himself. He dove underwater and swam as long as he could without coming up for air. Only when his lungs felt as if they would burst did he allow himself to emerge from the black water. Inhaling again, he ducked his head again and kept swimming.

At last he reached the south bank of the Thames. Wearily, he climbed out into the marsh. Then he ran.

Tripping over the uneven ground and the tangles of reeds, he pushed forward in a southwesterly direction to the woods, past the marshland. He had to reach them by daybreak or he'd be seen. There was little time left! He felt chilled now that he was in the open air, and he was exhausted from swimming against the tide, but fear didn't allow him to rest. Stumbling and falling, scratched and bruised, he pushed on. For the night was filled not only with the hooting of hunting owls, but with the distant baying of hounds, and the shouts of men.

Chapter 13

Winds of Winter

Richard made it to the woods as the faint light of day touched the earth. And still he ran. When he could go no farther, he leaned his weight against a tree and slid down to the ground. Gasping for breath, he covered his face in his hands and gave vent to wracking sobs. It seemed to him that he'd been running from the hounds for most of his life—with one glorious, and all too brief respite. Scotland. Catherine's face rose before him. *My love, do not weep, 'tis but an evil dream, and see, you have awakened now and all is well.*

But only death could relieve this nightmare. He knew that now. His life was penance for the sin of spurning death at Taunton. He had run from Taunton because life had held such sweetness then, such hope—but why was he running now, when he hated life, when it brought only despair?

The Tudor's own great-grandfather had run from the king's men, as he himself was doing now, and had made it to safety and freedom. It was because that ancestor of his arch-foe had cheated death that Richard found himself under this tree now. Meredyd Ap Tudor was a Welshman wanted for debt and murder in England. His son, Owen, had bedded the young queen, Katherine of Valois, widow of Henry V. She had produced Henry's father, Edmund, out of wedlock, and Edmund had wed Margaret Beaufort, also of bastard descent. Now a thorough bastard sat the throne of England and hunted down a king's son.

Richard laughed until he wept.

When his tears finally subsided, he looked around. The balmy air was scented with flowering hawthorn and elderberries, and above him stretched the most beautiful sunrise he'd ever seen. Crimson, violet, and orange stained the heavens, shining a rose glow over the earth and all creation. He heard the gurgle of a stream nearby. For a brief moment, a deep peace found him. He had never felt such harmony with the world, except at Loch Lomond, and still this was different. He felt a oneness with God that he had never known before.

The baying of hounds along the river broke into his thoughts. He scrambled to his feet. Pushing aside the branches that blocked his way, leaping over the brambles and nettles in his path, he ran.

Ran for his life.

*   *   *

A fitful morning light broke over the Tower. In her bed, Catherine turned her face to the window. As usual, her sleep had been marred by bad dreams. No wonder, for her mind had been filled with dread since she had given Richard her blessing to escape three days ago. Each night when she went to bed and each morning when she awakened, the same thought came to her: *Was this the day?*

Something mingled with the ravens' ugly cries this morning. Something unsettling. The clanging of arms. The shouts of men. Catherine hurried into her slippers and wrapped her chamber robe around her with trembling hands. She stepped over Alice, who was still asleep on her pallet on the floor. She went to the window and looked out. An army of small craft barred traffic on the river, and the wharf swarmed with men-at-arms. *This is the day!* Catherine thought.

This is the day.

* * *

With Alice's help, Catherine's toilette was nearly complete. Her hair had been twisted and looped into her silver net at the nape of her neck, and her headband and veil were barely secured in place when the dreaded knock came at the door. Alice opened it to reveal Henry's squire, James Strangeways. Her mouth tightened to see him, and behind her, Catherine's did the same. He was the one who had brought her the king's gift of a gown, and Catherine hadn't forgiven him for it.

"My lady," James Strangeways said courteously, with a formal bow, "the king requests your presence in his privy chamber."

At least he isn't wearing his usual smirk, Catherine thought. She acknowledged him with a brusque nod, and swept past him with her head held high. Hurriedly, he fell in behind her, quickening his pace to match hers as she led the way to the king's privy chambers along the twisting passageways. When they arrived, one of the two hundred yeomen guarding the area threw the door open to the royal chamber. Strangeways announced her to the king and she sailed past him into the room.

Catherine saw Henry turn from the window. His face wore a hard expression. She did not know as she approached and fell into a curtsy that, like her, he had not slept all night. While she feared Richard would be caught, Henry feared he wouldn't. His plans had gone awry during the night, and somehow the prey that should have been delivered safely to him by now had eluded the net he'd thrown over London. He worried that Margaret of Burgundy had finally succeeded in getting a plot past his spies and that the Pretender had already been spirited to safety aboard a ship bound for Burgundy. The calm demeanor he presented to Catherine was a calculated stillness that he had honed over the years; it had served him well by unnerving the subject of his scrutiny. But in truth, he was restless with anxiety.

Henry didn't stir or speak as Catherine rose from her obeisance and waited before him. He merely stared at her.

For Catherine it was as if she had gone back in time and was a child again, face to face with the serpent in the field. Her father had slain the hideous creature, and saved her then. But who could save her now? No one but herself. She lifted her chin.

As Henry looked at her, he wondered what it was about this girl that he found so utterly entrancing. He had seen beauties before. He'd taken what he'd wanted, given them a few groats for their service, and dismissed them without another thought. But Catherine Gordon he could not dismiss. She was an intoxicating perfume that lingered around him; she had struck his very soul and would not fade away, no matter how hard he tried to be rid of her. She kept her eyes down, yet he sensed her defiance. Was her confidence placed in him, or in herself? Did she think he could never hurt her, or did her royal blood give her the strength to defy him—and deny him? She was a Huntly, after all, and came from the finest stock of Scotland. Was this the reason he couldn't intimidate her the way he did everyone else? Was her noble birth the reason he desired her so desperately— to prove himself her equal? All his life, he had been taunted for his bastard blood and made to feel inferior, and now that he was king, he distrusted those better-born than himself, and favored those who, like him, shared his bastard lineage. In her veins ran the noblest blood of Britannia, and if she took him as her lover, it would mean he'd proved himself her equal.

Yet there was more. The girl had a courage he'd never seen before in any woman except his mother. But in overcoming her challenges, Margaret had grown hard and brittle as an old broom, while Catherine had a vulnerability about her that tugged at him. He longed to protect her, to gratify her every whim, to share with her his earthly treasures—if she would but let him. His need for her was so great that he'd toyed with the idea of taking possession of her body against her will, but doing so would have proved a hollow victory. She would elude him still, and hate him more.

"What have you to say for yourself?" he demanded coldly.

"I do not understand, Sire. What am I accused of?"

"Don't play games with me! You knew he was planning to escape!"

said Henry. For the first time in an audience, he found he was the one unnerved.

"Nay, my lord, I tried to dissuade him from it."

"I don't believe you."

"'Tis the truth."

"You helped him. You sold your jewel. You gave him money!"

"It was my duty to do so. A woman's property belongs to her lawfully wedded husband."

Henry slammed his fist on the table. "After all I have done for you! All the kindness I've shown you—I have been merciful beyond belief—and this is how you repay me!"

"I could not stop him, Sire!" Catherine cried, suddenly fearful, for Henry trembled with rage.

"Who helped him?" Henry demanded.

"No one."

"You lie—tell me the truth for once!" In two quick strides he had closed the distance between them. He seized her by both arms.

Catherine dropped her gaze and turned her face away from his. "I swear by my mother's soul, 'tis truth. No one helped him. He did it alone."

"How could he evade so many men if he did it alone—" Henry broke off, suddenly realizing that he was giving himself away. *No one must see your hand in this,* Morton had warned. He released her. "If he was alone, then he shall soon be caught. Do you know what I shall do to him when I get him back?" He spoke the words in a hiss, and it was the serpent in the field that Catherine heard.

She turned her head and looked at him then. He was watching her with a chilling smile on his lips.

Henry read her thoughts. *No, don't tell her—if you hope to ever win her affections, she must never know.*

As Catherine waited, Henry's demeanor changed. The mad look that had flashed in his eyes vanished, and in an instant he was again the cold, calculating man she knew.

"You must pay for what you have done," Henry said calmly. "Your allowance will be reduced, and your status diminished. As for your ladies-in-waiting, henceforth you are permitted only one. I leave to you the choice of which shall be put into the streets."

There was no doubt whom Catherine would choose to stay. Alice was kin, friend, as well as servant. The Tudor spies would find good homes, but what about dear Agatha—she had no one, and Catherine had no money to give her. What would become of her? "My lord, I pray you to reconsider—"

"Perhaps I will . . . On one condition," said Henry.

Catherine waited.

"That you divorce him and look on me with favor."

Catherine gasped. Through the roaring in her head, she breathed, "No!" She closed her eyes to steady herself.

"You will be sorry—you will regret this—I will make you pay!" Henry shouted, trembling with rage. "And when I catch him, know that he will pay—pay dearly—*dearly*, you hear me? *Dearly*—" With each word, he took a step closer to Catherine, forcing her to edge backward. "Now, go!"

She turned and ran, sobs stifling her breath, tears running down her cheeks.

"Go!!" she heard him shout after her.

*   *   *

Richard emerged at the edge of the woods, drained by the night's ordeal. Beads of perspiration streamed down his face, stinging his eyes with salt and blurring his vision. He wiped them with the back of his torn sleeve and pulled down a branch to see what lay in the distance. His heart pounded so violently in his chest, he was afraid he would collapse if he didn't find help soon. Where could he go? Who would dare give him shelter? There had to be someplace—

He saw that he had made it to Richmond. There on the hill at the edge of the riverbank had stood the palace of Shene that he'd burned down in his bungled attempt to escape at Yuletide. Now only a few charred remnants of towers and a few walls remained as monument. Soon these would be torn down to make room for an even more splendid Tudor palace. He scanned the rolling hills and spied the tower of a church on the north edge of the royal property. Standing next to it was the Carthusian monastery known as the Charterhouse of Shene. His heart missed a beat. There—they would help! The place had Yorkist connections! A prior of Charterhouse had been an executor of his mother's will! The men who dwelt there were true men of God. They had renounced the world for solitude, hair shirts, and endless prayer—

The yapping of hounds sounded again, more distantly now, but fright overwhelmed him. There was no time to rest—no time to think! He threw a glance behind, expecting to see them leap from the woods, but the forest was still. He ran from the covering of the thicket and dashed across the fields. He leapt over stone walls, and pushed through hedgerows. He had seen the prior once at Shene, but only from the distance when he came to deliver a Yuletide gift. Prior Ralph Tracy was held in high favor by the tyrant.

The few peasants in the fields paid him scant attention as he stumbled past the monastery's high wall into the outer courtyard where the cells of the monks were clustered. Dragging himself past the next building that housed the forge, the carpenter's shop, and the kitchen, he burst into the inner courtyard, yanked open the great door, and hurtled into the church, reeling from pillar to pillar until he crashed into a monk at the altar and fell to the floor at his feet. The man recoiled with shock. He was not accustomed to intrusions of such violent nature in this quiet place. Guests were never welcome, for the Carthusians were a reclusive order that had already withdrawn from the earthly world and lived only for the day when their bodies would join the souls they had already given over to heaven. They preserved silence and left their cells solely for mass and to attend their duties. They even avoided one another; each monk's cell had a tiny walled garden where he could sit in total privacy.

Into this holy order had Richard crashed. He tried to release his hold of the man's legs, but his arms were frozen and he could not move them. "Forgive me—" he panted, licking his lips, for his mouth was suddenly as dry as parchment. "The prior, I pray you— 'tis urgent—urgent—"

The man pried Richard's fingers loose from his leg and freed himself. Dimly, Richard became aware of his surroundings. A few smoky candles of mutton fat flickered around the interior, and from these emanated an unpleasant odor and more shadows. Shivering, he shrank back. In shadows lurked danger and death. He seized a corner of the crimson altar cloth as if it could protect him, and lifting his eyes to the cross, sent a rushed and feverish prayer to heaven.

A door creaked open. Two monks entered, one old, one young, both clad in white. The older one was gaunt, his face deeply wrinkled with thin silver hair around his tonsure.

"You wished to see me, my son?" Prior Ralph said gently, his compassion stirred by the quivering mass sprawled at his feet. The monk at his side extended a hand to Richard to raise him up.

Richard gradually managed to come to his feet, though he listed to one side and had to lean on the altar rail for support. Prior Ralph was taken aback to see a young lissome body in the prime of life struggle so, flinching as if every movement hurt. When the young man looked at him, he was shocked by the fear he saw in his blue eyes. The cuts and bloody bruises on his face, head, arms, and legs suggested a wretched story, but he didn't look like a thief or a murderer.

"Son, whoever you are, before you try to tell me what is wrong, let us go to my chamber and take a cup of wine together. It will restore your strength."

When they arrived at the prior's cell at the end of the cloistered walk, Richard collapsed onto the pallet bed as they entered. Above the bed hung a vibrant painting of the Passion, and a crucifix. A small window gave light, and a hatch in the wall allowed delivery of food. Richard's labored breathing filled the room, and he closed his eyes, willing himself to stop shivering, embarrassed not to be able to catch his breath. The prior placed a blanket around his shoulders and passed him a cup of wine. Richard's hand shook so violently that he had difficulty holding it. He used both hands to try and steady the cup.

"Fetch some bread, and if we have any meat, bring that also," the prior told the young monk. "We do not eat meat unless we are ill," he apologized, rising to his feet. "Meanwhile, I shall leave you to rest."

"Nay—" Richard cried, clutching at him and nearly falling from the bed in his panic. "Pray, do not leave me—no one must know I'm here—do not tell anyone—do not go!" His eyes darted anxiously to the door.

Prior Ralph was shocked into pity as a new thought occurred to him. Was the young man not of sound mind? The prior knew little about the outside world, but he had difficulty believing it was truly as dangerous and menacing a place as this lad believed. Yet, if his presence lent the boy solace, what was the harm in remaining with him? The prior sat back down in the only chair in the room, suspending judgment until he could fathom the truth of the matter.

And so they remained quietly together in the little cell while Richard drank his wine. When two monks entered, bearing food, he exhaled with relief. He tore into the meal as if he hadn't eaten in weeks. Indeed, the simple repast of sliced cucumber, cheese, and nuts, with thick barley bread and cabbage soup, tasted incredibly delicious to him. The prior watched, his curiosity growing about this handsome young lad with the graceful bearing who had evidently fallen on desperate times.

With his hunger staunched, Richard sighed tremulously. "I am grateful to you, Prior Ralph, for your great kindness to me."

"Would you care to tell me what is troubling you, my son?"

Richard dropped his head into his hands. "'Tis a long tale and I know not where to begin."

"I have patience, and we have time. Why not begin at the beginning?"

Richard swallowed hard. "The beginning . . . aye . . . the beginning—" He wiped his face with his hand, and met the prior's eyes.

"I was born at Shrewsbury on August 17, 1473. I believe you knew my father, and perhaps my mother also. Prior John Ingilby certainly knew her. He was an executor of her will when she died in '92."

"Who were your parents?"

"King Edward IV, and the queen, Elizabeth Woodville."

The prior stared at him, mouth agape. "You are the false prince?"

"That is what Henry VII would have you believe."

"What are you saying?"

"Look at me and tell me you do not see my father. That you do not see my mother."

The prior scrutinized him for a long moment. He'd met King Edward once, but it was long ago. The monk, Brother Oswin, high in years, might be called upon to verify a resemblance, however, for in his youth he had known King Edward. As to the Woodville queen, Brother Ralph remembered her very well indeed. Who could forget her? Time had erased much of her beauty when he'd seen her at Bermondsey toward the end of her life. She'd been confined there for plotting in the '87 rebellion. Strangely, it was her mouth that he remembered most vividly. The upward tilt at its corners gave her face the appearance of a permanent smile though she had been in pain and near death. He had wondered about that at the time, and it was the reason he recalled it now, for it was thus with this young man. Despite his lamentable predicament, there hovered about his lips the shadow of a smile. And what of his strange left eye that drooped and held a glassy look? He searched his memory. As he recalled, two Plantagenet kings been marked by the same fault. As to that cleft in his chin, his uncle, King Richard III, had it, too. Could so many marks of Plantagenet royalty be combined in a false prince?

Perhaps.

"You bear a strong resemblance to those you claim as your forbears, but that alone is not sufficient. What proof can you offer me that you are indeed King Edward's son?"

"Perhaps my education," Richard said. "I was raised a prince. I can speak, read, and write Latin, am fluent in French, Flemish, Portuguese, Italian, and the German tongues. I have studied the classics, and can recite to you from Ovid, Virgil, Aristotle, and Plato. I have met the pope and conversed with him about theology and philosophy. I can do so with you, if you wish . . . All the crowned heads of Europe, including Charles of France, and Isabella and Ferdinand of Spain, have accepted me as King Edward's son, and I was proclaimed King Richard IV in Vienna . . . See here, I have a silver penny that was minted in my image on that occasion—"

Richard dug deep in his breast pocket for the coin that Catherine had given him as a good-luck piece, and handed it to the prior. Brother Ralph turned it over in his hands as he examined it.

"King Richard gave me a letter of identity bearing his royal seal when I left England on the eve of the battle of Bosworth. That was handed over to my aunt, the Duchess of Burgundy, and I do not have it in my possession. As for any other documents, I have none. But I ask you, Prior Ralph, if I were a false prince, would King James and the Earl of Huntly have allowed me to wed royalty? Would the Holy Roman Emperor have offered to abdicate his claims to the English throne and pay an enormous royal ransom he can ill afford merely to get me back? If I were a 'feigned boy,' would King Henry not have put me to work in the kitchen, like Lambert Simnell? If he didn't fear my royal blood and see me as a threat, why did he take away my son and unman me by denying me the right to sleep with my lawfully wedded wife? Why does he fear a second generation from me? Why am I a threat to him when I have disgraced myself by—by—" Even after all these months, Richard had difficulty putting his shame into words. "By abandoning my men at Taunton? I am no threat to him, for no man will ever follow me again in battle, so why does he not release me and take Maximilian's gold and send me back to Burgundy? Freedom is all I want now—not the throne, not anything more—except my wife and child! I tell you why he doesn't release me—because he wants what is mine—my throne, and my wife—aye, Prior Ralph, my wife, too! My wife who is a princess of Scotland, and for whom he lusts most wickedly. Would she love me if I were a boatman's son? He lures me into an escape so that he is not bound by the pardon of life he gave at Beaulieu. He wants me dead—he wants me dead! O Prior, why—if not because he knows I am the true prince of England and the son of my father, King Edward IV, and he a usurper while I breathe?"

Richard dropped his head into his hands and sobbed. The prior watched him with soft eyes. The young man had made a persuasive argument. He sighed inwardly. Man's world was indeed a dangerous place. He had always known it, and yet not known it—not like this. This young man's predicament was so terrible, it bordered on Hell.

At last, Richard wiped the tears from his eyes. He fell to his knees and seized the old man's blue-veined hands in his own. "Help me, Prior Ralph! I want to live—I know not why when life has taken so much from me, but I want to live—I pray you, in God's name, help me!"

The prior did not speak for a long moment. Gently, he said, "I am instanced lamentably by your piteous motions. But I know not what I can do, my son. I cannot help you to escape, for to do so would be to disobey King Henry's commandment and risk great punishment. What would become of my thirty charges? Many have been here since their tender years. They are aged now. They know no other life. I must think of them, too . . . Let me pray over this. Maybe God will send me an answer. Meanwhile, I will show you to your room, such as it is, for we have no guest quarters."

The tiny cell at the end of the cloisters looked much like the prior's room. It had a bed, a crucifix, and a small window that let out onto a private walled garden. A jug of wine and a cup had been set on a small table.

"Is there anything I can have sent to ease your discomfort?"

"A lute—or any instrument—if music is allowed—"

"I have never heard music here, but I saw an old lute somewhere, so it must be allowed. But only after vespers, and before matin prayers, my son. I shall have it brought to you."

Prior Ralph locked Richard into the cell and sent a monk brother to find the lute. He proceeded along the cloister to Brother Oswin's cell, for he had need to consult with the old man. The boy—prince, more likely than not—had touched his heart, and he hoped to find a way to help him. As he related the matter to Brother Oswin, there floated over the cloisters the most beautiful, melodious music he had ever heard.

"Interesting," murmured Brother Oswin softly. "I recall that the little prince, Richard of York, had a beautiful voice and a fondness for music, especially the lute. He played it well . . . even as a boy."

* * *

Prior Ralph found his answer in the night. Locking Richard into his cell again, he left to see King Henry after prime, taking a lay brother with him. They rode to London on mules, for that was the creature that had borne the Lord Himself, and arrived at the Tower well before the hour of sext to find the river lined with barges checking the small boats that sailed past them, and stopping many for search and close examination. Throngs of men-at-arms crowded the wharf and messengers galloped in and out of the raised portcullis of the Tower. Something was afoot, and it struck him as strange that, otherworldly as he was, he should be numbered among the few to know what that was, and the only one to be able to provide the king with his heart's desire.

Two guards blocked his path as he rode into the gateway with his companion. "Your business?" one demanded roughly.

"I am Brother Ralph Tracy, prior of the Carthusian monastery at Shene. I come to see the king on a matter of utmost urgency."

"What matter?" The guard eyed him suspiciously as he cast his gaze over his white garb. He knew the order as one that lived on its knees, groveling like beasts by day and night, performing no useful work and achieving nothing.

"That is for the king's ears alone, my son."

"Wait there," the man commanded, indicating the outer ward. He disappeared into the fortress.

The great paved courtyard was as noisy and full of confusion as the streets and the river. Horsemen galloped in and out with purposeful expressions, and hard-faced men-at-arms strode to and fro, their eyes watchful.

Prior Ralph trotted his mule to a quiet corner where they could be out of the fray. He and his companion dismounted and gave their reins over to a stable urchin. When the constable of the Tower appeared to escort them to the king, they wove their way through the bustling inner courtyard to the White Tower. It had been many years since Prior Ralph had visited the fortress, and it seemed to him that the complex had grown even larger in the meanwhile.

In his bedchamber, King Henry waited for the prior's arrival. The Carthusians didn't leave their abode but once a year, and that at Yuletime, to bring him a gift. This visit, therefore, was most unusual, and he suspected the reason for it. He prayed that the prior was bringing him the news he desperately craved—that York was apprehended. For three nights he had not slept since he'd learned that the Pretender had conjured an escape past the hundreds of guards he'd set over the city and along the roads.

"Prior Ralph," said Henry pleasantly, when the prior was ushered in and the door was closed behind him. "We thank you for the tablet of imagery you sent us. We have much enjoyed the sacred paintings in our private meditations."

"Sire, you are kind, and I am gratified to hear that we have been able—albeit humbly—to give pleasure," said the prior, cupping his hands together and giving a slight bow.

"So what brings you to the Tower?"

"Sire, you know that for us, as Carthusians, the soul has almost escaped the prison of the body, and it is our practice to dwell only on the beauty of the kingdom to come."

"'Tis what we most admire about your order, Prior Ralph."

"For us, our privations are a release."

"Indeed," said Henry, wishing he would get to the heart of the matter. Did he, or did he not, have the Pretender?

"We feel we are all royal in that we are the children of a king, and that king is God."

Henry waited.

"One such child of God has come unto us, but he believes himself the son of another king. An earthly king . . . King Edward."

Gladness exploded in Henry's breast and a smile burst across his gaunt face. So joyful was he that he forgot to be still, and he both moved and spoke in the same moment. "You have the false prince, Perkin Warbeck!"

"He claims to be the true prince, my Liege."

"And you know that he lies, do you not?"

"He may well dissemble, yet I cannot be certain of it."

Henry's face darkened. "Are you telling me that you believe this feigned boy to speak the truth?"

If the prior were afraid of death, he would have cringed at this change in his royal master, but he feared only the wrath of God. "I believe he may speak truth, for he bears a marked resemblance to those he claims as his parents—King Edward and Queen Elizabeth Woodville."

Henry did not break his silence for a long moment. At length, he said, "Clarify that for me, if you will."

"There are those among us Carthusians who knew the late king and his queen—God assoil their souls—and they have remarked upon the similarities."

"Such as?"

"They are in the lineaments of the young man's face. He has King Edward's jaw and nose, and the queen's mouth. He has King Richard's cleft chin, and the drooping eye that marked his forbears, Edward I and Henry III."

Henry slammed a fist down on the table beside him so hard that he could not speak for the pain that shot through him. When he had recovered, he stared at the monk, taking his time and rubbing his jaw. In a steely tone, he said, "Are you aware, Prior Ralph, that some might construe your words as treason?"

"Indeed, I am. But I must impart what is in my heart."

"Welladay, now that you have done so, you may deliver him up to us."

"That, Sire, I can only do on one condition."

Henry stared at the old man and his hand balled into a fist at his side. He clenched and unclenched it, as if he would strike the old monk. Prior Ralph saw the motion, but did not flinch.

"What is the condition you demand?" Henry hissed.

"Sire, the affairs of this world are of no concern to us. Only life and death matter to us, for God gives life and takes it in His own time."

"And your point is?"

"We cannot deliver the young man up to you except on promise of pardon for life."

"By God's Bloody Nails! How dare you? After the favor I have shown you—" He turned away, fighting for composure. He swung back on the priest. "And if I refuse, what will you do? Help him to escape?"

"Nay, Sire. We shall enter him into the custody of an eminent cleric."

"Cardinal Morton?"

"The Bishop of Cambrai. When he comes to England from Burgundy in September."

"You do that, and I'll smash your monastery into dust! I'll obliterate your order! I'll—" He broke off. He had forgotten himself and used the personal "I" instead of the formal "we," and what could he threaten them with anyway when they didn't fear death or the torture of their body, or privation? Death would take them to God; torture would bring them closer to the earthly suffering Christ; and privation they already knew, for they deprived themselves.

Henry saw that the old man was looking at him strangely, and he struggled to regain his royal composure. These people couldn't be reasoned with, and they couldn't be threatened; they valued nothing except their faith, and their faith made them immune to fear.

"We cannot grant your demand," Henry said more calmly, "but we urge you to consider the consequences of defying your king."

"Sire, you are our earthly master. We have no desire to defy you, but our obedience is to a higher King, one that is also your King, Sire. We wish to deliver the young man up to you. We ask only for his life."

"You ask too much!"

"Sire, consider what *you* ask. God does not condone killing. The giving and taking of life belongs only to Him. If this young man is the true prince as he claims, you would be committing regicide by taking his life, a sin that God Himself may find difficult to pardon. For your own soul, I beseech you to show mercy to this child of God."

"I have shown him mercy—I have been kind! But he is the devil on my back—I must be rid of him!"

"Better to bear a single devil on the back than to have a hundred devils invade your body, Sire. To have them take you by the throat and tear out your soul from your innards, and to do this over and over for all eternity. Better one devil on the back, Sire, than to be cast out by God into darkness and oblivion, and the monstrous Hell of the damned."

Henry sank into a chair. He felt drained. He put a hand to his brow. He had to have the Pretender back, whatever the cost. Once he had him back, he would find a way to deal with him. But first, he had to have him back.

Henry dropped his hand with a sigh. "Very well. Deliver him to me, and he shall have grant of his life." He rubbed his eyes and turned his gaze to the window. A line from the Greek Euripides echoed in his mind: What glory can compare to this; to hold thy hand victorious over the heads of those you hate? And he smiled.

* * *

Ringed by the king's men, Prior Ralph rode back to the monastery, his heart sore, burdened by sorrow. He should have been relieved that he had secured mercy for the young man, yet he felt naught but grief and a dreadful heaviness. The king's rage had revealed what lay in his heart, and what Prior Ralph had seen in his eyes he would not forget for as long as he lived. In his wrath, the king had taken on the look of a wild man. For a fleeting second Prior Ralph had glimpsed madness in those narrowed, cruel eyes—and something else. Something he could not put his finger on—a flash—a glint—of something vile . . .

What had the young man said? That the king lusted for his wife, a princess of Scotland . . . Prior Ralph had not known in his ignorance what evil lurked in the world of man. Even a predator in the woods would not look that way upon his prey before he pounced for the kill. Nay, he did not relish putting back into his king's hands the hapless captive who inspired such depths of hatred, of envy, of fear.

As the men-at-arms waited outside the monastery wall under

the sharp eye of their captain, Simon Digby, Prior Ralph went to inform Richard of the outcome of his meeting. He found him in the church, prostrate on the stone floor before the altar. When he arose, his breath reeked of wine. Pity overwhelmed the prior. Would that he could empty his cellar of the king's prized wine that was delivered to him every Yuletide, he thought, and give it over to this lad—this prince—to take with him to the Tower! Doubtless he would have need of it. Compassion twisted his heart as he looked upon the young one standing unsteadily before him. The prior rested a gentle hand on his shoulder.

"My son, I bring good news. The king has given grant of life."

Relief washed over Richard and he grabbed the prior's hand. He took it to his lips and laid a kiss on its withering skin. Oh, to live— what it meant to live—how good it felt to know that he would live! That he would see Catherine again! "Thank you—"

"Now, my son, let us pray before you go."

Together they knelt at the altar. *"Quia tu es, Deus, fortitudo mea . . . Emitte lucem tuam—"* they intoned together. For You, O God, are my strength . . . Send forth Your light and Your truth; they shall lead me on and bring me to Your holy mountain. *"Quare tristis es anima mea?"* Why are you so downcast, O my soul? Why do you sigh within me? Hope in God!

"Gloria Patri, et Filio, et Spiritu Sancto," they ended, making the sign of the cross.

They walked together from the church into the small courtyard, where the splashing fountain lightened Richard's heart. From inside his shirt, he removed the pouch of coins Catherine had given him and handed it over to the prior. "Father, take this—I regret it is not much, but it is all I have." He dropped to a knee before the old monk. "Do not forget me in your prayers, Prior Ralph."

Prior Ralph looked at the pouch in his hand that constituted all the worldly possessions of this destitute prince, and turned his gaze to Richard, to the eyes that were as blue as cornflowers and to the mouth that lifted even in distress, and he was moved to deepest pity. For the young man's teeth were for laughing round an apple, and his arms were for raising high the girl he loved, and these things would never be again. He watched him mount his horse in the sunshine as birds sang in the branches and rabbits hopped through the lettuce. He watched him turn his reins and throw him a salute. Then, he watched him disappear over the green hills into the distance, surrounded by the army of guards that would take him to the Tower.

Chapter 14
Tower of Hell

It was an easy pace that Digby set, and Richard enjoyed the journey back to London on the beautiful summer's day in June 1498. Delighting in his gift of life, he savored with heightened joy the world around him. The flight of the birds across the sky, the flapping of their wings, and the sound of their song all brought him renewed pleasure, and he marveled that he had given so little thought to God's creation before. In the forest, he breathed deep of the scented air, and plucking a blossom from a wild fruit tree, inhaled its fragrance. As he passed through the rolling fields that bordered the city, he delighted in the fresh smell of the earth and of the feel of the wind in his face that stirred the trees into sighs. He thought what music there was in nature's creation and was amazed he had not noticed it before. He thought about Catherine, and wondered if he would see her before supper.

Bells were ringing for nones when the Tower rose up on the north bank of the River Thames, its many stone towers and turrets marking the line of the sky. As soon as he arrived, he would wash and change and give thanks to God in the chapel. Then he would go in search of Catherine.

They trotted into the outer courtyard of the Tower and handed their reins over to the stable boys. With purposeful strides, Digby led the way into the inner court and Richard followed, ringed by the men-at-arms and wondering at the sudden tension he felt around him. Why were the men-at-arms not dismissed now that he was safely delivered to the Tower? "Where are we going?" he asked.

"The king wishes to see you," said Digby, not slowing his pace.

Richard fell silent. He had forgotten about Henry. He would have to thank him for his pardon, but Henry was probably angry, and the meeting would be unpleasant. The knowledge dampened his excitement as he entered the White Tower and climbed the stairs to the king's apartments. The customary two hundred yeomen and men-at-arms lined the halls, and he was met with a hiss when he appeared. Picking at their teeth, they leered at him, shoved and heckled him. Someone called out, "Perkin's back!" and someone else replied, "Not for long!" and everyone guffawed. A man put his foot out to trip him, and almost succeeded. By the time he reached Henry's council chamber, Richard was as tense and unnerved as if he were walking into a lion's den.

Henry sat at the table, playing solitaire. His monkey sneered at Richard from where he sat watching his master with a cup of wine in his hands, but Henry didn't look up. He continued to lay his cards down thoughtfully, now and again removing one to the side. Richard shifted his weight from foot to foot, wondering when Henry would see fit to put an end to his little game. Finally, Henry gathered up the deck of cards and shuffled them expertly from one hand to another.

"I won," he said, acknowledging Richard's presence at last. "I always win."

Richard didn't reply.

"You should know that by now."

Richard still made no response. He could see Henry was in an evil mood, and he didn't know what reply to make.

Henry rose from the table and slammed a hand down so hard that Richard jumped.

"Finally, a reaction. So you still live . . . and breathe . . . You are not dead yet I see. Pity—for you, I mean."

Richard decided it was time to defuse the animus that was building in Henry. "I am indeed alive, thanks to your great mercy, King Henry."

Henry closed the gap between them until he stood uncomfortably close. "Mercy you do not deserve, but never mind. That will soon be remedied."

Richard lifted his gaze to Henry's eyes. They held a fearful glazed look. Richard shuddered inwardly and his legs went weak beneath him. He held himself erect by force of will alone.

"You persuaded that old man that you really were Edward's son, didn't you? With your pretty mouth, and your perfect jaw, and your golden good looks. But mark my words, by the time I'm through with you, you'll look nothing like Edward—and I'll have you begging for death! Begging, you hear me?" He struck Richard a blow to his ear that sent his senses reeling. Richard nursed his injury and Henry continued talking, but his voice faded in and out as he paced to and fro. Richard couldn't hear what he said for the throbbing pain on the side of his face until he caught the name "Catherine—" He dropped his hand, momentarily forgetting his injury.

"Catherine—how is she? I beseech you to tell me how she is—"

Henry in the motion of striding away turned to stare at him, his hands behind his back. "You are well matched to one another, I daresay. For she is as much fool as you. She refuses to divorce you, but she'll change her mind, I've no doubt. She is not accustomed to living like a pauper, and now that I've cut her allowance and dismissed all her attendants save one, she will come to realize you're not worth the cost to her. What kind of a man are you? You can't even provide for your wife."

For the first time since he'd entered the room, Richard felt a moment's joy. Catherine had refused to divorce him despite everything. Despite everything—*Oh, my beloved, my dear heart, my God-given angel,* he cried silently. *You are with me in bliss, and in woe. How I love you—*

He came out of his thoughts to find Henry watching him silently, his face as dark as thunder, a muscle twitching at his jaw. "You may smile now," he hissed, "but not for long. Mark my words, I shall wipe it off your face very shortly." He went to the door and yanked it open. He turned back to Richard. "I will make you rue the day you were born." He ground the words out between his teeth and the thin smile that hovered on his mouth sent chills down Richard's spine.

At the door, Simon Digby snapped to attention. "Sire!"

"Take him away. You know what to do with him," Henry said.

"Aye, Sire."

Richard's blood went cold.

Digby was Constable of the Tower.

*   *   *

Richard spent the night in a small windowless room in the Salt Tower and awoke the next morning to a strange silence. It was the Feast of Corpus Christi, yet he heard nothing of the revelry or noise of the pageants he knew were taking place all over the city. From the guards he learned that court had moved to Westminster in his absence. His most bitter disappointment was that he didn't see Catherine.

"Will I be going to Westminster?" he asked one of his guards. The man looked up from the game of cards he was playing. "Aye. Tomorrow," he grinned, exchanging a look with his companion.

Tomorrow, Richard told himself, forcing himself to be patient. *Tomorrow.*

At daybreak, he was taken to Westminster Palace with his hands bound before him and his feet tied beneath the belly of his horse. As they had done since the first time they'd seen him, the common folk in the streets of London tormented him, and the homeless who slept in the streets sat up to marvel at the sight of someone more wretched than they. But Richard paid them little heed; he knew Catherine was at Westminster.

At the palace, Digby helped him dismount and led him to the gigantic hall that served as both a concourse and a meeting place. It was thronged with people. The props from the pageants of the day before had been left up and still divided the large chamber into three areas. He looked up at the gilt signs hanging over the displays that declared PARADISE, PURGATORY, and HELL.

"Sorry, Perkin, it's not Paradise for you, but Purgatory," said Digby as they passed boughs dressed with leaves and flowers, decorated with golden hanging cages of chirping, colorful birds. He followed Digby as he led him farther away into a dark and gloomy place lit by few candles. A scaffolding of barrels stood among huge rocks and burnt-out tree branches.

"Climb up, Perkin," Digby demanded. "You're to be in the stocks in Purgatory for two days." He locked Richard into place with chains around his hand and feet. "I have a message for you from King Henry," he said. "He said to tell you to prepare yourself well here, for on the third day you shall descend into Hell."

Richard swallowed hard.

People soon began swarming around him, jumping up and jostling one another to gain a better look. Some spat at him, and cursed. Since his neck was secured into the stocks, he could only shut his eyes to shield himself from their phlegm. When the day finally ended and he was released, Richard breathed a sigh of relief: his joints ached from the enforced confinement.

As he lay down on his straw pallet in his windowless chamber that night, his thoughts were of Catherine. She had to know that he was there at Westminster, and she had to know, too, that he would never want her to see him this way. *Beloved Catryn*—He wished the room had a window so he could see the stars; the night with its beautiful stars always reminded him of her. He was awakened by a harsh shove. A bowl of gruel was thrust into his hands, accompanied by a crust of dry bread teeming with weevils.

"Breakfast, Perkin." Digby laughed in response to the expression on his face. "Food straight from Purgatory."

Richard put the bread down. He had little appetite in any case.

Digby shrugged. "It's worse in Hell." When Richard was on his feet, he chained his hands and took him back to the stocks. On this day, however, he was made to stand on the barrels and read his confession to the crowds who came to see him.

"First it is to be known that I was born in the town of Tournai and my father's name is called John Osbeck . . ."

On the third day, Richard was taken to the Tower. The sun was shining brightly as he rode past Cheapside and St. Peter's Church, and along Mark Lane in the greatest ignominy, cursed by many of those he passed in the streets and laughed to scorn. But at the Tower gates, a nun regarded him with tears, and a sob broke from her throat. "Pray for your king—" he called out to her with the last ounce of courage left in him. One of the guards at his side raised his weapon to strike him, but then dropped his arm, confused. *Do you really think I mean the bastard you call king?* Richard thought, allowing himself a small smile as he passed beneath the portcullis into the outer ward.

The rope that bound him to his horse was cut, and he was helped to dismount. He followed Digby to the Salt Tower, but at the entrance he came to a halt, blinded by the darkness. The torches had burned out. Digby and his men-at-arms waited for a man-at-arms to bring replacements. A flame was put to them and the entry flooded with light.

"This way—" said Digby, leading the way down a stairwell.

Frozen with horror, Richard looked into the black pit that led to the dungeons. An evil stench of dampness and slime wafted up, and with it a strange dull roaring sound. Here was a chorus that mingled together all the cries, screams, pleadings, and moans that torture could elicit from a human throat. "Why are we going there?" he cried.

"Hell is always underground," Digby replied as his men snickered.

"I won't go!" cried Richard, pushing back in terror.

"You have no choice, Perkin." Someone gave him a hard shove.

Richard fought them, but they seized his elbow and twisted it behind his back until the slightest resistance elicited an unbearable pain. They forced him down into the curving stairwell. He couldn't see for the shadows, and kept losing his footing on the wet, narrow steps. The terrible din from below grew louder until it burst on his ears with the force of blows.

"You don't have to do this!" Richard cried desperately, struggling in the arms of his captors. "I'll say whatever you want! Tell me what you want me to say!"

"Not *say*," replied a man with a hatchet-face who came forward to take him. "But *give*."

What did he mean? Was he mad? He could scarcely breathe; every part of his body vibrated with terror. "Tell me what you want—" he cried again, louder, more urgently. "I'll say anything you want— anything at all! Money—is that what you want? I have friends— powerful friends—they'll get you gold—tell me what you want—"

"Too late for that, Perkin," said Digby. "Now I must leave you. Bear your fate as bravely as you can, son."

Someone guffawed. "Bravely, eh? Not likely, that 'un. I smell the urine already."

Richard turned to look at the one who spoke but his vision had blurred and he could see nothing except a hideous set of grinning teeth. His gaze went to Digby's retreating back and panic flooded him. "Don't leave me, Digby—help me—Digby! Why are you doing this?—O God . . ." Richard cried as men dragged him to a wooden table and strapped him down. He fought until they slipped his wrists into iron gauntlets, first one hand, then the other, and manacled his feet in place so that he lay helpless, and spread-eagle. The man with the hatchet-face took out a long dagger and ran his finger along the edge. The blade glinted in the torchlight. He laughed again, sending ice down Richard's spine.

"The king has ordered a very special treat for you," he grinned.

Wide-eyed, his mind a tumult of terror, Richard stared at his tormentor. He struggled with all his might. His chains rattled but the irons held fast.

"Tell me what you want—" he begged.

Someone tied a blindfold around his eyes. Moments later, such a tempest of pain came over him that he screamed in agony, and knew no more.

*   *   *

Sounds of weeping came to Catherine from the antechamber as she lay dry-eyed on her bed. Agatha had cried every night in the past week since Catherine had given her the news that she would be let go. She'd ached for her lady-in-waiting, but at the same time she felt gratitude that Henry had left the choice up to her. What if he had appointed Meryell as her sole lady-in-waiting? Somehow, she would find placement for Agatha. Cecily would help. Already she was spreading the word.

A week later, as Catherine watched children play in the garden, the Scottish ambassador crossed her path and took a seat beside her on the bench. Whether from intent, or pure coincidence—but likely the former—the dear man happened to mention that he had a vacancy in his service. She offered him Agatha, and he accepted.

"I hope she won't mind leaving England, however?"

"Leaving?"

"I must return to Edinburgh next week and shall be gone for a month. She will have to come with my party. She may return to England with me in September, if she wishes."

Catherine had taken his hand into hers mutely, and gazed at him through a blur of tears. He was going to deliver Agatha home, and James would give her a position in his court. Agatha would be safe in Scotland again. *There are still good people in the world,* she thought. *I must never forget that, no matter what happens.*

For all the blessings of those good people, however, there was unspeakable evil, too. For Richard, Catherine had sobbed until she had no more tears. She knew that if he were caught, no one would be able to help him—not Margaret of Burgundy, nor Maximilian, nor her cousin James, no one in this world, not even if they offered up their entire kingdoms to Henry. The king would wreak a terrible vengeance. The memory of her last meeting with him rose before her and again she saw his narrowed eyes flashing with a hideous glint as he deluged Richard in a torrent of epithets.

All lies in the hands of Fate, she had thought with a shiver, for Fate had proven itself a malignant force in their lives.

When the tidings came of Richard's capture, Catherine had lain in seclusion in her room, ill with fever and fear. She had heard that he was put to shame in the stocks at Westminster Hall for two days, and was committed to the Tower on the third. Horror, black and chill, froze her breath and she bolted upright in her bed. Thrusting the blankets off, she rose. It was still dark, barely five of the o'clock; it had been a bad night. The queen had suggested she not report for her duties until she felt better, but she could no longer stay away. Time was poison to her; it gave her too much chance to think.

With Alice's help, she dressed quickly, and picked up her basket of silk thread, and together they made their way to the queen's privy chamber. They exchanged a look of surprise as they entered the ante-chamber of the royal bedchamber. Light flowed from beneath the queen's door and voices drifted to them, low and muffled. Catherine was disturbed by the anomaly. While the queen might stir from sleep at this hour, it was far too early for her to be up and entertaining company. Catherine approached anxiously. She couldn't clearly make out what they said.

"You don't want to know." Cecily's voice.

"Tell me," Kate insisted. "I have a right to know."

Kate was there, too? How strange.

"He could be my brother, too," Kate added.

So it concerned Richard! She tiptoed closer and laid her ear to the door.

"You'd be looking into a very ugly corner of the human heart, Kate." It was Cecily who spoke.

Catherine peeped through the keyhole. Cecily stood in the middle of the room, her face close to Kate's. They lowered their voices. Catherine strained to hear but she only caught mumbling, and then she heard Cecily utter words that would never leave her for as long as she lived: "For the love of Heaven, Elizabeth, how can you defend him! Do you not understand? Henry had him *castrated—*"

Catherine screamed and dropped the basket of silk thread she carried. She put her hands over her ears and screamed again. She kept screaming, because only screams could blot the words from her mind. Arms grabbed her around the shoulders, around the waist; she let herself drop into them as the cold marble floor rose to meet her. "N-n-no-noooo!" she cried, reaching out to them.

As she lay on the ground, moaning and writhing wretchedly, she saw Cecily and Kate staring down at her in horror.

"Let it not be true—" she begged.

Footsteps sounded distantly and voices came from along the passageway. The queen's other ladies-in-waiting were arriving. They rushed to her side and helped her up, but she could barely stand for the shattering pain in her stomach. "What can the matter be?" "What has happened?" "Shall I fetch wine?"

"Hush, hush," Cecily told them. She took Catherine's hand into her own. "'Tis her monthly cycle. She suffers from fierce pain, poor thing. Here, Catherine, come with us. Help me, Kate—come with us—that's it, Catherine, one step at a time—" She took her into the bedchamber and Kate shut the door behind them, locking everyone out.

Catherine looked at Cecily and took in the anguish on her face. *Cecily is the only one who cares in this cold, heartless world,* she thought. "O Cecily," she wept. "O Cecily, Cecily . . ."

* * *

A month had passed since Richard had been dragged back to his cell. He had lain for days in his own blood, groaning with pain and wishing for death. He remembered clutching his belly when he first arrived; remembered his legs giving out from under him; remembered falling to the floor. He remembered writhing in his own stinking vomit as he wept for what was lost forever.

Catryn, he'd screamed into the blackness that surrounded him.

But Catryn was gone, and if God was kind, she would never see him again. Not this way. Let her remember him as he had been.

What was it she'd said about the mirror of the mind reflecting the past back onto us? Aye, memories helped; and prayer, too, though prayer could not fade his bodily agony. Oh, to fall into a deep sleep and never wake up! But sleep did not come as faithfully as he wished, and thirst was always with him. "Wine—" he had begged, barely realizing that he spoke, or that he pushed his cup through the steel bars of his cell. "Have pity—"

One of his four jailors, Roger Ray, whom they called "Long Roger," did show compassion. He filled and refilled Richard's battered tin cup each time Richard passed it to him. And after drink had revived him, Richard always asked himself the same question. *By what path did I find my way into this hell?* The answer that came to him was always the same: *The mistakes I made brought me here; one reckless step after another. And failure brought me here; one miserable failure after another. But most of all, pride brought me here . . .* Hubris, the first deadly sin, the most dangerous of sins because it blinds our understanding.

"From pride all perdition took its beginning, is that not right, my friend?" he asked, rattling his chains as he waved his empty tin cup through the bars of his cell. Long Roger undid a flask beside him and poured him more drink, his movements enlarged by the shadows he cast in the candlelight. "That's right," he mumbled. "'Tis what they say."

"*Right* you are, my friend—" Richard upturned his cup and downed a long swallow. Ah, that was better . . .

He had committed the deadly sin of pride, and for that he had fallen into perdition. He had thought that all he needed to do was show himself to his people, and they would recognize him as the son of his father and restore him to his father's throne. He had thought to prevail because he had righteousness on his side—and God, too. For how could God side with a tyrant? It was inconceivable.

Pride had blinded him to the truth. Might, not right, won earthly kingdoms. He laughed uproariously into his half-emptied cup. God had not taken care of him, but the Devil had not failed his disciple, Henry Tudor. He shook his head in wonder.

"The Devil takes care of his own, isn't that what they say?" he demanded of his jailors. They threw him an indulgent smile, and went on with their card game.

He had come into the tyrant's lair as blind as a bat, without an army, and worse—with his heart stuffed with the pride of righteousness. And when he was brought face-to-face with the truth at Taunton, he ran from death. He was a coward—and not merely a coward. A stupid coward who had not seen the truth until it was too late.

A stupid coward. He laughed uproariously, drained his cup, and held it out again.

"How much wine does it take to knock you out, mate?" Long Roger demanded, slapping his cards down with annoyance this time, for now the flask was empty and he had to get up and refill Richard's cup from the barrel of wine standing in the corner. Another jailor, Thomas Strangeways, perhaps a relative to the fellow James Strangeways of the king's chamber, passed Long Roger the flask while he stood there, and Long Roger filled that also before returning to the table. "Here you go. This is the last time tonight, understand? I'm not getting up again." He gave Richard his wine.

"Understand—aye, I do understand—*now,"* Richard laughed. "Now I surely do—" In an abrupt change of mood, he cried out suddenly, as he had many times before, "I thought it was a blessing to be born a prince! All my life, I took pride in my royal Plantagenet blood, but Dear God Almighty, how happy I would be now to be a simple peasant—to be tilling the fields in rain and sunshine—to look up at the stars and kiss the girl I love! Like you—Long Roger—and you, Thomas Astwood, and you, Strangeways—and you, Walter Bluet! Do you know how blessed you are? Give thanks, all of you—give thanks for your low birth, that you were not born the son of a king, like me!" Abruptly, he covered his head in his hands, and sobbed.

And this is your penance, you accursed son of a king, Richard thought. A penance sent by God, and delivered by the Devil's disciple into whose hands he had delivered himself—that other coward, Henry Tudor. The one who'd fled Bosworth. The one who, in

Brittany, had trembled so violently to return to England that he'd almost died of fright in the dockyard at St. Malo.

His sobs ceased abruptly and he grinned, imagining Tudor's terror. Then his smile faded. The tyrant had lived because the Duke of Brittany had taken pity and rescinded the order to send him back to England. But where was the tyrant's pity, where his humanity? He who had trembled to die did not shrink from acts of unspeakable cruelty and the taking of life in abominable ways. Like the poor friar who had burned at the stake when a word would have spared him. Like William, the sergeant-farrier, who had challenged the tyranny of his rule—

William's face floated before him. He screwed his eyes shut and put out his hand. "Go, William—go!" he yelled, waving him away. "I cannot bear to see your face, nor to know how many others I have sent into this hell that binds me now. Go, my friend—"

He broke into sobs once more. Reckless, stupid fool that he was, among these others that he had delivered into the Devil's hands were his wife and child. *Catryn*— he cried softly. *Forgive me, my beloved— Dickon, my beautiful son, wherever you are, forgive me—*

He lifted his eyes, and lo! through the tears that blurred his sight he beheld the glory of what had been his wedding day. He, in white damask and gold, and Catherine, in velvet the color of snow, were swinging one another around with wild abandon, arms linked, eyes only for each other, and Catherine was shaking loose the lilies in her black hair as they danced to the frenzied beat of a Highland melody blown on bagpipes and clashing with cymbals. The vision vanished as if the golden bubble that encased it had ruptured in the air before him. But then Catherine came to him again from out of the shadows. He heard her silvery laughter and she took his hand, and together they threw caution to the winds and galloped out of the castle gates over the moors, to picnic in the heather and run on the windy hills. Once more he saw himself holding her in his arms at Huntly Castle, loving her in the tenderness of the night, with a love that he had not known existed in the world and an ecstasy that had lifted him to the fringes of Heaven. Together they had mingled their blood and begotten children . . . beautiful children . . .

Oh, how I miss you, my beloved Catryn, and you, my Dickon, my sweet Dickon, angel child that you were—

And how he missed the simple things of life: the stir of the wind through the trees, the smell of the earth on a cool spring morning, God's creatures in the forest, delighting in the brief joy of their brief existence. The sun, the stars, the moon, the fragrance of flowers, the touch of the rain on his face—

He laid his head back against the dank stone wall of his cell and closed his eyes. *This hell is my penance but, Father in Heaven, it should not be theirs.* Stupid coward that he was, he had not only come unprepared into the tyrant's lair, thinking he had the protection of God, but had brought his wife and child with him. There was not penance enough for that.

The jangle of keys in the lock broke into his thoughts. Two men were entering his cell, the whites of their eyes glowing strangely in the darkness, their burly shoulders blotting out the little bit of light from the candle on the table. Now he saw that Long Roger, Thomas Strangeways, and the others were gone. Terror gripped him. His gaze went to their hands, and he broke into a fit of violent shaking. Dragging his chains, he shuffled backward along the floor until he slammed himself up against the cold wall. For they held clubs in their hands, and he knew not what evil they had come to wreak.

Chapter 15

Season of Death

The sun bore down on Henry's back as he dismounted and made his way to the inner court of the Tower of London to see the Pretender, surrounded by the two hundred armed guards who never left his side. The thought of the Plantagenet tightened his mouth into a line that cut across his face like a blade. Sick of hearing how much he resembled King Edward, he'd taken care of it so that no one would ever see King Edward in his face again. Sick of worrying that he would escape and scatter his seed, he'd taken care of that, too—his son was as good as dead, hidden away where no one would ever find him, and there would be no more progeny from the father. Henry was determined to have it end, and he had ended it. He'd stamped the Plantagenet threat into oblivion.

If all this was not enough reason for what he'd done to him, there was still one more. *Catherine.* Sick of seeing her gaze at his rival with adoring doe-eyes when she coldly spurned him and his gifts, he'd made certain to wipe the face she'd loved from the face of the earth— as best he could, without going against his oath to God before Prior Ralph. A brilliant stroke, even if he said so himself.

Damn Margaret of Burgundy! he thought as he conducted the

delegation from Archduke Philip the Handsome to the White Tower. Her support for the Plantagenet was a thorn in his side that had kept his nerves on edge for well over a year now. There was only one way to force her to stop plotting to free him. Show her that the Richard she knew no longer existed.

He'd wanted to punish her for her myriad plots against him, but Philip and his new archduchess, Juana of Spain, sister to Prince Arthur's betrothed, Catherine of Aragon, wouldn't permit trade sanctions against Burgundy. Therefore he'd agreed to this meeting. Led by the archduke's foremost councilor, the Bishop of Cambrai, the delegation had come to discuss trade, but for Henry, the Pretender eclipsed the trade issue. He had invited the Spanish ambassador, Dr. de Puebla, along to join the delegation. All the royal blood of Europe had to know how closely the Pretender was guarded and to see that his cause was dead. That included Isabella and Ferdinand of Spain.

He strode purposefully up the steps into the entrance of the White Tower, accompanied by the Bishop of Cambrai and the members of his delegation. Henry's thicket of soldiers peeled away to secure the premises as he crossed to the northeast corner. He took the turret staircase up to the chapel of St. John. Built by William the Conqueror in white Caen stone, in the Romanesque style, with thick, round pillars and a stunning two-story curved gallery of stone, it was an impressive place for what he hoped would be a decisive meeting. Guards thrust the doors open.

"Truly magnificent," murmured the Bishop of Cambrai, gazing around him reverently.

Henry offered him a smile and led the way along the vaulted nave up to the altar where de Puebla already waited for them.

As Philip the Handsome's austere councilor, the Bishop of Cambrai, followed the king, Prince Richard was at the forefront of his mind. The trade agreement that had ostensibly brought him to England was not of sufficient importance to drag him away from his duties in Malines. He had a secret and more pressing purpose for this visit. To see Prince Richard, gain his freedom, and conduct him back safely to Flanders had been the sole true aim of his embassy to England. If that failed—God forfend!—then he wished to return to the Duchess of Burgundy with words of hope, and to assure her that her beloved boy was at least well.

He bowed to the Spanish ambassador. When the crosscurrent of greetings had subsided, Henry spoke.

"Whenever you are ready, the false prince, Perkin Warbeck, shall be brought before you, Your Highnesses, so you may hear the truth from his own lips, as sworn before you and God Himself."

The Bishop of Cambrai inclined his head.

"Bring him in," Henry said, turning to Digby.

Digby left to fetch Richard, and Henry knelt before the altar in prayer. The bishop's thoughts turned to Duchess Margaret. All her efforts so far to rescue her "dear darling," as she called her nephew, had met with failure, and Cambrai knew that the only hope she had left resided in him. In his mind's eye, he saw the duchess waiting for Prince Richard's return, sitting by her writing desk of solid silver in a study where green velvet covered the table, purple taffeta hung on the walls, and her cherished companions, the books she loved, were laid out behind a grille. Few were admitted entry to her sanctum, but her nephew had always been welcome. Every evening they had taken a cup of wine together in solitude, two lonely souls united in blood and love, finding refuge in one another. Since his capture, she had fallen into a frenzy of soul, weeping, praying, and pleading with everyone on earth and in Heaven to return to her her beloved White Rose. Aged, ill, and lonely, she dreamt only of him, and of his release.

A sudden commotion sounded. The bishop's thoughts fled as the chapel doors were thrust open. At first, he did not comprehend what he saw: a man-at-arms, and something that resembled an animal in tow. The creature, clad in hose and a shirt, was emaciated and hunched over, and balanced a contraption of metal across its shoulder and chest in the manner of a performing bear. From this nexus a plethora of iron chains ran down its body to the shackles on its feet, its wrists, and to the collar around its neck, encumbering its movement so that it shuffled along with difficulty, jangling and dragging its heavy chains on the stone floor.

The bishop peered into the distance. *Christe Eleison*, it could not be! Father in Heaven—but it was—it was indeed—Without being aware that he did so, he who hid all emotion behind an impassive facade shrank back with a gasp and made the sign of the cross. All that was left of the glorious young prince he had known and loved, whose friend and confessor he had been, was a mass of matted fair hair, bloodshot eyes ringed with black and blue, and a face disfigured by a broken nose and the loss of teeth, and swollen with congealed blood and pus. It was a young face from which every vestige of youth had been torn. Here, in this terrible shell of humanity, dwelled the once magnificent son of King Edward IV, the darling of his Aunt Margaret's heart, the last of her illustrious male line. What would he tell his poor dowager duchess now; she who had longed for a child and been barren; she who had known too much of grief and loss, and emptiness? This would kill her.

He tore his gaze from the wretched creature that had been Richard, to the king who stood beside him, watching with cold gray eyes and a triumphant smile. At that moment, it was not the Devil that Cambrai feared as much as Henry Tudor. His gaze, moving back to Prince Richard, touched on de Puebla. The Spanish ambassador had turned a sickly green as he gaped slack-jawed at the prince.

The guard gave Prince Richard a nudge, and he knelt down, slowly and awkwardly, rattling his chains as he moved. Henry stared at the bowed head before him for a long moment before he broke the dread silence that held them in thrall.

"Why did you practice such deception on the archduke and his country?" he spat.

The Bishop of Cambrai held out the Bible, and Richard laid his hand on its gilt and jeweled cover. With great effort, he forced his broken and still-painful jaw, swollen tongue, and bruised lips to form the words he had rehearsed: "I swear solemnly before God that the Duchess Madame Margaret knew, as I did myself, that I am not the son of who I said I was." His voice was rough and guttural, and no longer bore any resemblance to what it had been, but he hoped the too-ready answer to a different question would send his aunt a message. He wanted her to understand his meaning, and appreciate his guile. He lifted his head and met the bishop's eyes, praying that his double-entendre was not lost on him: *I am not the son of the boatman of Tournai.*

"You see, Your Highnesses," said Henry, "that the pope, and the King of France, and the archduke and the King of the Romans and the King of Scotland and the Duke of Milan and the Doge of Venice and all Christian princes have been deceived."

The bishop did not speak as he mulled over what had been said. The young prince had not denied his birth under oath but spoke a riddle. Aye, the duchess knew as the Pretender did himself that he was not the son of the one he said he was. But whose son was he? Before his capture, he had said he was the son of King Edward. After his capture, he had said he was the son of John Osbeck. Under torture, anyone would say anything. Cambrai had met the prince's eyes, and the message in them was clear. Prince Richard's reply might content King Henry. But to the duchess these same words would convey exactly the opposite meaning. He, Cambrai, would report to her that even under these fearful circumstances, her beloved nephew had found the courage—and the wit—to smuggle out a laugh at the usurper's expense.

Beside him, de Puebla stood silently. Though his sovereigns, Ferdinand and Isabella, had not been mentioned, they, too, believed in the young prince, and Henry knew it.

Henry turned to the Bishop of Cambrai. "You said you had news for this—this fraud?"

Cambrai recovered his composure. He cleared his throat and regarded Prince Richard. "Her Grace the Duchess Margaret of Burgundy sends greetings and wishes you to know that she sorely misses your presence and prays for you daily. You live in her heart, and her remembrance. She will remind you, in case you forget, that God is Love, and that reward and joy await the righteous in Heaven. She also says to tell you that the wretched hound you rescued from the streets of Malines has birthed a litter of pups."

Richard caught the soft gaze of his old friend and confessor, and gratitude swam in his heart. The Bishop of Cambrai had understood. He hoped the bishop could see his smile, though it fluttered on a mouth now misshapen and contorted by the shattered bones of his face.

*   *   *

July was a hot month in the summer of 1498. The drought parched the cornfields and thinned the grass, but the sun shone brightly every day. Catherine did not notice. For her, since Richard's escape on Trinity Sunday, it was night, and never would the darkness lift.

Many times she would go to the hall in search of him, forgetting that he was not there. At other times, tears would assail her at unexpected moments—in the midst of unrelated conversations, during a stroll in the garden when birds sang brightly, or when laughter erupted at the clever antics of a fool. Then she would plead a headache and excuse herself. At night, she kept to her room and stitched her embroidery feverishly, as if Richard's own life depended on its completion. She knew that to be ridiculous, yet she felt driven by some inner force.

Catherine spent Richard's birthday—on the seventeenth day of August—walking alone in the gardens of Windsor. Now that Henry's spies were not watching her every move, Alice sometimes accompanied her, and they spoke of him, and Dickon, and Scotland and the days of yore when they had been girls together in Huntly Castle, and life had been sweet. The summer passed and October came, bringing the nip of impending winter.

"'Tis a beautiful season, autumn," said Cecily as they strolled together in the garden. She had just returned from the Isle of Wight, where she'd been visiting a friend over the summer. When her husband had visited her there, he'd brought news of the Bishop of Cambrai's visit to the Tower on the last day of July, and the uneasy rumors that came with it. "De Puebla could not fathom how Perkin could have changed so much in such a short time," her husband had reported. "It seems he's been horribly disfigured. De Puebla doesn't expect him to live much longer."

Cecily was overcome with grief and revulsion. She was not one to weep often, but she wept now that this should be the cruel fate of the merry little brother she remembered from the days of sanctuary, the boy who had loved to sing. On her return to Westminster in October, she'd sought out Catherine, thinking she might have need of a friend, and was taken aback to find that Catherine was unaware of any of these happenings. Cecily didn't want to be the one to tell her, and so she spoke of light matters.

"The leaves turn into rubies and gold," she said, "and the sky is never so blue as in autumn."

"I used to think autumn was beautiful," Catherine said, lifting her gaze to the sky, turquoise like Dickon's eyes. "My child was born in September."

Cecily took her hand into her own, and gave it a squeeze. For a while they walked along in silence, arm in arm. Then Cecily said, "My sister the queen hates the fall, though her beloved Arthur was also birthed in September. She calls it the season of Death." Cecily hesitated for a moment, and added, "You see, the man Elizabeth had loved had been born in October, and autumn is always a heavy time for her."

The season of Death. "'Tis an apt nomer," Catherine murmured. Last year at this time she had bid Richard farewell on the beach at Marazion; her golden child had been ripped from her arms; and her unborn babe had died in her womb.

They both fell silent, mulling their thoughts. A pair of lovers strolled past, laughing, eyes only for one another. Catherine's gaze went to a group of young people gathered around a fountain ringed by roses and a low hedge. Three fresh-faced youths sang to a lute and pipes as girls danced for them. They drew near to listen. Catherine regarded them, wondering how many of them would ever know the happiness of living with the one they loved, as she had done. Probably none. "Court is a place of broken dreams," she heard herself say, speaking her thought aloud.

Cecily had been feeling bereft as she'd listened to the lament sung by the young people, and Catherine's remark made her realize why. Neither of her husbands had touched her emotions or awakened any intimacy of body or spirit. She had missed something of great value, and she yearned for it, not knowing precisely what she yearned for.

"What is it like to be wed to the one you love?" she asked.

"That sweet ditty touched a chord of sorrow in you, did it not?" Catherine asked.

"Aye, 'tis always so with a beautiful melody of love."

"Nay—" Catherine murmured softly, seeing a campfire on the shores of Loch Lomond. "There was a time when such a melody made me feel the exquisite beauty of Creation. For I was whole, and my heart was full to bursting with happiness. To be wed to the one you love is something sacred and as close to Heaven as it is possible to get on this earth, Cecily." After a hesitation, she added, "Emptiness for me, when I had Richard, was but a memory."

Cecily averted her gaze. Once there had been a young man for her, too. Once, long ago, when she'd been fifteen. She'd wanted him from the first moment she's laid eyes on him—wanted him as unquestioningly as food to eat, or wine to quench her thirst. For eight months, he'd been her guard in sanctuary at Westminster Abbey, ready to escort her along the cloisters to the small green turf where she sat watching over her playful little sisters and her young brothers. Even now she could see every detail of his face, his brooding gaze, his drowsy smile; the tilt of his fair head as he stood looking down at her; the shine on his boots, the gray of his fine woolen doublet that matched the color of his eyes. She would climb out the impossibly high window of the Chapter House and flee into his arms almost every night, and she could remember still, with vivid sweetness, the touch of his lips on hers when he kissed her. Her mother had never caught her, and her sister, Elizabeth, had never noticed. She'd evaded them all. To her deep regret, they'd never made love, but many times in the years since, she'd made love to him in her dreams.

She looked out into the distance, seeing there among the

withering flowers the glorious days of her imprisonment. Her sweetheart had marveled at her skill in climbing from such a high window.
"How in God's name do you do that? I didn't think it was possible
for a monkey to manage it!" She always laughed at his amazement.
"I can do anything—almost," she liked to boast. And it did seem
that way to her then. Life had held an excitement that had made her
feel vitally alive. Everything had seemed possible to her then, but
her uncle, King Richard, had married her to some dumb-knuckle
friend of his in Yorkshire who could never get two sentences out
without stuttering whenever she looked at him, and life had taken
a sharp turn for the worst. She'd felt as if she'd been buried alive in
that dreary place, and she was certain she'd come near death many
times from simple *ennui*. There was no one to dance with; no one
to flirt with except the laborers; none to pass the time with except
ancient people whose hands trembled when they raised their goblets to their mouths, and who mumbled endlessly about the Cause
of York. There was only her bumbling idiot husband, smiling at her
everywhere she went.

The only good thing about King Richard losing the Battle of
Bosworth was that she finally got back to court. She lost no time
befriending Henry Tudor's mother, and Tudor's mother had her
marriage annulled. Her merriment and celebration was short-lived,
however, for Tudor's mother married her off to her bald and tiresome
half-brother, Viscount John Welles, who was even worse than her
first husband, Ralph Scope. At least Ralph hadn't been a hundred
doddery years old. What a fate for someone who had almost been a
queen!

She turned her gaze back on Catherine. "What is King James like?"

Memory brought a smile to Catherine's lips. "He is charming,
handsome, generous to a fault, and the most chivalrous king in Christendom. He keeps a lion as a pet, collects guns, and adores warfare."

"I could have loved such a man," Cecily sighed wistfully. "I
wanted to be queen very much, you know—and to think you and
I would have been"—a hesitation—"sisters in Scotland, had I come."

"Aye, we would have been—sisters—" She lifted her gaze to

Cecily, and Cecily looked into her eyes, and both knew the other's thoughts: *As we are now, in England, dear sister.*

"Life does have a way of twisting on us, doesn't it, Catherine?" said Cecily.

"Always."

A silence ensued as both followed into their thoughts.

"Did you know a man called 'O'Water'?" Cecily asked at length.

Catherine jerked her head up. "John O'Water, the Mayor of Cork?"

"He's been caught in Ireland and will die at Tyburn."

"Sweet Mother of Christ—" Again Catherine heard him calling across the years in his Irish lilt, *Me lord, I bring ye news—good news! A delegation has arrived from Penzance in support o' the Yorkist cause!* Kind, gentle John O'Water, who had been loyal to the House of York through its many battles for the throne— She shut her eyes. Oh, how she wanted her father! When she'd been a child mad with fear, she'd buried her head in her father's shoulder and cried until she felt better. More than anything in the world she wanted to bury her head in her father's shoulder now.

Cecily stole a sideways glance at her, wondering if she should tell her about Richard. The news of John O'Water had been a blow, but it might cheer her to know about Cambrai's visit and Aunt Margaret's efforts to gain Richard's release—though she'd have to hold back on Richard's condition. He had been *defigurado,* the Spanish ambassador had said, and was unrecognizable. More he would not say. Neither would her husband. All she knew was that Aunt Meg was still trying to gain his release, or at least to ameliorate his conditions. She had written Henry offering to apologize for her past conduct, promising she would never make trouble again for him, if he would only send Richard back to her. "I won't send him back," Henry had replied. "But if you do these things, I may not kill him."

Aunt Meg would never abandon him. Surely it would be a comfort to Catherine to know that? Cecily inhaled deeply. "Aunt Meg sent the Bishop of Cambrai here to report on—on—Henry's prisoner."

Catherine stared at her wide-eyed.

"She wanted to know how he is, and she managed to get Henry to agree to let the bishop meet our—your husband."

"When?" Catherine whispered.

"They met four weeks ago, on the last day of July. You heard nothing?"

"Nothing." So that explained the looks she received each time she walked into a room: the silences, the fading smiles, the looks of pity, the averted eyes. Henry had forbidden her to see him in prison, though it was a wife's duty to visit her husband under such circumstances. Filled with terror of losing his throne, he feared that she might somehow help Richard escape, captive and pauper though she was. *Perhaps with the aid of the magic arts?* she thought bitterly. "How is Richard, do you know?"

"The Bishop of Cambrai says Aunt Meg has offered to apologize to Henry and to promise never to support another venture against him if it would help Rich—your husband."

Catherine regarded Cecily thoughtfully. She had avoided answering her question, and that was answer enough. Richard fared so poorly, she could not tell her. Catherine gave a cry and covered her face with her hands.

"There is still hope, Catherine—dwell on that." Placing a gentle arm around her friend, Cecily led her to a bench sheltered by dense foliage, away from prying eyes.

*   *   *

The leaves of autumn were swept away by the winds of winter, but in February 1499, before spring blossomed over the land, Cecily's husband, John, Viscount Welles, died. Cecily donned the black garb of mourning and tried to pretend she was sorrowful. But she wasn't. It was the most natural thing in the world that he should die. He was old, and his heart had given out. Why should she have to pretend hers went into the grave with him? She was alive, and never had she felt more exhilarated! Everything was possible again!

Beneath her black gown, she tapped her toes to the music of the minstrels as she watched others dance, and looked forward to the end of the official mourning period when she could join them. Then her eyes moving over the hall would alight on Catherine, and an ache would tug at her heart. For some there was no new beginning. She had a sense that Catherine could be in black forever and ever.

Spring did come, and so did summer, but joy did not follow, not even for Henry. He stood at the window of his council chamber, gazing absently over the beds of crimson gillyflowers and delphinium that decorated the royal garden, his lightness of mood and peaceful slumber after the recapture of his rival a forgotten memory.

The Plantagenet had been rotting in the Tower for nearly a year, but he was never far from Henry's mind. He had proved himself a valuable bargaining chip and had secured for Henry many important concessions from the royal blood of Europe—all surrendered in the hope that he, Henry, might spare his rival's life. Using the Plantagenet as a pawn after Taunton, he had pushed James into a truce with England, and after Cambrai's visit, the Duchess Margaret had groveled before him in the hope of gaining better treatment for her "White Rose." Henry was still milking them both for concessions. James had sent missives protesting the treatment of "his cousin, the Duke of York" and the Scottish ambassador had conveyed his complaints about Henry's penurious punishment of Lady Catherine, urging him to send her home to her native land. But Henry had made it clear to James that would never happen; Lady Catherine, he said, would never be allowed to return to Scotland, not even within a hundred miles of it, and he cared not a whit for James's objections. If the King of Scotland wished to better his royal cousin's position at the English court, he should consider marrying Henry's daughter, ten-year-old Margaret.

All this would be cause for celebration if not for the fact that plots were constantly being hatched to free the Pretender. Despite his confession, his humiliation, and his degradation, men still believed in him. Many had been at the Plantagenet's side from the first. They had received Henry's pardon, but kindness had failed to win them over. Men such as John Heron from the Plantagenet's days at Beaulieu refused to change, and would never change. They were an incorrigible lot, undeserving of his mercy. The shaming and imprisonment of their prince made no difference to them—as it made no difference to the Plantagenet's supporters outside England.

Henry's thoughts turned to Catherine, and he gave an audible sigh. *I can't let her go.* He'd tried to banish her from his mind but he still loved her as desperately as he ever did. He was a tortured man, suffering a disease for which there was no remedy. When he looked at Catherine now, it was with ice in his eyes while in his heart raged a fire that would not be put out. As long as he kept her beside him in England, he had hope she would come to care for him one day. As he had expected, his treatment of her husband had exacted an enormous toll on her goodwill toward him, and now he faced another decision that could cost him what gentle sentiment might still remain. His rival was no longer a viable threat, but clearly, he couldn't be allowed to live indefinitely.

Catherine was not the only impediment that stayed Henry's hand. He had granted the Pretender a pardon before Prior Ralph. Though this presented a small problem that could be circumvented, there was still another more urgent reason to proceed with caution. Regicide was a mortal sin, and he had a superstitious fear of committing the deed. If the responsibility could be transferred to someone else, however—if he could cleanse his hands of blood—that would be a different matter.

At his urging, de Puebla had written Isabella and Ferdinand of Spain on his behalf several times during the past year asking for their advice on the matter of the Duke of York. He had hoped they would recommend that he be put to death. In that case, he could do so with a clear conscience, absolved of the sin, but they had ignored his inquiries on the matter, and worse, they had delayed sending their daughter, Katarina of Aragon, to England to wed Prince Arthur.

Now, at last, the Spanish ambassador had sent word that he wished to see him on a matter of vital importance. Nothing was more vital and important to him than the Spanish marriage—and the Pretender. As Henry waited for him to arrive, his heart hammered in his breast.

Voices sounded at the door as de Puebla was announced. Henry turned. The one-armed ambassador entered, and the door closed behind him. Henry watched him approach, his empty sleeve tucked neatly into the silver belt of his tunic. He inclined his head in greeting.

"Majesty, my sovereigns, Ferdinand and Isabella, have written you with the reply you have been awaiting."

Henry's heart raced as he accepted the rolled parchment de Puebla offered him. He unfurled the document, and bent his head. It was what he wanted to hear, yet he felt himself grow pale as he read. He looked up at de Puebla. "King Ferdinand and Queen Isabella state that the marriage cannot take place, and they cannot send their daughter to England, as long as the royal blood of the rival line survives in England," he said, lowering himself into a chair. They meant not just the Pretender. They also meant young Edward, Earl of Warwick. Orphaned by the age of three, he was now a young man of twenty-four. He had been a ward of the Woodville queen's relatives and they had mistreated him until they fell from power when he was nine. Henry had been obliged to imprison him in the Tower when he took the throne, and there he had remained. By all accounts he was a lonely and gentle soul, obedient to a fault. In mind, he was still an innocent, a child who couldn't tell a goose from a capon.

Henry put a hand up to his brow, and swallowed on the constriction in his throat. He gave a nod, and managed a wave of the hand. The door closed behind de Puebla.

He looked up at the sky with moist eyes, his heart aching. *O God, I don't want to do this! Let there be another way, I beseech you . . .*

* * *

Richard sat on his pallet, drinking wine from his battered tin cup, his eye on Long Roger and Thomas Astwood playing cards with his other two jailors by the flickering light of the candles. These two had offered to help him escape, and he had turned them down.

What was there to escape to? Catherine was lost to him, unmanned and unrecognizable as he was now. He had no hope of ever seeing Dickon again, and he was of no use to his aunt anymore. He downed another swallow of wine. He had long suspected these two of Yorkist sympathies, for Long Roger and Thomas had shown him kindness. Nevertheless, he was surprised that they would be willing to risk their lives again. Long Will had suffered in the Tower before he had received a pardon, and Thomas had nearly died on the gallows. In one of those dramatic gestures Henry liked to make, citing the boy's youth, he reprieved Thomas at the last minute as he stood with the rope around his neck, to the cheers of the crowd. No doubt Henry had smiled, thinking himself merciful in sparing this one life while taking hundreds of others.

Richard brought his cup of wine to his lips and was about to down another gulp when strange voices broke into his thoughts. He looked up. Long Roger, Strangeways, and the others had laid down their cards and stood conversing with another man whose face he could not see in the dim light. He edged closer and peered into the darkness. The voice sounded familiar.

"Aye, sir—" Long Roger said to him, turning to look at the others.

They all filed out as the man watched them leave. The door shut with a thud. There was a jangle of keys, and from the shadows a second man emerged. He was burly, with broad shoulders and bulging muscles. Richard recoiled, recognizing him as one of the ruffians who had broken his face. Shaking and limp with terror, he dropped his cup, splattering his wine. He scooted backward until he slammed against the wall, and looked on in horror as they unlocked his cell and entered.

"Have no fear, we're not here to do you harm," Digby said.

Richard could barely hear him. Digby's voice seemed to come to him from far away. He dragged his eyes to his face.

"I bring an offer from the king."

Richard could not speak, even if he had wanted to.

"I shall be blunt, since you are clearly uncomfortable with our presence. Below your chamber is that of Edward, Earl of Warwick.

For reasons of state, Warwick must die, and the king wishes you to help bring about his demise."

Richard found his voice then. "You're mad! I will never do such a thing!"

"You haven't heard the offer the king makes you."

"What can he offer me that is worth having anymore?"

"The life of your son," Digby said quietly.

Richard gasped.

"He is offering you the life of your son, in return for the life of the Earl of Warwick. If you do not do this, your son will die."

Richard stared at him, scarcely breathing, his heart pounding. "What kind of a monster makes such an offer? My son is not yet three years old. Warwick is still a child at twenty-four!"

"I will not tolerate any more insults to my king. Make no mistake about it, you and Warwick are going to die, the only question that remains is how."

Digby's words fell on Richard like burning stones. How many times had he prayed for death in the nearly two years since his capture? How many times had he lamented that he fled death at Taunton? Yet now, as sentence of death was pronounced on him, he knew he still wanted to live. *To live!*

"You will ensure the life of your son by getting Warwick to agree to escape the Tower with you."

"I know not if my son is even alive."

"We are prepared to prove to you that he is."

A long-forgotten pang of joy came and went. "How?"

"We will bring him to you."

O Almighty Father—to see my son one last time! To know he lives— to kiss his sweet face—to hear him laugh—Dickon, who wouldn't know and didn't care that he was deformed—

Digby was waiting.

"What would I have to do?"

"If you agree, a hole will be bored in the corner of this chamber so you can speak with Warwick. You will lay out your plans. Whatever you need will be brought to you. You will escape, and before you leave the Tower premises, you will be caught. You will go to your death at Tyburn."

Richard put a hand to his roaring head. "Tyburn," he echoed, barely aware that he spoke.

"If you do this, the king is prepared to be merciful. Death by hanging, instead of evisceration. But for that, you must comply in one more respect."

Richard dropped his hand. He couldn't see Digby and the rogue with him; he had trouble with his vision. He wanted them gone. The words they spoke made him feel sick to the pit of his stomach, but these men were the only earthly link with his child, and he wanted to see his boy.

"In return for the commutation of your sentence, before you die at Tyburn, you will confess again that you are not the son of King Edward IV."

Richard was silent for a long while. At length, he lifted his head and looked at them. "When I see my son, I will give you my answer."

* * *

Richard drank all night on the eve of his execution. He needed courage, and thankfully, his guards did not deny him the wine to blur reality. The next morning, fortified and somewhat inebriated, he confessed his sins to the priest they sent, chief among these his involvement in convicting poor, innocent Warwick of treason. All else he had done in his life paled in comparison to this, the greatest of his sins. Whatever misery this day wrought, he hoped it would help him atone in God's eyes for bearing false witness against an innocent.

He stood calmly, bare-legged and clad only in a white knee-length shirt of the condemned as his hands were bound with rope. Someone threw a blanket around his shoulders and his captors led him down to the boat that would take him to his death. For fear that Yorkist sympathizers might mount an escape effort during the four-mile journey from the Tower to Tyburn, Henry had wished Richard to make the longest part of his journey by river, but he was not to be permitted to sit, for the crowds needed to see him. Standing up in the small craft, surrounded by boatloads of armed men, they pushed away from the shore. Each time the vessel lurched, Richard lost his footing and almost fell, to the amusement of his guards. "Can ye swim, Perkin?" they would ask, and then answer their own question: "He's a boatman's son, ain't he?" and they'd burst into riotous laughter.

Richard ignored them. He wanted to savor his last look at the world he was leaving behind in the springtime of his life, and never had it looked more beautiful. It was the twenty-third of November, 1499. On this day four years ago he had met Catherine at Stirling Castle. A light snow had fallen during the night and London shimmered in the morning sunshine. A line came to him, *Like snow in the river, for a moment white—then melted and gone forever.* Life was like that, glistening one moment; vanished in the next.

The bells of St. Paul's pealed for terce and were echoed across the city like a bright melody. So they had chimed when he had held Dickon in his arms, filling his heart with joy. His son was three years old and came into his cell holding Digby's hand, a sight that so wounded him, he had to avert his gaze.

"May I have time with my child alone?" Richard had asked, and Digby, to his credit, had allowed him that.

"Little one, come to me—fear not—aye, that's it, that's it—" Richard had murmured to his wide-eyed little boy when they were alone together. There was a knot in his throat as he watched Dickon close the gap between them with wobbly steps. "May I hold you in my arms? May I kiss you?" Dickon gave him a nod, and Richard scooped him up and laid his head against the child's soft hair, his tender cheek. He closed his eyes, overcome with the sweetness of him, and rocked with him back and forth. He released him from the cradle of his arms and took his child's face into his hands. "Dickon, we have not much time, and I know you do not remember me, but I have to tell you something—something important—something I want you to try and never forget—"

The child stared at him with eyes that reminded him of his

own as they had once been. "Dickon, I want you to remember that your father and your mother love you very, very much. Do you understand?"

The child nodded solemnly.

"I know that because I am your father, Dickon, and I love you more than life itself—"

There was a commotion at the door and Digby came in with a man-at-arms. Richard's heart pounded in his chest—so soon! He'd barely had a minute—

The key jangled in the lock. Richard bent his head to Dickon's ear. "Remember, my son—"

With tears blinding his sight and grief rending his heart, Richard had surrendered his boy to the men who came to take him away.

Richard looked up at the blue sky as the boat cut across the waves. He inhaled deep of the cold morning air. He had seen his son. He had saved his life. To do it, he'd given up his own, and also offered Warwick's. The simple young man had been like butter in his hands and had agreed to escape with him from the Tower, though it was clear Warwick did not understand why he should flee, and only assented to please his new friend. He was a sweet and gentle lad, and when Richard recounted his sorrows, he had tried to comfort him. Comfort him—he, Richard, the vile betrayer! He could hear Edward's voice in the wind speaking through the hole bored in the vaulting, "How goes it with you, Cousin Richard? Be of good cheer. All will be well."

Richard turned his gaze to the riverbank. The only aspect that spoiled God's creation, he thought, was man, and he himself was no exception. He should die, and he should suffer, both in this world, and in the next. He had much to answer for.

Wherever he looked, crowds of people hugged the shore, some jostling one another, others standing waist deep in the icy water to gain a better view. Across the river they hurled stones at him and cupped their mouths to bellow insults. London Bridge loomed ahead, swarming with ravens. He could hear their ugly cawing as they stood atop human heads and pecked out bits of rancid flesh.

He closed his eyes. They would be feasting on his soon enough. A gust of wind blew, banishing the stink in his nostrils. How he had missed the touch of the wind on his face; the smell of the river; the cry of the gulls! So had it been on the deck of the *Cuckoo,* when he'd stood with his arm around Catherine, gazing at St. Michael's Mount taking shape before them. All things had seemed possible then, but he had lost the throw before he had even cast the dice. He found it strangely fitting that the gamble he had put in motion by water should end by water. Perhaps, he thought, it was Fate's last jest, her way of bidding him farewell.

The boat changed direction. He opened his eyes to see Westminster Palace drawing near.

"You'll be transported by cart from here," Digby said, "to Tyburn."

Tyburn, where common criminals are butchered. Richard didn't bother to acknowledge him. He was preparing to meet his Maker and his mind was already beyond the reach of the world of men. He climbed meekly out on the dock and looked up at the Palace. Catherine was at Windsor, not here; there would be no farewell, and her beloved face would not be in the crowd. Not that he wanted her to see his ugly end, but his heart ached that he would never see her again on this earth. How different England would have been had he been allowed to rule. Kinder, gentler, in many ways. Full of music, instead of terror. But God had judged, and it was not to be.

Richard climbed into the cart. He tried as best he could to keep his balance as it rattled its way to Tyburn, bearing him along, his bevy of armed guards riding at his side. He wondered vaguely what it would feel like to be hanged. He had heard his jailors talking. If a man was lucky, they said, he broke his neck as soon as he fell, and death was quick. But if he wasn't, death came by slow suffocation, and men gasped and gagged and turned red, their mouths opening and shutting like a dying fish until they choked. That could take as long as an hour.

They turned into Tyburn Lane. On this day, a Saturday, he would meet his doom. Henry had always regarded Saturday as his lucky day. Richard allowed himself a faint smile. Why did a king need to hang a boatman's son on his lucky day? Did anyone wonder?

His execution on the Feast Day of Saint Clement, the first pope, meant that everyone could attend, and the crowds, held back by wooden barriers, were thick, lining both sides of the streets west to Tyburn. So many had come that, in some places, they were slammed up against the doorways of the squalid, tottering houses and taverns that populated this area of Middlesex. They booed and threw rotted stuff at him, and often landed a blow, like the wormy apple that had struck him on the cheek, and the piece of stinking pig intestine that had landed at his feet, fouling the cart.

The village of Tyburn drew into view. A special scaffold had been erected to raise him high above the crowd. Etched against the blue sky, the noose hung waiting. Digby helped him dismount and led him to a crude staircase. But light-headed with wine, his hands tied, his legs blue and almost numb from cold in his thin shirt, he could scarcely manage the climb and a guard had to help push him up each step. When he reached the platform, the executioner placed the noose around his neck. The rough hemp scratched his skin. A silence fell. He scanned the faces around him, and saw that Kate's husband, William Courtenay, was there, richly clad and riding the war-horse he remembered from Exeter. Far more humble mounts bore the Spanish ambassador and an alderman and chronicler of London named Robert Fabyan, whom he had met in passing at court. Their expressions were impassive, yet strangely, he sensed sympathy from all three. In the crowd, not all were hostile. Some had been weeping, and all their faces were upturned to him. He thought of a field of sunflowers gazing at the sun.

It was time, and he was prepared.

With the salvation of his soul hanging in the balance, he was ready to confess the truth. The words he would use were the ones that he had used in the Chapel of St. John; they had worked with Henry then, and they would work now. They would save his body from being cut down alive from the gibbet, butchered, and eviscerated, with his bloody entrails burned before his eyes. They would save his immortal soul. And they would save the life of his only child.

King James's words rang in his ears: *Far from recognizing you as their king, they don't even see you as an Englishman!* That was what counted in the end, wasn't it? To his people he was, and would remain forever, a foreigner, and if Henry was successful, a false prince. He braced himself, and spoke.

"I stand by my former confession that I was never the person I said I was, and that I came to the shores of England a stranger." He did not lie. Each would hear in his words what they wanted to hear—what the Tudor willed them to believe—that he was not the son of his father, King Edward. Few would ever suspect the truth he meant: *I never was Perkin Warbeck, and I never was an Englishman, for the people of the land of my birth rejected me.* Even fewer would wonder why he who was not born an English subject should die a traitor's death for treason to an English king. He lifted his eyes to the November sky and murmured Christ's last prayer on the cross: *In manus Tuas, Domine, commendo spiritum meum*—

The executioner released the trapdoor beneath his feet.

A shattering pain shot through him, and he felt as if his head would burst from the burning in his ears and the blood that gagged his mouth. He tried to cough it out or swallow, but he couldn't. As suffering invaded every pore of his body, he was back on the table in the Tower, writhing and shivering. *No—help me, Jesus! I am not brave or strong—I pray you, take me from this place—* And all at once he was on the beach at Loch Lomond, laughing and running along the sand, and Catherine was stealing backward glances at him as he followed in her footsteps, his pants rolled up to his knees. He caught her and they fell down together in the water, wrapped in one another's arms, and he felt the heat and the joy of her body. *Catherine, how I love you*—he said, but he was not with Catherine any longer. He was with his uncle's man, Edward Brampton, and he was ten years old on a stormy sea, and Brampton was at the helm, drenched to the skin, yelling for all hands on deck, and the wind was whipping the sails, and the ship was tossing and groaning in the roaring waters, the great lantern swinging wildly. In its narrow illumination he saw with horror that the black sea had turned white with foam, and he was thinking they were going to die—

But they didn't die, for Aunt Meg smiled at him in her green velvet–draped study, and opened her arms wide to receive him, and he ran into them and she held him tight against her breast, and he felt a warmth such as he had never known before in life, and the wet of her tears fell against his face when he looked up at her. "My dear darling—you are safe—you have come back to me—my beloved, darling little White Rose—"

He saw himself going through the wicket gate in Picardy and someone was calling, *Pierrequin, come to the river!* and someone else was jangling a set of keys as he watched his foster-father, Jehan, standing in a rocking boat, loading sacks of flour. But instead of the river, he was in Brabant, riding beside his friend, Philip the Handsome, and the streets were hung with tapestries and silks, and horns were playing. Like a king, he was passing out the silver coins that Aunt Meg had minted for him in Flanders, bearing his image with the words *King Richard IV* on one side, and *O Mater Dei, memento mei* on the other. Remember me, O Mother of God—and Catherine was examining one in her palm, and smiling at him. "May I keep this as a memento, my love?" Before he could reply, he was a small child again, being wed to a little girl, and he was marveling at a lion someone had brought him as a gift, and one of his uncles, clad in black velvet, was jousting at his wedding. Then there was more black, and he was at the funeral of the little girl he'd kissed at the altar. He fled, and peeking through an open door, he saw the damask hangings of his royal bedchamber and a page dragging a dog away by its studded collar. He opened his eyes to object. A black shape turned to look at him. *Let him stay,* he cried, gasping for air; *he is my friend—*

But the black shape made no move to obey, and he closed his eyes again. Now he was with King James in the tent where they had written out their agreement before their invasion of England. "You must give me Berwick," King James was saying, and he heard himself reply, "My country needs it more." Choking and gasping for air, he opened his eyes again and the scene around him swam dizzily before him. Faces stared up at him, silent, immobile, a tableau frozen in time, and then it was night, and he was in Artois, and before him stretched another multitude come to celebrate a great feast day, each carrying a candle in their hand, and they seemed to him a burning sea of light beneath the starry sky.

Catryn, see that star, it is my star—And Catherine's face rose before him, radiant with joy. *I will always love you, Richard.* She turned to smile at him, and she was in her wedding dress, and Dickon was at her shoulder. His son put out his arms to him with a shriek of delight and pushed away from his mother to come to him, and Catherine laughed, and he laughed with her. *O Catryn, you have been my joy on this earth.*

The executioner standing beside the gallows looked up. The prisoner's murmurings and little gasping movements had ceased and his lips had turned blue. Silence reigned. His soul had departed to God.

He took out his dagger and moved to cut down the body. It had taken a full hour for Perkin Warbeck to die, and never before in twenty years had he seen a hanged man endure his death agony so calmly, without a struggle. That took courage, and they had said he was a coward. But then, they had said a lot of things about this man.

PART II

1502–1526
A Rose for All Seasons

Chapter 16

Mirror of the Mind

1502

When Catherine awoke each morning since Richard's death, for a drowsy moment she was at St. Michael's Mount and the gulls were crying, and the surf was pounding and Richard was stirring at her side. She had no illusions. Richard was dead. But his ghost haunted the great hall, and from the castle passageways and the palace gardens, she saw him smile at her with his brilliant blue eyes, while every evening she felt his presence in the shadows of dusk.

She found it strange that she shed no tears, and attributed this to the soothing sense of his presence. He felt so close to her that she communed with him each day. Sometimes she withdrew into that secret place in her mind where she lived in another time and another place, when Richard had been alive and there had been laughter and smiles. When memories of the past failed to comfort, she laid Dickon's coif against her cheek, drank in his sweet scent, and moved into the future, into that shining spot where, one day, she would once again enfold her child in her arms.

She had been afraid that time would erase her memory of Richard's face but that fear was gone, thanks to the queen, who had stolen Richard's portrait for her from the king. It had been made for

Henry by his spies in Scotland. "He will think his monkey ate it, just as he ate his memorandum book." Elizabeth had smiled as they sat together shrouded in mist one cold afternoon at the river's edge.

Seated on the same bench at Windsor in the first week of April 1502, Catherine fingered the portrait that was hidden between the pages of a Book of Hours, and smiled up at Richard, who she knew was somewhere behind the glorious curtain of the sunrise that drenched the water with gold at her feet. Strangely, her memory of the day of his death and the immediate aftermath remained dim; she recalled only the few hours of that terrible morning when a great weariness had weighed her down, as if she wore the same metal chains that had shackled Richard's limbs.

On the morning of his execution she had stolen away deep into the snowy woods of Windsor, and sat down by a brook edged with half-melted snow. The trees, covered with ice, had sparkled with bridal beauty in the sunlight, and the sky was as turquoise as Richard's eyes had been. "I won't let you be dead, Richard," she had promised him, calling out to the sky, the earth, the water. "I will keep you alive for as long as I live, my beloved—"

And she had.

She told him everything as it happened. How Edward, Earl of Warwick, was beheaded at the Tower, five days after Richard had died, with no one to weep for him except Heaven, and how Heaven had sent down howling winds and torrents of rain to drench the land and swell the river over its banks as soon as his head was severed from his body. Even Henry knew that Heaven was displeased, for his mental anguish was such that he aged twenty years within weeks of the executions. Catherine told Richard how Kate's husband, William Courtenay, and the Spanish ambassador, de Puebla, who had witnessed both deaths, had been overwrought after Richard's execution, and refused to talk about it. "They said you died bravely, that is all they would say, Richard," she had told him, knowing that would please him. "So bravely, my love."

She told him how, for weeks afterward, white roses had appeared around her, sometimes on her pillow at night; sometimes in the spot where they used to stand together in the great hall. Sometimes they were flung over hedges into her path as she strolled in the garden, or through an open window to land at her feet. "Once a dove brought a white rosebud to my windowsill," she said, smiling at him in the sky. "There were many who loved you, Richard, but they were afraid."

She told him that his grieving Aunt Meg had kept a room for him at Binche, and celebrated mass for him every day. On the first anniversary of his execution in 1500, she spent three times the usual sum to burn candles in her chapel.

She had told him how the queen banished her husband from her bed after the executions. "She knew you were her brother, and wanted to save you, but there was nothing she could do," she had explained. "And Henry fell so ill within the month after you died that his death was expected, and the succession was murmured. Whether from conscience, or to appease God for his regicide, he had you buried at the Church of the Austin Friars on Broad Street, where executed nobles are buried, not at All Hallows on Bread Street where commoners are interred. He knows what he did, Richard . . . He knows who you were."

And she gave him joyous news about his sister, Cecily, who had fled court after the death of her husband, Viscount Welles, and married Thomas Kymbe on the Isle of Wight, surrendering all her estates and titles for the obscure country squire she had loved as a girl in sanctuary. "She writes me of her happiness," Catherine had told Richard, turning her face up to Heaven. "She says it is because of us that she did it. Because of us, Richard—"

Across London, bells pealed for prime. She stirred from her reverie. She might miss Richard and need her visits into the past; she might cry out to him now, and hear him crying out to her in her mind, but there was one thing she could not deny. There was no going back. She was going forward, to Dickon.

"You've made a habit of living in the past, but you're not dead," said a voice behind her.

She turned with a start.

"You have a life before you, God willing, a long one. Live it,"

James Strangeways said. He stood looking down at her, his dark hair ruffled by the breeze, his dark eyes holding hers. He was a massive, self-confident presence in black and silver, and she resented every inch of him.

She rose angrily. "How dare you speak to me in this fashion! Who do you think you are?"

"A friend."

She was so breathless with fury at this intrusion on her privacy that she could find no voice to answer. He was right, of course. She could not reclaim the past, and there was no guarantee she would be able to shape her future and find her child. The present was all she really had, and she chose to reject it. She opened her mouth to retort in anger, then shut it again, flooded with remembrance of his many kindnesses since Richard's death.

Shortly before the execution, he'd offered to take Richard a message from her. "No one can get through the guards the king has set upon him in the Tower. How can you?" she'd demanded with the suspicion that came so naturally to her since her arrival at the Tudor court. "I cannot tell you that," he'd replied. "Not because I don't wish to but because I cannot endanger the one I shall ask for the favor. You will have to trust me." Catherine had regarded him with disgust and asked, "Did the king put you up to this?" "The king would no doubt have my head if he knew," Strangeways had replied. Despite the impishness that stole into his smile, she knew he spoke the truth. He was putting himself at risk for her—she didn't know why, and she didn't care. It was enough that he would serve her needs at this moment. She'd given him her message, and he'd brought the one Richard sent back. The last she would exchange with her beloved on this earth.

"This world has been my prison and I do not regret to be leaving, my beloved Catryn," Richard had written. "As I prepare to meet my Maker, I return to you the token you gave me for good luck. One day I will see you again, my Celtic princess, and we shall be reunited. Until that day comes, think me not gone, for I will always be with you and Dickon. Remember your promise to me at St. Michael's Mount."

Catherine had stared at the tiny silver coin stamped with Richard's image, the one she had given him at the Tower before his escape. *King Richard IV*, it proclaimed on one side. She had turned it over in her palm. *Remember me, O Mother of God,* said the inscription on the back.

Remember me ...

She had squeezed the coin in her hand and closed her eyes on the pain.

Strangeways's kindness had not ended there.

On that first Yuletide following Richard's death in 1499, in despair and forsaken by God who was deaf to her pleas, she had sought refuge in the garden at Windsor. All she had to sustain her were the few treasures of her past: the gold locket of diamond fleur-de-lis, Richard's love letter, his silver groat and portrait, their babe's little coif—and hope. Hope that her son lived, that one day she would see him again. If that day came, it would mean that Richard had not died in vain and that she did not live in vain. But what if it didn't come? What if this suffering were for naught? Such had been her thoughts when Strangeways found her hidden in the shrubbery. He had fallen to a knee before her. "Pray accept my condolences," he'd said, his voice surprisingly gentle for such a powerful man. "I cannot pretend to know how hard this Yuletide is for you, but I know it must be frightening to find yourself as alone as you are, far from kin and kith and everything familiar at this time of year when others make merry with those they love." He had laid in her lap a sprig of holly that was covered with fresh snow, its red berries glistening. "You need a friend at court, my lady. Everyone does. I beg you to think of me as one."

"No one is my friend," Catherine had replied.

"You are mistaken. Many would be your friend, if you'd but permit them."

She had lifted her head and looked at him then. Gone was the mocking grin that she had detested, and the bold look in his eyes that earlier had offended her so deeply. Since the day she'd refused the king's gift of a gown, respect and concern had crept into his attitude toward her, along with a deference that she knew owed nothing to the gulf of their births: she as a royal and he as a commoner. His deference was to her suffering, and to Richard's.

Later, Strangeways had escorted her to Richard's grave at the Austin Friars. Henry had left it unmarked, perhaps to save money on the engraving, as he had done with King Richard, or perhaps to prevent the grave from becoming a shrine. And perhaps for both reasons. The Austin Friars was where executed nobility was buried; where dukes, and earls, and knights were interred. Henry had granted Richard that one small boon in death, expecting no one to notice.

Aye, James Strangeways had proved himself a friend, and she owed him the courtesy of one.

"You are never to take such liberty with me again," she said with a toss of her head.

* * *

As soon as Catherine stepped into the palace, she knew something was wrong. Pandemonium had broken out and courtiers, servants, and men-at-arms rushed about in a state of alarm. She stopped one of them. "What's happened?"

"Prince Arthur—he's dead!"

"Dead? What—how—" cried Catherine.

"No one knows—'twas sudden—my lady, I must go!"

Catherine reeled. She turned and rushed up the tower stairs. She had to get to the queen!

The rooms were crowded with the stunned faces of Elizabeth's ladies-in-waiting. She ran past them to the royal bedchamber and pulled up short at the threshold. Elizabeth had collapsed on the floor in a frenzy of grief, crying out for her boy. "Arthur—Arthur—O God—O God . . ." she sobbed, her body heaving. A priest knelt on the floor beside her, murmuring soothing words she didn't seem to hear. Catherine watched in pity. How well she remembered— She heard herself say, "Is there nothing that can be done?" and knew the answer even as she spoke: Nothing.

Lady Daubeney said, "We've sent for the king."

Catherine turned away.

* * *

Events moved rapidly after that fateful day in April 1502. Fifteen-year-old Prince Arthur was buried at Worcester Cathedral barely five months after his wedding to the Spanish princess. His young widow arrived from Wales soon afterward, her future in disarray. Henry didn't wish to send her back to Spain, since to do so would require him to return her dowry, so she hovered at court, huddling miserably with her ladies, cutting almost as lonely a figure as Catherine, for few spoke Spanish, and she spoke no other language but Latin. While Arthur's devastated parents grieved in seclusion, eleven-year-old Prince Harry, the only member of the family not mourning Arthur's death, paid court to her and wrote sonnets and poems for her amusement. Sometimes Catherine heard them laughing together. "Fret not, Katherine," young Harry would comfort her, "I shall be king now, and marry you, and you shall be Queen of England. Would you like that, Katherine?" To which she always responded, *"Es cierto, mi príncipe galan."* Truly, my charming prince.

From the window where she used to stand with Richard, Catherine's gaze went to Katherine. The Spanish princess was desperately homesick and unhappy and well Catherine knew how lonely she must be. Each woman had lost her country and her husband both. But she found herself devoid of sympathy. It was for Katherine's royal marriage that Richard and Edward had died.

With Arthur gone, it was Harry who sat with Katherine on the grass. Strange, how Arthur had died so suddenly, and at Easter, too. The English throne had claimed yet another royal at Easter, for Elizabeth's father, King Edward IV, had died at Easter in 1483; and it was at Easter exactly a year later that King Richard's only son and heir died. *Poisoned*, so it was rumored. Now Arthur was taken in April, by who knew what means and what hand? Six months before his death, that worm, John Skelton, had predicted Harry would be king. Only one way could that happen—and it had. For his prophecy and the dedication of his treatise, *How to Rule*, to Prince Harry, the king had sent Skelton to the Tower. A smile lit Catherine's lips at the thought.

She turned away from the window, aware of approaching footsteps. James Strangeways gave her a deep bow.

"I have brought you some items, my lady," he said, handing her a small wooden box.

She removed the velvet cloth cover to reveal the contents. Some yardage of black silk ribbon; a few embroidery needles; a small dagger; and a collection of fine yarn in different hues of red to pink.

"I am leaving this afternoon on the king's business, and will be passing Fleet Street. Should there be anything else you need, I can stop and pick them up for you. Or perhaps, you would like to accompany me?" He regarded her hopefully.

She looked up at Strangeways, remembering the secret he had confided to her on the riverbank at Windsor two years after Richard's death. First, however, he'd required her to take an oath on the Bible, swearing never to impart it to anyone. Then he had revealed that Dickon had been brought to London to see Richard at the Tower, and had given her the reason. Her legs could scarcely maintain her when she heard his words and she had collapsed on a bench. Strangeways, mistaking her tears for sorrow, had tried to soothe her until she'd lifted her face to his and he saw the tremulous joy that lit her features. "My babe lives," she'd murmured in an awed whisper. Not only had Richard seen Dickon—not only had Richard been allowed this one grace—but now she knew their babe lived!

Dickon, her beautiful boy, still lived!

"Where—" She could not form another word, but Strangeways had understood. "Wales," he'd replied. "I have family in Wales. I shall visit them, and make inquiries." Now her dream had a name. *Wales.* And Strangeways had connections in Wales.

He spoke again, jolting her back into the present.

"You are departing for Wales with the queen in a few days, and this may be the last time I can take you to the Fleet before you go."

Wales, she thought, savoring the sound of the word. She looked at him as he stood before her, and realized that he'd mistaken her silence for refusal. "I shall be happy to accompany you to the Fleet. Perhaps you can also find a way to come to Wales?" she said with a meaningful look. "Wales is very beautiful, so I hear."

"Indeed, it is. I shall try my best, my lady."

Gratitude warmed her heart.

*   *   *

After an abstinence of three years that she had imposed following the execution of her kin, Queen Elizabeth was with child again, for she had taken Henry back into her bed after Arthur's death in April 1502. The babe would be born in February, the month of her own birth. The royal household had borne witness to her words to Henry. "We are still young," she had said. "We can have more children." And fertile as ever despite her thirty-six years, she lost no time conceiving a child.

But Catherine had no doubt as she moved about the royal chamber helping to dress the queen and prepare for their journey to Wales that Elizabeth would never recover from the loss of her firstborn son. The queen went through the motions of daily living like a waxen figure, unaware of this world, only of the next, and more and more she was to be found at her devotions. The child she had carried in her womb these four months brought her no smiles, and music wrung only tears. Patch failed to draw her laughter, and feasts failed to delight as she pushed a fork around her golden platter as if she didn't know what the instrument was for.

She will not survive long, Catherine thought, watching Lady Daubeney set the queen's gable headdress over her bound hair. A vision of herself after Richard's death flew into her mind. *I will never eat again; I will never sleep again,* she'd thought, but she did. Had she ever looked like the queen with eyes that held the dazed look of pain, like an animal dying in a trap? Elizabeth was as fragile as a precious crystal figurine that one feared to touch lest it shatter in one's hand. Somehow Catherine had survived the loss of her son, for she had hope to cling to. But Elizabeth had no such hope. What little joy had been hers in marriage had come from Arthur, and now he was gone.

Catherine watched her make her way to her prie-dieu, as was her custom before leaving her chamber to attend her royal duties. Her eyes went to the Book of Hours Elizabeth carried. She had sent her one just like it after Richard's death; indeed, she sent anyone suffering a loss the same gift, expecting them to find the comfort there that she did. But Catherine had barely touched hers. She drew her solace from nature, where the hand of man was unseen. There she communed with Richard and watched the butterflies and beautiful birds, especially white ones, for they made her think of a white rose whenever she saw one flit across the palace gardens. At night, she worked on her embroidery. The tapestry that depicted Hell now wrapped nearly one half turn around her kirtle, and would go on endlessly thickening as the years passed. For the artwork that gathered in her skirts served to cushion her like armor, reminding her daily of the dark depths she had trawled. And survived. She had borne the worst that could ever happen. She could bear anything now.

* * *

The journey to Ludlow proved slow and ponderous, for the queen was unable to travel far in a day. Their accommodations were the best that abbeys, castles, and wealthy subjects could provide, but Catherine found herself too anxious to sleep. She was going to Wales, and Wales was where Dickon was.

As they rode along, Catherine watched Elizabeth. She was the golden-haired Tudor queen instead of the raven-haired Plantagenet queen Catherine would have made. Like her own child, Elizabeth's first son was conceived out of wedlock at Yuletide; like her own, he was born in September. Instead of her own, he had been heir to the throne. Now both the queen and the captive, united by marriage as sisters, but not daring to embrace as such, mourned their firstborn children on a pilgrimage to the place that had devoured them. Elizabeth's marriage had been unhappy and brought her a stream of losses, and many whom she had loved were now gone forever. Catherine's own marriage had been the happiest this world could bestow, and yet it, too, had brought suffering and woe. Death had stalked them both for so long, no doubt it seemed an old friend to Elizabeth, just as it did to Catherine. Like her, Elizabeth felt abandoned by God. Her motto, *Humble and Reverent,* came from a treasured book of an Augustinian friar named Walter Hilton, who died in 1396. "Wise and well-grounded is the lover of God who behaves himself humbly and reverently," he had written, "and who remains patient and calm, without despair and bitterness, when He is absent."

Absent, indeed. Arthur had been Elizabeth's hope, and God had taken him from her. Catherine marveled that Elizabeth, weary with the weariness that comes when hope is gone, could still find comfort in Him who had deserted her. *I may not have God*, Catherine thought, *but I still have my Dickon.*

So ran her thoughts as she trotted her palfrey to Ludlow beside the queen, crushing the drifting leaves of autumn underfoot.

In Tewkesbury, she was pleasantly surprised to see James Strangeways and a party of the king's horses riding toward them.

"My lady queen," said Strangeways, "we have received instructions from King Henry to accompany you to Ludlow."

"It contents us much to have your company, but we hope it does not inconvenience you, since you had hoped to return to London long before now," Elizabeth replied graciously.

"Quite the contrary, Majesty. We are delighted to be charged with this task." Strangeways's dark eyes sought out Catherine as he spoke.

Soon Catherine found him riding at her side. "How do you feel now that you are close to Wales?" he inquired.

"What is it like there?" If she could know more about the place, know what kind of skies Dickon saw when he woke up in the morning, what the ground was like that he played on, it might help her feel closer to him. She bit down hard, flooded by a sudden torrent of emotion that she held back by will alone. If her resolve ever broke, she knew she would weep forever.

But Strangeways was not to let her off easily. "It surprises me that you are not happy to see Wales."

"It is my fault he is in Wales," Catherine said in a choked whisper. She felt his stare.

"No, it's not. There are things in this world beyond our control. We try to blame ourselves to make sense of them."

Again, Catherine turned her gaze on him in gratitude.

* * *

They crossed into Wales, and immediately the sea of undulating meadows and lines of tall poplars gave way to the rugged terrain of gorge and thistle, cliffs and rocky rivers, and a succession of border strongholds and mountain ranges that soared and dipped across the horizon. There was a wildness to the place that lifted her heart, for it made her think of Scotland, and of home, and of her father, who had died the previous year, and whom she missed more now that he was gone from this earth than ever before.

Bells were pealing for evensong when they arrived at Ludlow. They were met by an entourage of officers led by the constable of the castle, a man of stature and noble bearing dressed in a blue velvet doublet with hanging sleeves, high boots, and a fur hat with a large feather. He introduced himself as Matthew Cradock and gave an eloquent welcome to the royal party. An instant liking ran through Catherine at the sight of him and she felt a strange connection, as though she'd known him before. Like her father, there was an air of command about him, but also a courtly refinement. He was older, with sandy hair flecked with silver, but handsome. His eyes were as blue as the thistle she had picked as a child, and there was a chivalry about him that reminded her of Richard and brought to mind the knights of the Arthurian romances. He turned around to look directly at her, and she averted her gaze with a blush. She had been staring.

They dined elaborately that evening on boiled wheat in venison, cured tongue, roasted swans and herons covered with their own feathers as in life, and for dessert, tarts, cheese fritters, and quince dumplings. But peace did not find Catherine that night as she lay on her featherbed. *Nor would it find the queen in this place*, she thought, turning her eyes to the window that stood open to the frosty stars. *Both our sons were born in this month, and here in this castle Elizabeth's took his last breath. And somewhere out there, I pray my little one is celebrating his sixth birthday.*

*   *   *

After two weeks in Wales, the queen decided to return to London. She was ailing and the pilgrimage had not helped her grief, nor had all the prayers she had murmured in the chapels and churches and cathedrals of Wales. Her son was gone, leaving behind no trace but her broken heart.

At Westminster, it was the same. Except for one thing. Cecily came to visit. Catherine ran to take her into her arms, laughing and teary-eyed at the same time.

"Cecily, Cecily! I have missed you so! How is married life? How do you like the Isle of Wight? How long will you be here—" The questions were endless, and never in many long years had her heart felt so light. Cecily was the only one who could make her smile. She was a sister. The two women linked arms and went into the garden, taking care to steer toward a secluded corner.

"Tell me—tell me everything—are you happy?"

Cecily grabbed both of Catherine's hands into her own. "Oh, Catherine, you were right—I am so happy—deliriously happy—if I were a bird, I would burst into song! Never did I know what happiness was until I married Thomas!"

"You didn't last long in widow's weeds," Catherine smiled, admiring her green velvet gown with a plunging neckline.

"Frankly, I know not how you do it, Catherine. I hated looking like an ugly crow." Quickly, so as not to offend, she added, "But you're so pretty, you give black an allure."

"No need to temper your words. I wear black because I choose to." She remembered her promise to Richard at St. Michael's Mount to find happiness. Impossible then, she thought; and impossible now. Maybe one day, when her child was restored to her, she could fling away the mourning gowns.

"Oh, Catherine, thank you for making me understand love! For making me see what I was missing. You and Ri—"

Catherine placed a warning finger to her lips. Nearly four years after his death, it was still not safe to speak Richard's name. *Maybe in a thousand years*, she thought sadly, *but not now*. "I am glad, Cecily. No one deserves to be loved more than you."

"Oh, I can think of others more deserving—but not one who enjoys it nearly as much as I!" She winked, leaving no doubt that she meant the bed sport. Into Catherine's mind flashed Richard, sweeping her into his powerful arms, passion written all over his face. For an instant she felt a surge of desire; then it was gone, and she was back in the present. "I miss that so much. It's like a giant emptiness inside me that nothing can fill. But love has cost you much, Cecily. I hope it makes up for the deprivations you have known since the king confiscated all your property."

"Oh, we are as poor as church mice, but I care not, Catherine! I care not! I had to borrow to make this trip, we are so poor—" She laughed. "I could use some money. I came for Elizabeth's sake, of course, but I hope to weasel some of my lands back from Henry. For soon there will be another mouth to feed."

"Another mouth?" Catherine's joy for Cecily bubbled in her laugh as she clasped her friend and held her close. So pure was her happiness that anyone watching would have found difficulty declaring with certainty which one of them imparted happy tidings, and which received it.

Cecily's merry eyes grew thoughtful as they rested on Catherine. "I just realized that never in all these years have I heard you laugh. You have a beautiful laugh, Catherine . . . Catherine, did you find anything in Wales?"

She swallowed hard. "No, nothing. But one day—"

Cecily gave a nod, and changed the subject. "I heard Strangeways came with you."

"He's been very kind. He takes me to visit Richard at the Austin Friars. The grave is unmarked. I would never have found it, but he knew where to go."

"He loves you, you know."

Catherine smiled. "Nonsense, Cecily. Why ever would you think that?"

"I saw it in his eyes when I was at court, and I've heard about it since I've returned."

"You're wrong. He's just a friend. He's never made an untoward remark."

"Of course not. He values his head, and he knows the king is watching."

The king. She had no desire to dwell on that unpleasant subject. "You've heard that your niece, Margaret, will marry King James?"

"Oh. When?"

"Henry wishes it to be immediately, but the queen deems twelve too young. She has extracted a promise from the king to wait until Margaret is fourteen before he sends her off. I have been instructing Princess Margaret on what to expect. She's learning the customs of the Scottish court, and our poetry, and our dances—and about James, of course, his likes and dislikes. She is fortunate to wed such a man."

"Once I would have been jealous," Cecily said. "But now I wish her well. Will you go with her to Scotland?"

"The king will not permit it. He has informed me that I will be accompanying her as far as Northamptonshire, and will take my leave there and return to London. But I look forward to seeing my cousin, Patrick Hepburn, the Earl of Bothwell. He will stand as proxy for King James in the marriage ceremony."

"Henry still loves you, Catherine, as desperately as ever. He's terrified you might leave him. If he lets you loose near the border, he's afraid you'll bolt for it."

Catherine did not answer. She was thinking how different she was from the girl who had left Scotland with Richard in search of adventure. She could never go back, not until she knew what had become of her son. That was all that mattered now.

"You are Henry's obsession. Even when you are not here, he speaks incessantly of his black swan."

She winced. Deep in her heart Catherine believed that Henry had made Richard suffer so brutally because of his passion for her. The thought haunted her.

"You are, you know . . . A black swan, gliding in dark waters, all alone."

Catherine dropped her gaze to Cecily's hand, clasping hers in her lap. *No one is your friend,* she had told herself so many times, and here was Cecily, a peerless friend.

"Not always alone," Catherine said softly. "Sometimes I hear Richard whisper to me . . . Sometimes I even feel the touch of his hand on my cheek. You think me mad. I've said too much—"

"Poppet, don't be silly. Go on, I beseech you. There is much I have experienced myself and cannot explain."

"It could merely be my imagination—I know not. 'Tis not exactly his voice I hear, you understand? Mostly it takes the form of coincidences. Some people pay not much heed to coincidences, but I see them as messages. They comfort me, and help me bear what I must. I'll be out in the garden, for example, and all at once everything rushes back in a torrent and the pain is unbearable, and at that moment, I'll hear a bird singing. I'll look up, and there's a warbler perched on a branch, as close as he can be to me, staring directly at me, pouring out his heart to me. And I'll think of Richard, that it's him, that he comes to comfort me. Or I'll say a prayer for Richard, and when I open my eyes, there is a white butterfly flitting around me, gliding the same speed as I am walking, first on my left, then on my right—as if to guide me, as if to kiss me . . ."

Cecily winced, thinking of his suffering at the Tower. "Dear Richard."

A silence fell.

In a low tone Catherine said, "And William Courtenay is sent to the Tower, and for naught but supping with his two de la Pole cousins on the night before they fled England." She gave a shudder, thinking of Kate's husband locked away in that dread place. Now that Henry had steeped his hands deep in royal blood with the murder of

Richard and Warwick, no one was safe. Certainly not the de la Pole brothers, who stood too near the throne for his comfort. It appeared they had good cause to flee since even William Courtenay fell under suspicion merely for breaking bread with them.

"I always blamed Elizabeth for what happened to us," Cecily resumed, "but I know now that I was wrong. It was never her fault. She did her best, and she suffers, too. She sacrificed her heart to unite the country. Arthur was her great hope, and her gift to England."

To banish memories that pressed too close, Catherine said, "What about that extra mouth—how will you manage?"

"I have a plan." A sparkle came into Cecily's eyes.

"Tell me—I promise not to tell a soul."

Cecily laughed. "Silly monkey—you have no one to tell even if you wanted to!"

"I have Henry," Catherine retorted.

Cecily burst into a flood of laughter. Then her voice sank to a whisper. "As I've said, I hope to get my lands restored to me—at least some of them. 'Tis one of the reasons I'm back."

"Good fortune to you. Once the king has his hands on money, he will move Heaven and Hell to keep it." Katherine of Aragon had come to England with great wealth, and now darned her clothes like the queen.

"You forget. The king has a mother."

"Who sues poor men for the small debts they owe and takes away their ploughs if they cannot pay. She even pursued a debt owed her great-grandfather a hundred years ago. What can you hope to squeeze out of her?"

"I know a secret!" she whispered coyly. "She loves love! She approves of what I did and would have done the same had she been in my place!"

"Fascinating! Do tell—"

"You know how she came to wed Edmund Tudor, don't you?"

"Something about a vision. I never paid attention."

"She was eleven years old and was told she had to wed the dull son of the Duke of Suffolk, but she wished to wed handsome Tudor instead. One night she had a vision. Saint Nicholas came to her and told her she had to wed Tudor." She smiled knowingly. "So she said."

"How very—blessed." Catherine was going to say *convenient,* but best to guard the tongue. Punishments often followed careless words, and a man who had called Margaret Beaufort "that strong whore" had paid for it with all his worldly goods. She doubted Cecily would have much fortune with the king's mother, but maybe the old cat wouldn't be able to resist her charms once she turned them on full force. "When is the babe due?"

"April."

"The queen's child is due in February."

Cecily's face grew somber. "I had not expected to find her so ill, Catherine. I fear Arthur's death will kill her. It takes great resolve to keep going in the face of such grief." Then she reached for Catherine's hand and gave her a squeeze, for no one had known more grief, or shown more resolve, than Catherine.

Chapter 17

A Rose in Winter

Elizabeth the queen died in 1503, on her thirty-seventh birthday, the eleventh day of February, giving birth to a daughter. Some said that death was God's loving gift to her, for her life had been naught but a chain of sorrows and heartbreak. Henry christened the babe Katherine, and she followed her mother to the grave three days later. Then he locked himself up to grieve, leaving instructions not to be disturbed for any reason.

Not only did Henry stagger beneath a stunned sense of loss, but also with the crush of remorse that comes from a suddenly awakened conscience. For the first time in his life he was regretting things he had done and things he had not done. To this was added a heavy superstitious fear. *I've killed her*, he thought, overcome with agony. *I never cared if she lived or died after she gave me my sons, and I wished her dead when I met Catherine. And God heard me, for now she is dead. Dead!*

The silent room pressed in on him heavily as he mulled his wine. With a quivering hand, he poured himself a full cup from the flask on the table, and drained it. Ah . . . that was better.

He had wronged Elizabeth dreadfully. He had married her coldly and used her coldly, and now he had killed her as surely as if he had thrust a dagger into her belly, for she had died giving birth to his eighth child. God would punish him for that, he was certain of it. Why had he not been kinder to her? She had always done what he wanted without argument, and she had never asked for much money but had made do with what little he had given her, even though it meant tin buckles on her shoes and wearing the same gown until it was too threadbare to be mended any longer.

He remembered how desperately she had pleaded for the life of two Stafford brothers she had known whom he had condemned to death at Tyburn for treason after Bosworth. He had granted half her wish, making her choose which one would live, and which would die. Yet she had never begrudged him the comfort of her companionship and the warmth of her bed—except when he executed her brother, Richard, and her cousin, Edward. How hard that had to be for her—both relatives dying in the same week! He ran a hand through his hair miserably. Trembling, he filled his cup again and emptied it once more, spilling more than he swallowed.

Even so, he could tell her anything and she would quiet his fears with her harp and her lute, and her beautiful voice. She'd always banished his cares, his fury, and his heartache with her compassion. She soothed him when the evil dreams came to poison his sleep, and cradled his head in her lap, murmuring gentle words that banished his sweat of terror. Now she was gone, and the calm with her. Now there was no one to turn to. Oh, there were flatterers aplenty at court to fan him, and there was still his mother to rely on, but she was as hard as he was, and he could not go to her in pain. Without Elizabeth, where was comfort in this cold, cruel world?

Oh, Elizabeth, forgive me . . . forgive me!

And then he looked out at the winter landscape, as desolate as his heart, and saw Catherine seated by the river.

* * *

Henry sent Catherine an elaborate new black gown with a fashionable plunging collar, flared sleeves, and cuffs trimmed with fur for his queen's funeral. On the final day of the ceremonies at the Abbey, Catherine performed the last act she would ever do for Elizabeth and laid the fourth of thirty-seven palls on her coffin, one for each year of her life. She received the long velvet cloth from Strangeways at the choir door, and as she took it from him, their eyes met, and something she couldn't explain passed between them. For an instant, she forgot the solemnity of the occasion and it was as if they were the only two in the world. She took the cloth from him, walked to the foot of the coffin, and made an obeisance. She kissed the pall and laid it over the coffin. As the words of the mass filled the chapel, Catherine bowed her head in prayer. *Forgive me, Elizabeth, for resenting you,* she entreated silently. *Forgive me for blaming you for not helping Richard. I know now that they kept you captive and nearly as helpless as he. Thank you for the sketch of him that you stole for me, and for the many kindnesses you did me in life. I shall cherish your memory always. May the peace that eluded you on earth find you now, and may you be reunited with all who you love . . . Bless you, Elizabeth, my dear sister.*

As she rose, her teary gaze fell on Henry's stiff, grieving figure standing erect, his face white and pinched in the gloomy light of Windsor Chapel. He held a dazed look, as if he didn't know where he was, or what was happening to him. For an instant, pity stirred her heart. In the space of a year, he had lost two pillars of his life: his favorite son and his queen, and soon his daughter, Margaret, too, would leave to wed King James, and never would they meet again.

He shifted in his chair and his gaze fell on her. Life flickered back into the empty eyes.

The day after the funeral a melancholy silence enfolded the castle. No one came or went, and no one made a sound. If they spoke, it was in whispers, and if they moved, it was on tiptoe. Deliveries stopped; there was no music, no proclamations, no bugles. Even children mysteriously disappeared from the palace, and hounds lay silent in the halls, their chins on their paws, their eyes mournful.

Catherine sat in a window seat in the empty great hall, listening to the cold wind that blew outside, and thinking how brief was life. She wanted to believe it was all for some purpose, that life mattered and God cared, but a deep apathy weighed her down, and the question seemed too burdensome for her weary mind.

A voice came at her shoulder. "My lady."

She turned from the window. Sir Charles Somerset, captain of the king's guard, gave her a bow; he whom Richard had called villain to his face in Brabant. Somerset stood courteously before her, awaiting permission to speak, and she inclined her head. "My lady, the king requests, if you are able, and willing, to favor him with the honor of your presence."

Never had Catherine heard a royal summons worded so meekly. Still, she knew she could not refuse, and in any case, what did she have to do now that the queen was gone? Sit and wonder if life meant anything, or made any difference to anyone other than the one who lived it? Anything was better than this, even, perhaps, spending time with Henry. She rose to her feet. "Of course."

As Somerset escorted her to the royal privy suite, sympathy engulfed him for the pale, touching figure beside him who bore herself so nobly. In the six years he had known her, she had surprised him in many ways. Any other woman would long ago have abandoned her widow's weeds for bright taffetas and gems, and acknowledged the heads she turned and the adulation she inspired in the male sex, but not Catherine Gordon. She had even won the admiration of his wife and the other women of the queen, setting for them all an example of grace under duress. The Gordon motto was *Animo non Astutia*. By Courage, Not by Craft, and this she embodied in full measure. She had stood by her husband every step of the way, her head held high, and met each of her griefs with a courage that Somerset, a warrior, could only envy. She was a remarkable woman, as unforgettable as she was beautiful. He nodded to the guard, and the man thrust open the door to King Henry's chamber. Somerset bowed. "Lady Catherine Gordon, Sire."

Catherine entered. Henry was seated at a table, a jeweled flask and two golden wine cups set before him. He gave her a wan smile. "Here, my dear, come and sit—" He pushed a chair out with his foot. "Shut the door, Somerset."

Catherine advanced carefully and took a seat, folding her hands in her lap.

"We are both alone now, you and I," he said.

She did not reply. What was there to say?

"You loved her, too, didn't you?"

"Everyone loved the queen," Catherine said.

"They are calling her Elizabeth the Good. The people are not usually so generous with their rulers, Catherine." He gave an audible sigh and threw a glance at the window. "It makes me wonder what they'll call me when I'm gone. Henry the Crafty. Henry the Cold. Henry the Miser?" His mouth quirked into a bitter smile as he looked at her. "How do you see me, Catherine?"

He was dropping his mask, clearly grieving, and not himself. She felt as if she were back in her nightmare, the ground perilous beneath her feet, emitting smoke from invisible fires in its belly, like a dangerous beast that would rise up and devour her if she took a wrong step. She decided to hold herself inscrutable so as not to make a mistake that might prove fatal. She had to think of Dickon. "Sire, how do you see yourself?" she asked gently.

"As a great ruler . . . one who has brought peace to a divided land roiling in blood. But I know 'tis not how they'll remember me." He waved a hand. "I wish I could pretend it didn't matter—that I didn't care, but I do. I care what they think . . . I care what you think."

Catherine's eyes went to his half-empty cup. *He's drunk*, she thought, wishing suddenly that she'd found some excuse to stay away, that she could excuse herself now and leave.

"Perhaps I've had too much wine, but it doesn't happen often," he said, following her gaze. "Here, have some with me. 'Tis not good to drink alone."

She watched him pour. He lifted his cup in a toast. "To Elizabeth—"

"To Elizabeth," she whispered, lifting hers.

"She was the only truly kind person I ever knew," he murmured, a faraway look in his eyes.

"That she was, my lord."

"And I was not kind to her."

She tensed. He shouldn't be talking about such intimate matters with her. "Sire, I pray you—"

He leaned forward urgently and seized her hand. His grip was hard, and he hurt her, but she dared not remove her hand from his.

"I want you to know how it was between us. We married one another for reasons of state, and for many years I cared nothing for her. In time, affection came, but not love. Never love. I gave my love to you, the day I saw you."

"My lord, I pray you—speak not these things!" she exclaimed, withdrawing her hand and blushing wildly.

"Why not? Why should you not know, now that we are both free? I wish you to know. After she died, I realized that I did love her—but not the way I love you. We must speak of these things, Catherine. I want you to know what it takes to survive in the world I live in!"

"'Tis not meet, my lord."

"Meet, meet! What do I care about meet? Do you think I know not that I am held in hatred? I have no friends, except my monkey, and my mother—"

Catherine almost burst out laughing. *This is a farce*, she thought. But it wasn't. It was more like a dangerous game, one she had no wish to play. She bowed her head quickly and wiped from her mind any thoughts of laughter.

"Elizabeth was my only friend, and now she is gone. I could talk to her freely about my troubles, and she did not judge me. There is no one now who doesn't judge me. Do you think I enjoy being friend-less, Catherine? Do you think I enjoy being alone on the summit of the world, in this empty place where I sit?"

"The air is always thin at the top, yet the wind is fierce. So they say."

"True! I am held in hatred and I must fear everyone and every-thing. Conspiracies abound against me, and I must be constantly on watch, like a hunted animal who sleeps with one eye open. It has always been that way for me. When the Yorkists held the throne, I was a boy, and my childhood was spent in imprisonments and flight."

Catherine lifted her gaze to his face. He may have been a hunted animal once, desperate and fearful, but his eyes were hard now, his smile wintry, and his face had the look of the predator, not the prey. She wondered for a moment if this was what would have happened to Richard had he won the throne, but she dismissed the thought. Different people were changed in different ways by the same experience, and Richard had been very different from Henry.

He took her hand again. He must have read something in her expression, for he said, "Everyone wants peace and security for his land, and for himself. I do not relish sending men to the Tower, Catherine, but it is a necessary evil."

Catherine felt that this was as close as he would ever come to making her an apology for what he had done to Richard. *But what good does it do me, even if he grovels at my feet? Richard is lost to me, because of him.*

"When his country is at war, a man is no longer bound to respect the sanctity of life. When his country is in danger, it becomes his duty to defend it. I am at war with war, Catherine. Without my hand on the rudder, and without the Tower to enforce my will, England would sink back into civil strife. When a body is sick, we give it medicine to cure the malady, do we not? But sometimes, the malady cannot be cured and will claim more lives if not halted. Then a king must have the courage to prescribe poison. That is what the Tower is for. To purge those who think differently, who do not agree with me, who challenge me. For they are the disease."

His words raged like a storm over Catherine's head and fell on her ears with the strength of blows. That he could turn evil into good, and justify what could never be justified!

He must have guessed something of her thoughts, for he said, "You think your husband would have made a better king than I, Catherine?"

She dropped her lids. "That question is for God, not for me."

"I know what you think! You think he would have been a gentle king over a gentle land. Let me tell you the kind of king he would have made—a weak king—a disastrous king! Every man would see an opportunity for himself, and strife would be without end. Whether you realize it or not, we live in a world that has gone mad! Every man is enemy to every man, and there is a war of all against all! He had poor judgment as a general, and he would have had poor judgment as a king." He took a moment to compose himself before he went on. "You see, Catherine, a king must deal with men as they are, not as they ought to be. Take my predecessor, Richard III. His mistake was to treat men as they ought to be, and look at him now—one of the shortest and most useless reigns in history. He made a profession of goodness in everything and came to grief because so many were not good around him. He died fighting valiantly, but to what avail was all his honor, his valor, his idealism? Those times are dead with him."

And you bought peace for yourself with my Richard's torment and inhuman suffering, she thought. Aloud, she said, "And you brought peace to England."

"Precisely. God put me here to rule, and He protects me, Catherine. What chance had I to be king—my great-grandsire a man wanted for debt and murder, fleeing for his life, pursued by the king's men? My grandsire a groom of the wardrobe? My lineage on both sides stained by bastardy? 'Tis a miracle worked by Divine Will no less! God Himself has smitten down my enemies. It has to be so; no other explanation suffices. *Dei Gratia Rex.* By grace of God. I know the reason God put me here. To save England. I have done so. I have saved her from herself and ended the great civil strife that rent her into two for so long. The land has peace, and it prospers." He heaved a long breath. "What I have done, I did for the good of the realm. Sometimes you have to do the wrong thing for the right reason, Catherine."

He toyed with his cup. Abruptly, he looked up. "I have decided on the date for Margaret's proxy marriage to James. It shall be a summer affair on the eighth of August. Then she will leave for Scotland." He had given his promise to Elizabeth that he would not send Margaret to James until she turned fourteen. That would not happen until November, but it was close enough, and he did not wish to wait. Besides, Elizabeth was dead and would never know.

"You will miss her."

"Catherine, it would please me immensely if you would supervise her wardrobe. I wish her to have magnificent attire, as befits a future queen of Scotland."

"I will attend to it, my lord."

"And Catherine . . . thank you for supervising Margaret's training. She is proficient in the lute and clavichord, in dance, in Latin and French, and is skilled in archery. Much of what she knows has come from you. I know she will be a gracious queen to King James, and shall make England proud." He kept his eyes on her face, and they were strangely alert and expectant, as if he waited for something.

Catherine gave him a small smile. "It has been my pleasure to instruct the Princess Margaret, my lord. May James love her to distraction."

His eyes left her face. "Aye," he said in a voice that seemed almost downcast. "Aye."

All at once, in spite of herself, Catherine felt a tide of pity for him. She wanted to ease his grief and bring a smile to his face. "My lord, perhaps I should amend my wish. Love her, but not to distraction."

Henry lifted his questioning gaze to her face.

"I once heard of a man who loved his wife to distraction. He was always jealous, and so he beat her often. One day he followed her, and found that his wife went to confession. When the priest was about to lead her behind the altar to be disciplined, he feared the worst, and cried out to him, "Hear ye, Master Parson, I pray you let me be beaten for her!" His wife, on hearing her husband's words, knelt down before the priest. "I pray you," said the wife, "strike him hard, for I am a great sinner."

Henry threw his head back and roared with laughter as Catherine smiled.

*   *   *

Catherine lay in her bed, staring up at the dark sky, and pondering Henry. Few stars were out, and hard as she tried, she couldn't find Richard's star in Orion. In spite of herself, she realized Henry's confession had changed her opinion of him. His crown was won by the sword and kept by the sword, but somehow, between the time he'd murdered Richard and last night, he had become human to her. He was selfish and ruthless, yes, but he was also a man—one who loved, and feared, who had a conscience, scruples, and something that could pass for compassion. He could not kill a child, even to secure his crown. On that, she realized, she had come to rely.

But it did not mean she approved of him, or that she could forgive him for what he had done to her. Still, she knew her own survival and that of her child depended on her dissembling that hatred and overcoming the fear, and so she did. She made him laugh, and found smiles to bestow, and kind words to soothe him when he invited her into the solar to dine and play cards with the family and friends, and to listen to music and poetry readings, as he had done often in these weeks since his queen's death. He was a good father, she realized, patient with his children and indulgent with flighty Margaret, whom he loved to spoil with jewels, for she could never have enough of them. *But someday when I am safe and he can no longer hurt me, I'll tell him what I really think of him.* She would rest her cheek on Dickon's little coif, and savor the faint scent of him that still lingered there. What pleasure that would give if that day came. Until then, she had to mask her true feelings, for Dickon's sake. If that made her a hypocrite, so be it. At least she wasn't a fool.

On the first day of March, Catherine awoke before daybreak, unable to sleep for excitement. Cecily was arriving! She had gone home to the Isle of Wight after Margaret's proxy betrothal in January, but had returned three weeks later when Elizabeth died. She had left with her three sisters immediately after the funeral for Framingham Castle, the Howard family residence of her sister, Anne, Duchess of Norfolk, to mourn in private. Cecily had invited Catherine to come with her, but she'd declined, not wishing to intrude on their grief. Now that Cecily was back, she'd have her all to herself, to speak of things that she wouldn't dare broach except in total privacy. Yet she knew, even as this thought came to her, that she would not tell Cecily how Henry had bared his soul to her.

"Dearest Cecily!" Catherine cried. The two women embraced and twirled one another around like two maidens instead of old princesses of royal blood. "You look wonderful! Peach becomes you—and I like the tight sleeves—how elegant."

Cecily cast a quick look around and swept off her headband. She shook her ringlets loose around her. "I can't stand these things anymore!"

"But Cecily, you cannot wear your hair loose," exclaimed Catherine, eyes wide with shock.

"Fiddle-faddle. At home I run around in a kirtle and wear my hair unbound every day—you cannot know how liberating it is not to have to coif and braid and wear headbands. Why, I've even done laundry with the servants!" Linking her arm in Catherine's, she marched her off to a secluded corner of the royal garden.

Catherine finally found her voice. "Laundry? With the servants, truly? No—"

"Indeed I have! I leave the heavy work to them, naturally, but 'tis so good to be out on the riverbank, standing in water to your ankles, with the wind blowing through your hair, the river birds screeching in your ears, and the fresh clean smell of soap in your nostrils!"

"Cecily, you make laundry sound better than a feast. How I have missed you."

"And you, what have you been doing since—since—what have you been doing?" The unspoken words hung in the air: *since Elizabeth died.* The laughter went out of her, and Catherine frowned. "Not much. Preparing Margaret for Scotland, mostly."

"And Henry? Has he . . . ?" She gave her a look full of scrutiny, leaving the thought unspoken.

Catherine knew what she meant. *Has he made overtures?* She dropped her gaze. "He has been grieving deeply for Elizabeth. It has been hard for him. 'Tis strange, but sometimes he touches my heart."

"Be careful," Cecily whispered. "He covets you."

"I can take care of myself. I have done so all this time."

"But he is king. I fear for you, Catherine. Do you have feelings for him?"

"Feelings? What is it they say—first you hate the sinner and the sin. Then you pity the sinner and hate the sin." *Pity, aye; but forgive, never,* she thought. Not after all he had done. She thought of sweet Kate, his wife's favorite sister, his latest victim. Kate had served as chief mourner at Elizabeth's funeral, and Elizabeth's death, coming as it did a mere seven months after that of Kate's five-year-old son, had struck Kate hard. Then Henry threw her husband into the Tower. Now there was talk of an attainder to seize Courtenay's inheritance. That would leave Kate and her two children destitute.

"How is Kate faring?" Catherine inquired.

"Not well. She worries about William in the Tower, with the rats, and the cold, and the diseases so rampant there. Many die from—" Her voice trailed off.

Catherine reached for Cecily's hand. "He's young. He's strong. He will survive. Never give up hope."

"Elizabeth arranged their marriage, you know. It was a love match. They were so young when they wed in '95—she was sixteen and he was twenty—and they had such a short time together." Realization washed over Cecily. Here was one whose monumental suffering and loss exceeded even Kate's. "How you do it, I know not, Catherine. You are so brave, and so strong. Everyone admires you. I pray Kate can find the strength—"

"I remember William at the jousting for Margaret's betrothal tournament in 1502," Catherine said quickly to lift the melancholy. "He and Kate were so happy. I can still hear them laughing. There was such feasting and dancing, and so many bonfires." Catherine smiled quickly and bit down to banish the memories. She had always known it would come to this. Each would regret in turn that they hadn't helped Richard, all those nobles who had failed him then, but she hadn't bargained on coming to care for them. There would probably never be an end to the murders, as long as a Tudor held the throne, for the shadow of usurpation and bastardy tainted their title. *I hate Henry!* she thought. *He cares nothing for anyone's happiness. I hate what he does, and I pity him, but I hate him, too!*

Aloud, she said, "What about Katharine of Aragon? She is unhappy in England, and there is nothing here for her any longer. De

Puebla says Henry won't allow her to leave England. Why does he not send the girl back to her family?"

Cecily grinned suddenly. "She has too much gold. I am so glad I have none!"

Catherine's brows arched with surprise. "Who would ever have thought that poverty could be a blessing?"

And they both covered their hands as they burst into childish giggles, laughing till they cried.

*   *   *

In April 1503, Catherine heard from Cecily that she gave birth to a beautiful girl-child and that the king had granted her some lands for her lifetime use, alleviating for Catherine some of the melancholy that had settled over the castle following the death of the queen. In the weeks that followed, Strangeways was always at her side when Catherine needed him. She knew that he complied with Henry's orders to make certain that she was well cared for, and this he did with meticulous care. He brought her posies and little gifts from town: silk thread for embroidery, ribbons for her hair and other bric-a-brac, but the most important service he rendered was to accompany her to Richard's resting place at the Austin Friars. She had just returned from a visit there and had gone to her room to freshen up when a knock came at her chamber door. She was annoyed; Richard was still on her mind and she wished to be alone with her thoughts for a while. She cracked the door open.

It was Strangeways. "My lady, the king needs to see you most urgently."

"Now?" She would see him at supper, and Henry normally issued an invitation to the solar after the meal was concluded. Catherine found it curious that Strangeways wore such a downcast expression, and that he wouldn't meet her eyes. He escorted her to the royal chamber in silence, and she realized that she missed his light banter. *What can it be?* she wondered, stealing anxious glances at him as they walked together.

Clad in his favorite crimson and gold, Henry stood at the window, awaiting her arrival. The door closed behind her.

"Catryn," he said.

She was jarred into stunned, frozen silence. The name swept back the years and returned Richard to her side, and again they were stepping in one another's footsteps in the sand, drunk on joy.

Back in the present, she saw Henry moving toward her, his eyes alight with love. He was about to take her into his arms when she found her voice, and cried out in panic, "Sire, I am Catherine."

He halted abruptly, the smile gone from his face. He wanted to take Richard's place and she had just told him he could not. His features tightened in fury. Again, she thought of the snake in the meadow of flowers. Even as a child she'd understood that one wrong move, one little sound, and the snake would strike. Her father had diverted that serpent, but there was no one to divert this one; no one to slay it with his sword, and save her. She was alone and had to rely on herself.

"But perhaps you may call me Cat," she said. It was the nickname she had hated all her life and it seemed somehow fitting that she should allow him use of it.

His face lightened and he resumed his approach. "Cat. 'Tis a pretty nomer. It shall be mine alone for you."

She had saved herself from the snake and would always be reminded of it. So relieved was she that she scarcely noticed him take her hand in his.

"Pray, let us sit together, Cat."

His rough skin and the bony feel of his hand were unpleasant, and she dared not breathe for his sour breath fanned her face as he placed his arm around her shoulders and led her to the settle. She sat where he indicated, and he took a seat beside her. He seemed nervous, and suddenly she was overcome with apprehension. She took her time smoothing her skirts, hoping to delay whatever he was preparing to say to her. When she looked up, he was watching her with a strange expression, and his breathing was labored. Abruptly he rose from the settle and went to the table, and she had the feeling that he, too, was stalling for time to compose himself. He poured two goblets of wine and brought one to her, but he did not sit again, nor did he drink. Keeping her eyes averted, she accepted the cup, her unease growing.

"I have considered sending you home to Scotland, Cat, but I cannot. What would I do without you?"

Catherine took the cup to her lips, a sick disappointment gripping her stomach. *You'd do without me in a minute if you knew what I really thought of you.*

"A prophecy foretold that you would be queen, Catherine. One word from you, and you can be queen. My queen. Queen of England."

Shock slackened her grip on the cup she held and it dropped from her hands, spilling wine on her skirts as it fell to the floor and clattered across the marble. She leapt to her feet as a vision of the wise-woman's brown, wrinkled face rose before her. The words she'd uttered resounded in her ears, "You have a destiny unlike anything I have ever seen," the old woman had said, examining her palm. "You will be loved by a king . . . I can make out nothing more. Except that you will be loved by a king." In her happiness with Richard, Catherine had remembered the prophecy incorrectly; she had thought it said that she would be queen, and that meant her husband would be a king. Only much later, when it was too late, did she realize her error. Her misplaced confidence in the prophecy, like a jest of Fate, had guided Richard to his doom.

She lifted her eyes to Henry's face. "No, my lord, you are mistaken. The prophecy was not that I should be queen, but that I would be loved by a king."

"A detail."

A detail indeed. One that had ripped her life to shreds. Henry was speaking again. She forced herself to concentrate.

"Think of it, Catherine—queen at my side. To have anything your heart desires."

"Anything?" she heard herself say.

"Anything."

Trembling, she moved to the window. She clasped her hands together tightly, as if by so doing, she could brace herself with a steel girder.

She turned to face him. "My son?" she demanded through parched lips.

Henry blanched and the bright look went out of his eyes. "'Tis the only thing you cannot have."

A silence.

Fate is mocking me, Catherine thought. One word, and the crown of England would be hers. If the Devil himself stood there with his horns and tail, he wouldn't frighten her as much as this man with a smile on his face. He was a king proposing to the woman he loved, as nervous and fearful of rejection as any man in his place would be. Yet despite his royal robes, his air of command and assurance, all he inspired in her was dread and fear, chastened by a touch of pity. If Henry had Richard's gallantry and ardor, or even Strangeways's endearing impudence, she might be able to force herself to endure him for Dickon's sake, but he shared so little with the one who lived in her heart. Even without his throne, Richard had been every inch a prince born to rule, and though Henry had once been a hunted animal like Richard, and had known terror and loneliness like him, his eyes were as hard as flint now, and behind his royal regalia he was simply a bastard who had the good fortune to win himself a throne and the ruthlessness to keep it. The thought of wedding such a physically and morally decrepit man swept her with a repugnance she was careful to hide beneath averted eyes. He couldn't help how he looked, but she must never forget how dangerous and duplicitous he was, and what evil lurked in him. That evil could be turned against her son, just as it had been turned against her husband.

"Cat—" Henry grabbed her, held her close.

She averted her face; she did not move. She could scarcely breathe.

"Tell me you care for me—" he murmured into her hair.

When she did not reply, he released her. "Do you not wish to be queen, Catherine?"

She swallowed hard. "I thought I did, once, but I cannot live in your world. The things that must be done to survive, I am not fitted to it."

Henry began to pace, his hands behind his back. How to explain, that was the question, he thought. How to make her understand why he had done the thing he'd done. He had pardoned many of those who had betrayed him, only to kill them in the end. Creatures of habit, they would not mend their ways. To protect himself, he had learned to anticipate betrayals, and end them before they had the chance to begin. As he had with William Courtenay.

He paused, looked up. "'Tis simple, Cat. We all make mistakes, but if we are wise, we learn not to make the same one twice."

"Indeed, Sire, experience is a wonderful thing. It enables you to recognize a mistake when you make it again." Catherine smiled at him.

Henry grinned, then grew serious and Catherine realized that she had failed to divert his thoughts.

"Cat, sit quietly, and listen for a change without interrupting." He paused to gather his rampaging thoughts. "If I can make you understand why I do what I do, and teach you to do the same, would you change your mind?" He gazed at her with desperate, pleading eyes. When she didn't reply, he slammed his fist on the table. "The truth is simpler than that, is it not? Richard may be dead, but his shadow will always lie between us!"

Catherine gave a start. His mood had changed again. Icy black fear swept her. *Dickon. Think, think!* she told herself. *You must not anger him—serpents strike when angry—you must buy time to think!* "Nay, my lord—'tis not the reason!" she cried, but she couldn't think of an explanation, for he had hit on the truth. In desperation, she flung herself on the settle, and covering her face, burst into tears. When Henry said nothing, she wailed louder, and when she dared, she stole a sly peep at him. He stood helplessly, an anguished expression on his face. Finally he stepped forward and offered her a handkerchief. She dried her tears and blew her nose hard, for effect.

He spoke again, and this time his voice was gentle and held

entreaty. "Power is the only protection against fresh calamities, Cat. I am offering you the certainty of a life without fear. Take it, my dear. Take me."

She looked up at him with moist eyes and pushed to her feet. "Sire, I beg for time to consider the great honor you have done me."

He smiled. She thought, *There is a coldness about him even when he smiles.* She forced into her mind the image of Richard on Loch Lomond and her lips softened tenderly as she rested her eyes on Henry.

Chapter 18

A Leaf of Hope

When she returned to her room, Catherine flung herself on her bed and wept in earnest. It was one of the few times she'd given vent to tears, but the great reservoir of sorrow and regret that filled her soul did not cease to exist because she cried. She stayed in her room the next day, and the day after that, until she lost track of time and the days ran into one another. She always awoke from her dreams in an agony of grief. Remembering Cecily's warning, she also remembered her own reply: *I can take care of myself. I have done so all this time.* What arrogance! God must have sent this latest trial to trample her pride. Never, even in her darkest moments, had she anticipated that Henry would propose. Oh yes, she had thought of the other things he might do—she had not failed to consider that he would attempt rapine. Then she would have made some pretty entreaty about honor and love, and warded him off with words to evoke guilt. But this—this offer of marriage—this, she had never anticipated!

Strangeways came hourly to check on her, and when Alice had told him that she was unwell on that first day, Henry sent his royal physician to see her and Alice had the thankless task of turning him away. Catherine had heard them outside her door. "My lady demands not to be disturbed," Alice had said. "Does she have fever?" the doctor had asked. "I know not, for she sleeps, and I dare not wake her." "But if she has fever, I must see her. Her life may be in peril." "If she wishes not to be disturbed, I dare not disturb her, even for the king's own physician," Alice had insisted.

Henry had contented himself by sending her a daily basket of marchpane, truffles, and other delicacies, but she couldn't bear to look at them and sent them to Lady Daubeney. Nor did she touch food of any kind, for her stomach had tightened into a ball. All the while she pondered what to do, and how she might avert this latest disaster. The idea of sleeping with the man who had castrated Richard and broken the bones of his face, who had taken his youth and crushed his spirit, who had stolen her babe and refused to restore him to her, horrified her to the depths of her being. She had thought she had survived the worst that could happen to her, but now she feared the worst was yet to come, and that it would last all of her life. Raising her eyes to the sky, she had cried out to the heavens, *God, where are You? For which of my sins do You turn away all my pleas? God, will You not answer me this one time—one time? Richard, are you there—if you exist somewhere—anywhere—can you not help me in my calamity?*

But all she saw was darkness; all she heard was the screaming of the wind.

She knew she risked Dickon's well-being by defying the king, and the thought struck new terror into her. She could not hide forever, nor could she abide the fate that lay in wait for her. One night, as she turned over in bed, her eye fell on her tapestry that lay on her tawny kirtle. Death wore a crown of horns, but behind its dread figure sat her mother, embroidering on a beautiful hillside in radiant light. If she died, perforce he might forget about her child and she could buy her babe's life with her own. She dried her tears and rose from bed. She took her cloak down from the peg where it hung and drew the hood over her head. Noiselessly, she stepped over Alice's sleeping form and, moving carefully in the darkness, cracked the door and crept out. Shadows danced on the crooked walls of the empty stairways and corridors she passed, and she thought of Richard, how afraid he had been of shadows. "I am not afraid of shadows when I am with you, Catryn," he had told her. "You banish them all, like a beautiful light." She quickened her pace.

She slipped out of the palace unnoticed by the patrols. The wind whipped her clothes and her breath made mist on the frigid air as she followed the path down to the Thames. Across the city, church bells marked the hour of matins with three long chimes. She hurried along the deserted riverbank until the walls of Westminster Palace and the sound of its patrols were swallowed up in the night. No oars splashed on the Thames. No fishermen were out. There were only the sounds of night critters and the dank smell of the water, punctuated by the rhythmic lapping of the tide. She advanced to the river's edge and looked down into the black water. Long reeds swayed in the wind, and above her a willow tree waved its bare branches to and fro, sighing heavily. She begged God for forgiveness and closed her eyes. She raised her arms over her head. She was about to fling herself headlong into the water when she heard something—a flutter—a cry. She looked up. A small white bird sat on a low branch, gazing at her. It burst into a beautiful, melodious song and she listened in wonderment, balm spreading over her anguished spirit.

The song ended; the bird flew off with a flap of wings. How could this be—birds were not out at night. She fell to her knees. *Domine, et clamor meus ad te veniat*—O Lord, let my cry come to you—hear my prayer—

Church bells pealed, but she heard them only dimly, for she was seeing Richard in her mind. He stood before her as something stirred in her, a memory, words, she knew not what, and then realization washed over her, bathing her in comprehension and light. Her heart thundering in her breast, she staggered to her feet with the awesome knowledge.

The king's mother, wishing to wed Tudor instead of Suffolk, had seen a vision in which Saint Nicholas had commanded her to marry Tudor!

Catherine turned. She fled back to Windsor, her feet flying over the rutted ground, the small pebbles and rough grasses. There was still hope! She had been blessed with an answer! She had been given a way out and saved from the mortal sin of suicide!

She would endure, but endure on her own terms. First, however, she had to get back to the palace! The clock was striking the hours: One ... two ... three ... It was four o'clock, and soon dawn would break over the world.

*   *   *

A bird had saved her life. Catherine stood quietly as Alice dressed her, pondering the ridiculous truth. A bird had saved her life, and that bird had been a white bird, the kind of bird that had grown special to her over the years, and it had come to her at night, when birds were not out. Was it coincidence or a miracle that it had landed on the tree and broken into song just as she was about to cast herself into the water? Was it coincidence or a miracle, the knowledge that had come to her then? She didn't know, and would never know, but she had begged Richard to intercede for her with God. And the bird had come.

If Alice had wondered at the mud that caked her shoes and the condition of her gown and cloak, she said nothing. She had merely taken down another black gown from the peg, helped Catherine into it, and brought her another pair of slippers. She set Catherine's veil on her head and secured the velvet headband to the abundant coils of her black hair.

"There," she said absently. "'Tis not possible to believe you've been so ill when you look as beautiful as a vision from a dream."

Catherine jerked her head up.

"Did I say something wrong, my Lady Cate?"

"Why did you use that word—vision?"

"I know not. 'Tis just what came to mind—"

"While I was ill, I received a vision."

"Oh, my Lady Cate! Can ye speak of it? Does it bode well?"

"I shall tell you in good time, but the king must be the first to know."

Alice looked at her with wide eyes.

"I pray you to inform Strangeways that I need to see King Henry."
She went to her prie-dieu, conscious of Alice's stunned gaze, for it
had been many years since she had knelt in private prayer. But all
Alice said was, "Will you not be coming to breakfast, my Lady Cate?"

"Nay . . . I need a different kind of sustenance this morning."

It was shortly after breakfast that Catherine found herself beside
Strangeways, making her way past the armed men that massed
along the hallways leading to the king's royal chamber. Only this
time it was Catherine who was silent at his side, ignoring his curious
glances.

Henry came rushing up to take her hand as soon as the door
was thrust open, as solicitous as a loving husband. "My dear Cat,
I am relieved to find you well! I have been worried about you. You
wouldn't see my physician, and you refused food—I know not why.
But I am relieved that you are well now."

Catherine gave him a curtsy.

"You have an answer for me, do you not—I see it in your face.
Here, come—sit . . ."

"I thank you, my lord, but with your indulgence, I prefer to stand.
What I have to say requires all my will."

"Beloved Cat, stand if you wish—sit, if you wish—your wish is
my command—"

He was excited and smiling broadly, but when Catherine didn't
return his smile, his expression changed.

"Sire, you know that I have been ill, and fasting. I have also been
praying. Many times in my illness I came near death." She drew
herself erect and lifted her chin. "Sire, I have received a vision that
concerns you."

Henry didn't move.

"Saint Margaret, Queen of our Scottish King Malcolm III,
came to me with my lord husband, Richard, at her side," Catherine
resumed, "and behind them stood a dread figure, stained with blood
and crowned with a horned serpent. This specter was neither male
nor female, and its waist was bound in cords of spotted snakes. I saw
it through a mist of foul-smelling vapors that stung my nostrils. The

ground beneath its feet was of scorched earth, broken by fissures that emitted the fumes, and I realized that I stood in a cemetery, one choked with weeds and crowded with crooked tombstones clustered closely together. Shapes of men and horses passed to and fro, carrying pale banners that fluttered vaguely above their heads like shredded veils. This, I knew, was the kingdom of the shadowy dead."

Catherine broke off to draw breath and saw that Henry was staring fixedly at her.

"A fearful hissing came to me then, and I looked up. Above my head, the wind was making an arc, and caught in its circling currents were foul black things with birdlike forms resembling dragons with scaly wings. One, more hideous than the rest, bore the face of a man in torment as he whirled about in the dark wind with the half-gnawed carcass of a child in his coiled tail.

"I shrank in horror from the sight, and Saint Margaret spoke. 'This soul,' she explained to me, 'is the soul of a babe-killer who has just begun his journey. Far worse awaits him below. As you have no doubt guessed, this grim terrain where you stand is but the threshold of the domain of the horrors of Hell.'

"My lord husband said nothing, and Saint Margaret went on, ' 'Tis by God's Grace that I bring you this warning. Listen well, and take heed. To wed, or to couple with the tormentor of your liege lord here, Prince Richard of York, shall deliver you and the earthly king into the clutches of the creature you see behind me, one of the minions that serve the Devil, his Master. You may tell the earthly king of what awaits should he choose to disregard this warning. His punishment shall begin at the moment of death when a thousand damnable esprites invade his throat to tear out his innards and seize his soul. They shall drag him screaming into the depths of this terrible place, and he shall suffer there through fire and ice, blackness, torment, and terror for all eternity. Tell the earthly king that he defies this warning on peril of his immortal soul.' Saint Margaret and Richard faded away into radiance, and I awoke from the evil place where I had been."

The color was gone from Henry's face and he was as white as

a phantom. Heavily, he lowered himself into a chair. The hand he raised to his head shook visibly, and he seemed suddenly a very aged man. For a long time he said nothing, nor did he look at her. Then, at last, he lifted his eyes to her face, and in them she saw a grief so profound that she was flooded with pity.

He nodded. She curtsied, and let herself quietly out of his chamber.

* * *

Catherine was swept with a joy she was careful to hide from all eyes. She had saved herself, and she had saved her child. God had not turned away from her, and if He had, He had seen fit to embrace her once more. And somewhere in Heaven, she knew Richard survived and that he waited for her. She had always believed that, but not with the depth of conviction she had been newly granted. Not since Scotland had she felt so free, so light. She understood now the weight of the burden she had shouldered since captivity, and the blackness of the cloud she had struggled beneath since the day Richard had died. She remembered, as if in a dream, how she had stood at this same windowsill in her room at Windsor listening to Alice's muffled sobs. She had been frozen and dry-eyed, as if she, too, were dead with him, and it had seemed to her that her very soul had seeped from her body and vanished into mist. "Gone," she had whispered to her reflection in the glass. "Gone forever."

But now another image rose in her mind, more real, with more substance. Richard was chasing her down a woody embankment. She heard herself giggling and heard him cry out in jest as he threw himself backward into a waterfall for her amusement and emerged looking like a drowned rat. Seizing her hand, he pulled her down with him into the cold water.

This was what she would remember whenever she looked back. The laughter. The happiness. She smiled and lifted her eyes to the scene outside her window. She felt as if she were seeing it for the first time. Doves and wagtails chirped loudly in celebration of the coming spring, swooping and diving from the branches of trees already bursting into bloom. It had rained fiercely that morning, she realized, but the sun had come out meanwhile and the raindrops that were caught in the foliage sparkled like diamonds in the thickness of the evergreens.

She opened a window and drew a deep breath of the cool, fresh air. *Aye, 'tis a new day. A day unlike any other. I have survived and I will survive. Someday, with God's Grace, I shall see Dickon again.* A sound from behind broke into her thoughts. She turned to look. Alice was gathering the linens from the room and bundling them into a pillowcase.

"Where are you going with that?" she asked.

"Why, to do laundry in the river. 'Tis Friday."

Catherine smiled. "I shall come with you." Ignoring Alice's stunned expression, she took her by the arm and led her out the door.

* * *

Catherine wore black for Margaret's proxy wedding to James in August 1503, but for the first time since her arrival in the Tudor court, she changed the color of her headband to a bright and beautiful shade of red. At the festivities, which were sweetened with strawberries, cream, spice cakes, and seven cartloads of cherries, Catherine welcomed her kinsman, the Earl of Bothwell, Patrick Hepburn. She took his arm and led him off to a secluded corner of the hall where they might converse alone. Patrick, the first Earl of Bothwell, was married to Margaret, one of her many sisters, and she wanted news of her family.

"The years have scarcely touched you, dear sister. Ye look as beautiful as ever, Catherine."

"But not as beautiful as Meg, I'm sure." Catherine smiled.

"Ah—are ye still nursing a broken heart over me?" he demanded, with dancing green eyes.

"Aye, and never shall you be forgiven for choosing to wed my sister instead of me when my father gave you the chance to choose between us." She threw him a sly smile.

Patrick chuckled. "Ye know why I chose Margaret. She was two years older than ye and would have been mortified had her younger sister wed before her."

"No, Patrick, that was not the reason. You were both in love . . ." *And my destiny was to love Richard*, she thought. Aloud she said, "Though I may not have told you, I have always been happy for you both. Tell me, does Meg still play the bagpipes?"

"Not for many years now. Can't deny I'm glad. Always thought it an odd choice of instrument for a woman."

Catherine grinned. "I asked her once why she chose to play the bagpipes. You know what she said? 'Because ye don't.'" Catherine and Patrick both burst into laughter at the same moment.

"Sounds like Margaret," he said, catching his breath.

"We were very close in spite of our rivalry. I miss her."

Patrick patted her hand.

"How is Adam?" Patrick's little red-haired firstborn had been three years old when Catherine left Scotland.

"A devil still. He manages to get into mischief daily."

"And Alexander?" Catherine asked, inquiring after her eldest brother, who had inherited the Earldom of Huntly.

"Doing well, and I suppose it can be said to be good that I have naught to report about him. Likewise yer brothers, Adam, William, and James . . ."

"And my sisters?"

"Now that would take all day, but in a nutshell, the Gordons are well and flourishing. Yer six sisters are thriving—and multiplying. They send their love and beg to be remembered to ye."

Catherine reached for his hand and her face took on a grave expression. "Pray tell my fair cousin, James, how deeply his noble gesture has touched me. He is in truth the most chivalrous king in Christendom." As part of the marriage negotiations, James had demanded that Richard's body be taken back to Scotland. Henry had agreed but wanted the knowledge to be kept secret. Naturally. It would be too hard to explain why a boatman's son was laid to rest with kings and queens, even in a foreign country. Harder to explain than the Austin Friars in London, where executed nobles, not commoners, were interred.

"James feels great sorrow that he failed to save Richard's life. He says it is precious little that he does for him now but 'tis better than leaving him in England. He will be interred in the royal vault where James's parents are buried, and one day he and Richard shall lie together, as befits their ties of royal blood and friendship."

"It means I cannot visit him," said Catherine sadly, "but he loved Scotland. 'Tis meet that he return to rest at Cambuskenneth Abbey." The abbey was a stone's throw from Stirling, that happy place where they had met, and wed, and conceived Dickon, and known the greatest joy that life could bestow. "If Richard could have had his way, he never would have left Scotland. Now he shall rest there forever."

"'Tis time to dance again, Catherine," said Patrick softly, as the beat of a popular tune came to them.

"Indeed, it is." She gave him her hand. They took the floor as the minstrels picked up a gay tune. Twirling and parting, they came together, and hopped hand in hand. Catherine was aware that Henry's eyes were riveted on her.

"King Henry does not seem happy," Patrick whispered when they drew close, but they parted before she could reply. Catherine's eyes went to Henry's glum expression. She twirled and drew near. "'Tis a bittersweet occasion for him. He is losing his daughter, even if she is to be queen."

Patrick was unconvinced. That Henry was besotted with Catherine and called her his black swan was the talk of Britain and the Continent. "Perhaps."

They gave a clap and placed their hands on their waists. The melody drew to an end. He bowed to her, and she gave him a graceful curtsy.

"It has been so good to see you, Patrick. I shall miss you."

Patrick took both her hands into his own, and lifted one to his lips. "Ye are indeed the brightest ornament of Scotland, and also of England. Whoever said that spoke true, Catherine."

Catherine's hand strayed to Richard's love letter that she kept over her heart. She gave Patrick a soft look. "Whoever said that was in love. Love is a wonderful thing. I am glad you have it still, Patrick."

The minstrels broke into a Celtic melody, one she had danced with Richard years ago at Stirling, stirring another round of painful memories in her heart. She saw Patrick staring behind her, and turned to see the crowds parting, making way for the king, who was striding toward them.

Henry came to a halt before her and inclined his head. "My Lady Catherine, would you care to dance?" He offered his hand.

"Sire, pray forgive me—but I only dance with kin, and never to Highland music."

"But I sent for the bagpipers to please you."

Catherine made no reply and held herself stiffly so she would not tremble or flee. "Forgive me, my lord."

Henry's expression tightened. He dropped his hand, gave an angry nod, and spun on his heel. "Women," she heard him mutter under his breath as he left.

At her side, Patrick sought her hand and gave her a squeeze.

*   *   *

Catherine lost track of time as the mundane and familiar days folded into one another. The court fed on idle gossip and the flare of an occasional spicy scandal. First came Henry's treatment of Katherine of Aragon. He had never allowed her to go back to Spain. In fact, after Catherine refused him, he considered marrying the Spanish princess himself. But he was forty-six, and she was seventeen, and her parents were outraged. He was her guardian, and her father-in-law. They threatened violence. Harry, too, protested fiercely.

"You can't wed her! You're too old!" Harry shouted at his father one night in the privacy of the solar. He had been infatuated with his older brother's widow since the age of eleven when he'd met the ship that had brought her to England, and he wished to wed her himself.

"How dare you?" Henry said to his son, rising to his feet with rage.

"I'm only telling you the truth you clearly have no wish to hear!"

"This is a state affair, and of no concern to you."

"You're a lecher! I hate you! I can't wait till you're dead! Then I'll do the opposite of everything you have done!"

"And you'll pay a hefty price for it if you do!" shouted Henry. "Every action I take, every groat I save, I do it for you—to secure the throne you shall sit on one day—and this is the thanks I receive? Get thee gone from my sight! Get thee gone—" Henry took a step forward and raised his cane to strike him, but Harry was too nimble. He sprang out of his father's range, strode red-faced from the room, and slammed the door behind him. Catherine, bearing witness to this scene, watched Henry sink slowly back into his chair. He was an old man now, frail and ailing, and in cold weather he had need of a walking cane. She rose and went to him. She placed her hand on his shoulder.

"He doesn't care for you much, does he, my lord?"

"If only Arthur hadn't died . . ." Henry managed in a choked voice. "I was about to give Harry over to the Church when Arthur died."

"Harry is but a child, my lord, brilliant as he is. Someday he'll appreciate what you have done for him, and thank you for it."

Henry placed his hand over hers. "I wish we could have wed, Cat."

Catherine made no reply.

*   *   *

Beneath the burden of his worries, Henry became stingier, more distant and more melancholy.

Through his various illnesses and emotional suffering, Catherine was with him. She sat with him in the evenings, playing chess and cards with him. Sometimes she won, and he had to pay her a gold noble or two, much to his great chagrin. This she sent to Cecily's little daughter, Margaret Kymbe, whom she visited each year, and who was dear to her heart. On occasion, she played the lute for Henry, and sang, but she knew that her musical talents didn't compare to Elizabeth's, or to Richard's, and she resisted more often than she agreed, deferring to his younger daughter, Mary Rose, who was an accomplished musician.

That Henry was growing increasingly distrustful, bitter, and lonely, Catherine knew, but the full extent of the fear and dread that he lived with eluded her until one evening when Simon Digby paid him a visit, accompanied by a manservant. Catherine stiffened when she heard his name. Digby had been constable of the Tower while Richard was imprisoned there, and had played too close a role in his torment. Digby's eye fell on her, and he colored and almost stumbled as he bent a knee.

"Sire, I bring you this with my own hands," he said, turning to his manservant, who offered Henry a bronze goblet. "'Tis from a different source, for the other died."

"Has it been culled with wine?"

"It has, my lord. Other ingredients have also been added. The royal physician and the royal alchemist have conferred together on the combination, and the elixir has been declared fit in their estimation."

"And the donor was young, and in good health?"

"He was, Sire."

"Very well." Henry accepted the cup and gave a nod of dismissal. Digby and his servant quitted the chamber. Henry took the cup to his mouth and drank carefully.

"What is it, Henry?" Catherine inquired, wondering about this mixture that required Simon Digby to bring it to him from the Tower.

Henry didn't reply right away. "You know that my health has been deteriorating for many years," he said as he gazed into his cup thoughtfully.

Catherine gave a nod. He had almost died after Richard and Edward were executed, and Elizabeth's death had taken a further toll, as did her own refusal of his offer of matrimony. Though not yet fifty, he fell sick every spring with a variety of maladies. Employing more and more physicians, he craved exemption from the Lenten fast, consulted the finest doctors from Germany and Italy, and prayed longer and harder as the years passed, but nothing had helped.

Henry spoke at last, not taking his eyes off the cup. "My alchemists have been searching for the fifth hidden element after air, earth, water, and fire, and it is my hope that they have found it, Cat. They assure me this elixir shall preserve my body from rotting and restore it to youthful vigor." He swirled the liquid around, lifted the cup to his lips, and drained it.

"What is it, Henry?" Catherine inquired again, watching him grimace at the taste.

"Human blood, from sanguine young men. They must be sanguine, you see. To give their health to me."

Catherine's stomach lurched.

Henry spoke again, almost to himself, mulling over his empty cup. "But I fear there is no elixir of youth."

She regarded him coolly, the pity gone.

* * *

When Catherine received the anguished tidings from the Isle of Wight in that cold winter of 1507, she packed to leave London with hurried urgency. These days she had a little money, for Henry had elevated her status and given her three more ladies to tend her. He also reinstated her annuity and even granted her small gifts from time to time. More precious was the measure of freedom she was allowed. Spies were everywhere at the Tudor court, but not for many years had guards been set to watch her.

Catherine sent Alice for Strangeways while she packed her belongings into a small coffer with careless heed—a few black dresses, some ribbons for her hair, a black veil or two, slippers, a mink collar, and her tawny kirtle. The knock at the door came as she was nearly done.

"James," she said, for in recent months she had taken to calling Strangeways by his Christian name. "Lady Cecily is taken gravely ill. I must go to her immediately." Catherine didn't meet his eyes, for she could not bear to see in them a sympathy that might weaken her composure. "Pray tell the king I have left for the Isle of Wight and know not when I shall be back."

"May I help you with your coffer, Lady Catherine?" His voice was soft, and Catherine raised her eyes to him. This man she had once despised for his arrogance and insolence was now the one she most relied on, the one she turned to first for help in ways large and small. In those dreadful days after Richard's death, he was there. As she sat alone and lonely, watching the court, his voice had come in her ear, "Bend with the wind, Catherine, and you won't break." Aye, she had fondness for him now and turned to him when she needed encouragement, or support, or simply a friend to offer her escort. She was grateful for his friendship, which had seen her through some difficult times. She gave him a nod, and he lifted the coffer up in his arms as if it were as light as a babe. Alice fell in behind them.

The sea voyage to the Isle of Wight took only a day and a half, but Catherine was in agony for every minute of it. Cecily's husband, Thomas Kymbe, had written that she was so ill that she was not expected to survive long. What if Cecily died before she got there? A swell of pain choked off her breath. She had to live—she had to see her again, if only for one last time! She had not had the chance to bid Richard farewell, or Dickon. That Cecily should be taken from her without a farewell embrace cut her to the heart. Catherine thought about little Maggie Kymbe, Cecily's four-year-old daughter who would be left motherless. Her heart turned over for the child. No nurse could take a mother's place and well she knew that the void would be with her for as long as she lived. Then there was Cecily's husband, Thomas. How devastated he would be! So ran Catherine's thoughts as she stood at the prow of the boat that took her across the sea to the Isle of Wight. It was the first time since St. Michael's Mount that she made a sea voyage, and her memories were bittersweet.

Thomas Kymbe was standing on the dock to meet her boat. He gave Catherine and Alice a warm welcome, though his face showed strain. He hoisted the coffer on to the litter and they climbed in.

"What sickness does Cecily have?" asked Catherine.

"We know not. She has been under the care of a physician monk from Quarr Abbey. He comes daily to check on her and has tried all the remedies he is familiar with, but nothing helps—" He broke off.

Catherine threw him a look of sympathy. Fair, in his early forties, Thomas was lean and tall and his face was weathered by wind and water. Beneath the years that etched his face, she saw the young man who had won Cecily's heart at Westminster, and she approved of him. She reached out and took his hand, and their eyes met in quiet understanding.

Chapter 19

Stars of Fate

In August 1507, five months after Catherine's arrival at the Isle of Wight, Cecily died. Catherine had intended to leave shortly after the funeral but found herself unable to abandon Cecily's grieving husband and little daughter.

"Why does it hurt so much?" four-year-old Maggie had asked her, with tears in her eyes.

Catherine had pressed the little girl to her bosom and kissed her soft cheeks. "My darling little one, there is a hole in your heart now, for your mother has taken a piece of it away with her to remember you by in Heaven. That is where the pain comes from, but it will heal, I promise you." Gently smoothing the little child's fair curls, she'd added, "Though you can't see her, she is up there with the angels, watching over you. She will always keep you safe from harm. Yet there is something I must warn you of. Something important."

Maggie's wide blue eyes were fixed on Catherine's face.

"'Tis a dangerous world we live in, and though your mother is always with you, she cannot guard you from all evil. So I would like to ask a favor, if I may?"

The child nodded solemnly.

"I am your aunt, and I love you as if you are my own little girl, but never call me 'Auntie' in front of others, at least not now. Harm may come to you if you do, and I couldn't bear that."

"Why?"

"When you are grown, you will understand, my sweeting."

"What should I call you then?"

"Lady Catherine."

"But that's like a stranger!"

"Think it as a game of pretend. We shall pretend to be strangers, knowing that we are not. It shall be our secret."

"Will I ever see my mother again?"

"One day ... one day ..."

Maggie went off with her puppy, and her father came to sit beside Catherine on the beach. "Thank you," he said.

"'Tis nothing, Thomas."

"Your kindness to Maggie is not 'nothing,' by any means, and I do thank you for it. But that is not what I meant."

"Then for what?"

"Cecily married me because of you and Richard. She had thought the gulf in our births an insurmountable impediment. You changed her mind. You showed her the power of love. When she agreed to wed me, she said that love was all that mattered, that it leveled mountains, that it made you see dismal gray as sparkling silver, that it made you believe leeks give honey. She gave up everything for me, and claimed never to regret it. I am so grateful to her—and to you—for the blessing of the years we had together."

* * *

Catherine received news of court through the missives Strangeways wrote her. She was distressed to learn that Spain, where Edmund de la Pole, Earl of Suffolk, had sought refuge, had surrendered him up to Henry on pardon of life, and he was now imprisoned in the Tower. Thus reminded of the doings at court, she delayed her return. She took long walks with Maggie on the white chalk cliffs that jutted out from the golden sand, and searched for dragon skeletons and footprints in the rocks, for many had been found on the Isle. *I'll go back in the spring*, she thought as she plaited little Maggie's fair hair by the fire in the cottage, where Cecily's presence still hovered.

When spring burst over the isle and fields of lavender bloomed purple, waving in the wind and perfuming the air, Thomas's large herd of sheep gave birth to a multitude of bleating lambs. With soft eyes, Catherine watched the mothers fondle and nurse their young on the grassy meadows. On warm evenings, they dined outside in Thomas's vineyard amid the ripening grapes, and she thought, *I'll go back in the summer*. But in the summer, she wanted to stand with Maggie, looking out to sea as the wind whipped their hair, and to picnic with her in the forest, where they might spot a red squirrel or find a flower the locals called "orchid," said to be the favorite flower of the ancient Greeks. She wanted to wash clothes in the river with Alice, and stand on the rocks and gaze out to the horizon. She wanted to visit Cecily at Quarr Abbey in Rhyde, where she was buried, and remember the laughter they had shared.

And so she stayed. Soon it had been a year since she had arrived. In late March 1508, a summons arrived from the king. "Come quickly, my Cat," his scrivener had written, "I need to see you, and I fear there is not much time."

Catherine looked up at the royal messenger. "What is the matter?"

"The king is ill, my lady. He is not expected to live long."

Catherine tore herself from the family she had made her own and journeyed back to Westminster with Alice.

The king's chamber was darkened, quiet, when she entered. Sir Charles Somerset sat in a chair by the gold-canopied bed, and a physician and two favored monks hovered by the fire. A musician strummed his lyre in a corner, trying vainly to dispel the distress and suffering that claimed the room. Henry lay on a huge four-poster bed hung with gold and crimson brocade and painted with his motto, *Dieu et Mon Droit.* God and My Right. A deep blue coverlet embroidered with golden dragons covered his gaunt frame.

Catherine approached, knelt, and kissed the bony hand he held out to her. His fingers were cold. "Cat, 'tis you—you have come at last . . . Sit here, leave me not, my dear . . ." He spoke the words like a sigh.

"Why did you stay away so long? . . . I have missed you . . ." His voice was faint, little more than a whisper. She gave him a smile.

"Talk to me, Cat . . . Tell me what you did while you were gone . . . tell me a story . . . anything to take away the pain—" He squeezed her hand and lowered his voice so that she had to lean close to hear his words. "I am so afraid, Cat—" A choked sob escaped from his throat.

She stroked his wispy hair back from his brow. "Now, now, Henry . . . it shall be all right. I shall tell you tales, and I won't leave you, if that is what you wish. Do you know the one about the miller and his wife?"

Henry shook his head.

"A man was talking to his neighbor, a miller, who had newly married a widow. 'Do married life agree with ye?' the man asked. The miller replied, 'By God, me wife never agreed with her first husband, but we agree marvelously well.' 'I pray ye, how so?' said the man. 'Well, I shall tell ye,' said the miller. 'When I am merry, she is merry, and when I am sad, she is sad. For when I go out of my doors, I am merry to go from her, and so is she. And when I come in again, I am sad, and so is she.'"

Henry laughed. But it was a shadow of his old laugh, punctuated with coughing and spasm, and Catherine was swept with pity. She launched into another tale, and by the time she was done, he had fallen asleep.

Catherine sat with him each day and tried to calm him with her presence and her words. One evening, she fell asleep in her chair and was awakened by a bloodcurdling scream. Henry was sitting up in bed, a look of terror on his face. He put out his arms to her, and she clasped him to her bosom like a suffering child. The physician came running from the hearth where he, too, had fallen asleep, and moved to prepare him a potion. Henry waved a hand. "Leave us."

The friar looked from Henry to Catherine, but if he thought it unseemly to depart, he dared make no objection. When the door had shut and they were alone, Henry gazed at her. "Cat, you know I have loved you since the moment I first beheld you. Now, before it's too late, I want to know what you feel for me."

Once, the thought of flinging the truth into Henry's face had lit her dreams and guided her way, but now there was nothing she desired less. She didn't know why this should be, except that the hatred in her heart seemed to have been washed away, leaving behind only pity. She despised much of what she saw in Henry, but he was not wholly evil; there was goodness in him, and sometimes even kindness. It was just as Elizabeth had said it would be that day on the riverbank when she'd given her Richard's portrait. *The anger dies away, but the loss is always with you.*

"Cat, tell me how you feel about me—" Henry persisted urgently.

Cat. Here was her chance to tell him how she really felt, to remind him of the malicious role he had played in her life. Perhaps he would show remorse that could benefit him in the afterlife. Perhaps he would even choose to make amends for the pain he'd caused her.

She rose to her feet and drew up the outer skirt of her velvet gown. Henry watched in bafflement as she untied the black silk panel that lay over her tawny shift.

She held the panel close to her heart as she spoke. "You wish to know how I feel, and I have decided to tell you, Henry. Let me say first that I do not judge you. That is for God to do. We are told to confess our sins and do penance for them in sorrow and contrition. It is for this reason, and because you have commanded me to, that I shall unfold the truth to you now, for the sake of your immortal soul."

Fear flickered on Henry's face.

"You remember the vision that I related to you?" she said in a gentler tone.

"... cannot forget ... never forget—" Henry wheezed, averting his eyes, as if to avert the memory.

"Over the years I felt compelled to capture it on silk. I embroidered the dream through my loneliness and grief on the many nights when sleep would not come, and I believe now that I must show it to you. Not to torment you, Henry, but to permit you the chance to do penance to one you have greatly wronged. If you understand the weight of your actions, and make restitution here on this earth while you still live, God will surely take it into account when your sins are weighed on His divine scale. Do I have your permission to proceed?"

He managed a nod. She unfurled the silk, and waited. He turned his head and raised his eyes to the tapestry. A look of horror passed over his features. "That face . . . the one of the demon bird with the carcass of the child . . . that looks—like me!" he rasped, panting.

"I had to render it as I saw it, Henry. I know not what child this creature held in its coiled tail, for the face was eaten away. Perhaps it was King Richard's son, or King Edward's son—or mine—"

"No, no!" he screamed. "I did not kill your son, Catherine!"

Catherine closed her eyes and put out her hand to the bedpost, for her breath had caught in her chest. "What did you do with my Dickon?" She brought her gaze to his face.

"I had him taken to Wales."

Catherine's hand went to her beating heart. "Where in Wales?"

"I cannot tell you."

"I must know!"

"You cannot know."

"You have much to answer for before God, Henry! This is one matter you can still rectify, if you choose to—"

"I . . . cannot do it . . . he is a danger to my throne, and my son's throne—"

Catherine bent down to his ear. "What is more important now, Henry? Your throne, or your immortal soul?"

Henry clutched her arm tightly with more strength than she thought he had left. "If I tell you . . . he will be in danger from Harry—"

"Harry need never know. You have stolen my child from me, Henry. Release him to my arms now. I give you my sworn promise that he shall be my secret. All I want is to see him again—and for him to live. Tell me where in Wales he is."

"I know not—" Henry groaned.

Catherine's eyes narrowed. Could he have lied about Dickon

being alive? Had he killed him after all? Henry must have seen in her face her disgust for him for he protested, "I speak truth, Catherine— I gave him over to Daubeney's care—and he placed him with a family in Wales . . . He took him to see your husband before he died . . . He was returned to the family . . . I know not what happened to him after that. He was of no use to me any longer . . . I did not keep track of him—"

Of no use to me. Like a piece of trash, thrown into the moat! Catherine felt sick. Daubeney had died last year, taking his secret with him to the grave. She raised her hand to her brow, sank down into the chair, and forced herself to breathe. Then she turned her gaze on Henry. "You speak of love, but you do not love. How can you be so cruel? If you do not rectify this wrong that you have done us, you will suffer, Henry. Do you really wish to have a horned devil dive into your throat to seize your soul and take you away to unspeakable horrors? Do a last good deed now, while you can."

"I—" he wheezed. "I speak truth, Cat . . . I love you, and I will help . . . If anyone can find him, 'tis Somerset . . . I have made him the most powerful man in Wales. He can find out anything."

"Will you demand he do this for me? May I send for him?"

Henry gave her a nod. Catherine rose and placed a kiss on his brow. "Thank you, Henry."

"There is one more thing—" he whispered hoarsely.

Catherine waited.

"I wish to make provision for you, Cat . . . A manor house somewhere . . . and an annuity, so you need not fret about money . . ."

His voice drifted off, and he closed his eyes. Catherine bent down and adjusted the coverlet. She took a long, last look at him, this man who had shattered her life. Then she went to summon Somerset.

*   *   *

Catherine pulled another weed from the thousands that choked the grass around her new manor house. She stood up, and grimaced at the pain in her back. The August sun was hot and she had been hard at work since morning. She wiped the perspiration from her brow with the back of her hand and looked up at the sky. Not a cloud any-where and blue as lupine in spring. Or as Scottish thistle ... or as Dickon's eyes. Always, behind her hard work, was ever the thought that drove her: she had to make Fyfield beautiful, for this manor was Dickon's, too. One day he would come home.

Henry had died on the twenty-first day of April, 1509, after many frenzied offerings for his soul. England did not mourn him. All over the land, Harry's ascension was hailed with jubilation and hope. The new king inherited a throne made secure by the stern hand of his father, a fortune greater than any amassed by any previous king, and a kingdom beaten into submission by the bloody ordeal of the Wars of the Roses and Henry's repressive measures. King Harry was handsome, young, happy, and full of promise; he had at last wed the princess he loved, Katherine of Aragon, and on the second day of his reign, amid the rejoicing of trumpets, he rounded up his father's two most hated tax collectors. They now languished in the Tower, await-ing execution. He had also freed Kate's husband, William Courte-nay, from the Tower. There was much to celebrate. "Avarice has left the country, and everything is full of milk and honey," one of Harry's nobles announced in a burst of enthusiasm. "Our new king is not after gold or gems, but virtue, glory, and immortality."

Catherine bent back down and pulled more weeds.

The bells of the St. Nicholas Church on the other side of the yew-tree hedge chimed the hour of five. Soon it would be time for vespers. She rose and gazed over the scene that fanned out before her. Cascading meadows, golden wheat fields, and green farmlands undulated into the distance, covered with red wildflowers and dot-ted with sheep as far as the eye could see. The estate Henry had given her lay near the Vale of White Horse in Berkshire, eight miles from Oxford, in the midst of rich arable soil, and the area sustained an extensive trade in wool. It was a lovely place, and she was grateful for the serenity she had found here in these months.

Henry had died full of fear to the end, tormented by his sins. Terrible memories and imaginings assailed him, and he implored the Virgin to save him from his ancient and ghostly enemy, so that no damned spirits or horned devil would dive into his throat and seize his soul. It was clear to those around him that it was Richard he feared.

Catherine was surprised to find that she missed him. Even more surprising, his death brought back memories of Richard's own. Like a scab on a wound that bled again when picked. But it also meant her freedom, and once she'd grasped the concept that no one cared anymore what she thought or where she went, she reveled in her newfound independence. This manor was her home; it had given her a new life and a future that offered hope. All that had happened at court no longer existed, except in memories that had to be fought back in weak moments.

As the sun began to set, Catherine made her way to a chair placed on the lawn near the house. It was a peaceful hour. She still couldn't believe her good fortune to be here, in her own home, on her own land. Sixteen hundred acres. She loved to sit and listen to the thrushes and watch the light dim over the earth. Somewhere along the long road that had wound through the years, she'd left the carefree girl she'd been behind, and became the frugal woman she was, one that did not shrink from menial tasks, who counted pennies, treasured birdsong, and cherished solitude. *'Tis a beautiful world*, she thought, *and now a corner of it belongs to me and Dickon.*

The property had not been occupied since the owner's death a century earlier. When she'd arrived in May, she had been disheartened to find the grounds returned to wilderness and many buildings in need of repair. She'd bought ploughs and carts to till the fields, and hired a steward. Thomas Smyth was a man in his forties, competent, responsible, and hardworking, and a great asset in the management of her estate. She had a lady's maid, too, Phillipa Huys, whose husband, Alan, was assistant to the steward.

As more servants were hired, and their families came with them, the house filled with the laughter of young people. Sometimes Catherine would close her eyes just to listen, thinking of Dickon. But those moments were few. There was never-ending work for every pair of hands: animals to feed, floors to sweep, clothes to wash. Soil to till and land to clear and buildings to restore. Her expenses were heavy, and the annuity Henry had left her was almost gone for the year. Still, Henry had chosen the estate well. The sprawling manor house was a hundred and fifty years old and in all these years it had had but two owners: Sir John Golafre and, more recently, John de la Pole, Earl of Suffolk, who had died in the first rebellion against Henry. On his attainder, the property had passed to the crown, and there were no claimants fighting over it. Henry knew she would have no legal worries, for a woman alone was easy prey in the courts.

Meanwhile, her days of hard work were brightened by regular missives from Thomas and Maggie, and an occasional visit from James Strangeways, who brought news from court. He was now in the service of Henry VIII and enjoying the new king's lavish banquets and entertainment.

"Sir Charles Somerset has appointed me usher to King Harry," he said, sitting in the garden with her in the full sunshine of the late August day, taking a goblet of wine as she embroidered a square of rose silk for a chair cushion. He was particularly proud of his appointment, for Lord Daubeney had never done much for him, though he was kin.

"That is splendid, James. I wish you great honors." Catherine smiled as she drew her needle carefully through the silk.

"I wished to visit you earlier, but I couldn't get away. The new king keeps me busy twelve hours a day running his household, meeting with his messengers, assigning men to their daily duties, overseeing all the meals, and maintaining the records of expenses to submit to the counting house each day. You may remember his father took care of that detail?"

"Indeed he did. He would entrust that task to no other."

"'Tis how he came to leave his son such a monumental inheritance."

"Henry was a careful man in all things."

"King Harry is the opposite in many ways. Take war, for example. King Henry feared war, but King Harry dreams of the glory of another Agincourt. He has already declared himself desirous of an invasion of France to win back the duchy of Aquitaine that Henry VI lost."

Catherine did not reply. The young and the rash always tended to rush into war heedless of the consequences. She thought of Richard, who had dreamt of war on England when he'd been little older.

"Court is a gay place now, Catherine, and filled with pleasure," James resumed, carefully removing a dandelion seed from his brown furred mantle. "King Harry believes in enjoying himself."

"So I have heard."

"Did you also hear that the king's mother is dead?"

Catherine was taken by surprise. She lowered her embroidery. "When?"

"Two weeks ago, at Westminster."

"So she survived Henry by only two months?" Catherine exclaimed. "One would almost say she died of a broken heart—although they did quarrel in the last year of their lives. And over a manor house, no less." The manor of Collyweston in Northamptonshire had been Lady Margaret's favorite residence, but Henry had grown jealous and decided he wanted it for himself. His mother, however, had no intention of relinquishing her property. As avaricious as her son, and as determined to keep her property as he was to get it from her, she fought him in court every step of the way until he died.

"No, indeed, she didn't take kindly to the confiscation." His eyes were dancing merrily, and the impudent smile she knew so well lifted the corners of his mouth as he watched her. "As soon as the king died, it was awarded back to her, but it proved a hollow victory. She may well have died of a broken heart, for no one did more to secure King Henry's crown, except perhaps Morton, and she may have felt she'd lost her purpose with his death."

"Henry was very bitter about his mother at the end. He was used to having his way, you know."

"Not entirely. I can think of several occasions when he didn't have it." James was staring boldly at her, leaving no doubt what he meant.

Catherine blushed. "But I imagine the judges are relieved?" she said to divert his thoughts.

"Very," he said, not taking his gaze from her face.

"Still, to die so soon after her son's death. 'Tis curious . . . Almost as if Fate is playing her games again. James, stop looking at me that way."

"What way?"

"You know what I mean."

He grinned. "I am perfectly innocent of any crime. I was just thinking how well it agrees with you to be here, in your own home. Are you happy?"

"Happy enough. I am grateful to have found a good steward, and I think that Alice is, too."

He lifted his eyebrows.

She lowered her voice and threw a smiling glance over her shoulder. "I believe there is a romance blooming between those two—indeed, I hope so. I would love Alice to wed, and to have children before it is too late . . ."

A silence fell.

"Something is still missing, then," Strangeways said, giving her a penetrating look. "Is it of Wales you think, or of the past?" He stared at her as if everything hung on her reply.

"I have taken your advice, James. I live in the present now, and have let go the past. It is Wales that I think of with longing."

"Have you heard from Somerset?"

"No. Nothing."

"I think you will soon, Catherine."

Catherine drew a sharp breath. "Have you learned something—did he say something?"

"He gave me a message to give you. He told me to tell you he has not forgotten his oath to the old king."

Tears rushed to her eyes. She seized his hand. "Oh, James—how wonderful it would be—what it would mean—"

James looked down at her hand, and Catherine saw that his color had deepened. A sudden thrill passed through her. She pulled her hand from his. "I am glad you are here, James," she said softly.

"Are you?"

"I am." And Catherine realized with a jolt of surprise that the words she had spoken were true.

* * *

Sir Charles Somerset arrived late one winter afternoon, surrounded by his entourage. Catherine saw him from the window of her upstairs bedroom as his procession came down the long gravel path between the hedges. She smoothed her hair beneath her headband and veil, and straightened her gown as she ran downstairs, calling for her ladies.

"The king's lord chamberlain, Sir Charles Somerset, is coming! Make haste—have the servants get the rooms ready—have we food? Tell the cook to slaughter a pig for dinner—and have them bring us cheese and sweetmeats and wine in the great hall—quickly!"

Catherine drew a deep breath and stepped outside to greet the man she hoped would bring her news of her son.

"My Lord Somerset," she said, holding out her hand to the gray-haired gentleman clad in the rich velvets and furs of a courtier, and wearing the gold chain of office around his chest. His crinkly blue eyes took sharp appraisal of her, and she hoped anxiously that she met with his approval. "'Tis a great honor to see you again."

"I am on my way to Oxford on the king's business, and thought to stop briefly and pay my respects. It has been a long time, Lady Catherine."

"Ten months," Catherine replied.

"I regret I have been unable to come earlier. I was in France. We have begun negotiating the marriage of Princess Mary Rose to the Dauphin."

"'Tis most kind of you to come here now, as busy as you are with royal matters. Shall we go inside?"

They spent a comfortable evening remembering the old king, and his good queen, Elizabeth. Over dinner they took on literature, and history, and the fall of Troy, the sorrows of the vanquished, and the birth of Rome. The trestle tables were dismantled, and they moved into the solar, where a fire blazed and they could talk more privately over wine. Somerset took a seat across from Catherine.

"And so it has been since the time of King Arthur—nay, since the time of Scripture it has been so," Catherine mused. "Old ways give way to new, and lost hopes are buried or bury those who pine for them. The cycle has been part of life since Adam fell from Paradise. Nothing changes much, does it?"

Somerset regarded her, his old blue eyes thoughtful, kind. "What you speak is called wisdom. You were very young when you lost your world. Yet you continued on with your head held high. And if you mourned for that lost world, no one knew it but you. I should like very much to learn your secret, Lady Gordon. For I find you quite remarkable."

Catherine turned her head to the window. Twilight was falling; the earth had grown still. Soon it would be dark. "Someone much wiser than I once told me that when darkness falls, the stars come out. Sir Charles—" She leaned close and lowered her voice so that no one would hear her words but him, "My star is my little boy. He is my secret. Do you have news of him?"

Somerset was silent for a long moment. Then he nodded. "Shall we go into the garden? I believe Orion can be seen this evening."

Catherine froze in her chair. "Orion?"

"You know the hunter? He races across the night sky, fleeing Scorpio, but never the twain shall meet. Come summer, it will be Scorpio that rises, and Orion that falls."

She rose and led the way, her heart thundering in her bosom. Coincidence, nothing more, she told herself. Coincidence. And yet—

The wind had risen and the night was chill, and from all around them came the chirping of night critters. They followed the long grassy path to the point where it fell steeply down into the meadow. Stars sparkled in the vast expanse of sky overhead, and from the sleepy village in the far distance came the faint flicker of light.

"There is Orion—see?" said Somerset, pointing over his head.

"I see indeed." Fixing her gaze on Richard's star, she sent a brief prayer heavenward, and turned her attention back to Somerset.

"I have made inquiries, Lady Gordon, but this is a sensitive matter that demands utmost discretion. Therefore, I must warn you that progress will be slow."

Catherine waited, not daring to utter a sound.

"That said, I have established that your babe was taken to southwestern Wales. 'Tis only a matter of time before I narrow it down and learn exactly where in Gower he was sent. You will have to be patient, Lady Gordon. As I said, 'tis a most delicate matter."

She nodded, and raised her eyes to Richard's star sparkling above Somerset's head. "Thank you," she murmured to them both. "Thank you."

*   *   *

It was a glorious October day. Breezes swept the trees, scattering fallen leaves like jewels across the walks and pathways. From the chantry across the road there drifted the periodic chant of monk-song, while the bells of St. Nicholas on the other side of the yew-tree walk rang loudly, marking the hours. Catherine was in the garden supervising the laying of the flower beds when she heard the sound of hooves, and as she peered through a tangle of rose vines, she saw James Strangeways's tall figure riding up to the house on his ebony horse. She wiped her hands on her skirt and, smoothing the hair that was caught in a net at the nape of her neck, walked to the path to greet him. He was almost at the porch when he saw her.

"Catherine," he said with a low bow, his dark eyes dancing, "my, how fine you look this day. You are a vision for sore eyes and a potion for my heart."

"And you, James Strangeways, are full of fiddle-faddle," she said, surprised at how pleased she was to see him. *He looks well in gray,* she thought; *it complements his dark coloring.* Linking arms with him, she led him to the back of the house, where chairs had been set to face the view. She called for wine, and took a seat.

"God's knuckles, you have cleared the entire stretch here up to the fields!" he exclaimed, throwing a glance around.

His stance emphasized the force of his thighs. She had forgotten how well built he was. Catherine blushed and looked away quickly before he noticed. "Aye, we've made good progress, haven't we?" she said. "Everyone has been working hard."

"What do you have in mind for this area? More flower gardens?"

"No, an orchard. Apples to sell, and cherries. Anything that makes money."

He laughed. "I hope you can spare a few cherries to bake me a pie? I happen to be very fond of cherry pie." He caught her gaze and held it until she blushed and looked away. She found herself suddenly tongue-tied. It was James who broke the silence that fell between them. "I would have come to see you before now, but I had business in Wiltshire and Salisbury. My properties needed tending. How have you managed here?"

Catherine's face fell. She remembered how angry she'd been to hear the steward tell about certain tenant-farmers who were continually delinquent in their rents. She'd assumed it was because she was a woman, and had personally marched down to one of the shacks and pounded on the door. There she had found the tenant's wife on her knees on the earthen floor, sobbing beside the lifeless body of their child.

She banished the memory. She dreaded demanding rents, and avoided doing so, and too many unscrupulous tenants were taking advantage of the knowledge.

"Since you ask, James—" she began. And from there, she found herself speaking of the difficulties administering her large estate. "There are problems with revenues. My tenant farmers tell me they need more time to make the payments they owe me and claim a variety of setbacks—sickness with their animals, or bad weather for the crops, and so on. Some lie, but not all. I have not the heart to be harsh with them, though the steward assures me that if I am to win their respect, I must be seen as a taskmaster."

"The king's mother was respected because she never forgave a debt," James said. "Not even one owed to her grandfather a hundred years ago. She fought in the courts for every groat she deemed owed to her. She would even take away a man's plough if he could not pay, and send him to prison."

"James, that is dreadful! I believe in fair dealing and concessions to help those in need, but many of the excuses I am given are outright fabrications. I know I should press those who deceive me for their own gain, but it takes a great deal of time and money to pursue a claim in court—time and money I do not have. I will fight them as soon as I am able, but court is a hard place for a woman. 'Twas different for the king's mother. She was who she was, and I am a foreigner, a woman alone now that Henry is gone. Besides, men side with men. 'Tis common knowledge that King Harry hates the Scots and did not favor me with a position in his queen's household. I fear I can expect little success in the courts where influence is all that matters."

Now a far more serious problem had reared its ugly head. Henry had given her Fyfield because it was clear of debts and claims. However, a claimant to the manor had emerged who was a distant relative to its onetime owner, John de la Pole, Earl of Suffolk. Suffolk had died in battle against Henry and been attainted, and his property and titles had been forfeited to the crown. No one would have dared present such a claim during Henry's lifetime, but with a woman owning the manor—and a rich manor at that—she was fair game for unscrupulous men. She had never shied away from a fight, and fully intended to give as good a punch as she got, but there were only so many hours in the day.

James listened patiently to her troubles, then reached over and took her hand. "Do not fret anymore. With the exception of the claim on the property, these problems can be dealt with fairly easily. I shall stay and do what I can to clear them up for you."

"How kind of you! But—how can you possibly stay? You must get back to the king."

"I required leave for urgent personal business, and if this does not qualify as urgent person business, I know not what does." He turned her hand over and pressed a kiss into her palm. His touch leapt through her, warming and thrilling her body, stirring old memories of love beneath starry skies. For a moment she wanted to run her hands through his hair, and feel the hot stir of passion in her loins.

But he is not Richard. Bewildered, blushing furiously, she withdrew her hand from his.

Chapter 20

A Rose in Bloom

During the months that followed and the year 1510, James Strangeways was no stranger to Fyfield. He visited regularly and stayed at least a week each time, riding with the steward to the farthest reaches of Catherine's sixteen-hundred-acre estate. As good as his word, he resolved many of Catherine's problems. What he told her tenant farmers, Catherine did not know, but she received few excuses from them for nonpayment of their debts, and those that did plead for an extension due to hardship proved genuine. All her farmhands suddenly became cooperative and hardworking, and yields went up. In addition, there was injected into the townsmen who dealt with her a new attitude of deference. She began to receive good value for the money she paid them for goods and services, and the merchants who bought her wool no longer offered her low prices for her bales. Her worries eased; revenues increased; she slept better and ate with more appetite, and she began to look forward more avidly to James's visits.

Always, when she caught sight of his tall figure riding up to the house on his ebony courser, followed by his manservant, William Sholson, her heart leapt with excitement. Why this should be, she didn't know. Surely it wasn't love. Love came but once a lifetime, and she belonged to Richard. Never would she love again.

"James!" she called, hurrying from the great hall to the front door. "'Tis so good to see you!" She did not venture out from the shelter of the porch, for the December day was cold and snow flurries fell.

James dropped down from his horse and threw the reins over to Phillipa's boy, who disappeared in the direction of the stables with Sholson. James's powerful, well-muscled body moved with easy grace and his laughing eyes were filled with admiration as he came crunching over the snow toward her. When she looked up into his face, she felt suddenly young, buoyant, and happier than she could remember. Taking his arm, she led him into the house, which was bedecked for Yule, with greenery in the niches and ribbons and holly boughs in the windows. In the great hall, where a fire roared welcome, they took a seat together on a settle by the hearth. They were chattering about the weather when Alice entered, bearing a tray laden with wine and pasties.

"Alice, my sweet, not married yet?" James teased. "You do give these lads a run for their money, don't you? The talk in the taverns is all of you, my dear."

Alice blushed beneath his charm and smiled a gap-toothed smile, for she had lost a tooth in the past year. "There, there, ye know I won't be believin' anythin' ye say, Master Strangeways," she announced in her Scottish brogue. "Why, ye tell that to all the girls, whether they be fifteen or fifty."

Strangeways roared merrily. How wonderful it was, Catherine thought, to hear such a hearty, joyful male laugh in her quiet home. That Alice was fond of James pleased her, too. Often he smacked her rump, sending her into fits of giggles like a maiden. When she caught her breath again, she would pretend to be offended, and he would present her with a gift.

"Such a nice gentleman, that Master Strangeways," Alice would say after his visits. "What a difference he makes at Fyfield. And he's sweet on ye, he is, my Lady Cate," she'd say.

"Alice, what are you suggesting?"

"I'm suggesting the obvious, my Lady Cate. Anyone who has eyes in their head can see it for themselves, and ye'd have to be blind to miss it." Pointedly, she would add, "Ye shouldn't be single, m'lady. 'Tisn't natural. Ye be too young for one thing, and it'd be nice to have a man about the place."

"Master Strangeways is not the marrying kind, Alice—no man is who's nearly reached fifty and never wed. And a good thing, too, for I shall never marry again either. You know that as well as I. In any case, that's enough prattle, Alice. You have work to do, don't you?"

Now Catherine watched Alice set down a bowl of nuts and meat pasties on the coffer. She arranged two goblets and a flask of wine within easy reach, and curtsied her departure, giving Catherine a knowing glance as she shut the door behind her. Catherine smiled helplessly to herself. *As if we need privacy,* she thought.

James missed neither Alice's glance nor Catherine's indulgent smile. He watched her pour wine, and accepted the cup she gave him. He had something important to say, and now, on the spur of the moment, he decided not to wait until after dinner, as he'd planned. He downed a long swallow, and put his goblet back on the coffer.

"Have you missed me, Catherine?" he said, his eyes alert, expectant.

"I have, James. 'Tis always good to see you. I am happy you came to Fyfield for Yule. I want little Maggie and her father to meet you. They are family to me, you know."

"Catherine," he said, taking her hand into his, "I would like to be family to you, too."

Catherine knitted her eyebrows together in puzzlement. "I don't understand."

James fell to a knee before her. "Catherine, I want to marry you."

She stared at him in astonishment.

"I have loved you for a long time, Catherine. While King Henry lived, I dared not speak of my affection. The day he proposed to you was the worst day of my life, for I thought I would surely lose you forever. Never could I have imagined that you would refuse a king! I admire you so, Catherine, and I love you in a way I could never have imagined loving anyone. There is no one like you in all the world. I beg you to say yes to me. Marry me, and make me the happiest man in Christendom!"

As Catherine stared at James, it was Richard she saw, golden-haired, blue-eyed, full of princely dignity, bending his knee before her. She leapt to her feet and withdrew her hand. "James, I cannot marry you. Not because I don't care for you—I care very much. 'Tis just that I will never marry again."

"Your husband has been dead for eleven years, Catherine—"

But he is not dead to me, she thought, dropping her lids so he wouldn't read her thoughts. "And you!" James exclaimed. "Catherine, you are alive! Let yourself live!"

Before she could stop herself, she was in his arms and his lips were pressed down hard on hers, hot, demanding, urgent. Richard's face blurred and dimmed into the deepest recesses of memory and there was only the present moment, and James's hard body burning into her. She dissolved in his arms as ice melts before fire.

"Say yes! Say yes to me—yes, to life—yes, to love!" he demanded, holding her tightly to him. He slid his mouth along her neck, smothering her with kisses, his breath scorching her skin.

"Yes," she murmured faintly, then with increasing fervor as fire surged through her once again, "yes—yes . . ."

He took her hand and kissed her palm. Dizzy, she closed her eyes, savoring the tingling heat. She never wanted it to stop. Oh, for it to go on like this forever, and never to stop— She didn't know she could ever feel like this again. Through her giddy senses, she heard him speak.

"You won't be sorry, my Catherine."

*   *   *

In a hurry to wed, James pressed Catherine for a January wedding, but she resisted. That month was sacrosanct, for it was in January that she'd wed Richard. Claiming to need more time to plan the wedding, she avoided giving James the real reason. Reluctantly he agreed to wait until March.

The Yule of 1510 was a happy one at Fyfield. Catherine found that the thrill of living had returned. The scene inside the house was of domestic tranquility. She hired two minstrels to play until Twelfth Night, and they made merry while the manor prepared for the arrival of their Yuletide guests. Alice and the servants took much time to celebrate the tidings of her betrothal by consuming barrels of ale, malmsey, and wine, for they all liked James and wished to ensure his health by frequent toasting. It became such a problem that Catherine complained to James about it.

"Your popularity is costing me much money, James," she grumbled one evening when they were alone in the solar together. "All the servants do is get drunk toasting your health. I've been considering limiting them, for they're not getting enough work done. Our guests will soon be here, and we are not ready."

"I'd say you were jealous if I didn't know better—" James laughed, kissing her brow. Then, in a change of tone, he added, "Forget about expense, Catherine. A betrothal should be celebrated in rowdiness, and joy should not be curtailed. Think of it this way—can there be too many nightingales singing at night, too many rosebuds in May, too many dawns in life? Let them rejoice, my sweet. Lenten is around the corner. They'll make up for it then."

Catherine saw then the truth of what he said, and let the servants alone. In fact, she found herself smiling when they grew boisterous and staggered carrying out their tasks. In one way or another, James's presence had benefited everyone at Fyfield, she thought, not only her. From the advice he dispensed, to keeping the young and unruly farmhands under firm control, his manly grip had eased their lives. They all had reason to celebrate.

Thomas and Maggie finally arrived from the Isle of Wight two days before Christmas. Maggie took to James immediately and was invariably found on his lap having her hair smoothed, or enjoying a card game with him by the fire. Local gentry came to pay their respects and brought gifts of homemade jellies, wine, or sweets, and often stayed to dinner, so that the house filled with laughter and dancing and the pleasant hum of conversation. But there was one neighbor Catherine could have well done without, and that was Francis Fremont. With his strange glinting eyes and unpleasant way of holding her hand too long, he unsettled her in a most discomforting way. He was unmarried at thirty-two, his reputation as a gambler, drinker, and lecher having preceded him all over the county. No self-respecting family would give him their daughter. James favored him, however, and so he came too often to Fyfield.

To offset this blot on her happiness, Catherine was pleased to find that Thomas and James got along well together. Cecily's marriage to "an obscure man of no reputation," as Henry's historian, Vergil, had put it, had made Cecily an outcast among the royals, but Catherine remembered with a smile how her friend had declared, in her usual high-spirited and mirthful way, "And do I care a whit for their opinion?"

Sometimes, during dinner, they played Maggie's favorite game of "Pass the Parcel," where a package tied with a ribbon would be passed from person to person between courses. When the music stopped, whoever held the parcel would open it, and they would either find a gift or a forfeit. This was accompanied either by yelps of joy or groans of disappointment.

"I have a ring!" Maggie exclaimed in delight on the first day of Christmas, lifting her hand for everyone to admire the sparkle of a pink crystal stone set in gold.

"God's blood, I have a dare," James complained. "I must leap in the air three times, like a tumbler!" And when he fell flat on his face on the third tumble, Maggie squealed with laughter.

One evening, when they were between guests in the solar, Catherine stole a glance at Cecily's family over her embroidery, and said a silent prayer for her friend. *How dear to me you were, my sister, and how dear your family is now. If only you could have lived to see how well Maggie is turning out, you would have been so proud.* Then she chased the sadness away with a smile, for life had taught her not to let the losses of the past blight the happiness of the present. She turned her attention to James.

"Now that the old king is dead, the mood at court is much

changed," he was saying. "'Tis an almost unbroken round of daily revels, disguisings, mayings, pageants, tilts, and jousts, interspersed with long days in the saddle hawking, and long nights banqueting, gambling and dancing, and making music. Since it falls to me to arrange these matters, you can imagine how weary I am some days," he smiled.

"What is a pageant?" piped little Maggie.

"Mummers perform scenes from the Bible," James explained. "Or sometimes, from tales of chivalry. I remember one where beautiful maidens danced around the roses and pomegranates of England and Spain that were growing out of a golden stake set on a hill. The girls wore colorful tulles and silks that you would love, Maggie—and in their hands they held pieces of wood they clicked to mark the beat of the music as they twirled. It was quite splendid."

"I've never seen a pageant," said Maggie.

"Is that so, little lady? Then I shall make sure that you receive an invitation to the very next one."

Maggie beamed.

"Court sounds delightful," hinted Francis Fremont, who was present on this occasion.

"It has its charms," James agreed. But he didn't promise Fremont an invitation, and Catherine wondered if James was afraid his friend's reputation would reflect poorly on him among his peers.

"Is the king handsome?" continued Maggie.

"King Harry is as handsome as a god, my little lady. He's tall and well built, with auburn hair and a round pink face. At seventeen, he's not much older than you. And he is a gifted prince. He rides like a knight, and plays the lute better than the best minstrel. He'll probably compose a song for you when you come, but you'll have to make me a promise before I allow you to meet him."

"What is that?" Maggie asked sweetly.

"That you will not steal his heart."

Everyone chuckled, and Maggie beamed.

"I hear that King Harry is contemplating war with France," said Thomas, moving to a more sober subject. "Is it true?"

"True indeed. King Henry followed the arts of peace and had no use for the sword. But King Harry is different. He has no wish to be a quiet working monarch. He excels in deeds of arms, and desires to prove himself in the field."

"I presume Spain will be our ally in the venture?"

"Aye. King Ferdinand is interested in annexing Navarre."

Thomas fell silent, and Catherine, too. Harry had inherited a throne his father had made remarkably secure, and a fortune greater than any in history, as well as a kingdom that was the most obedient and peaceful in Christendom. And England had welcomed Henry's son with a jubilation not known in living memory, for Harry's father and grandmother had been grasping, stern, and much hated. To his people, the amiable young monarch represented deliverance from their oppressive rule. Few reigns had begun amid such promise and hope, but Catherine knew Harry too well. He was selfish, volatile, and jealous; he had quick-silver changes of mood, and he possessed a strong streak of cruelty. She remembered how he had taunted Richard. She remembered, too, how he had enjoyed watching and discussing executions. That he lost no time executing Edmund de la Pole and his brother, William, as soon as he was king came as no surprise. His playthings, in addition to the lute and pen, were hatchets, blades, and other instruments of death.

No, she could not celebrate his ascension to the throne. Cruel as Henry had been, he had not been without scruples, and she suspected his son had none. Shortly after ascending the throne, Harry had executed two of his father's most devoted ministers. Never mind that they were hated by the people. The fact that he could take life so carelessly boded ill for his reign.

"When do you think he will take us to war?" inquired Thomas.

"Soon."

"As gentleman usher, you will accompany him, I gather?" said Francis Fremont.

"No. When I marry"—he reached for Catherine's hand—"I shall request a position as Justice of the Peace so I can live here, with my wife."

"You will not miss the excitement of court life?" Fremont quirked an eyebrow.

James laughed. "It shall be exciting enough here at Fyfield."

Blushing, Catherine smiled and dropped her lids. When she looked up, she saw Fremont leaning on a coffer in a corner of the room, staring at her with a flagon of wine in his hand. On his face was such a look of raw sexual desire that she recoiled.

She left James on the settle and approached Fremont. She put her hand up to her lips as if to whisper a secret, and announced in a loud voice, "Master Fremont, I hate to tell you this, but your codpiece is slipping."

He colored to the roots of his hair.

"What's a codpiece?" Maggie asked from the other side of the room.

"I'll show you on your hound tomorrow," Catherine said, smiling sweetly.

* * *

A few days before her wedding, after communing with Richard in the garden and praying for him at St. Nicholas, Catherine removed the gold fleur-de-lis of diamonds that he had placed around her neck on their wedding day, along with his letter, and gently laid them to rest in a secret compartment of her jewel coffer. She didn't abandon her widow's weeds for her wedding, however. "Until I find my child, I can wear nothing else," she had explained to James, but she made concessions. She added white ribbons and a pearl headdress to her veil, and white fur to her collar and cuffs, and carried a bouquet of white narcissus.

For these past three months, Catherine had been beset with misgivings. To wed, or not to wed? Should she cancel the wedding before it was too late? Before she made a mistake? But what of the scandal that would ensue if she did? And what reason could she give for such a step? True, she didn't like James's choice of companions, but every wife in the land had to put up with disreputable relatives, or friends whom they would rather not see. Maybe it wasn't Fremont but Richard who held her back, she thought. She didn't love James the way she'd loved Richard, and it had been a long time since she'd slept with a man. Sometimes the thought of intimacy filled her with dread, and sometimes remembrance would flood her with the heady feeling that was hers each time James took her into his arms. What if she gave him up and he never came again to Fyfield—could she bear never to see him again? And what of the manor? Memory of the months when she had struggled as a woman alone rose up to torment her sleep. Without James, how would she fight off the de la Pole relative who litigated against her in court? That headache had not yet been put to rest, and posed peril to her hold on Fyfield.

Aye, what of all this—how would she keep her manor without the help of an influential man?

In the end she buried her doubts and wed James on the tenth of March, 1511. It was a small affair, for James had no relatives, and she had only Thomas and Maggie. She had invited Cecily's sister, Kate Courtenay, but she had declined. She was in mourning for her husband, William, whose nearly eight years of captivity in the foul Tower had led to death nine months after his release.

In other news that dampened Catherine's spirits, their honeymoon had to be deferred. Young King Harry was anxious to begin his campaign against France, and James had to help Somerset plan the invasion.

"I'll be back as soon as I can, my sweet," he whispered in her ear as they took their leave of one another in front of the servants. "And as often as I can." With a kiss farewell, he trotted off on his ebony courser, Sholson following behind.

James proved as good as his word. Since Fyfield lay but a half-day's journey from London, he sometimes came for a night or two without being missed at court. And Catherine was mostly happy. Life had been so serious and bitter before, and now it was light and pleasant. She had done the right thing marrying James, she thought. He was amusing company and their nights were glorious, filled with delightful lovemaking that brought a blush to her cheeks with remembrance. Still, his frequent visits to Francis Fremont distressed her. Often he stayed all night and came back drunk and disheveled. "You know I like to gamble a little," James would say when she pressed him. But she knew there was more to it than that.

James made progress with the claim against Fyfield, however, and assured of Somerset's support with the litigation and a good outcome, he was able to put her mind at ease on that issue. And in July he returned to Fyfield with heartening news.

"Somerset's inquiries about Dickon have proved fruitful," he said. "He's established that he was in Swansea for a while. He is pursuing some leads and is hopeful he'll have more information soon."

Catherine closed her eyes. Bowing her head, she gave a prayer of thanks.

* * *

One afternoon in August, returning from a check of the crops in the fields, she found James in argument with another man in one of the small rooms off the hall. "I told you never to come here!" he was saying in an angry voice. "Get out and stay out! I never want to see you here again!"

"James?" she said, coming into view.

Both men fell silent and turned to her. The stranger gave a bow. "The famed Lady Gordon, I presume? 'Tis an honor to meet you."

Catherine glanced from the stranger to James, whose face had darkened as he fought for control.

"Allow me to introduce myself," the young man offered when James said nothing. "I am Giles Strangeways, a cousin to James."

Catherine extended her hand as she threw James a look. Should they not invite the young man to stay? But James glared at her and she dared not extend an invitation.

Catherine turned on James after Giles left, claiming business in London. "Why would you treat kin in such a shabby manner?"

"'Tis not your business!" he exclaimed. "And I'll thank you never to mention his name again."

A few weeks later, a stranger rode up to Fyfield and pounded at the front door, yelling for James. Catherine leaned out of the bedroom window and looked down. Clearly, the man was drunk, for he waved his hands around and cursed her steward, Thomas Smyth, demanding to see James as he tried to push his way in. She reached the bottom of the staircase just as an altercation was about to break out between them.

"'Tis all right," Catherine called from the stairs, hurrying down. "I will see him, Thomas."

The man recovered a modicum of civility when she appeared, and removed his hat. He gave her an awkward bow, for his legs were unsteady from drink. "M'lady, me thanks to ye. Ye be a lady, not an uncouth, kettle-faced scallybag like this knave here—" Smyth's face darkened and Catherine feared they would come to blows in her presence.

"It would please me much if you would sheath your tongue long enough to inform me what this disturbance is about." She turned to Alice. "Pray fetch Jack and Piers, for I have business with them, as soon as this matter is dispensed with." Jack and Piers were two of the burliest young fellows she had working for her on the manor. They could be counted on to throw this ruffian out like a barrel of sour wine, if it came to that.

Catherine swept into the great hall and turned to face the man who followed her, but he had halted in his steps and was looking around in awe at the soaring, ornate roof, the silver candlesticks in the niches, and the tapestried settle and velvet chairs. "A fine place ye have here. Fine indeed, n'er thought to see James livin' in such finery." He looked at her. "And with such a beautiful lady like ye. He's done well fer himself, I'll give him that, the old skullmudgeon!" He guffawed. "Mighty well indeed, I'll say that fer him."

"State your business," Catherine demanded.

"Aw—ye don't approve o'me, do ye? No matter, no matter, a fine lady like ye, 'tis to be expected. I'll state my business fer certes—do ye 'ave a little something I can use to wet me mouth? 'Tis dry, my mouth is— I've ridden far this day, and it would help to have a little something—"

Catherine poured him a cup of wine from the flask on the coffer and held it out to him at arm's reach. She feared to catch lice or ver-min if she drew too close.

"Me lady, ye see it be like this, it be—" He took a long draught and smacked his lips. "Ah, that's better . . . Ye see, Strangeways owes me money."

"Owes *you* money?" Catherine reacted without thinking. This was such an abominable, impossible farce, she couldn't restrain from lashing out.

"I know I don't have the airs of a gentleman, but 'tis truth I speak—by the mass, it's truth. Yer husband owes me twenty pounds he lost to me gamblin' with the dice."

Catherine's hand went to her lips to quell the gasp in her throat. "Twenty pounds?"

"Twenty pounds he's owin' me. An' he's been sayin' he's goin' to pay, an' givin' me promises for over two years now, but he doesn't pay, and I've come to collect."

Catherine felt a chill creep over her as she listened to the man's speech, for now she knew that James's relative had come for the same reason. "I know nothing about this matter. You shall have to speak to my husband about it."

"See here, that be just the point. He's a lyin' bastard he is—"

"How dare you insult my husband to me!" Catherine demanded, raising her voice and balling her fists at her sides. "To come here with this damnable lie when you know my husband is not home to refute you. How dare you!"

"I swear it ain't a lie, me lady—I have here this piece of paper—and his promise to pay is in his own hand . . ." He held out a filthy, crumpled piece of paper.

Not taking her eye from the ruffian, Catherine moved closer. She cocked her head to read:

I, James Strangeways, gentleman usher to King Henry VII, do promise to pay this debt of twenty pounds within one year from the date given.

It was James's handwriting, to be sure, dated June 1509. But it had to be a forgery, for where in God's name would James meet such a scurvy character? "How did you come by this? Who gave it to you?"

"Master James Strangeways, he gave it to me hisself—in Salisbury, when he gambled at the Old Boar Inn—and whored, too, I might add—" He began to snicker, then remembered where he was. "Me lady, forgit that part—I didna mean to add that—'tis only the money I care about."

For the first time since the man's arrival, Catherine sensed he might be telling the truth. Salisbury was where James owned land and a few tenements. She had never questioned him about his properties, but now she wondered what else she didn't know about her husband. She felt sick. She put her hand to her brow to steady her head, and when she'd recovered her composure, she said, "You had best speak to him. He will be here the day after tomorrow."

The man was ushered out, and Catherine sank to the settle, trembling. Summoning the servants, she ordered them not to speak of the man's visit to anyone. "The master is not to know until I've had a chance to tell him. Is that understood?"

"Aye, my lady," they murmured with one voice, scattering back to their chores.

* * *

When James arrived two days later, she merely took his arm in silence. After he had rested and left to check matters with the steward, she took his key from his pouch and went to the coffer where he kept his private papers. Riffling through the stash, she found what she was looking for. Her strength ebbed from her as she read, and she leaned her weight on the desk, feeling weak.

No, there was no doubt. In November 1510, James had received a loan of sixty-six pounds, thirteen shillings, and four pence from King Henry VIII. And fresh from this monstrous debt, he had ridden to Fyfield and proposed to her.

Chapter 21

A Song in the Night

1512

When James returned from his survey of the estate, Catherine led him to the solar and confronted him with the promissory note. "Tell me the truth—did you marry me for my money?" she demanded, still pale with the shock of discovery.

"Have you lost your senses? What are you talking about?"

"This!" She threw the royal note at him.

He glanced at it, lying at his feet. "I didn't marry you for money. But perhaps you should tell me why you married me?" he said coldly.

She stared at him, incredulous. "I have no idea what you mean."

"You know exactly what I mean. You lust for Richard in your heart. Don't you think I can feel it?"

"What in Heaven's name are you talking about?"

"Richard! That's what I'm talking about. You pretend I'm Richard each time you're in my arms, don't you—don't you?" He was red-faced and shaking with rage.

"You're mad! I married you because I cared about you. How can you do this? I've been a good wife to you—"

"Good is not good enough!"

"What more do you want? To ruin us with your gambling? Is that what you want?"

"I want you to stop thinking about him! I want him gone from our lives!" He grabbed her by the arms and shook her as if she were a rag doll. "I'm sick of having three in our bed!"

"Stop it!" Catherine cried. His eyes held a wild look and she was suddenly afraid. "Let me go! You're behaving like a ruffian!"

He froze, then dropped his hands.

"We must discuss this, James! It's not going away."

"No. Richard has to go away—I can't take it anymore."

"Sixty-six pounds you owe the king! How many years do you think it's going to take to pay back that kind of money? If you loved me, you wouldn't be doing this. How can I trust a man who doesn't care that he's ruining us?"

"And how can I love a woman who wishes I were another man, and drives me to drink!"

"You drank and gambled before you met me! When are you going to stop blaming other people for your shortcomings? You are a coward, James Strangeways!"

He swung on her. "How dare you?"

"A coward you are, indeed. What else would you call a man who steals from a woman? If you had any guts, you'd find a way to pay back that money with honest labor."

He stared at her, his face ashen white with anger. Swiveling on his heel, he grabbed his cloak from the peg and strode out. She ran after him to the driveway and reached him as he mounted his horse. "Where are you going?" she called as he galloped away.

"Where I'm welcome!" he yelled back through the cloud of dust he left behind.

* * *

James didn't return for two days, and when he did, he was drunk. Sholson put him to bed, and Catherine went to the woods to find solitude, and to pray. Her relationship with God had been tested to destruction that night at the river, but it had come back stronger than before. She felt near to Him in nature where His hand was more evident than in a church built by man. Despite her faith, however, she was unable to shake her worry. She had to find a way to make James see reason, or they would indeed lose everything. This was the thrust of her prayer: that God would see fit to help her find a way.

That evening they dined alone, and in silence. When Catherine found the right moment, she went straight to the heart of the problem. "James, we have to do something, or you will be ruined."

"I? From what I recall, it was 'us' only the other day."

"I am the sole owner of Fyfield. They cannot come to me for payment of your debts."

"Then you have no worries, have you?"

"I do have worries. I worry about you. 'Tis a terrible thing to see your husband on an evil path and not to be able to help him." She raised her large azure eyes to his.

His broad shoulders sagged suddenly, and he gave a sigh and passed a hand over his face. "Oh, Catherine—"

"James—" she said, laying a hand on his sleeve. "Francis Fremont is part of the problem. You must cut him out of our lives."

"I cannot," James murmured miserably, his hand hiding his face.

"Because you owe him money?"

"Aye . . . him, and others."

"How much?"

"Thirty pounds."

Catherine's heart sank, but this was no time for self-pity. "I will help you pay off the debt, James, but you cannot attend his gatherings, and he is not to come to Fyfield again. Inform him that you will be making monthly payments until the sum you owe him is paid in full. I'll do the same with your other debtors. And James—"

He dropped his hand and looked at her.

"You must promise me that you will give up gambling and look for lucrative work."

"What do you suggest? The king pays me twenty pounds a year

for fourteen hours' work a day, seven days a week, and I get another twenty from my estates. What would you have me do, Catherine? Pirate a ship?"

"You have a sharp mind. You are energetic. You know how to manage men. You'll think of something."

James cut back on his visits to Francis, though he still went, and still came back drunk. And they still argued over Francis, and James's drinking. But he did think of something. Instead of requesting a post as Justice of the Peace in Berkshire so he could remain at Fyfield and manage Catherine's estates, he requested to accompany the king on his expedition to France. War afforded a chance to acquire riches from booty and ransom. Maybe, in this way, if they were fortunate, they could shed their terrible debt.

James was assigned the post of captain. He went to work raising men for the royal army, and Catherine didn't see much of him over the winter. She didn't think he was drinking as much because work claimed his energies. In May, he was busy gathering gunpowder, bows, arrows, and bowstrings for the master of the ordinance, and in June he left for France.

Four months later, he was back. From the upstairs window of the solar, Catherine saw him trotting up the drive with Sholson. Relief flooded her as she rushed down the stairs to meet him. But she halted abruptly in her steps, checked by the expression on his face. He began to dismount. Catherine ran to him.

"You're wounded, James! Here, let me help you . . ." She took his arm as he winced in pain. Supporting his weight on one side, as Sholson did on the other, she led him into the great hall. He let himself down heavily into a chair by the hearth. She poured him a cup of wine. "What happened?"

"I took a sword thrust to my back, and to my thigh. I was laid up for three months. And I caught the bloody flux."

"He almost died, my lady," said Sholson.

Catherine gasped.

James dismissed Sholson then, and together they watched him take his leave.

"Are you all right now?" Catherine asked gently.

"Depends what you mean by all right . . . I'm alive, at least."

Catherine fell silent. Clearly, James had no wish to talk about his injuries, or his ailments. Dysentery was a dreadful disease, debilitating and often fatal, but James had survived. He was strong. Surely, time would heal him completely. "What about the war with France?" she asked.

He took a gulp of wine. "It was a disaster."

Catherine sank down on the settle.

"King Ferdinand was supposed to be our ally against France, but once he won Navarre, he packed up and left, leaving our men to be slaughtered at Fuentarrabia. The army returned to England near mutiny."

"And King Harry?"

James shook his head, and his eyes darted to the open door of the great hall. Catherine understood. Harry had made a mess of things. "He wishes to mount a second invasion as soon as possible." He emptied his wine cup.

"There is something you should know, Catherine," James resumed after a silence. "King James has renewed the 'Auld Alliance' between Scotland and France."

Catherine's heart quickened. Despite Margaret's marriage to James, matters between Scotland and England had steadily deteriorated over the years. In contrast to the usual border squabbles, this was serious. France was Scotland's traditional ally, and Harry's hostility to France was bound to draw Scotland into the conflict sooner or later.

"What about you, James? You cannot sign up again." Her eye went to his leg, propped up uselessly before him.

"I have applied for a post as Justice of the Peace for Berkshire. There may be opportunities in county politics to augment my income. Meanwhile, Somerset has informed me there is only one way out of the legal action brought against Fyfield by de la Pole's relative."

Catherine held her breath.

"Your grant of lands from King Henry is not valid in law. You must surrender it, and the property will then be regranted to both you and me."

Catherine stared at him. Could this be true, or was it a ruse to transfer his debts to her? That she could even think such a thing made her realize how irretrievably the trust between them was broken. She rose to her feet and turned to the window so he would not read her thoughts.

"'Tis the only way, Catherine."

Her gaze settled on the autumn landscape and the orchard that she had so laboriously planted, where fruits now hung ripening on the green branches. She looked at the expansive west garden that had taken her two years of hard work. She had come to love every inch of her manor, and not merely because it represented such freedom to do as she willed. She had been homeless for so long, and this parcel of soil was a home for her at last. She had to know that James spoke the truth. She turned back.

"'Tis a long time since I've been to court," she said. "I shall leave tomorrow and visit Lady Daubeney—and use the time to think on this. I'll give you my answer when I return."

He flushed beneath her gaze, and his expression told her that he knew the true purpose of her visit. There was something else. Fear? *Oh, James,* she thought. *Where has it all gone—the hopes we had, the dreams we shared, the smiles we gave to one another?*

*   *   *

Catherine had been told often enough that court was a gay place since Henry's death, but never could she have imagined how festive it had become. How much gold it took to wage a war while turning daily life into one endless feast Catherine had no idea, but every day was a feast day for Harry, filled with music, song, and lavish banquets such as she had never seen before. Minstrels wandered the halls, playing their merry melodies, and troubadours sang sonnets in the garden. Wine flowed, and flowers bedecked the halls, and the nobles who moved among the palace rooms blinded the eye with their gems and rich brocades. Even the birds that ornamented the gilded cages now were not simple linnets anymore, but enormous creatures of gorgeous, jewel-colored plumage ferried at great expense from across the seas and the New World. But the largest and gaudiest of them all was Harry. He threw away huge sums of money gambling at cards and dice, and dressed lavishly, bedecked in priceless jewels. Every finger of his hand was a mass of gems, and from around his collar of gold hung a diamond as large as a walnut. *If Henry could see him now, he would surely die of apoplexy*, she thought. She saw Henry suddenly in her mind's eyes, sitting alone at his ledger at night, going through his expenses, trying to pinch a groat where he could. What he had scratched together, his son was now scattering to the four winds with both hands.

She turned into the passageway that led to Somerset's suite, marveling at it all. Here and there, those who recognized her dropped curtsies and bows. She acknowledged them with a graceful nod of her head. The antechamber milled with people, but the guard announced her immediately. Somerset looked up and broke into a smile. Though he was in conference with another man, he left the table to meet her and gave her warm welcome.

"My dear Lady Catherine, how kind of you to honor us with a visit." He bent over her hand with courtly grace. "'Tis always a great pleasure to see you." He led her forward to the other man in the chamber. She couldn't see his face at first, for he was in shadow. Then he moved into view.

"I don't believe you've met my deputy, Matthew Cradock of London and Wales."

Cradock raised her hand to his lips with courtly elegance. "We met once, but Lady Catherine would not remember," he said. His arresting blue eyes were heightened by the sapphire of his doublet.

Such was his charm and Catherine's immediate sense of connection that the word *Wales* did not fill her mind. She gave him a wide smile. "But you are mistaken. I do remember. We met in 1502, when I came to Ludlow with Queen Elizabeth."

Indeed, how could she forget the instant liking that had run through her at the sight of this vitally attractive man? She realized she was staring, but she was unable to tear her gaze away. Tall, with an aquiline nose and brown hair silvering at the temples, his face was bronzed by sun and wind, and etched by experience, and his generous mouth curled as if on the edge of laughter. Matthew Cradock exuded an air of command that reminded her of her father. But it was his eyes that held her. As blue as Richard's had been . . .

"You have a good memory, Lady Catherine," Matthew Cradock said. He'd been taken aback by the emotion that assailed him at the sight of her, for he was a grandfather, and a widower, and had thought himself immune to such feelings.

"Lady Catherine—" Somerset's voice.

They both caught their breath and turned to him at the same moment.

"Your visit is most fortuitous," Somerset said. "We were just discussing you."

"Indeed?" Catherine said, aware of Cradock's eyes on her. She forced herself to concentrate.

Somerset turned to the man-at-arms at the door, where men milled in the antechamber, awaiting their turn with the Lord Chancellor. "Shut the door," he called, then turned back to Catherine. "I have news regarding the matter entrusted to me by the old king."

Catherine became instantly alert.

"I have been given to understand that the search has narrowed in Gower to an area ten miles from Swansea. We have learned that the child in question was alive four years ago and it should not be long now before we get more details."

Catherine's heart lurched in her breast. Four years ago Dickon would have been twelve years old. "Thank you, my Lord Somerset."

"I have other news as well. Would you care to sit?" She nodded gratefully and sat down at the long, polished table in the chair he drew out for her. Somerset and Cradock followed suit.

"I have been deluged with royal business of late and it appears my responsibilities for King Harry are going to demand my full attention in the future. As a result, I fear I may not be able to pursue the matter in Wales as expeditiously from now on as I would wish."

Catherine tried to crush her disappointment, but said nothing.

Somerset resumed. "This does not mean, however, that it need drag on because I am unable to attend the details. In fact, my stepping back from the inquiry may actually help matters."

"My lord?"

"Matthew Cradock here is my personal deputy in Wales. It is Master Cradock who has been gathering the information on the—ah—the matter in question, and keeping me informed. Now that he is no longer present at court, and I am unable to visit Fyfield to update you, may I have your permission to turn the inquiry over to Matthew Cradock, and have him report directly to you?"

"Mind? Of course not. Lord Somerset, Master Cradock—I am in your debt."

"Matthew is Welsh himself and the most influential, respected, and trusted royal authority in Gower." Cradock made a murmur of appreciation and Somerset continued. "You may know that his daughter's father-in-law is the Earl of Pembroke? I myself have utmost faith in Master Cradock. I believe, Lady Catherine, that this is the most efficient way we can proceed."

"Thank you."

"Is that all, Lady Catherine?"

"My lord, there is one other matter. My manor . . ." When Somerset said nothing, she went on, "Regarding the title?"

"Ah yes, my lady. The king agreed to Master Strangeways's petition that the crown take back the property so it could be regranted to both of you. I thought I'd informed him of it before he left court?"

Catherine felt herself blanch as the blood drained to her legs. She was thankful she was sitting down, thankful she was able to hold her head high. It had been James's ruse, as she suspected, and now she was trapped, for she couldn't admit to these men here that her husband was a cheat and a liar and had married her for her lands. To cover the truth, she turned to Somerset. "My lord, he forgot to mention it to me. He has not been well—"

Somerset threw her a look of sympathy. "The injury in France," he said. *The drinking,* he thought. Pity for Catherine swelled in him.

Her husband had turned drinking into a fine art form and only cleared his head long enough to sit upright at the gambling table. If he hadn't been injured in France, it would have been only a matter of time before they had to let him go for inability to perform his duties. Maybe that was why Daubeney had paid him so little heed. The rogue was no good, and either wine would be the death of him, or another gambler would slay him over a debt.

The silence in the room lengthened until Catherine rose to her feet and held out her hand. "Thank you, my lord . . . Master Cradock. I must leave you now, but I look forward to seeing you at Fyfield."

When she'd left, Somerset turned to his friend. "Did you get the same impression I did?"

"Aye," Cradock sighed. "She had no knowledge of her husband's request. He tricked her, that scoundrel."

"Daubeney never had any use for Strangeways, and he was kin. I am sorry for Lady Catherine . . . Two husbands, and both of them a disappointment. She deserved better."

"Welladay, you never know," Cradock said. "She is still young."

Chapter 22

Raindrops and Rainbows

As Catherine traveled back to Fyfield, her emotions were in turmoil. She was consumed by disgust for James, and flooded with memories of Richard. There had been so much to survive—and just when she thought her struggles were behind her, Fate emerged with a malicious laugh. Now she was alone again, with no one to rely on but herself, and the dull, dreary days spread out before her like a limitless gray sea.

Nay—not alone, she thought, remembering the night at the river. *You are there, Richard; I know you are.* She turned her face up to the sky. *I may not see you, but I feel you near.* The thought brought her comfort, but when the manor came into view behind the church, James's face rose up before her and she was swept with despair. Her marriage was a disaster. If she lost the manor, she would be destitute. What then? Where would she turn? She had no family and knew no one in a position to help. Thomas would take her in, of course, but he and Maggie had little to live on now that Cecily was gone. And what of Alice and all the others who depended on her? Dear God, she had been such a fool!

When she arrived at Fyfield, she found James upstairs in the solar, half-drunk and refilling his cup. The room stank of wine. He looked at her with glazed eyes and set his drink down. He tried to rise and fell back. "Catherine—" he lisped drunkenly, unable to wrap his tongue around the word. She went to him, picked up his cup, and threw the wine into his face. "You are despicable!"

Leaving him to sputter, she turned on her heel and left the house, hurrying through the orchard until she reached the meadow's edge. The autumn day was brisk and the wind stirred the line of tall poplars against the sky. It seemed to Catherine that they waved a welcome to her, but that only reminded her how much Fyfield meant to her.

She managed to get through that day, and the next, and all the ones that followed, week after week. November arrived on a hailstorm, and winter passed into spring, bringing the news that King Harry was mounting a second invasion of France. James was not asked to supply men or gather munitions. And in June, when King Harry left for France, James did not go with him.

Catherine couldn't reason with him, and she gave up trying. Often, as they sat silently by the fire on cold winter evenings, a faraway expression would come over him. He was over fifty now, and she knew he was thinking of his lost youth. Their fifteen-year age difference had meant nothing to her when they'd been at court, but since he'd returned from France, his health had deteriorated. He had brought the bloody flux back with him, and each time they thought it cured, it returned with more severity than before. A myriad of other ailments plagued him as well, requiring constant visits by a physician. Some days he had difficulty even mounting his horse. Seeing how he suffered, she felt pity. If he hadn't proved himself so disreputable, she might have been able to forgive him, but the trust between them was irretrievably broken. Ever since she'd returned from the meeting with Somerset and Cradock, she had locked her bedroom door to him at night.

Had Catherine known the truth, she would have dispensed with the precaution. When she spurned his advances one night, he rode off to Fremont's house to drown his sorrow in bed sports with the baudy women ever-present there. But he found himself unable to perform. He thought the problem would pass, but it didn't. He was as useless as a eunuch. He could not admit to himself that he was only half a man now, and he didn't want Catherine to ever know. That was what kept him drinking. The pain. He needed to bury it, and he buried it in wine—wine and silent dinners and locked bedroom doors.

Itinerants came and went, stopping for a meal or shelter along the way, and injecting news and conversation into Fyfield. From a gray friar seeking harborage for the night, Catherine learned about the last de la Pole brother left alive. "Richard de la Pole, brother to John de la Pole, Edmund, and William of recent memory, is in France, and has sworn to fight King Harry when he invades, my lady," the friar said. "They call this Richard the last White Rose."

Catherine excused herself to escape to the yew-tree walk that edged the summer garden where she had cut an arched opening into the greenery and set out a table and chair for her pleasure. The secluded spot afforded her solitude along with a view of flowers, and she often sat there in quiet contemplation and prayer, for it adjoined the church grounds. The bells of St. Nicholas chimed more loudly there, the song of the chantry priests drifted more clearly, and the only eyes that watched her belonged to the sweet linnets and other small birds that sought refuge in the foliage as she did. Edmund de la Pole had not been one of her favorite people at court, but he had always shown Richard respect. Now his brother, Richard, was the only male left alive of the four de la Pole boys. The royal blood in their veins had cost them their lives, and Catherine knew it would not end with them.

*   *   *

Matters between Catherine and James deteriorated rapidly. Swept by memories of a time when the season of love had meant laughter and the pleasures of the flesh, James fell into a deep melancholy. Catherine tried to alleviate his spirits by taking him to the warm springs of Leamington, which were said to cure many maladies, and by sending for leeches to bleed him. Sometimes, when he fussed over the nasty potions he had to swallow or objected to something the physician had ordered, she would try to soften him with light banter.

"The only way to keep healthy is to eat what you don't want, drink what you don't like, and do what you'd rather not, James. Then you'll be well in no time."

Not that he would admit it to her, but James had tried all kinds of remedies himself, both for the flux that plagued him, and for his manly problem. He'd slept with a spider web across his brow and kept three candles burning beside him for three nights. He'd hung a wreath of garlic bulbs around his neck, and worn a bag of arsenic against his skin. He'd eaten crushed ram's testicles and swallowed viper fat and even dead man's flesh, dried and mixed with wine. But nothing helped. He grew convinced he had been cursed by the earl's daughter whose child he'd fathered years ago and had refused to wed. As his afflictions worsened, he grew angrier, especially at Catherine. For she was a constant reminder of what he desired most and could not have.

There was another grief that troubled him. Ill health and his bad leg had cost him an invitation to go to France with the king. His pride had been deeply hurt, and he felt discarded, forgotten, and useless.

Catherine took pains these days to avoid his company. More often, she sat alone among the yews and communed with Richard. *I do not search for happiness*, she told him, *only for peace*. As she drank in the flowery scent that wafted to her on the breeze, she decided to gather a posie for the great hall. On her way back to the house, she caught the clippity-clop of hooves from along the roadway. Shielding her eyes against the sun, she moved closer to the front path and peered into the distance.

"My Lady Catherine," said Matthew Cradock as he drew up to her at the head of his retinue. She stood before him, tall and statuesque, her head held high and a profusion of brightly colored flowers in her arms—a fairy queen in a jeweled tapestry of black silk. Her dazzling smile of welcome sent his pulses pounding. He dismounted and threw his reins to the boy who had come to take the horses, glad for the chance to recover his composure.

"I vow you grow lovelier each time we meet," he said, creases bracketing his smile as he kissed her elegant hand.

"Thank you, Master Cradock," said Catherine, noting that he had not let go of her hand. For a moment she was so lost in admiration that she forgot her duties as a hostess. She tore her eyes from his at last and sent Alice for wine and sweetmeats as she led Matthew Cradock and the members of his retinue into the great hall.

"Very pleasant," said Cradock, letting his gaze roam over the ornamented chamber with its massive hearth and multi-colored stone floor. Pointed archways decorated the walls on both sides and led into a honeycomb of smaller chambers only glimpsed from where he stood, and sunlight poured through the open windows on the south. What he found most interesting, however, was the soaring ceiling, supported with lovely foiled braces and an artwork of ornate wooden trusses.

"There is much work to keep a manor running smoothly, is there not?" Cradock said, settling in to dine on wine, sugar cakes, and sweetmeats. He watched Catherine's graceful movements with pleasure and admiration as she arranged the flowers into a brass pot.

But Cradock's comment had reminded Catherine of the prime reason she had wed James, and her hand, in the motion of picking up a peony, stilled. "Indeed there is," she said, her smile fading.

Cradock's sharp glance had missed nothing. But, reluctant or not, he had to bring up what he feared was a painful subject. "'Tis, in fact, estate business that brings me here," he said at last.

"Oh." She had hoped that somehow the king would forget, or the paperwork would get lost, but of course, that was merely an idle dream. She lifted her gaze to him.

Cradock dismissed the men in the great hall who had been conversing among themselves, and when the last of his retinue had gone, he took out a wad of documents from a leather pouch left on a coffer. "I shall need your signature, my lady."

Catherine stared down at the packet he brought to her as if she were a victim tied to a stake and here was the torch to ignite the flames. She wanted nothing to do with this—it was all being done against her will. *And whose fault is that?* a small voice asked in her head. *You brought it on yourself, you fool.*

She carried the papers to the desk by the window and sat down, drained. Her hand shook as she poised her pen over the paper, and she struggled to control her trembling. Then she forced the pen down and scribbled her signature hastily, furiously, before she could change her mind; before she could collapse and weep in front of the king's messenger.

The deed was done. She felt sick. Taking a handful of sand from the small crystal box, she scattered it over the parchment to dry the ink, then closed her eyes, her head dizzy.

Cradock had watched her keenly as she brought pen to paper. Her struggle served to confirm the initial impression he'd received at Westminster, that she had been tricked into this move by her husband. As a man of honor, he was offended by such conduct. His heart went out to her, and disgust for Strangeways flooded his mouth with a sour taste. Yet the mystery remained. Such a woman must have had many admirers. Why would she have married a man of ill repute: a known gambler, a drinker, a rake? A heartless rogue who, aware of what she had suffered in life, could strip her of her single comfort?

He looked at Catherine helplessly as she rose from the desk, her face pale.

"Tomorrow is the Feast Day of Saints Peter and Paul," she said, lifting her gaze to his face. "I would be delighted—I mean we would be delighted—if you could stay for the festival." She felt so bereft; she didn't want him to leave, this man who reminded her of her father.

Cradock had business in Oxford and could scarcely afford the time, but tomorrow was Sunday, and—as she had reminded him—a feast day as well. The king's business could wait. "It would bring me and my men much pleasure to accept your offer, Lady Gordon."

A silence fell between them again, for she could think of nothing more to say. "'Tis close in here, is it not?" she managed at last, taking a feather fan from the mantelpiece, and fanning herself.

"I was thinking the same." Cradock threw a glance at the window.

"There is a pleasant breeze outside. Would you care to go riding? I should like to see the estate—that is, if you have time."

A thrill of excitement ran through her. "Nothing would please me more."

Catherine escorted Cradock outside, and together they walked the length of the manor house, through the stables, the kitchen garden, and past the new bake house.

"How delightful," he said. "I've never seen a conical bake house, or a kitchen garden where woven willow twigs fence the herbs."

"In Flanders it is the custom to use such branches instead of hedges. My lord husband Richard described it to me. He would have liked to see it done this way."

For a moment, their eyes met and Catherine felt his sympathy. She turned abruptly and led the way into the orchard. "These are young trees, planted when I first came to Fyfield. And over there, by the church, are my flower beds." She waved a hand to the west. Leading him past the yew-tree walk, she entered the garden. "But now look—"

Cradock gazed at the expanse of lilies, hyacinth, hollyhocks, and Persian lilies laid at his feet like some gigantic, colorful Saracen carpet. Beyond bloomed golden narcissus as far as the eye could see. He turned behind him and threw a glance at the church. "Well, Lady Catherine, I must say that you and the Creator have between you done a grand job on this ground."

"Maybe so," Catherine replied. "But you should have seen it when the Creator had it all to Himself. It took two years to clear the ground of weeds, brambles, and nettles."

Cradock threw back his head and laughed.

She took him into the yew-tree walk. "This is where I love to sit—welladay, one of my favorite spots, for I have several. It affords me a view of the flowers and also of the birds that visit. We have kingfishers here, and heron, and larks." They quitted the walk through the opening in the hedge and passed to the lawn behind the house that was set with a table and chairs. "From here I can see everything all at once. Fyfield is beautiful, you know, even in winter. Especially in winter. Freshly fallen snow turns it into a fairy landscape then, and deer come up to the house to feed, but perhaps it is loveliest now, in spring. For as you can see, blossoms drape the branches and birds chirp loudly—aye, I do think spring is fairest of all the seasons." She thought for a moment. "Maybe autumn is even more splendid than spring, when pears glisten gold and ripe apples hang on the branches, shiny and red—oh, I know not which season is more beautiful!" she finally exclaimed, leading him back to the front of the house, where their horses awaited. "I love them all."

Cradock was enchanted by her delight in her property. He himself had many manors, far larger and more impressive than Fyfield, but none had ever engendered that kind of emotion in him. They were scattered mainly in southwestern Wales, and he had a few smaller manors even in England, as well as a large house in London. Mostly, however, he lived in the Welsh castles that he managed for the king.

They rode together through the farmlands and golden wheat fields, the wind in their faces, and passed into the meadows, where cattle mooed to see them.

"Cattle, too? Doesn't seem large enough a property for this many head."

"We had a large number of calves born last spring. We could use more land, but we must make do."

Catherine pointed out the crops of barley, beans, peas, and turnips, and paused to greet the peasants tilling the fields. Passersby along the road welcomed them with smiles, and tenant farmers brought apple-cheeked children out from their cottages to meet them. As she enjoyed the beauty of the scenery, the friendliness of the people, and Matthew Cradock's camaraderie, Catherine forgot her troubles. Laughing together, they cantered into the woods. The fragrance of fern scented the quiet air and trees embraced one another in the dappled sunshine. Picking their way through delicate underbrush, beneath trees overhanging with flowers and berries, they exchanged smiles over the deer and small creatures of the forest that drank from gurgling brooks and peered at them through shrubbery before darting away.

By the time they returned to Fyfield, the sun was setting in the west, and Matthew Cradock had come to fully understand how much this manor meant to Catherine. The delicate thread that had begun to be woven between them at Westminster had hardened for him into something of far greater significance. As he dropped down from his saddle in front of Fyfield and gave Catherine his hand, he knew that, somewhere along this ride, he had also given her his heart.

*　*　*

Trestle tables were set up for dinner in the great hall when they arrived back at the house, and James was home, awaiting supper. Catherine was relieved to find that he was sober and playing the role of gracious host with the old decorum she remembered. He'd had a keg of ale brought in for Cradock's men, many of whom he knew from court, and was engaged in light banter. Seeing an echo of the man she had married, she felt a rush of sadness that he'd changed so much.

James set down his beer mug and limped forward to give Matthew cordial greeting, for he knew him to be an influential man. Cradock's star had been in the ascendancy under three kings, and office after office with increasing authority had fallen to his lot. He had served Richard III with distinction as a young pirate when he was captain of a ship of war of the realm, and old King Henry had also valued him highly, granting him for life the office of constable of Caephilly Castle in Cardiff and many other lucrative appointments. In King Harry's 1512 war against France, which had proved so disastrous for James, Cradock had resumed his piracy with great success, capturing a French vessel and booty worth a king's ransom. His attachment to Somerset had garnered him a host of honors meanwhile, and he practically ran Glamorgan for him as his deputy in Wales.

James knew that all things Welsh greatly interested Catherine, and as he took in the heightened blush in her cheeks and the sparkle in her eyes, he suspected they came not so much from fresh air, but from Cradock's company.

At dinner, James took the high-backed chair at the head of the table. "What news of King Harry?" he asked Matthew as they dug into the sweet and sour spiced rabbit and frumenty that had been served. "Has he left for France yet?"

"King Henry departed for Calais a few days ago, leaving young Queen Katherine as Regent. Barring bad weather, he should make landfall soon, God willing," said Cradock, thinking that James had aged much since he'd seen him last. He'd shed weight and his doublet hung on him as loosely as if it belonged to another man, while his complexion had turned florid from drink. Deep furrows ran along his cheeks down to his mouth, giving him an ill-tempered expression, and clearly, vigor had seeped out of him. He had noticed that James never looked at his wife, and there seemed to be an excessive restraint between them. Here might be the reason.

"I heard at the court house that King Ferdinand let King Harry down again," said James.

"He did indeed. He concluded his own peace with France, just as he did last year."

"I assume you shall be leaving shortly to join the king in France, then?" inquired James, chewing hard to keep his emotion in check, for he had not recovered from the hurt and anger of not being invited to go. He had been made to feel old and useless, and he hated this man who had achieved so much in life, and who had everything he himself wanted and would never get.

"I leave next week on my own ship, the *Matthew Cradock*. I have been given charge of the Lord Chamberlain's retinue of a hundred soldiers and a hundred mariners."

James slammed his knife so viciously into the wheat bread that Catherine jumped.

"So you will be at sea during the entire campaign?" *Good*, James thought. It meant Cradock wouldn't be back for a long while.

"I shall come and go, for I will be ferrying munitions and supplies from London to Calais."

James stuffed his mouth with bread and chewed hard, but a sudden pain in his groin sent him clutching at his belly. He pushed away from the table with an oath. Doubling over, he stumbled out of the room as hastily as his bad leg would permit.

Poor Catherine, Matthew thought. *It can't be easy living with a difficult and ailing husband.* Beneath his sharp gaze, Catherine colored and looked away.

* * *

Catherine had gone to great expense to ensure that the villagers enjoyed their feast day. As it turned out, thanks to Matthew's presence at the Feast of Saints Peter and Paul in that year of 1513, the day became for her a dreamy haze of sunlight and pleasure, real life at its most charming, a world where nothing was sinister or dark. As she passed through the throng of peasants and town-folk, exchanging greetings and pleasant words, and performing her duties as lady of the manor, she was aware of Matthew Cradock with every breath she took. She had just admired a little girl with a garland in her hair when a voice came in her ear.

"Would you care to dance, Lady Catherine?" It was Cradock. He held out his hand.

She blushed furiously. "I cannot, Master Cradock—I have not danced in so long, I have forgotten how. It has been years—many years." The last time she had danced was with her brother-in-law, Patrick Hepburn, Earl of Bothwell, at Margaret Tudor's proxy wedding, and he had died soon afterward. The time before that, with Richard, at court, on the eve of his escape from the Tower. Then there was Philip the Handsome, with whom she'd danced in Calais. All dead now. She blinked to banish her memories.

"I must refuse, Master Cradock. Disaster seems to befall those I dance with."

He laughed. "My dear lady, then 'tis high time you danced, if only to prove yourself wrong. Come, life is short, and we must snatch our happiness where we may."

Catherine looked at the bright blue eyes in the bronzed face that gazed at her so earnestly. He drew her into the crowd of merrymakers and she went as if in a trance, for she had no power over her own body and her will seemed compelled by some force beyond herself. Together they clapped their hands and moved to the beat of the music, stepping to one side, then to the other; stepping behind one another, and back to back; stepping in front, and face to face. All the while she was aware only of his presence, his eyes, the touch of his hand on hers, and the brush of his shoulder against her sleeve. She felt the dance as a natural thing between them, as if they had danced together all their lives.

When the music ended, Catherine came back to the present with a jolt. The ground no longer seemed solid beneath her feet and her breath was uneven. A trifle dizzy, she hung on Matthew's arm with both hands and leaned into him as they left the rowdy crowd of merrymakers. As she turned her head, her eye fell on James, seated directly ahead, in the line of sight, beneath a fig tree. The laughter died on her lips. His face was stormy and a vein throbbed at his temple. She knew then that if he had been alone with her, he would have beaten her until life left her. Standing amid the throng of oblivious and happy villagers, her cheeks flaming with guilt, she dropped her hold of Matthew's arm. James pushed out of his chair and glared at her. Then he turned and went off with Sholson at his heels.

Too soon the sun was setting and it was time for vespers. Torches were lit and passed out to the villagers. Catherine and Matthew led the procession as it trooped across the meadow and past her manor house to St. Nicholas Church for prayers. Each time their gaze met, Catherine's heart turned over in response and a sadness came over her, for Matthew would leave immediately after the service. He had over an hour's ride to Oxford ahead of him in darkness, and she dreaded his departure. He made her feel safe, and as long as he was there, she feared no harm from James. But he couldn't stay forever.

Night had fallen when they quitted the church. The crowd

dispersed, and their voices grew faint. The countryside quietened, and there was only chirping of night creatures to break the silence as they walked back to the manor. James had not shown up for vespers, but when he was in the grip of the bloody flux, he had to stay close to the privy pit. He was still nowhere in sight when the horses were brought out of the stables by torchlight, but Sholson came to convey his message to Matthew. "My master bids thee farewell and safe journey. He regrets that his malady has grown worse and that it confines him to his rooms."

"Pray give my thanks to Master Strangeways for his hospitality," said Matthew.

Sholson withdrew with a bow, and Matthew turned to Catherine. In a low voice, he said, "My lady, 'tis with utmost reluctance that I leave you, but I pray you know that I will be back as soon as I can. There is the matter of the regrant of the manor to you, and I shall see that it is done without delay. There are also other matters of even greater import that you know I cannot entrust to hands other than mine—"

Aye, thought Catherine gratefully. *My Dickon*.

"Meanwhile, I am leaving my man Piers here to attend you. Should you have urgent need of me, dispatch him to London. He will know how to find me. Even if I am at sea, I shall come to you." Beckoning to Piers, he placed a hand on his shoulder and led him aside for a few private words before turning back to her.

Catherine lifted her eyes to his, and the tumult and chaos that had claimed her being ebbed away. She marveled that her heart, so filled with fear only a short time ago, should now be pervaded with such hope. "I understand."

From the upstairs window, James observed them: the hand that was kept too long; the glance that was held too long. He ground his teeth, and balling his hand into a fist, he smashed it into the wall.

*   *   *

Matthew lashed his horse as he rode furiously to Fyfield in the drizzle of the September afternoon.

Over the few months of the summer of 1513, he had managed to visit Fyfield twice more. Both times James had been drunk and causing problems for Catherine, but Matthew had brought good news that cheered her. Once he came to give Catherine the documents of the regrant of the manor and to inform her that Sir Charles Somerset had been created Earl of Worcester in February 1513. On that occasion, he had also presented her with the additional parcel of sixty acres of meadow in the parish of North More in Oxfordshire that he had obtained for her, so her cattle would have ample space to roam. As he galloped to Fyfield now, he remembered how she had looked at him then, her black-fringed azure eyes shining with a gratitude that melted his reserve.

On the second occasion, he had brought her news of the search for Dickon, which had narrowed to a stonemason who might have had him briefly.

But this third time was different.

Only the night before, he had been with the king in Calais, resupplying the army with munitions, when the tidings had come. He'd lost not a minute returning to London on the *Matthew Cradock,* giving as excuse for his abrupt departure from Calais the necessity of delivering posthaste the canons he'd left behind for lack of space. Fortunately, there was a fair wind and the voyage went smoothly. While the guns were being loaded onto the ship, he took a few men with him and rode to Fyfield. His only concern now was to get to Catherine before she heard the news from some itinerant seeking harborage for the night. He prayed he was in time.

Church bells were ringing for nones as he galloped through the manor gate and up the drive with his men. From her upstairs chamber, where she had been going over the books with the steward, Catherine heard the pounding hoofbeats on the gravel. Looking out the window, she saw her visitor approach. She rushed downstairs, ran through the great hall, and flew out the door, heedless of the rain. She watched him pull up to the house, but the smile that lit her face vanished when she saw his expression.

"Matthew—" she exclaimed anxiously, for some time over the

course of his visits this summer, they had fallen into given names. "What is it? What has happened?"

"Catherine," he said urgently, taking both her hands into his, "where is James?"

"He's upstairs, sleeping; why?"

"Is there somewhere private where we can talk?"

"The solar." She turned to lead the way inside and glanced back when he didn't follow.

"You may go in," he told his men. He drew Catherine back from the house. "Nay, outside. Somewhere we can be alone."

"What is it, Matthew?"

He took her by the elbow and led her to the garden. She stumbled along unevenly as he hurried her into the yew-tree walk. *Don't you see, 'tis drizzling*, she wanted to say. "Matthew, what is it? You're frightening me—"

They had reached the hedge. Matthew turned her to face him.

"Catherine, you know that King James issued King Henry an ultimatum in August demanding that he be recognized as Henry's heir in England if Henry died childless?"

"Aye." She looked in puzzlement at his hands for he held her tightly by both her arms.

He rushed on. "And you know James crossed the border and took Norham and some other English castles when he refused?"

What urgency in this? "Aye, but—"

Matthew cut her off. "And you know the Earl of Surrey marched north to give battle?"

Catherine had heard something about Surrey leaving Pontefract for Newcastle, but there were always border troubles. She didn't understand what made this any different from the usual skirmishes.

"Five days ago there was a battle at Flodden. The Scots suffered an appalling defeat—" Suddenly Matthew fell silent, at a loss for words.

A cold knot formed in Catherine's stomach. "James—"

Matthew nodded.

"James—no, no! Oh no, not James—tell me not James!"

"And, Catherine—Catherine—James, and others—"

"Others?" Her stomach was still clenched tight and now an icy fear began to creep around her heart.

"Catherine, your brother, Alexander, Earl of Huntly, is the only noble to survive the battle."

"What do you mean?" She stared at him in bafflement.

"Your brothers—and William—they were all slain—"

Panic exploded in her. "All—slain—William—" His name was almost a scream on her lips. Her beloved, favorite brother—her laughing brother—gone, out of the blue, in the flicker of an eyelash. She looked at Matthew mutely, unable to speak for the constriction in her throat. It couldn't be true. It had to be some mistake!

"Catherine, your cousin, William Hay, Earl of Erroll, is dead. There is more."

"More?" Catherine whispered hoarsely. She shook her head, backed away. "No! No, no, no—no more—"

Matthew tightened his grip on her arms. "A third of all Scots nobility perished in the Battle of Flodden."

Catherine stared at him, frozen with horror, disbelief, and bewilderment, unable to comprehend. "A third?"

"Your nephew, Adam Hepburn, Earl of Bothwell—"

"Stop it!" Catherine screamed, sobbing and twisting her head from side to side to escape the agony that gripped her. "Stop! Stop—" Not Patrick's son; not her sister Meg's child, that redheaded little one running in the wind with his ribbon banner blowing behind him at Huntly Castle. Not him! Not Adam. Oh, Adam! The tears she had held back for all the years in England found her then and poured out of her heart in a flood. All that kept her upright was Matthew. She collapsed against his broad chest and he wrapped his powerful arms around her, and she clung to him, and wept. There had been so many black days in her life, but this—this—

This was too much.

Chapter 23

Abide with Me

1513

Catherine fell into a melancholy for months after Flodden. Ten thousand Scots had died there. Among them she numbered many cousins and extended kin from the Gordons, Setons, Stewarts, Hays, Crightons, and Keiths. They had grown up together, and as children they had played and laughed and chased one another around the castle halls. All had danced at her wedding to Richard. In those long past halcyon days of their youth, they had toasted life, confident of victory in every battle, certain there was no obstacle they could not vanquish. Some had waved farewell to her at Ayr, and she saw them still in her mind's eye, standing on the dock as she sailed away to her destiny, leaving them to await theirs at Flodden. "Farewell, King Richard of England, farewell! Farewell, fair Catherine!" they had called. And James had smiled; James, who had blessed her marriage to the one she loved; who had espoused Richard's noble cause with all his heart. James, brave king; kind heart; beloved cousin.

James was gone.

His mutilated body had been taken to Berwick to be embalmed. From there it was brought south, to the Carthusian monastery at Shene. How strange that of all the monasteries in England, it should be there. Catherine laid down her pen and closed her ledger. She rubbed her eyes. Pushing away from the desk, she went to the window. Through the ice on the windowpanes, the winter landscape stretched to the horizon, as dreary as her spirit. The Carthusian monastery, where Richard had sought refuge after fleeing the Tower. For one night he'd dreamt of hope, if not freedom, before leaving the monastery for the most dreadful fate any man could ever face. Now those same four walls enclosed his friend, James. In his chivalry, James had had Richard's body brought to Scotland to be placed in the royal vault, thinking to lie beside his friend when the time came. But Fate, as always, had other plans. Now, Richard lay in Scotland, and James was here, an alien in an alien land.

She didn't know what she would have done in these months without Matthew. Despite the war, he'd managed to make a trip to Fyfield twice a month after Flodden. When King Harry finally abandoned his dreams of continental conquest and returned home to England, Matthew divided his time between his duties in Wales and royal business at court, coming often to Fyfield. Meanwhile, his man, Piers, never let her out of his sight until she went into her bedchamber at night and locked the door behind her.

Strangely, James had given her little trouble after the feast day. It was almost as if he were resigned to matters the way they were, or perhaps he was merely too drunk, or too ill, to care anymore.

With Fyfield, James left everything in her hands. For much of the year during his illness, there was naught but toil as linens fouled by vomit and offal were washed daily, and chamber pots emptied. Incense was burned to rid the house of odor, and when summer came, Catherine filled the rooms with garden flowers, boiled mint, and fragrant herbs, and opened every window. Still, James's spirits continued their decline, and constant pain kept him confined to bed.

At least Catherine had come to an arrangement with each of James's debtors regarding repayment of the money he owed them. She paid them monthly, without fail, and though the amounts were small, they knew they would receive their money in full someday. Reassured, the debtors no longer came to Fyfield in person, and the confrontations ceased. For the management of the estate in matters where the steward needed help, she turned to Matthew. Once the word went out that her protection came from the highest echelon of state, all those who might have thought to wheedle more money out of her for repairs or harass her in other ways abandoned their efforts. She found there was little to trouble Matthew about.

"You mean I am not needed?" he would demand, quirking an eyebrow.

"'Tis because of you that all is well, Matthew. If you fled the scene, I fear they would all rise up against me."

"Flee the scene indeed. The very thought strikes fear into my belly."

"Aye," she'd laugh. "And I see how you tremble."

He would smile and place an arm around her shoulders, and thus would they stand and watch the sunset together.

It was Matthew who took her to visit King James at the Carthusian monastery, where he lay unburied; it was Matthew who held her up when she visited the cell where Richard had spent his last night outside the Tower walls; and it was Matthew who stood at the back of the church as she prayed for them both. Through all the heavy days and months of her grief and difficulties, it was Matthew who was there beside her, who brought her news of the search for Dickon, who eased her worries, and paved her life with hope. And if Catherine had any doubts before that she loved him, she had none now. She did love Matthew. Loved him with all her heart.

* * *

By summer of 1515, James was bedridden. The bloody flux had caused him much grief but Catherine suspected he was suffering from other ailments, too. The excesses of his youth had taken a toll on his general well-being and his ability to fight disease. Through his protracted illness, she matched Sholson's devotion in tending to his needs, and in these days she helped to lift the wine cup to his lips, for drinking soothed his pain.

"How are you this morn?" Catherine would ask.

"I hurt," James would reply.

And she would try to lighten his spirits. "That is very good, James. After a certain age, if you don't wake up aching in every joint, you are probably dead."

And James would smile.

Still, his condition worsened. Though Catherine sought remedies for his belly cramps, his yellowed complexion, and his bloodshot eyes, it was all to no avail. On the eleventh day of November, 1516, he made out his will.

In his London town house in Southwark, Catherine bid the lawyer and the witness farewell at the door, and treading lightly, returned to James's bedchamber. Snow was falling and the day was dismal, but candles burned on the bedside table, somewhat alleviating the wintry gloom. She had expected to find him asleep, exhausted by the effort of making out his last testament, but he lay awake, his head turned to the window. When the door opened, he shifted his gaze to her.

"Catherine," he whispered, his voice weak.

She went to his side and smiled down at him as she smoothed his thin hair. He was an old man now, with hollowed cheeks and a shrunken frame. Pity swept her.

"Catherine . . . I didn't marry you only for your money—"

"Hush, James—hush . . ." She took a seat on the edge of his bed.

"No, there is not much time . . . We must speak of it . . . You must know."

"There is no need. 'Tis all in the past now."

"But the past matters . . . you know it does."

Her eyes grew moist as she looked at him, and she didn't attempt any more denials. He was right. The past mattered.

"I want you to know that . . . I loved you . . . and I love you still."

She nodded mutely, not trusting herself to speak.

"Will you forgive me, Catherine . . . for what I did . . . the manor, I mean—"

"I forgive you, James."

"I have been selfish . . . You deserved better, Catherine."

"No, James, say not these things. You were a comfort to me. When Richard died, I had no one and you were always there when I needed you."

It must have heartened him to hear this for his expression lightened.

"We had some good times, didn't we, Catherine?"

She took his hand into hers. "Many ... good times," she managed. "I was so alone. I couldn't have made it through those days without you, James."

"I have led an evil life, with no regard for anyone but myself ... but I am glad I did some good."

"Oh, James, you did—you did. I relied on you for everything in those early days after Richard ... and with the manor, in the beginning. But it was always more than that for me. I did love you." For there are many kinds of love, she had come to learn.

"I threw away your love, Catherine. I can't forgive myself for that—no, deny it not—I have many regrets ... especially about us."

Her mouth worked with emotion. "You enjoyed your life, James. You loved life. That is good. That is a good thing—"

A silence fell. They smiled at one another; she, tearfully; he, peacefully.

"Catherine ... I want to be buried before the image of the Blessed Virgin Mary at St. Mary's Overy ... behind the high altar. I always felt at one with God there."

She nodded.

"I know I leave you nothing but debts, Catherine ... but Sholson has been good to me ... I would like to make him a bequest, if you have no objection?"

Blinking back tears, she shook her head.

"Would you see to it that he does not want? He's getting old, too."

A suffocating sensation tightened her throat. She lifted his hand to her lips and pressed a kiss against the withered skin. "I will ... make sure, James—" Her heart ached for him, and for all the years that had been wasted. Years that might have been so different.

She laid her cheek against the back of his hand and closed her eyes. He gave a sigh, and when she looked at him again, he was asleep. Quietly, she rose, and tiptoed from the room.

*   *   *

Catherine had not expected to miss James as much as she did. The house seemed suddenly silent and very empty after his death on November twenty-third, but there was much to do for the funeral and that occupied her mind. Sir Charles Somerset and Matthew attended the ceremony at St. Mary's, as did many of those who had known James from court. Even King Harry made an appearance, sparkling from head to toe with jewels and rich damasks as he smiled and waved to the throng at Southwark that had gathered for a glimpse of their handsome monarch. In the evening when the mourners had left, Matthew remained behind to comfort her.

"You look tired, Catherine," he said.

"I am, Matthew. Yet I know I won't sleep this night."

"I hope you're not feeling guilty?"

"A little, perhaps, but mainly it's the memories. Richard died on November twenty-third, and James, too. Even Richard's Aunt Margaret died on November twenty-third in the year 1503. I thought it strange then that she should die on the same day . . . Now, with James, it is even more curious. Both my husbands, the same day, in the same place, and Richard's aunt who was so dear to me. I can make no sense of it."

"'Tis futile to try, Catherine. God moves in mysterious ways."

Catherine gave a sigh. "Perhaps there is nothing significant in these coincidences, but my life seems to have taken on a pattern, and 'tis not a good one. James pressed me to wed in January. Had I done so, it would have been exactly like my first marriage. Marry in January, die in November, weep at Yuletide."

"Catherine, you are too morose. You did not wed James in January, and I will not let you weep in December. You are going to make a sea voyage with me on the *Matthew Cradock*. I shall bear you away to the Isle of Wight, and there you shall be given cause to celebrate life."

Catherine's heart soared. "Maggie? Thomas? I shall see them

again! A sea voyage—oh, Matthew, I love the sea! I have missed the sea!" She seized his hand. "Thank you, Matthew."

*   *   *

Catherine stood on the forecastle, hanging on to a rope as the *Matthew Cradock* sailed the choppy seas in December 1516. She inhaled deep of the salty air, savoring the freedom she remembered when she'd sailed away with Richard on the *Cuckoo*. The wind blew her hair wildly around her and beat the king's banner that hung on the mast, sending it flapping noisily above her head. It was a cold but glorious December day, glittering with sunshine, and the sea was a deep blue. Birds followed them, squawking with excitement. She lifted a hand and pulled her hair back from her eyes to look up at them. How beautiful and carefree they were, these creatures soaring above! What joy it was to be here with them, out on the sea again!

"You make a lovely bowsprit, Catherine." Matthew's voice. He appeared beside her and put a hand on the rigging. He looked out over her head and she saw his profile in sharp relief against the blue sky. He seemed so natural, so at ease on the sea. "And you make a fine captain, Matthew. I would have no fear with you anywhere."

"You seem very comfortable aboard ship yourself."

"I have always loved the sea. If I were a man, I would have been a pirate like you."

He gave a chuckle and looked at her.

"I know it sounds strange, but the year I spent nursing Cecily on the Isle of Wight was my happiest in England," Catherine said. "After she died, I remember thinking I wished I could go to sea and never, ever touch land again."

"The sea is not always so welcoming, Catherine. There is nowhere to hide in a storm."

"But the storms on land are far more deadly, though they may not claim your life." Memory pushed Richard and Dickon forward and she saw their faces. The storm in the Irish Sea had changed her and taught her fear, not because it had threatened her life, but because it had threatened theirs. When they'd reached land, she had thought them safe, but it was in a storm over London that Richard had died, and in a storm over Buryan that Dickon had been rent from her arms, never to be seen again. She turned her eyes on Matthew, her smile gone. "At least 'tis how it seems to me."

"We will find him, Catherine. We are close now. Very close."

She never had to explain to him, she thought. He always understood. He knew her heart and her hopes and fears; he knew what drove her, and always spoke the words she needed to hear. A tear touched the back of her eye. She gave him a smile. "How wonderful it is to be with you, Matthew, to feel so light, and to have such hope. Anything and everything seems possible with you. I have not felt so protected since I left home and bonnie Scotland."

He wrapped his arms around her and drew her against him. He pressed a kiss to her brow. "When we are married, I shall make you feel you have come home, my lovely girl."

Catherine's heart warmed. This was the first time he had spoken of marriage, but it came as no surprise to her. She had always known, just as he had known, that they would be wed. She turned her head and looked up at him. "It cannot be soon enough for me, Matthew."

"Nor for me, my love."

"I am so pleased you will meet my kin, Matthew. You will like Thomas. His daughter, Maggie, is eleven now . . . She was already a little beauty like her mother the last time I saw her three years ago."

To this, Matthew made no reply. He had only one child, a daughter, also named Margaret, but to mention her now would be to spoil the moment. He pushed away the memory of her letter to him in which she'd called Catherine a Jezebel.

"There!" Matthew said. "The white cliffs of Dover. 'Tis the last sight of England for those who leave, and the first sight that greets them on their return." In the distance, the gleaming white cliffs of chalk that ran the length of the island drew into view, glistening in the sunshine.

"Beautiful," murmured Catherine. "I have seen the north, and I have seen the south, and now this. England has such beauty, and everywhere is different from everywhere else."

"And soon you will see my beloved Gower."

She gave him a loving smile.

They docked at Newport quay. Thomas and Maggie were awaiting them, Maggie's fair hair shining in the sun, her bright green eyes
sparkling with excitement. She flew to Catherine and threw her arms
tight around her. "Auntie—oh, Auntie—it's been so long! I thought
you'd never come!" She looked up at Catherine, and it was Cecily
that Catherine saw as she looked down at her niece's sweet young
face. "My dear heart," she said, holding Maggie out at arm's length to
admire her. "Why, how lovely you are—and how you have grown!"

"I am almost twelve," said Maggie proudly.

Catherine hugged her again and held her for a long moment. With
her arm around Maggie's shoulders, she walked across the uneven
ground to the cart that Thomas had brought for them.

"I fear I have only one extra horse," he explained, "and that is
reserved for Master Cradock."

They spent a happy Yuletide together, laughing and playing
games by the fire, as they had done while Cecily still lived. Many
times during those weeks, Catherine went to visit Cecily at Quarr
Abbey with Maggie. Afterward they always strolled on the windy
beach, where Catherine told Maggie stories about her mother and
what she had been like. Maggie never tired of hearing them.

"Your mother was betrothed to my cousin, King James of Scotland, but she fell in love with your father, and finally she ran away to
marry him—against the king's wishes. And it mattered not that your
father was no king, nor royal, nor even born noble. It mattered not
that he had no riches but only a farm. Love was all that mattered to
your mother. Your beautiful mother . . ."

"And to you, Auntie."

Catherine smiled. "I have married twice for love."

"Do you love Master Cradock?"

Catherine's smile widened. "Yes, my sweeting. Very much."

"Will you marry him?"

Catherine laughed, thinking, *From the mouths of innocents*—

"You are fortunate to live here," Catherine said, changing the subject, for she and Matthew had decided to make their announcement at dinner. "Even in the heart of winter, there is something magical about this isle in the sea." She looked around in wonder. Nothing but water and frothy waves whipped by the wind, and behind her the steep ridge of white chalk cliffs running to Alum Bay. Sea birds screeched as they circled for fish. *How magnificent nature is!* she thought. It had a raw power and never failed to touch her at some deep level that filled her with awe.

"I wish you could stay here with us forever, and wed my father, and never leave me."

So that was what was on the child's mind. "When you are grown, you will see that it is not as simple as that. Your father still loves your mother, and she lives in his heart. There is no room for anyone else but you, because you were her most precious gift to him."

"I want to marry for love when I grow up. It sounds like fun!"

Catherine chuckled. "As long as you marry someone of good character like your father, Maggie. If you wed the wrong person, it can ruin your life." Her own life would be in shambles now, but for Matthew. She shuddered to think how different it would have been for her had she not met him. Her eye went to Alice, and a new joy flooded her. How different it would have been for Alice had she not met Thomas Smyth! She had wed him just before James's death, shedding light and a moment's bright laughter into the gloom of those days.

* * *

For the Twelve Days of Christmas, Matthew took them all to splendid Cradistbrooke Castle to enjoy the lavish festivities and mummery at court, and Maggie was enthralled.

"Master Cradock has a daughter named Margaret also," Catherine said, in an effort to engage her interest.

"Is she nice?" whispered Maggie.

"I haven't met her yet, but if she's anything like her father, she is very nice." Catherine smiled.

During the celebrations, Catherine told Thomas and Maggie of her engagement. "Then you shall go to live in Wales?" asked Thomas.

"Aye . . . Wales," Catherine murmured.

Knowing what Wales meant to her, Thomas squeezed her hand under the table while Maggie exclaimed, "But Wales is far away and we'll never see you then!"

"Nay, my sweeting. All things are possible now. We shall come often to visit in Master Cradock's ship, and we shall take you to Wales by sea to visit the king's castles. Would you like that?"

Maggie covered her mouth with her hands to stifle her joy, and nodded vigorously, eyes wide.

Catherine's own eyes grew moist as she gazed at her niece. She lifted her goblet. "To life . . . to love . . . to hope," she toasted.

"To life. To love. To hope," they echoed.

* * *

Once the tidings of their betrothal reached court in January 1516, King Henry conferred a knighthood on Matthew in honor of his marriage to royalty. Catherine knew she had Sir Charles Somerset to thank for it and was pleased when he accepted the invitation to her wedding at Fyfield on May Day.

May Day, thought Catherine, when all the world was expectant, joyous, and gay, and celebrating the Feast of Love! Matthew had informed her that she did not need to concern herself with the wedding expenses or the arrangements, and that he had tended to every detail. She knew it would be a perfect day, and she felt as if she walked on a cloud as she prepared for her wedding. Only once did Catherine wonder why Matthew's daughter, Margaret, did not attend, but she did not allow herself long to ponder it. She would soon meet her.

In the morning, while it was still dark, Maggie came running into her bedchamber, delirious with excitement. In her hand she held a cup of morning dew that she had collected from the garden. Into this she had crushed the fragrant lavender that she had brought from their farm on the Isle of Wight.

"The perfume is ready!" she cried.

Catherine laughed, but she bent over the basin and held back her hair, as Maggie wished. The child had reminded her on the previous day that washing in dawn dew on May Day had to be observed, for it helped a girl wed the man of her choice. "Even when my wish is already coming true?" Catherine had asked. "Of course—you are not yet wed and 'tis best not to take chances with such things!" Maggie had replied. Now she carefully bathed Catherine's face in the lavender dew. Taking what was left of the precious mixture, she splashed it on herself. "There! Now I, too, will marry the man of my choice one day, but maybe not three like you, Auntie. One husband shall be enough for me, I daresay." She stood with her face dripping wet and her eyes closed as she groped blindly for a towel. Catherine laughed and put one into her hands.

"We must dress your hair," said Alice, picking up the brush, but Maggie grabbed it from her. "May I do it? I love Auntie's hair. 'Tis so soft, and thick." Catherine exchanged a smile with Alice and patted the hand Maggie rested on her shoulder.

Maggie brushed Catherine's rich black tresses until they gleamed and helped Alice dress her in her new black velvet gown, which Alice had sewn with tiny silver spangles. As Catherine stood patiently, they pinned the sleeves and collar with roses and ribbons of the palest pink hue.

"Now for your jewels, and the wreath for your hair, Auntie—"

"Not yet, Maggie," Catherine said. "First I need a moment alone."

Maggie looked at her in surprise, but Alice understood. She led Maggie out and shut the door. The room went silent, except for the song of the birds that poured in through the open window. Kneeling at her prie-dieu, Catherine murmured a prayer for James's soul, and one for Richard. Moving to the small jewelry coffer by the window, she unclasped the golden heart set with diamonds in a fleur-de-lis that Richard had placed around her neck on their wedding day and that she had worn since the day she'd learned of James's betrayal. With a kiss, she laid it gently to rest in the secret compartment and closed the drawer. She fixed her gaze on the golden dawn that streaked the sky. *Richard, my love, thank you for your blessing that you gave me on the beach at St. Michael's Mount, and for giving me permission to love again. I did not know then what a gift you were handing me, my beloved husband. Though I shall be wedded once more, think not that there is no place for you in my heart. Never will I forget you. Always you are with me. Take this kiss until we meet again—* And she blew to Heaven the kiss she pressed to her fingertips.

"Are you ready yet?" called Maggie from behind the door.

Catherine wiped her eyes. "I am ready."

As she stepped into the full sunshine of May Day, she was met by the bright and lilting tune of a piper leaping and dancing through the gate. A bevy of maidens with garlands around their shoulders, and leaves and flowers in their hair, skipped along behind him, waving ribbons. She gasped. All at once she was at Stirling, hanging expectantly over the parapet as minstrels played, pipers leapt, girls danced, and ribbons waved in the sunshine. She half expected Richard to follow through the gate on his white horse, but he did not come. She blinked. It was perhaps a coincidence; perhaps merely the May Day ritual, but she believed with all her heart that Richard had sent her a smile from Heaven. Lifting her eyes to the wide blue sky, she returned his smile. The merry group came singing up to the house, for it was the custom to beg favors on May Day. By this time, the entire household had gathered to watch them. Catherine nodded to Thomas Smyth, who carried the cup of coins, and he distributed them among the young people, giving one to each child, and double to the piper. Thus rewarded, the piper led Catherine and her procession to the village green, where a towering Maypole stood in front of St. Nicholas Church, made of the trunk of a birch tree and decorated with ribbons and bright flowers from the fields.

People were descending on the green from all directions now, and smiles were everywhere. Girls wore wreaths of flowers in their hair and men had flowers tucked in their ears and into their belts. Even the hounds were bedecked with posies and frolicked in celebration. Already Matthew's wine, perfumed with violets and wild rosemary, was being handed out to the crowd that was forming around the Maypole. Catherine thought they were celebrating the arrival of the May Queen, but when she drew closer, she saw that it was the male dancers they hailed. The Morris men, with deer skins on their backs and antlers on their heads, were dancing the energetic Horn Dance, celebrating the May as the ancients must have done in the days of Dionysus. Every so often they stopped to refill their cups. Suddenly, a cheer went up from the crowd of onlookers, and she saw that the May Queen, who had already been chosen from among the pretty village girls, had arrived. Seated on her flowery throne in a cart drawn by young men, she was followed by her maids of honor. The Morris men paused their dancing to do her homage and see her crowned. They helped set her up on her throne beneath an arbor bedecked with roses near the church, and from there the May Queen smiled down on Catherine and showered her bridal party with wild-flowers as they passed to the church porch, where Matthew and his party awaited with the priest.

Matthew stared at Catherine, spellbound, as she moved toward him. What he saw was a glittering vision of flowery beauty flashing silver in the sunlight. Again he was reminded of a faery queen in a glade of springtime greenery and he thought himself the most fortunate man alive as the ethereal creature took his arm and smiled up into his eyes.

Oh, how beautiful the world is! Catherine thought. *How grateful my heart is! The joy of my youth has been returned to me!*

* * *

The wedding celebration was shared by the entire village. At last night came. As the bells of St. Nicholas chimed the hour of midnight, they returned to the manor, where a rarely used upstairs room had been prepared for them. Together they stood at its open window, gazing at the stars and watching a few merrymakers still dancing around the bonfire, their distant laughter floating through the air.

Catherine looked up at Matthew. At last their time had come! Her heart hammered in her ears and desire left her trembling in his arms. In one swift, graceful movement, he swept her up and carried her to the bed. She watched breathlessly as he removed his clothes and lowered his body over hers. He tossed her shift from her and kissed her again with a savagery that wiped everything from her mind except the wild thrill of his body against hers. In a delirium of excitement, she felt his uneven breathing on her cheek and the surging, shocking contact of flesh against flesh as his lips seared a path down her neck, her shoulders, her stomach, leaving her burning with fire. As she drew him tightly to her, it seemed to her that her weary soul melted into his. There came over her a lightness that she had forgotten existed. Once she'd known this place of beauty, but she'd lost the way. Now love had found her once more, and the glittering secret place belonged to her again.

Chapter 24

In a Summer Garden

When Catherine had visited Wales with Queen Elizabeth nearly fifteen years earlier, its rough terrain of gorges, thistles, and mountain ranges reminded her of Scotland. Journeying there now with Matthew, she drank in the wild beauty that was so different from the gently rolling hills of grassy England, her heart lifting with memories.

She had lost no time leaving Fyfield after the wedding. Matthew's duties beckoned, and his firm hand was sorely needed in Wales to put down outbreaks of violence that were erupting with more frequency. Family feuds, local quarrels, and general discontent had led to the breakdown of law and order, and the region had become a place of rebellion. In addition to this heavy responsibility, Matthew was constable of several castles for the king. As Somerset's deputy, he also administered Somerset's holdings there, collecting revenues, approving payments, making appointments, and dismissing inept servants. Where Matthew went, Catherine would go, for the frightening thought always hovered at the back of her mind that he was fifteen years older than she and their time together was limited.

Upon their arrival, Catherine and Matthew took up residence in Swansea Castle, but when Catherine missed the privacy she had become accustomed to at Fyfield, Matthew bought a property near the castle on Goat Street, and built her a house. They named it "New Place." Like Fyfield manor, it had a spacious great hall, many windows to the garden, and pointed archways that led to a myriad of other chambers. New Place included everything Catherine treasured about her manor at Fyfield, including an orchard and lovely gardens. Matthew, however, made one improvement on the Fyfield design. On the northeast corner of the great hall, he added a tower three stories high for Catherine's privy suite. Spacious and secure, the tower was reached by its own stair turret through one of the archways in the hall near the fireplace.

Catherine was enthralled with her new place. She especially loved the solar, which stood above the great hall and opened to the roof—for while she had admired the openness of the great hall at Fyfield with its intricate foiled trusses, the hall's soaring height had made it hard to heat in winter.

Catherine fell in love with the beauty of Gower and the Vale of Glamorgan. Here, mountains met the sea, spacious beaches gave way to tiny, rock-bound inlets, and Roman ruins vied for attention with castles built on the edge of a cliff. Around Swansea the countryside was dotted with square-towered churches that overlooked castles, manor houses, forges, and mills, but the Vale of Glamorgan, called the garden of Wales, was rich in farming, with grassy vales crowded with sheep.

In addition to his estates in England, Matthew owned several in Wales, including a fair manor place called Cogan Pill. Each of these properties had to be visited and administered, so the couple found themselves traveling frequently, dividing their time between Matthew's properties in the south, Somerset's estates, and the king's castles across Wales. They interspersed these with trips to court and Fyfield, and squeezed in a visit to the Isle of Wight to see Thomas and Maggie whenever they could manage it.

And Catherine finally met Matthew's daughter, Margaret. Now she understood the reason for his reluctance to introduce them. Margaret came to visit in January, after Yuletide, on her way back to her estate at Ewyas with her husband, Sir Richard Herbert, the bastard son of William Herbert, Earl of Pembroke. Catherine had been acquainted with the young man at court when he had been an usher to Henry VII, and she had found him soft-spoken and inoffensive. It was an advantageous marriage that Matthew had secured for his only child, for Richard enjoyed a close connection with his noble kin.

As Catherine stepped forward to greet her stepdaughter, she saw that Margaret looked nothing like Matthew. Likely she favored her mother, Matthew's first wife, Jane Mansell. Margaret was only five years younger than Catherine, and a woman of wide berth whose face might have once passed for fair. But now her enormous fatty cheeks buried her small eyes and mouth, giving her the look of a blowfish. Nor did it help her demeanor that she wore a displeased expression. And displeased she proved to be, as Catherine discovered. Margaret did not approve of her father's new marriage.

Margaret assumed a stony stance as Catherine embraced her, and she did not return her smile.

"Lady Catherine," said Sir Richard pleasantly, ignoring his wife's glare, "it has been a long time since we last met. You look very well indeed." His two sons stood scowling behind their mother and watched him embrace Catherine as kin, but they made no move to emulate his example. Turning to his boys, Sir Richard brought them forward. "And this is my eldest, George, who is sixteen . . . and this is my younger boy, William. He is fourteen." Both of them, round-faced and plump like their mother, stared at Catherine sullenly.

"Charming," said Catherine, at a loss. "This is my cousin Alice Hay." She turned to Alice.

Sir Richard gave her a kin's embrace, but once again Margaret and her sons watched with displeasure. Entering the house with heads held high, they gave the servants their cloaks and furs, and passed through the entry toward the great hall. "Father, you used to have such good taste. What happened?" Margaret said, throwing a disdainful glance around, her little eyes glinting. "The ceiling in the hall is far too low, and the moldings have few carvings. Moreover, had you tried, I am certain that you could have found better carpets than these—" She looked with disgust at the Saracen rugs that Matthew had brought back from France.

A muscle twitched in Matthew's jaw and his face was as dark as a thundercloud. He made no reply. Instead, he turned to his son-in-law.

"I hope your journey from Ewyas was a comfortable one?" Matthew said, pointedly ignoring his daughter.

"Snow made the roads a trifle slippery, but it was nothing we couldn't manage," Sir Richard replied. "How do you like Wales so far, Lady Catherine?"

"Delightful, Sir Richard. In many ways it reminds me of Scotland," Catherine said, relieved by his courtesy. She led the way into the hall.

"Never been to Scotland, and never care to go," offered Margaret, her skirts swishing as she moved. "Belligerent lot from what I hear. Always fighting with one another. Oh—I am sorry—I forgot—" She looked directly at Catherine, a cold smile on her thin lips as she smoothed her skirts and sat down.

"Margaret, dear," Catherine said. "The reason we Scots fight so often among ourselves is that we're assured of having a worthy opponent that way." Then she returned Margaret's cold smile. A silence fell. Margaret went directly to the settle and Catherine saw that what she didn't take up with her ample girth, she covered with her skirts. Catherine called for a chair to be brought. She looked at Margaret, and said sweetly, "Since the settle has no room for two this day."

Servants entered with trays of sweetmeats and wine and passed them around as everyone watched in silence. Then the boys seized a fist full and began a food fight. "That is enough," exclaimed Matthew. "If you cannot behave like gentlemen, you need to go outside with the pigs."

The children made ugly faces, and Sir Richard, in an effort to keep the peace, sent them upstairs to play. "Boys," he grinned sheepishly. "Sometimes they can be a handful."

"Indeed," said Matthew, with a smile that didn't reach his eyes.

"It has been a long time since we saw you last, Father," said Sir Richard. "You have not come to Ewyas to visit us."

"We have been busy with the king's business, and other matters," replied Matthew, being only partially truthful.

"Speaking of the king's business, in Wales there is talk that King Henry wishes to set aside his queen," Margaret said, munching on a sweetmeat. "Any truth to the rumor?"

"There has been talk at court also, ever since the queen miscarried her second child in the autumn," Matthew replied.

"But the queen is with child again, is she not? She may have a son this time," said Margaret.

"That is everyone's hope," Matthew replied.

"There is also talk that King Henry is much displeased with the queen's father, King Ferdinand, and that there is friction in the royal family." Margaret popped another sweetmeat into her mouth.

"Friction is nothing unusual in families, royal or otherwise," said Matthew, throwing his daughter a hard look. "King Henry has reason to be upset with his father-in-law. Ferdinand of Spain has treated him with contempt."

"Indeed, I have heard that the king seeks revenge on the queen's father. Do you think the king will truly rid himself of his queen to wed a French princess, merely to spite Spain? After all, he hates France."

"If the queen gives birth to a son, the question will be mute," Matthew said. "Meantime, I do not think on such matters, and if you value your life and your position, daughter, you will not think on it either." Matthew would have to have yet another discussion with his son-in-law about his wife's tongue. Many a man had been sent to the Tower for less, and God forfend, should that happen, there was little he himself, or even Pembroke, could do to save them.

For a while, Sir Richard and Matthew kept the talk turned to more benign subjects such as the weather, and whether to plant cabbages and barley come spring, or invest in skins, or to add to the head of cattle, or to sheep for the wool. But Margaret finally found an entrée.

"I hear from my father-in-law, the Earl of Pembroke, that Sir Thomas More has penned a history of King Richard III, pointing the finger at Sir James Tyrrell as the confessed murderer of the little princes in the Tower. What do you think of that?" Margaret asked, directing herself to Catherine.

Catherine wanted to slap her face. She restrained herself with difficulty from leaping up and telling her exactly what she thought of it. More was a protégé of Cardinal Morton, a sworn enemy of King Richard, and only five years old when the king died. Many believed More's so-called "history" of King Richard's reign was Morton's own work, dictated to young More while he still lived. Since Morton died in 1500, and Tyrrell wasn't taken to the Tower until 1501, how could Morton have "known" such a thing before his death? But Catherine knew the perils of speaking out and saw the trap the malicious woman had set for her. She rose to her feet and, excusing herself, left the room.

"There must be something wrong with the design of this hearth," Catherine heard Margaret announce as she left. "The fire does not draw near as well as the Earl of Pembroke's, Father. You should have consulted him on the dimensions of the flue . . ."

Before her stepfamily left New Place, Catherine gave them the gifts she had laboriously prepared for Yuletide. For George, she had a sword of finest steel, and for William, an archery set with bows constructed of knot-free yew with solid wood shafts, set in a maroon velvet case tied with silk ribbons. For Margaret, she had spared no expense; with her own hands she had painstakingly embroidered on rose silk a peacock seated in an orchard, a work that had kept her up many nights. But she could never have anticipated what happened as a result of her gifts.

Soon after the exchange, the boys left for the garden, and when shouts and cries came from outside, everyone ran out to see what the problem was. The servants' eyes were wide in horror. They stood covering their ears and some wept, for the boys had decided to practice their skills on a hound. The poor creature was covered in blood and howling in agony with the most heartrending cries Catherine had ever heard from an animal. At last a servant came forward and cut the creature's throat to put him out of his misery. Blood poured into the sand and Catherine turned away, sickened by the sight. When the Herberts finally left, she found the gifts she had laboriously collected for them thrown aside in their rooms and the tapestry crumpled into a ball and smelling of urine.

She had never witnessed such boorish behavior before in her life. Though people at court might harbor malice, they were careful to mask their true feelings beneath a cloak of civility. But this! Catherine was so exhausted after their departure that she slept for days. But she was determined to do what she could to mend the relationship.

"Matthew, it is natural that Margaret sees me as a usurper of her mother's affections in your heart, but I wish to win her over," she said, broaching the subject that weighed on her. "What can I do?"

"Put her out of your mind, Catherine. She was always a troublesome child, but this is the worst I've ever seen her. I fear she is losing her wits with age."

Catherine dreaded every visit the Herberts made, but fortunately these were few, partly for Margaret's dislike of Catherine and anger at her father, and partly because Matthew was in truth so busy that they were rarely in a place long enough for anyone to arrange a visit. Since the beginning of the year, the pace for him had been frenetic. Often Catherine worried that it was too much for a man of his years, but he never complained. In March, they moved into their London town house so Matthew could attend his heavy demands at court.

During this time, she barely saw him. He came home late to their London house, for there was much to do. King Harry had decided to make an alliance with France in order to punish Ferdinand of Spain, and the necessary arrangements required the expertise that only a handful of men such as Cardinal Wolsey, Somerset, and Matthew could provide. Preparations were frenzied; there was not a moment to be lost. King Harry, it seemed, was a man in a hurry.

Before the meeting with France took place, he had pledged to meet with the Holy Roman Emperor Charles on English soil. Both

Charles and Francis disliked the idea of Harry meeting with the other, but Harry was determined to bring together these old enemies and get their support against his father-in-law. While they prepared for this important occasion, a vast number of details had to be arranged for the meeting in France in May. There were delicate matters of protocol to be decided; the king and his huge entourage had to be transported across the sea; they had to be accommodated on foreign soil in suitable royal style. And time was short.

After much debate, it was decided that Harry and Francis would meet on the Field of Gold in France. Matthew helped plan the tournament and dealt with the problems of transportation and accommodations. He worried whether it would be more expensive to buy flour in Calais or England, and whether there would be enough wine and beer; enough geese, storks, rabbits, quails, and cheese; enough fuel for the kitchens. He ensured the purchase and shipping of hundreds of pounds of velvet, sarcenet, satin, cloth of gold and doublets, bonnets, shirts, and boots for the royal household, and found tailors and dressmakers to make the garments. He ordered hundreds of tents and pavilions, and sent them to France, along with food for both men and beasts. He shipped mountains of plates, cutlery, and glass and hired six thousand carpenters and workmen to set up the tents that would house the English nobility.

They returned to Wales briefly in April, and Catherine gave herself one more chance to improve her relationship with Margaret. On a journey from Cardiff Castle to join Matthew in Hereford, she stopped at Ewyas with Alice and two servants. She arrived late in the afternoon to find the household in turmoil, for Margaret had chastised the servants in such an angry and humiliating manner that they could barely manage a curtsy without breaking into tears as they fled. Catherine had planned to spend the night with Margaret, hoping to find a chink in the armor of malice that surrounded her, but it was not to be.

"'Tis our custom to eat dinner at six of the clock. It is five now. Will you be staying?" Catherine was about to accept when Margaret added, "However, servants eat at five. Alice, you may join them now."

"But Alice is not a servant!" Catherine protested. "She is kin."

"No kin of mine," Margaret replied. "If she receives wages from you for her humble service, she is a servant."

Catherine made her regrets, mounted her horse, and they left for Hereford with only a brief stop to eat at an abbey, for there was no room for them there for the night. They arrived in Hereford disheveled and weary from nearly seven hours in the saddle, three of them after dark when it was most dangerous to be out. Matthew was furious. "This is the end. No more! From now on, the earl is their family, not I!"

"I'm sorry, Matthew," Catherine said, dropping wearily into a chair and removing her bonnet. "I wish it could be different."

"But it can't. Let it go. I command you to stop trying to win her over. Margaret has gone mad. She cannot be reached."

Late on the night that they arrived home at New Place, Catherine and Matthew were awakened before cock's crow by a messenger who had ridden without pause to bring them news. Matthew's mother-in-law, an old and gracious lady in her eighties, had been found murdered in her bed. The assailant was unknown, so the messenger said, but young George Herbert was suspected. The last time he'd left her house, he'd been overheard to say that he would see her dead soon, for she had lived too long already.

The old lady was found lying on bloody sheets, her body riddled with stab wounds, a dagger left in her back. Catherine gave a cry, and held up her hand over her eyes to blot out the image of the hound writhing in agony, pierced with arrows, a sword embedded in his back. The two deaths bore too much similarity. She sank down on the bed. "Matthew . . . if it is George, what will you do?"

"I must protect him," he said, running a hand through his hair. "I cannot let him hang." He looked at Catherine with stricken eyes.

"Matthew, it may not have been him," she soothed, although she couldn't convince even herself. "It could have been anyone."

"No one else would have dared. George has a fearsome temper and is gaining a bad reputation for violence. He is reckless and greedy. He coveted her goods. He is accustomed to having his way, and he knew he would get away with it."

Catherine laid her hand over his. "Oh, Matthew, my dear love, I am so sorry."

He held her hand between both of his and took it to his lips. He met her eyes. "I have you, Catherine, my lovely girl. You are my good fortune."

"And you, beloved, are mine."

*　*　*

Thanks to Matthew's influence, the investigation into the murder of his mother-in-law was soon dropped. Before he sailed to France, he obtained the verdict of death by assailant, or assailants, unknown. From then on, Catherine and Matthew celebrated every Yuletide with Thomas and Maggie on the Isle of Wight, or at Fyfield. Often, Matthew's three sisters and their children made the trip to be with them, filling Catherine's heart and her home with joy. She was happy not only for Matthew, but for herself. His sisters, unlike his daughter, had all welcomed her into the Cradock family, and she had grown fonder of them with every year that passed.

By May, 1520, Catherine and Matthew had been wed three years, and each year that passed brimmed with days of sunshine, love, and laughter. She had forgotten how happy life could be. At night when she fell asleep in Matthew's arms, she gave thanks for the blessings that had been hers that day. Matthew was shelter from the wind and protection from the elements. He was a place to run to when fleeing the hounds. In his arms, she felt safe—as safe as she had felt as a little girl in her father's arms. "Oh, Matthew, never leave me," she would sigh, drawing his arms tight across her breast, feeling his warmth pass through her body as the wind howled and rattled the windows. "I'll never leave you, my lovely girl," he would reply, and Catherine would close her eyes and fall asleep to dream.

In early May, he'd been home barely four days after his return from France when he had to make a trip to take care of business for

Somerset. He came galloping back the next afternoon, calling for her urgently. She ran downstairs, her heart beating wildly, expecting some grief, for life had taught her that nothing was more fickle than good fortune. Instead, Matthew was smiling broadly and his sapphire eyes held a dancing light. He put a finger to his lips, and extended his hand to her.

"What is it?" she said.

"Not here," he replied under his breath. "Outside in the orchard, where no one can hear!"

Catherine half expected to find a magnificent steed or some great luxury of that nature awaiting her there, but there was nothing but the apples and cherries ripening on the trees.

Matthew took her by the shoulders. Reminded of that day at Fyfield in the yew-tree walk when he'd told her about Flodden, her smile faded. But Matthew's held steady. Her heart took up a beat of anticipation.

"Catherine, what is your heart's desire—think—think! If you could have one wish granted to you now, in all your life, ever, what would it be?"

Catherine stared at him in bafflement. "You—to have you with me always."

"But you already have me, my lovely girl. What would you wish for that you don't have? That you desire more than anything else in the world."

She seized him by the collar, afraid to speak, afraid to think, in case it was not that for which she yearned. "Dickon?" She had not said it, not clearly, and no eavesdropper would have understood the half-formed sigh that came from her lips. Her eyes widened as she stared at him and she saw his smile break out across his face. Her hand tightened its grip on his collar.

"I've found the family that raised him."

It seemed to Catherine that her heart stopped its beating.

"They live in Reynoldston. A town near Swansea."

"Is he—" *Alive*, she wanted to say, but couldn't. What if she were dreaming? The dream might vanish if she reached out to it.

"Catherine—" She felt Matthew tighten his hold on her, as he had in the yew-walk. But this time was different—oh, so different! She gazed into his shining face.

"Catherine, he lives in Rhossili-Gellis. I am taking you to him."

* * *

On a sparkling day in May, they rode to the village of Rhossili-Gellis at the tip of the Gower peninsula, accompanied by a few men of Matthew's retinue. Peasants walking in the road scattered before them, and wagons pulled over to the side, allowing them to pass. From the orchards of flowering apple and plum came the laughter of children playing and the barking of their hounds as they gave chase. Trotting over hills covered with yellow gorse, purple heather, and thistle, the small party clattered over wooden bridges. Fields opened into forests, and closer to the ocean, as they neared Rhossili, the forests gave way to farmland where sheep grazed peacefully on the grassy green slopes. But Catherine barely noticed the beauty that normally delighted her, not the babbling brooks they crossed, nor the delicate loveliness of the lime green growth in the dappled forest. Wearing Richard's locket, his love letter, and coin token around her neck, with Dickon's little coif laid safely against her breast, her heart was laden with memory. They had named her son Richard Perkin . . .

Richard . . . Perkin . . .

Matthew rode silently at her side, secretly blessing the tall hedgerows that lined the roads and shielded them from the sea-borne wind, for he was cold even in his fur-trimmed cloak and beaver hat. But then, he was growing old. He was a fulsome sixty years old now, and what time he had left was short. He wished he could spend more of his days with Catherine, but then she would learn of his aches and pains and the various ailments he had kept from her. She would worry, and he didn't wish to burden her. He was simply gladdened that he had been able to find her son for her before it was too late. Behind him, his men talked boisterously and joked among themselves, and now and again they burst into laughter. *Ah, yes*, he smiled to himself as he stole a glance at Catherine. Life was good. There was much to celebrate.

They arrived at the cliff-top Church of St. Mary the Virgin. Bordered by a low stone wall, the small church dated from the sixth century. Bells were chiming for nones, for it was three in the afternoon. Jolted out of her memories, Catherine dismounted and gave her trembling hand to Matthew. Here, in this little church that belonged to the medieval Order of the Knights Hospitallers of St. John, her babe awaited. Little Dickon, who had been ripped from her arms before his first birthday and was now a grown man of twenty-five. Little Dickon, her babe with the wide blue eyes and white-gold hair who, as an infant, had borne such strong resemblance to Richard. Catherine was suddenly frightened. She froze in her steps and dug her fingernails into Matthew's hand to feel his flesh. Would her child know her? Would she know him? Or would they be strangers with naught to say to one another? She had dreamt of this moment for so long, had feared it would never come to pass, and here, a few short steps away, her past, present, and future mingled together, waiting to meet her. She turned wide eyes on her husband.

"Have no fear, Catherine. 'Tis the deepest wish of your heart . . . Come, my dear."

He led her forward and she moved to follow, leaning on his arm, her legs a leaden weight. As she went, her eyes touched on the tombstones that lined the path to the church, some decorated with white roses. How apt, for death and white roses had lined her life, just so, and pointed her forward to this moment. Matthew pushed open the stout carved door. They passed through the Norman archway marked by dog-tooth moldings, a chevron, and battered carved heads, and stepped into the nave. Matthew let the door close quietly behind them.

The little church was dark and smelled musty, for only a few half-melted candles still burned in the sconces, and there was no incense. Catherine stood still while her eyes adjusted to the low light. Then her gaze caught and held on a figure kneeling before the altar rail. His golden head was bowed and so absorbed was he in prayer that he had failed to notice their entrance. On him shone a ruby light from above the sanctuary, and she thought of a knight at vigil before the day's trial. She thought of Richard, his father. A soft gasp escaped her lips. Her hand tightened on Matthew's arm and she turned to look at him mutely. Matthew smiled, and gently, very gently, pried her fingers loose from his arm. As if releasing a dove to the sky, he turned her toward the young man.

She moved forward in the stillness. As she did, in her heart there rose the faint echo of an old beloved melody from long ago. The memory moved forward to meet her, engulfing her in tenderness, and there unfolded before her two young lovers by a campfire on the sandy shore of a Scottish lake. Barely realizing that she moved, she edged forward. Forward to that old, forgotten melody. The young man turned and looked at her, and a radiant smile spread across his handsome face. He rose from his knees. The fire danced over his features with a rose glow, throwing light and shadow across his bright eyes and dimpled mouth. She had thought it was long ago, but now she knew it was only yesterday. Tears stung her eyes and rolled silently down her cheeks. *Oh, Richard, you have come back to me—'tis you, my love!* A sob threatened as she put out her hands to the memory, and the memory came to her, enfolding her with warmth. She looked up, and stared into the deep blue eyes she remembered. She lifted her hand in wonder and touched his cheek, his hair, his brow. "'Tis you. 'Tis really . . . you, my love . . . my dearest, dearest love . . ."

"'Tis me, Mother. 'Tis me," he echoed, laying his golden head against her hair and drawing her into the circle of his arms.

Chapter 25

Field of Gold

1520

While Matthew went to the village to meet with tradesmen, Catherine and Dickon took the stony track that led down behind the church to a footpath along the ridge. Despite the lovely May weather, few fishing vessels were out, and the bay was deserted except for a group of men on the beach below, repairing nets. Catherine smiled up at her son as they stood together at the edge of the windy cliff. Matthew had alerted Dickon to his true identity a few days earlier on a separate trip, but for mother and son there was much to learn about one another, much to share. They had only a week's time, for soon Catherine and Matthew would sail to France for King Harry's meeting with King Francis on the Field of Gold.

"I have always loved the sea. It has such power, such freedom," Catherine said, taking in the wheeling sea birds and the fishing boats that appeared as black specks on the glittering water. "And your father loved it, too, Dickon. He was nine years old when he left England. By the time he was twenty-three, he had sailed many seas and visited many lands. He saw Spain, Portugal, France, Italy, Scotland, and Ireland before he returned to England to—" She broke off, forcing back the unwelcome images that came to her. "What about you?"

"The sea must be in my blood, for I feel the same. I am a sailor, Mother."

"A sailor?" The thought pleased her. "Matthew is a sailor. He owns several ships. Years ago, when he was your age, he gave the York-ist King Richard III devoted service as a pirate on the high seas. He even dabbled in piracy for King Harry in the first invasion of France—very successfully, I might add."

"Are you happy, Mother?" Dickon demanded abruptly.

Catherine gazed at his handsome face, so like his father's, even down to the cleft in his chin. "I am, Dickon—happier than I ever thought to be after I lost your father. At first I turned away from hap-piness, but then I realized it was a way to honor him. What about you? Matthew tells me you remain unmarried at twenty-five."

"I am not ready to wed, Mother. I want to make something of myself first. I want to see the world . . . Perhaps I take after my father?" He gave Catherine a shy smile, his eyes lit with dreams.

"Aye, you are like your father. He, too, had great plans . . . great things he wished to accomplish with his life." *And gambling all, he had lost all*, she thought sadly. "But know the risks, dear son. Do nothing heedlessly. The world is a dangerous place."

A silence.

Catherine said, "You met your father briefly when you were three years old. Do you have any memory of him?"

"I am not sure. I remember being taken to a strange, dark place where a man with bright hair held me in his arms, but I don't remem-ber what he looked like, or what he said."

Catherine closed her eyes. Richard's last moment of earthly hap-piness was taking shape before her.

"Sir Matthew is a good man," Dickon said.

"Matthew is your father's gift to me," Catherine said softly. "When he left for battle, he made me promise to leave my heart open to love. I didn't wish to make a promise I couldn't keep, but he insisted. He said he wanted to look down from Heaven and see me smiling, not weeping. He said he couldn't bear to see my tears—" She realized suddenly why she had found it so difficult to cry all these years.

"Your father and I, we were young, Dickon. Youth is a wonderful thing, but it can be costly. We were blind to everything we didn't wish to see—anything that didn't fit in with our plans." The dock at Ayr rose up before Catherine's eyes and she winced. "We made careless decisions, and as a result, we had one another for less than two years." She pushed back the memories that kept slipping through her mind. "I was older and knew something of life by the time I met Matthew, so it is different now, yet no less wonderful in its own way. He helped me through the burdens that were mine at the time I met him. I know not what I would have done without him." Turning her eyes to her son's face, she traced the line of nose and mouth with her fingertip, lingering on the cleft in his chin. "Matthew is my great blessing, Dickon—as you are—as was your father—" Her voice trembled with gathering emotion, and she dropped her hand.

"'Tis beautiful here," Catherine said, when she had regained her composure. The arc of beach shone gold in the dimming light and the water had turned from dark blue to pewter. "One day I should like you to visit St. Michael's Mount. I loved it there. Your father was so filled with hope there. It was on the beach at Marazion that I took last leave of him. Naught was the same after we met again, for he was Henry's captive when next I saw him . . ."

Catherine related a brief account of their lives together, ending with Richard's death but omitting the last eighteen months after he was delivered to the Tower. For there were things too evil to speak of and thoughts too wicked to entertain. "And you, my *son*—" she said, savoring the sound of the word. "What about you?"

"There is not much to tell. I have been raised by good people. I never suspected I had royal blood in my veins until Sir Matthew told me."

A sudden chill came over Catherine and she gave a shiver. Dickon adjusted her cloak and drew her close. "The secret of your birth is something you must forget now, my son. Never allow yourself to think of it. Never, ever speak of it—not to anyone. Not to your wife when you marry, not to your children, not to a single person—for if one person knows, you are never safe. Do you understand?"

"But think how impressed the girls would be." Dickon grinned. "Surely, after a time—"

"Never!" Catherine clutched his arm and did not return his smile. "Not in your lifetime. If you don't want a secret to get out, you must not tell a single soul." Catherine took a moment to compose herself, for the horrors Richard had endured flashed into her mind. *The fate of the father must not be the fate of the son!* She had to make him understand. "You have heard no doubt of the executions of Edmund de la Pole, Earl of Suffolk, and his brother, William?"

"No. I cannot say I have."

"My son, you have led a sheltered life. You know nothing of court or the terrors that await a man born wrong, as you are, but even you in faraway Wales will have your fill of such deaths with the passage of time. For the Tudors are of bastard lineage and fear those born better than they. They will not rest until they are all dead." She lifted her gaze to him. "Two days ago, Edward Stafford, Duke of Buckingham, went to the block. You may not have heard of his execution, but surely you know of him?"

"Indeed, for he owns Brecon Castle, and spent much time in Wales. What was his treason?"

"He had more royal blood in his veins than the king who sits the throne. So it shall be as long as Tudors rule England."

"Very well, Mother. I will keep the secret of my birth, but must it die with me? If I have a son, can he not know of you and my father— not know his noble heritage and the sacrifices made for him by his grandfather?"

"You may whisper to your son on your death bed, if you can make him understand what danger lies in the truth. If they are careful, the Perkins of Rhossili-Gellis will know the ancient blood of England and of Scotland runs in their veins, and perhaps one day they may even be able to speak openly of their proud forebears—" The castle courtyard at Stirling flashed into her memory and she heard the steward barking orders, "Make haste for the arrival of Prince Richard of England, make haste, I tell ye!" Someone exclaimed, "Gawd! What is that?" and the steward replied, "Naught but the king's lion, laddie!"

She saw James make a sudden entrance, dragged from around the corner by the lion he tethered with a golden chain, and heard the echo of her laughter as the steward hastily added, "And the king!"

She inhaled sharply at the memory of James, whose body lay at Shene, still unburied in all these years after Flodden. Sometimes the fate of kings was a thing to dread. "Tell me, my son, did you ever suspect the secret of your birth?"

Dickon gave her a smile, and in his smile Catherine saw Richard and felt the sun touch her face, banishing the chill.

"Every changeling hopes to be of noble blood. I was no different. I had those dreams."

Catherine leaned against her handsome boy. Twilight was falling and the fishing boats were gone from sight. The beach at Rhossili was deserted now except for two men far below in rough coats and boots, picking cockles on the tidal sandbanks. The wind blew, thick with the salty smell of the sea, bending low the tall grasses that grew along the dunes. Catherine closed her eyes and listened to the rhythmic pounding of the surf on the shore and the call of the birds. Time shifted and present moved into the past, and she saw Richard's face again: the bright, twinkling blue eyes she had loved, the curving mouth, the golden hair. Her blood soared with memory and she knew again the scent of him and recalled the smoldering passion that had thrilled her at his touch. She heard once more the thud of boots as men came by the hundreds to climb to the fortress on the mount and swear fealty to the cause of York. For a fleeting instant, she felt the hopes that had lit Richard's breast. Then it was Marazion, and she was bidding him farewell as the wind whipped them, and birds mewed, and the ocean roared.

The faint bleating of sheep startled her and her eyes flew open; there were no sheep on the Mount! The past vanished; the present took its place, and Dickon smiled down at her. *No, I am not there with Richard, but all is right with the world; all is as it should be.* Here in this little Welsh village by the sea had ended the long road that began for her at Stirling Castle; what must be borne had been borne, and she had survived to see her beloved son. He was safe, and at her side, and he would be a sailor and sail to faraway places on Matthew's ships without fear of the shadow of death at his shoulder.

It was dark now; the birds had gone to sleep, and the stars were coming out. She touched Dickon's cheek. "I always told myself that the day I found you, I would find peace. And I have, Dickon. This day has brought back to me a life much loved and bitterly lost, but also a life that is found anew. My husband here on earth, and my husband there in Heaven, have together worked a miracle. That miracle is you. Your father did not die in vain, and knowing that gives me rest. What more is there, when promises are kept, and dreams come true? Whatever the future brings, it could not be greater than this."

Dickon pressed a kiss to her brow. The bells of the little church began to toll for vespers. She turned behind her and looked up. Matthew had returned from the village and stood gazing down on them, his lone figure in relief against the sky, his thick silvery hair shining in the gloom, his dark cloak whipping about him. *'Tis over, Matthew*, she thought. *I have found my rainbow, and it is you and Dickon.* She could not see his face in the gathering dark, yet she knew he smiled. Just as she knew Richard smiled, high up there somewhere in that vast magnificence above. She raised a hand to her lips and blew Matthew a kiss. Then she raised it higher, and released it also to Richard.

*   *   *

Two days after the Holy Roman Emperor Charles V left England, the twenty miles of sea between Dover and Calais were crowded with ships carrying King Henry VIII and Queen Katherine and their entourage to Calais, emptying England of its nobility, hierarchy, courtiers, noble ladies, and treasure. The massive flotilla made Catherine think of a giant military expedition, but instead of fighting, for the first time in history these ships were taking men to joust and tilt, to feast and dance with their enemies. Catherine found that quite remarkable.

Standing with Matthew on the crowded deck of the *Matthew Cradock*, she felt again the exhilaration that always came to her at sea, heightened now by Dickon's presence. Her eyes went to him at the prow inspecting cordage that he had ordered repaired. When she had returned to New Place from her week-long stay at a cottage on the sea at Rhossili-Gellis with Dickon, Matthew had prepared a wondrous surprise for her. He had appointed Dickon boatswain on his ship so he could accompany them to France. Afterward he unfolded his plans for his stepson. "I intend for him to be first mate. Then I shall make him captain, and when he is ready, I plan to give him his own ship."

Catherine's cup had overflowed many times in recent years, but the memory proved too much joy for her heart at this moment, and a tear rolled down her cheek. She was on the sea she loved; with the man she loved; with her beloved son, once lost and now restored to her. Matthew followed the direction of her gaze, and smiling, kissed her tear away.

"I love you," she whispered, finding an answering light in his eyes.

When Catherine arrived at Guisnes, she was stunned at the sight that met her. A land of faery splendor lay sparkling in the noonday sun. The castle at Guisnes in the border town of Calais was decorated with Tudor roses and dragons and surrounded by a glittering array of hundreds of great silken pavilions studded with gems and cloth of gold. Here were the accommodations for the nobles, and behind these stretched thousands more tents for the rest of the English company. On the other side, in French Ardres, stood the French camp, equally lavish. In the center of these two magnificent encampments sat the empty field of Val d'Or, where the two kings would meet.

With their jewels flashing in the sun, gorgeously clad ladies and knights in sumptuous costumes of silks and velvets paraded through the grassy paths between the tents, nibbling sweetmeats and cakes laden with strawberry jam, and pausing to dip silver goblets into fountains flowing with fine malmsey and claret. As strolling minstrels played lilting tunes, and mummers, jongleurs, and men on stilts entertained, they laughed, danced, and made merry.

Since Catherine was royalty and Matthew was closely attached to Somerset, she found herself housed in one of the jeweled tents close to Harry's spectacular crystal pavilion. Not to be outdone, Francis I

was based in a golden tent on the French side embellished with diamonds in the design of fleur-de-lis. Each day the English and French
courts vied with one another in offering splendid entertainments
and there followed much dining, good cheer, dancing, and tilting.
Then, on the fifth of June, days after their arrival, King Harry and
King Francis set out to meet one another.

The two kings halted at the edge of the field of gold and sat in
silence facing one another, their men around them in battle array.
Catherine caught her breath. There had been rumors of treachery
and a French ambush, and for a moment it seemed that these were
true and the two sides would charge one another. Then trumpets
sounded. Both kings spurred their horses and galloped forward to
the center of the field where a spear marked their meeting place.
As they dismounted and embraced, the people of their two nations
cheered madly. Laughing, they strode into a pavilion, followed by
their lords. Now the celebrations began in earnest.

Catherine cherished the moments with her son. Matthew found
frequent cause to summon Dickon on pretext of ship's business
so she could see him every day. Dickon was with her at one of the
masked balls, and Matthew even managed to get him a good seat
at the tournament where Queen Katherine sat beneath a canopy of
estate entirely lined with pearls to watch her husband joust against
King Francis. He was present at several feasts, and afterward, mother
and son had stood together watching the fireworks in the night sky.
Matthew slipped Dickon into the royal pavilion for the wrestling
match between the two kings, and though Catherine and Dickon
could not be seated together, as that would draw unwelcome attention, Dickon stood in Catherine's line of sight and they exchanged
many a smile across the distance. There was a moment of tension
when Francis threw Harry to the floor, to Harry's great displeasure,
but he rose, laughing. Catherine heard the Venetian ambassador
murmur, "These sovereigns are not at peace. They hate each other
cordially." A snicker met this remark and was quickly stifled.

Lavish entertainments followed daily as each king tried to out-
shine the other, and so much cloth of gold was in evidence that the

site of the meeting, Val d'Or, the Field of Gold, came to be called the Field of Cloth of Gold.

After two weeks of pleasure and amazing pageantry, Catherine returned to England with a renewed sense of awe for her husband and those who had helped Cardinal Wolsey and Somerset shape this meeting. The ceremony would live in her heart always for it was coupled in memory with Dickon, and Matthew. But no alliance came of it, and the expedition was deemed a wasteful extravagance. A failure. Catherine didn't agree. Old enemies had mingled and tasted of friendship; they had partaken in a solemn act of reconciliation. She saw this as a new beginning for the world.

As she boarded the *Matthew Cradock* for England with her husband and her son, Catherine's heart could not have been fuller. Standing alone at the prow of the vessel, her eyes sought her silver-haired husband and her golden-haired son, who stood together at the stern, watching the sailors assemble on deck. Matthew nodded his head, and Dickon blew his boatswain's whistle, conveying his orders to the ship's crew.

Catherine smiled. Life with Matthew was always a whirlwind of activity, for he served a demanding and energetic king, but with few exceptions, the days of her marriage had been wrapped in glitter. "Field of Cloth of Gold" might be the nomer of the place where kings had met, but it was also what Catherine would call her time with Matthew. He had banished the dark past and shed light over the present. With soft eyes, she watched him come to her across the deck, and it seemed to her that the future was spread before her like a field of cloth of gold.

* * *

For Catherine and Matthew and Dickon, the years after the Field of Cloth of Gold passed peacefully, bringing many blessings. In 1526, however, Matthew found his energies depleted by his duties and officially resigned his responsibilities.

"I shall miss you sorely, Matthew," said Charles Somerset, Earl of

Worcester, "but I understand. We are the same age and my heart is not what it used to be either." He gave Matthew a wan smile. "This court with its young king belongs to those whose hair is not as gray as ours, and no doubt 'tis time to let hale and hardier men take our place."

Matthew gave him a smile as he picked up his gloves. "We have seen much in our time, my lord of Worcester, and are blessed to have lived as long as we have."

"Speaking of which—" Somerset lowered his voice so that it was barely audible. "Did that matter I put into your hands ever resolve itself?"

"It did, my lord. Most splendidly." He exchanged a long look with Somerset. "My wife is ever grateful to you."

"'Tis good—very good. Give your beautiful wife my fond regards, Matthew. She is quite a woman. I daresay you know that better than anyone. 'Tis not for nothing she is called the Pale Rose of England, and indeed she is. A rare and most splendid rose . . . A rose for all seasons."

Matthew's eyes grew moist as he bent to kiss Somerset's hand, but Somerset restrained him, and instead, drew him close in an embrace.

"We know not when we shall meet again, Matthew, or whether it be here, or there—" He threw a glance at the sky. "So I shall bid thee a fond adieu. It has been an honor knowing thee."

Matthew nodded mutely, unwilling to trust himself to speech.

The journey home to Wales took longer than normal, for Matthew's heart beat more erratically than usual and he tired after only a few hours' ride. Nor did it help that he worried about Catherine. She was twice a widow and might manage well enough the third time, except that she had no kin to help protect her and was getting old herself. Fifty now. No one would know it to look at her—though her skin was not as firm as once it was, she still had all her teeth, and walked in beauty. A pale rose, still, that had fought many a fire and emerged unscorched.

When he arrived back at New Place, Catherine rushed to give him welcome. Leading him to the solar, she made him stretch out on the settle beneath a fur blanket by the fire that roared in the hearth, and poured him a goblet of warm, spiced wine.

"Somerset sends you greetings, my lovely girl," Matthew said.

Catherine smiled her radiant smile. "I will be fifty-one in November, dearest. Scarcely a girl."

"If you were a hundred, you'd still be my lovely girl," replied Matthew. He let his gaze rest on her for a long moment, then he put out his hand to her. "Come, I have something to tell you."

Catherine drew a cushion beside him and sat down. Taking his hand into both her own, she waited.

"The time has come to build my tomb," he said.

A cry escaped Catherine's lips. She tightened her grip of his hand and bit down hard to hold back the emotion that flooded her.

"You must be strong, dear heart."

"I am so afraid," she breathed on a sigh.

"You have been afraid many times before, and always—always— hope has trumped your fear. This time will be no different, Catherine."

"Oh, Matthew—why can we not live together forever? Why must it end? I am not ready for it to end."

"Now, now, my dear. We've had nearly ten years together, longer than most people I know. God willing, we may have more time yet, but I need to be ready. You understand?"

Catherine nodded.

"Catherine, I would like you to stay here at New Place and be laid to rest beside me when your time comes. It gives me much comfort to think you will be near, and that we shall be reunited in this world, as well as in the next. May I have your permission to design the tomb for us both?"

Catherine didn't dare look at him, but she nodded her head vigorously, stifling the tears that threatened. He pressed a kiss to her brow and the tide of panic that had engulfed her began to recede. She lifted her hand and touched his beloved face.

* * *

On the fifteenth day of April, 1526, only weeks after Matthew had bid Somerset farewell, came the tidings of Somerset's death at the age of sixty-six. While on a visit to the Chapel of St. Anne in Swansea Church to check the progress of their effigies, Catherine and Matthew lit a hundred candles for him so that the church blazed like the bursts of fireworks that had lit their nights in France. Catherine murmured silent thanks to him anew for the son he had helped her find.

Standing at the foot of the tomb Matthew had commissioned, Catherine gazed at their effigies. They were so lifelike—and yet so dead, so empty. She and Matthew lay recumbent; he in armor, his head resting on a helmet with a boar on the crest, and she in her gown, her head on a pillow supported by angels. Two boars were at their feet, and one held a portion of her train in his mouth.

"It is lovely, Matthew," she said, deeply affected by the knowledge of their mortality.

With the effigies vivid in her mind, Catherine never took a single day of her time with Matthew for granted. She relished having him home with her and cherished the fact that he no longer had to ride to court or across Wales each week to tend to his duties. His declining health coupled with Somerset's death stressed to her the urgency of savoring what time they had left. They made another trip to the Isle of Wight in the spring, and went for long walks together over the hills and dales that dazzled with wildflowers. They rode to the seaside and picnicked on the beach, and ambled through woods where delicate fern-lined paths were sprinkled with sunlight. They paused to rest by brooks with water so clear, they could see the pebbles at the bottom, and on their return to New Place, they strolled arm in arm through the orchards, where boughs bent low with blossoms shed petals over them like blessings. Sometimes Catherine picked posies and fashioned the flowers into wreaths with which to crown Matthew's silver head, declaring as she did so, "Hail Poseidon, King of the Sea!" And always, wherever she was, she would be gazing about her, dwelling on the details of the moment so she could capture their memory forever.

* * *

They celebrated Matthew's sixty-seventh birthday in September, and with great anticipation, Catherine prepared for Yuletide. As was customary for them since that disastrous Yule with Matthew's daughter, they would spend the sacred season with Maggie and Thomas on the Isle of Wight, and Dickon would take them there, his expert hand guiding the *Matthew Cradock* as she and Matthew sat and watched. When winter arrived, they lingered by the fire, reading poetry or chatting about nothing in particular, and marveling at the great doings at court, which now seemed so distant and irrelevant to them. Sometimes Dickon would come to visit, and these were the best times of all. Her joy in showing him his room the first time he'd come to Fyfield was a memory that would live forever in her heart.

In the four years since they had found Dickon, Matthew had taught his stepson everything he himself knew about trade, and Dickon had proved himself an apt pupil. He still didn't marry, however, though he could well afford a wife.

"Later, Mother. I am having too much fun," he would laugh when she teased him about his single state. Catherine always smiled, thinking of his father, who must have broken hearts by the cartloads as he roamed Europe as a young man. Matthew, meanwhile, continued to make secret provision for Dickon. There was always the danger that his daughter might learn of the monies he had given his stepson, and discover Dickon's dangerous connection to Richard of York. To protect him, Matthew hid Dickon's ownership of the ship he had given him by setting it up as a Genoese vessel under a code known only to them.

By December 1526, the talk at New Place, Fyfield, and the Isle of Wight had invariably turned to a different secret, one that had come to be called "The King's Secret Matter." But it was no secret at all, for naught in the realm was more widely discussed than Henry's desire to disown his queen, Katherine of Aragon. He had fallen in love with another woman named Anne Boleyn.

"She is beautiful, intelligent, and much younger than his queen," reported Matthew as they sat in the solar at New Place on a cold wintry night. "A headstrong and ambitious woman who refuses to be the king's mistress. It reminds me of someone I know." His eyes twinkled as he looked at her.

Catherine lay down the thick black velvet cloak she was embroidering as a Yuletide gift for Thomas. "You do me an injustice, sir," she bristled. "I refused to *marry* the king. There is a difference, you know."

"Indeed, you did, my dear girl. I don't believe another woman in history can lay claim to refusing a king. I always knew you were exceptional and without peer."

"Exactly," said Catherine, only partly mollified. "And I wasn't ambitious either. At least, it depended on the king." She grinned suddenly. "Henry wasn't worth the taking."

Matthew laughed.

"Nevertheless," Catherine resumed, "Anne Boleyn has my sympathy. All marriages are happy—it's the living together afterwards that causes all the problems."

"I hope you're not speaking of us?" Matthew said anxiously.

"No, merely thinking of dear James." Catherine smiled. She fell silent as she took another few stitches with her load of turquoise silk thread, and laid the cloak down again. "I've walked in Anne Boleyn's shoes. I know what it takes to tread those hot coals at court. These Tudor kings have a way of burying their queens. I survived only through sheer guile. I do not envy her, nor do I believe she has any idea what she is getting herself into. Harry is a whited sepulcher, beautiful on the outside, rotten on the in-. I know him. At least Henry had scruples. I fear Harry has none. Anne Boleyn had better watch her step."

"She has many enemies, and they are powerful ones. I've heard her called every epithet there is, but Henry is a man besotted. He claims divorce is diplomatically expedient, dynastically urgent, and theologically necessary. He says his queen is barren because his marriage to Katherine was never lawful. According to Henry, the two books of Leviticus forbade the very marriage he had entered with his brother's wife. He sees it as his duty to his people and to God to cast aside Katherine and marry the woman he loves. But Wolsey is sluggish in pushing the divorce forward, and in this he stands to incur the king's mighty wrath."

"How can she be called barren when she has birthed her daughter, Mary?"

"She has given the king no son, and is past childbearing age. As far as Henry is concerned, that makes her barren. He has a fear of dynastic failure. He's sent to Rome for an annulment."

"I remember Katherine's wedding to Arthur—" Catherine paused, her needle in the air, her mind burning with memory. "What do you think Henry will do if the pope does not grant him the annulment he seeks?"

Matthew sighed heavily. "Henry is nothing if not determined. He will have his way, whatever the pope decides. I have no doubt he will wed Anne Boleyn without the pope's blessing, if he must. If that happens—God forfend—there could well be civil war."

"Katherine once said that her marriage was made in blood." *Aye, drenched in Richard's blood, and Warwick's.* She blinked to banish the dark memories that leapt in the shadows of her mind.

"Well, my lovely girl, 'tis no use to dwell on things we cannot change." Matthew poured two goblets of wine and handed her one. "Here, let's drink to us—and to those we love—be they with us, or up there."

He lifted the silver goblet she had given him as a birthday gift, and she followed his example. They sipped the sweet malmsey thoughtfully.

"Dickon is twenty-nine now, and I am thinking he should marry soon," Catherine said. "And Maggie has not yet wed." She smiled at Matthew over the rim of her cup.

He gave a roar of laughter. "What are you plotting, my lovely girl?"

"A marriage made in Heaven," smiled Catherine. "Speaking of those up there, Matthew, and those down here, it would please me, and Thomas, I am sure—and no doubt Richard and Cecily—if such a match could be arranged between Dickon and Maggie. Cecily believed in Richard, that he was her brother, you know."

"As did many others," Matthew replied softly.

"Do I have your blessing, Matthew?"

He reached out and took her hand. "You have my blessing, my lovely girl," he chuckled.

"Thank you." She rose and gave him a kiss on his cheek. "And now I daresay 'tis past your bedtime."

Outside the wind banged the shutters while Catherine basked in the warmth of Matthew's body. "Oh, Matthew, never leave me," she sighed aloud, drawing his arm tightly across her breast, as was her wont.

"Never," he mumbled sleepily.

Catherine snuggled close. Soon it would be Yuletide, and Yuletide was always wonderful. They would sail away to the Isle of Wight. Dickon and Maggie would be with them. What a blessing if they wed . . . They would need a papal dispensation since they were cousins, but that shouldn't be a problem . . . How marvelous to think that she, and Cecily, and Richard, and Thomas would be united that way for all time—

"Will . . . you . . . speak to . . . Dickon, Matthew?" she murmured drowsily.

"Hmmm . . ."

"About . . . the . . . marriage . . ." Her lids were growing heavier with each word.

There was no response; his breathing had changed. Matthew must have fallen asleep. She made a mental note to ask him in the morning. She pushed up closer against him, feeling warm, and so very blessed. Her lids grew heavier still and she felt herself fading away into sleep. *Thank God for Matthew*, she thought, drifting off.

Thank God for dreams . . .

Thank God for hope.

Epilogue

WESTMINSTER, 1532

The year since Matthew's death was fraught with sorrow and difficulties, and his loss plunged Catherine into a depth of loneliness she had not known since Richard had died. Though she was grateful to have had five years more with him after he built his tomb, she missed him sorely. Alone she labored beneath the weight of the administration of her estate, and alone she walked in the woods where Matthew's gentle companionship had brought solace and brightened her life.

At first, nature proved healing, but then solitude turned into an enemy. So heavy was the despair unleashed in her that she returned to court, that place where swirling memories, both joyous and bitter, tangled in her heart in a knot as heavy as lead. Better to be alone with strangers than to be alone with nothing but emptiness, or so she had thought. But in the passing days here at court, she had learned that whether alone or with others, all was the same. Nothing helped.

She made her way along the torch-lit passage to the king's privy chambers, where the royal festivities were in progress, presided over by Henry and his new queen, Anne Boleyn. Thus had she walked many times since Richard's capture. At the end of the long road, a king awaited once more, but the familiar face was gone now, and the new one that had taken his place had changed the old ways. Now the walls that encircled her resounded with merriment, instead of dole, yet dole and merriment were the same to her, and at the end of life, there was only memory, nothing more. That much she knew.

Sudden emotion overwhelmed her. She cut short her steps and turned into an empty alcove. The window stood open to the dark garden, and though she could still hear the voices of the merry-makers, they were fainter here. She lifted her eyes to the moonlit sky. Her mind drifted into memory, and before her eyes she saw herself at Castle Huntly, with her beloved Richard. They were dancing to a tempestuous Highland melody that was charged with energy. She had eyes for no one but him. As she leapt from side to side, pointed her toes, and shook her skirts, the music reached a feverish, almost violent, pitch. Drunk on joy, they followed the dance, clapping their hands, swinging one another around, laughing with wild abandon. Linking arms, never taking their eyes from one another, they moved to the ferocious tempo, drawing close, drawing apart, determined to wring from each note its full measure of ecstasy.

She came back to the present abruptly. A woman's voice was raised in a song without words, a poignant, melodious lament that ushered forth a fathomless despair from the depths of her being. She'd not given it much heed as she'd made merry with Richard on that immortal evening forever imprinted in her mind, but those Highland pipes had vibrated with martial fervor, hinting at darkness and war for those who strained to hear. It had been, she realized, a warning of what was to come.

She closed her eyes against the grief. *Richard, I miss you. Matthew, I miss you . . .*

"Lady Catherine," said a resonant voice from behind her. "Your husband, Sir Matthew, and my father, were good friends."

She swung around. She did not know this young man. "Forgive me—have we met?"

"We have. Clearly you don't remember, but I have never forgotten."

She gazed at him in puzzlement, trying to recall.

"Christopher Ashton, my lady." He swept his plumed cap from

his fair curls, and gave her a low, elegant bow. "Son of Thomas Ashton. He remembered you from the early days and always spoke of you in most glowing terms."

"Ah yes, I remember your father," she lied. "That was kind of him. How is he these days?"

"He died three years ago."

"I am sorry."

A silence.

"I see you have returned to court. How long will you stay?" he said.

"I know not. Until I have need to return to my manor at Fyfield, I suppose—or until I tire of court." She gave him a smile. Time had marked his eyes and mouth, though gently so, she suddenly realized, and he was not as young as she'd first thought. Even at forty, however, he was young to her. "I am alone, as you may know—" She blinked to banish the ghosts who were suddenly all around her. Matthew had left her all his worldly goods, excepting the provisions he had made for the inheritance of his daughter and her sons. He had even granted her New Place for her lifetime use, but Margaret and her sons had challenged his will and threatened her with violence if she stayed. Mindful of the fate of their other grandmother, she had fled Wales, leaving everything behind that had belonged to Matthew. Fyfield had proved a lonely place, empty of memories, except those of James, whom she did not wish to remember.

"Solitude is a good thing," she said, "if it is not overly done." She looked away. She had no desire to say more to this man who was making conversation with her out of pity or curiosity.

"The minstrels play a delightful melody, Lady Catherine." He threw a glance over his shoulder at the passageway. It was a love song that did nothing to assuage the ache of loneliness running rampant through her this night. Not trusting herself to speak, she turned her gaze to the open window. The night was somehow tender in its darkness. A roomful of strangers and the laughter she would have to endure with them seemed suddenly most unwelcome. Sleep rarely found her anymore, but perhaps it was time to return to her chamber in case it should decide to visit. She was about to bid Christopher Ashton a fair evening when his voice came again.

"The stars are unusually bright tonight, are they not? Especially that one—"

She followed the direction he pointed and astonishment washed over her in a flood of disbelief; he was indicating Richard's star, shining bright in the heavens. Awestruck, she said softly, almost to herself, "'Tis only when darkness falls that we can see the stars."

"Beautiful. Something the poet Thomas Wyatt wrote?"

She shook her head. "Something someone told me a long time ago."

"A very wise soul."

Averting her gaze, she struggled for composure, her mind in tumult as she sought to make sense of the coincidence. That, she thought, was no doubt futile. Life was filled with coincidences.

"King Henry has arranged lavish entertainment this night. I should like to escort you the rest of the way, my lady, if I may? For I would claim a dance."

Her head shot up in surprise. "A dance?" She stared at the hand he offered her, but she did not take it. Even at forty, Christopher Ashton was nearly seventeen years younger than her. Pity she would not accept, but what else could there be? "Master Ashton, such a dance may cause gossip that would not reflect well on either of us."

"Let them gossip. I care not a whit. I did not think you did either. Am I wrong?"

She regarded him thoughtfully for a long moment. "I do not worry about what people think. For I have found they don't do it very often."

He laughed for a long moment. "'Tis what my father admired most about you. You are a woman of spirit and courage, Lady Gordon."

"'Tis not courage, dear sir, 'tis necessity. We do what we must."

"We do what we must, indeed. It takes all kinds of courage to get through this world." He fell silent, and their eyes met. There was far more to this young man, she realized abruptly, than fair curls and an intriguing smile.

"Let us not dwell on dismal thoughts. Life is brief. Let us dance and make merry, my lady."

A faint memory echoed in her mind, and she realized Matthew had spoken similar words on the feast day at Fyfield. She lifted her eyes to him. Something about Christopher Ashton reminded her of Richard. Maybe in the line of the jaw, or maybe in the way he held his head. *Remember me in happiness, not in tears; smile for me, Catryn; laugh for me. 'Tis how I want to see you remember me.* What was wrong with recapturing a semblance of that happiness, if only fleetingly? He spoke truth, this young man. Life was short, and joy so very precious.

"Let us dance—" she said. She broke into a smile for the first time since Matthew's death, and accepted the hand he offered her.

Author's Note

Except for her dazzling beauty, the lifelong passion she inspired in King Henry VII, and the general facts of her life, nothing endures of Lady Catherine: no portrait, no letters, no observations she made or that were made of her. Only ten words that she spoke were recorded for posterity: "It is the man, and not the king, I love." These words, spoken at a young age, at a point in her life when she was under unimaginable duress, live in tribute not only to her love for her first husband, but also to the remarkable and courageous woman she was. Devised at short notice, it is a reply addressed to both a king and his captive that gives no offense to one, while offering encouragement to the other, and that speaks to both simultaneously, while conveying volumes to each.

From these ten words, and her refusal of a king's gift, I derived my portrayal of Lady Catherine Gordon.

Since the story of Lady Catherine given here omits the time period of January 1502, which includes the betrothal of Princess Margaret to James IV, I plead artistic license for depicting the proxy wedding as taking place in 1503, and for consolidating the Earl of Bothwell's visits of 1501 and 1502 into one.

Catherine's fourth husband, Christopher Ashton, was a much younger man, born around 1500, and a widower with two small children. Of his ancestry little is known, but he may have been related to Sir Ralph Ashton of Yorkshire, who had been a staunch supporter of King Richard III. Several Ashtons died in the Pretender's cause, and if Ashton was related, he would have harbored strong Yorkist sympathies.

As noted by Ricardian scholar Wendy Moorhen, Christopher Ashton was a courtier of unknown origins, sufficiently well connected to obtain a post at court as gentleman usher to the king. He supported Queen Anne Boleyn, whom he described as "one of the bountifullest women of her time or since" and was a man of forceful personality who made his mark in local politics, battled with his neighbors in and out of court, fought for his country in Scotland and in France, and finally challenged the rule of Bloody Mary.[1]

Ashton, a ringleader in the Marian Conspiracy directed at "Bloody Mary" Tudor, was one of eight hundred men to flee England after the plot failed. Although there is no record of a pardon on the accession of Elizabeth I, he is thought to have slipped back into England and avoided attention by living in obscurity. There is a tradition that he was buried at Fyfield with Lady Catherine, but the date of his death is unknown.

In her will, Catherine describes Christopher Ashton as her "most intierlist[2, 3] beloved husband" and her third husband, Matthew Cradock, as her "dear and well-beloved" husband. Sir Matthew's will evinces a high regard for his wife, whom he named as his executrix. It also suggests a coolness in his relationship with his daughter. That Catherine didn't stay in Wales as she and Matthew had planned,

---

1 Wendy Moorhen, "Four Weddings and a Conspiracy, Conclusion," THE RICARDIAN, pp. 494–96.

2, 3 Wendy Moorhen, "Four Weddings and a Conspiracy, Conclusion," THE RICARDIAN, p. 498.

and that she wasn't buried there, shows a change of heart that came abruptly after his death. The reason has to lie with the Herbert family. Matthew's grandson, George Herbert, enjoyed a violent reputation, and George's grandmother Edith Mansell met with foul play. Catherine had problems with her Welsh inheritance, and since her stepgrandson was the ultimate beneficiary of her estate, she may have feared for her own life. In later years, Christopher Ashton is known to have harbored antipathy for Sir Matthew's younger grandson, William Herbert, who, unlike his brother, survived his violent childhood to become Earl of Pembroke later in life. This may have stemmed from what Ashton learned about them from Catherine.

Little is known about James Strangeways, Catherine's second husband. In her will, she describes herself in less than endearing terms as his "some tyme wife." Twenty years after his death, when she herself died, she was still engaged in litigation with his relative, Giles Strangeways, and still trying to pay off his debts.

It is not known whether Catherine was ever reunited with her child, but certain clues suggest this was the case. The Perkins of Reynoldston and Rhossili-Gellis traced their descent back to the Pretender. If they knew their ancestry in the nineteenth century, they must have known it in the sixteenth. In a curious coincidence, Catherine settled ten miles away in Swansea. Such a remarkable coincidence cannot be insignificant.

Readers may be aware that Lady Catherine Gordon's maternal descent is disputed, and historians are divided as to whether her mother was Huntly's second wife, Princess Annabella Stewart, or Elizabeth Hay, his third. I have elected to choose Princess Annabella, daughter of James I, over Elizabeth Hay, who was descended from two daughters of Robert the Bruce.

A question to be addressed concerns Catherine's marriage to Richard. The reader should know that detractors of Prince Richard deny the idea of a prearranged marriage. They believe Catherine and Richard fell in love on sight, and married from lust. Other historians—those who believe "Perkin Warbeck" was the younger prince in the

Tower—regard the marriage as prearranged by James IV before Prince Richard's arrival in Scotland, as behooves a royal contract. They base this belief on three things: the fifteen ells of velvet James sent Catherine on the eve of Richard's arrival in Scotland; the fact that no sooner was Richard in Scotland than he was married; and the fact that the subject of a marriage with some undetermined royal princess had already been raised while Richard was still in Burgundy.

There are, however, two considerations that do not entirely support either of these arguments: the situation of Catherine's father, the Earl of Huntly, which suggests he would not have favored the alliance, and Richard's love letter to Catherine that suggests he had met Catherine and was in love with her when he wrote it. Regarding Huntly, historian Ann Wroe states:

> Huntly's most famous son-in-law was to say, later, that Huntly had believed him to be Richard, Duke of York. The aged earl was in James's privy council, and had therefore heard Richard's heart-rending account of his life. Yet marriage was essentially a business and financial contract, made without emotion, especially by the brides' fathers, and there was little in a marriage to Prince Richard of England to secure—let alone advance— Catherine's position. Her husband-to-be was an exile and a wanderer. His kingdom was a dream, and his only income was the money James allowed him . . . He in turn offered nothing but his titles (on paper), and himself, the perfect image of a prince. From Huntly's point of view there was nothing solid to be gained from this alliance, and everything to lose.[4]

Richard's love letter to Catherine in which he calls her "the most beautiful ornament of Scotland" is preserved in the archives of Spain. As his biographer notes, this was "a work of maturity, passion

---

4 Ann Wroe, *The Perfect Prince: The Mystery of Perkin Warbeck and His Quest for the Throne of England*. New York: Random House, 2003, p. 265.

and independence" that stands in sharp contrast to the love letters between Prince Arthur and Katherine of Aragon with their stilted expressions and their sense of hovering parents. Richard's love letter expresses a prince's desires, but is couched in the language of the heart. According to Wroe, if Richard hadn't already met Catherine when he wrote it, he had "dreamed her to distraction."[5]

Between these two positions in support of, or against, a prearranged match, lies a third that could explain the apparent conflicts in the evidence. The marriage may have been prearranged, but final approval was withheld until Richard came to Scotland. King James played Cupid, but there was to be no coercion. He gave his consent in principle before Richard left Burgundy, and arranged the meeting between Catherine and Richard on the understanding that his royal approval would be granted if his council found merit in the Pretender's claim to be the Duke of York, and if Catherine herself desired the marriage. Huntly may have complied with the same understanding. When Richard and Catherine met, they fell in love at first sight. This would explain the emotional intensity of Richard's love letter, their speedy marriage, and their life-long devotion to one another; all without compromising the Pretender's claim to be the true prince, Richard of York.

Regarding the Pretender's claim: Was the so-called "Perkin Warbeck" the younger prince in the Tower, or not? Volumes have been written on the subject and a select bibliography is provided for those interested in pursuing the subject further.[6] *Pale Rose of England* presents the Pretender's case, but in this note I wish to address some points in more depth and highlight a few considerations not raised in the story, or missed in the historical texts, or not enhanced by them.

At this great distance in time, there can be no definitive answer

---

5 Ibid., pp. 254–70.

6 Some of the books listed in the Bibliography are of interest not only for the belief that the younger prince survived, but for alternative theories of what became of him. However, the reader should bear in mind that it is a select Bibliography and far more has been written on the subject than can be included here.

to the mystery of the survival of the princes. My research and review of the facts and the inconsistencies surrounding the Pretender have convinced me that he was the lost prince in the Tower. Francis Bacon, writing in the 1620s, expressed the general bewilderment of his contemporaries, and called the case of the Pretender "one of the strangest examples of a personation that ever was."[7]

The official narrative of the Pretender given under torture contains many elements applicable to the life of the real prince, Richard, Duke of York. The two worlds of the Pretender, so far apart, should never have touched, yet they did, time and again. Here is a child who resembled King Edward IV and bore the marks of Plantagenet royalty in his strangely defective eye and drooping eyelid; whose name meant "real" and "orphan"[8]; who was of no known address or clear parentage; who moved all over Europe, always in the company of English people (to explain his fluency in the English language); and who lived for a time in Portugal, somehow managing to attach himself to the wife of one of Edward IV and Richard III's most loyal retainers—the Portuguese Jew, Duarte Brandeo, known as Sir Edward Brampton. Even Edward IV makes an appearance in "Perkin's" tale, acting as his godfather.[9] Both princes are linked by a common thread of wandering, jeopardy, and sorrow.

That Henry VII allowed Brampton to be named in "Perkin's" confession is evidence that this information was well known, could not be suppressed, and therefore had to be explained away. In order to denigrate the connection to Edward IV's loyal retainer, Brampton's wife was substituted as the contact, but the tale is startling

---

7 Francis Bacon, ed. F. J. Levy, *The History of the Reign of King Henry VII*, New York: Bobbs-Merrill Company, p. 151; and Ann Wroe, *The Perfect Prince*, p. 397.

8 Wroe, see p. 407, and pp. 412–13. In his letter on October 13, 1497, from custody in Exeter, to Nicaise Werbecque, identified by Henry VII as his "mother," the Pretender signed himself "Pierrequin Wezbecq." *Wezbecq* was a Flemish-French play on words, with the Flemish *wezen* meaning "real," and *weze* meaning "orphan." To quote Wroe, "This was the orphan Perkin speaking."

9 Bacon, pp. 152–53.

nevertheless. The child, whoever he was, went to Portugal in the company of Sir Edward Brampton's wife in 1487, after the Battle of Stoke and the failure of the rebellion against Henry VII led by John de la Pole, Earl of Suffolk—a most curious coincidence at the very least. At the time, Bruges was infested with plague and seething with political unrest and would not have provided safe refuge for a fugitive prince.

According to Brampton's testimony given in 1496 to Henry Tudor's man in Portugal, he didn't wish to keep the boy, for he had nothing to offer except *a talent for music*. This talent was so extraordinary that, in later years, it drove John Skelton to a fever pitch of jealousy. Most remarkably, this talent for music was shared by the younger prince in the Tower and noted by a variety of observers who had met King Edward's younger son.[10] It is also a talent that seems to have run in the family, since Elizabeth of York was musically gifted.

As noted by a chronicler unfriendly to the Yorkist cause, the Pretender passed as Prince Richard for a very long time, and without a mistake, deceiving everyone.[11] The probability that a false prince could be found who not only resembled Edward IV and bore the marks of Plantagenet royalty, but could play the part of a prince with aplomb, and who also shared with the younger prince in the Tower a talent for music, is so small that it surely deserves little credence.

In the account of his life given before his capture, the Pretender said that he hid in various countries with two men who were sent to guard and govern him. These guards disappeared from his life when one died and the other was sent back to his own country (suggesting that this man was not English). As noted by Wroe, Brampton received a reward from Richard III in 1484 for services rendered. A similar reward on the same day was also given to Christopher Coleyns, Esquire. He, like Brampton, had been a gentleman usher to

---

10 Wroe, p. 59. Rui de Sousa, councilor to the king of Portugal, was besotted by the singing of the seven-year-old prince.

11 Ibid., p. 397. Comment is attributed to Jean Molinet.

King Edward IV, and was also a seaman who would know how to get goods—or a child—out of London. Like Brampton, he was granted a pardon by Henry VII, but disappeared from the historical record, perhaps owing to his death. Meanwhile, Brampton returned to his own country, Portugal.[12]

One striking feature of the Pretender's life is the loose connection between him and his family in Tournai. The Pretender's confession is riddled with errors in family names, occupations, and general information, as if it had been a memorized account, and neither the Pretender nor the Werbecques exhibited any great affection or concern for one another such as would be expected from a family in these circumstances. "Perkin's" letter to his mother written in captivity is notable for its stiff courtesy and lack of feeling. Furthermore, and most curiously, Henry's obsessive spy-work never established, to anyone's satisfaction, including Henry's own, that "Perkin Warbeck" was the son of the boatman, Jehan Werbecque, or even that Jehan Werbecque had a son named Perkin.[13] There is no record or evidence of his birth except a reference that was drawn up after his death that said his parents were poor and suggested they were unknown. The child, "Perrequin," simply appeared in Tournai at the age of ten, was soon sent away to fend largely for himself, and never returned.[14] His parents weren't interested in him and seemed to play no part in his upbringing.[15] To explain the loose family bonds, some surmised that the Werbecques had played foster parents to a fugitive prince.[16]

Among the many inconsistencies in the tale of "Perkin Warbeck" is Henry VII's own ambiguity about the Pretender. The Pretender

---

12 Ibid., p. 109.

13 Ibid., pp. 392–420.

14 Ibid., pp. 392–93.

15 Ibid., p. 409.

16 Ibid., pp. 417–18.

was someone whose real name and real parents the best labors of Henry's spies could never quite uncover. The city of Tournai never claimed him, and Henry never asked for confirmation.[17] As Henry noted himself, nothing explained the endurance of the Pretender's reputation as the true prince or the unwavering support of the great names that backed him, such as James IV of Scotland; Margaret, Duchess of Burgundy; Maximilian, King of the Romans; Philip the Handsome, King of Castile; and Charles VIII, King of France. Both he and his backers seemed to feel themselves under an obligation to one another that had not been invented and that the confession did not change.[18]

Henry VII lived in terror of the reappearance of the younger prince in the Tower, suggesting that he knew both princes had not perished. Sir Thomas More admits, "Some remain yet in doubt whether they were in (Richard III's) days destroyed or no."[19] Polydore Vergil, Henry's own historian, records, "It is generally reported and believed that the sons of Edward IV were still alive, having been conveyed secretly away and obscurely hidden in some distant region." Francis Bacon, another faithful Tudor supporter, also records these doubts regarding the death of the princes: "It was still whispered everywhere, that at least one of the children of Edward the Fourth was living."[20]

Today's informed reader may point to the bones that were found at the foot of the Tower stairs and put into an urn at Westminster as proof of the murder of the two princes. It should be borne in mind, however, that there has been a human presence at the Tower of London for over two thousand years and finding skeletal remains is

---

17 Ibid., p. 419.

18 Ibid., p. 518.

19 A. J. Pollard, *Richard III and the Princes in the Tower*, p. 120, states that the similarities in More's tale to the story of the *Babes in the Wood* powerfully suggests a literary rather than a factual inspiration. Pollard is worth reading for a review of the case against Richard III.

20 Bacon, p. 82.

neither surprising nor uncommon. The bones in the urn could date from Roman times, or they could be female. Until a DNA study is conducted, they can be given no validity. The 1934 forensic examination was flawed and didn't even check for gender.[21]

The subject of "Perkin Warbeck" is fraught with controversy in England, where he tends to be dismissed as a fraud, so much so that Ann Wroe's biography *The Perfect Prince* was entitled *Perkin: A Story of Deception* for the UK market. Yet Wroe states that no explanation or piece of evidence offered up by Henry and his spies could explain who "Perkin" was, and Henry knew it.[22] Many contemporaries of the Pretender agreed. The poet and chronicler Jean Molinet found his English, his manners, and his knowledge of the Yorkist court formidable.[23]

Mary Shelley, the author of *Frankenstein,* also believed in the Pretender. In the preface to her novel *The Fortunes of Perkin Warbeck, A Romance,* she states:

> It is not singular that I should entertain a belief that Perkin was, in reality, the lost Duke of York. For in spite of Hume, and the later historians who have followed in his path, no person who has studied the subject but arrives at the same conclusion. Records

---

21 See Peter Hammond's *Richard III: Loyalty, Lordship and Law,* pp. 104–47. This comprehensive and detailed academic study reexamines the forensic examination of 1934 and the evidence for the deaths of the princes. It is noted that the examiners of 1934 by their own admission presumed throughout the investigation that the bones were male and those of the princes. However, evidence is found to suggest the origin of the bones is likely female. Other finds of "princes'" bones prior to the "authentic" find in 1674 are also discussed. Audrey Williamson's *Mystery of the Princes,* a Gold Dagger Award winner, offers a compelling and very readable account of the subject and presents a convincing case for the survival of the younger prince, pp. 161–73. Diana Kleyn's *Richard of England,* pp. 36–48, discusses the discovery of the other bones at the Tower thought to have been the princes and presents reasons why the bones in the urn could not be theirs. Kleyn also lists further reading on the subject. Bertram Fields offers a clear and insightful analysis in *Royal Blood,* pp. 238–57. Also see Paul Murray Kendall, *Richard the Third,* pp. 465–95.

22 Wroe, p. 399.

23 Ibid., p. 397.

exist at the Tower, some well known, others with which those who have access to those interesting papers are alone acquainted, which put the question almost beyond a doubt. This is not the place for a discussion of the question. The principal thing that I should wish to be impressed on my reader's mind is, that whether my hero was or was not an imposter, he was believed to be the true man by his contemporaries.[24]

Mary Shelley's novel covers the fugitive prince's story until his arrival on the shores of England. *Pale Rose of England* picks up the tale from there. To my knowledge, *Pale Rose of England* is the first fictional exploration of Lady Catherine Gordon's four marriages. Along with Mary Shelley and some professional historians and scholars, I believe that Richard III did not murder his nephews; that he did indeed send the younger prince abroad for safety; that the child survived to adulthood and that the so-called "Perkin Warbeck" was this prince, the son of King Edward IV. *The Rose of York: Fall from Grace* gives the scenario for how his survival may have been accomplished using a page-boy substitution for the younger prince in the Tower.[25] English novelist Philippa Gregory, who holds a doctorate in history, agrees and comes to a similar conclusion in her novel, *The White Queen*. She explains her reasons:

Then there is the historical evidence. A very interesting book by Ann Wroe, *Perkin*, suggested to me that the so-called pretender Perkin Warbeck might well have been the surviving prince, Richard. Her case for it is very compelling, as others have

---

24 Mary Shelley, *The Fortunes of Perkin Warbeck, A Romance*, 1830; reprinted by Kessinger Publishing, p. 3. The documents at the Tower that Mary Shelley refers to have not been mentioned by other sources. They may be waiting to be discovered, or they may have been destroyed, or may be lost.

25 Sandra Worth, *The Rose of York: Fall from Grace*, Yarnell, Ariz.: End Table Books, 2007; the third book in a trilogy of three stand-alone novels is a multiple award-winner in its own right.

suggested too. There is other persuasive evidence that both boys were not killed as the traditional history (and Shakespeare) suggests. Even the traditional history—of them being suffocated in their beds in the Tower and buried beneath a stair—is filled with contradictions. If Perkin was Richard—and this is speculative history, as indeed all history around this genuine mystery must be—then Richard must have somehow survived.[26]

That Henry VII believed the Pretender was genuine seems to be the case. As late as September 1497, he still referred to him as the Duke of York.[27] He would not give him up even for the astounding terms offered by the Holy Roman Emperor Maximilian, which included renouncing—*in perpetuity*—for himself and "his cousin of York, and all their heirs and successors" all rights in the kingdom of England. Although plagued by massive financial troubles, Maximilian offered enormous riches to anyone close to Henry VII who could persuade Henry to surrender the Pretender. When these efforts failed, Maximilian hoped to launch an invasion of England to free him. He abandoned his plans only when civil war broke out in his own kingdom.

In spite of these threats and offers, Henry VII would not relinquish the Pretender, even when the Pretender, broken, beaten, and exposed as a coward, no longer posed any viable threat to him. Nor would Maximilian abandon his efforts to gain the Pretender's release long after he could gain any political advantage for himself, and even at his great personal expense.

Fearing a second generation from the Pretender, Henry did not allow him to sleep with his wife. The Pretender's escape from the Tower caused Henry genuine distress, and on his recapture, he engaged in a strange drama of sending him to "Purgatory" for two days, and delivering him to "Hell" on the third.

---

26 "Conversation with Philippa Gregory," philippagregory.com, January 2010.

27 Wroe, p. 407.

In reference to the Pretender's escape, it is interesting to note that he chose to escape from the Tower.[28] This may have been due to the proximity of that fortress to the sea, but if he were the true prince, it may have owed more to the psychological terrors that the Tower held for him.[29] In the end, the Tower proved to be the Pretender's "Hell" in many ways, not least of which was the punishment he suffered within its walls. The idea of castration as set out in this novel is profoundly repulsive, but not gratuitous. I was driven to suggest it for several reasons.

Castration was a horrific punishment commonly practiced in ancient times against the captured enemy, and Henry VII would have been aware of this. Given the vengeful nature of the Tudor monarchs, it would have provided a fitting end to the little drama of "Hell" that Henry VII devised for the captive who was his rival both in love and war. Whether or not Henry castrated the Pretender can never be known, but Henry VII's agony of mind during the Pretender's escape from the Tower was noted at the time. The disfigurement mentioned by the Spanish ambassador and the ambassador's shock that anyone could change so dramatically in so short a time also suggests some great violence. Henry's fear of the Pretender politically led him to break the bones of his face so he would not resemble his father when he was brought out for execution. In the same vein, his need to eliminate the danger of a second generation in the event of a future escape, and his jealousy of the Pretender's claim on Lady Catherine's affections, might have driven him to complete the Pretender's "Hell" in this manner. Another frightful consideration is that here might lay the reason why the Pretender was not eviscerated alive. To do so would have meant exposing his private parts to the view of the crowd and raising questions Henry VII preferred to leave dormant, such as why a king would need to castrate

---

28 Ibid., p. 455.

29 Ibid., p. 449. As his biographer notes, the question of why he escaped seemed unanswerable, since he had to know Henry would track him down and kill him.

a boatman's son when the fraud Lambert Simnell was permitted to lead a normal life.

The difference in Henry VII's behavior with regard to Lambert Simnell and the Pretender indicates his different view of them. With Simnell, he used straightforward and reasonable methods to prove him an imposter, but with the Pretender, his strange behavior suggests that he considered him a viable threat to his throne. An obvious fraud could never have engendered such fear.

Most conveniently for the Tudors, Henry's captive, Elizabeth Woodville, the mother of the princes, died in 1492 as soon as the news first broke that one of her sons was alive, eliminating any possibility of a definitive verification of his identity. Queen Elizabeth of York might have done so in her mother's stead, but the Pretender was never allowed to confront any of the princesses who might have been his sisters. Neither did he confront Sir James Tyrell, who Sir Thomas More later claimed had murdered the two princes in the Tower. At the time, very curiously, Tyrell was in Henry VII's good graces and in charge of the Guisnes garrison.

It is generally accepted that the Tudors were ruthless and had little compunction about eliminating those who stood in their way. Since Isabella and Ferdinand of Spain considered the Pretender to be the Duke of York, they would not have sent their daughter to England without the death of the one they considered the legitimate heir of Edward IV. Henry VII executed Edward, Earl of Warwick, and "Perkin Warbeck" within five days of one another. He aged twenty years in a fortnight as a result and fell so ill he was not expected to live. This has generally been attributed to his execution of young Warwick, but the sin of regicide would have taken a heavy toll, if as suggested, Henry believed the Pretender was the true prince.

In this connection, I must add a few words of explanation regarding the Pretender's death at Tyburn. Most authorities speak of the Pretender being drawn on a hurdle from the Tower, and others have him walking beside O'Water with a halter around his neck. I plead artistic license in not documenting this last indignity and in depicting him as being taken partway by boat. This unfortunate young man had already endured deplorable degradation, and I felt no need to add more such instances to the reader's burden.

As a foreigner, the Pretender could not be pardoned his offenses since he didn't owe Henry VII an oath of fealty. Instead, he was "pardoned of life," with no paper record needed, like a prisoner of war. Yet he was executed as a traitor at Tyburn. To quote Ms. Moorhen, "It is ironical, or even an indication of King Henry's true belief of Warbeck's origins, that he was condemned as a traitor. Warbeck's confession made him a native of the low countries and, therefore, a subject of the Duke of Burgundy. How could he be considered a 'traitor' to the King of England, unless he was born an Englishman?"[30]

Henry VII's choice of burial place for the Pretender is also curious. He was said to have been buried in the Austin Friars on Bread Street, but the Austin Friars was reserved for executed nobility. It could be said that there was an error in the records, since the Austin Friars was located on Broad Street, not Bread Street, and it was Bread Street that was meant, not the Austin Friars. There were two churches on Bread Street where commoners were interred: All Hallows and St. Mildred's, and it would have been strange not to name one of these churches instead of the street. It is specifically the Austin Friars that was mentioned as the Pretender's place of internment, and that church is on *Broad* Street, easily confused with *Bread* Street.

A seventeenth-century chronicler listed all those interred at the Austin Friars before the dissolution of the monasteries, and found no record of the Pretender. Assuming the Pretender was buried at the Austin Friars, why was a boatman's son buried with nobility, and why was his grave left unmarked? Did Henry VII hope no one would notice that a low-born commoner shared a resting place with nobility if his grave was unmarked? Curiously, neither did Henry VII identify Richard III's grave at the Grey Friars in Leicester, choosing to leave it unmarked. Thus, a legitimate Yorkist king lay in an

---

30 Wendy Moorhen, "Four Weddings and a Conspiracy, Part 1," THE RICARDIAN, p. 418.

unmarked grave in a friary, as did the one who claimed to be a legitimate Yorkist prince.

There is, of course, yet another possible explanation for an unmarked grave. There was a belief among the people of Scotland that their chivalrous king, James IV, brought his friend Prince Richard back to rest in the royal vault at Cambuskenneth Abbey. In the end, any of these interpretations further enhances the idea that the Pretender was the legitimate prince.

"Perkin Warbeck" came to fight for a crown but he came without an army, and he came bringing his family. Either he was astoundingly dim-witted, and so were the crowned heads of Europe who supported him, or he was the genuine prince gambling that all he had to do was show himself to his people and they would know him. An imposter would never have dared what this young man dared. In his courage in coming alone to claim his father's crown, I find final confirmation that he had to be who he claimed he was.

Mary Shelley makes the following observation: "The various adventures of this unfortunate prince . . . and his alliance with a beautiful and high-born woman, who proved a faithful, loving wife to him, take away the sting from the ignominy which might attach itself to his fate; and make him, we venture to believe, in spite of the contumely later historians have chosen, in the most arbitrary way, to heap upon him . . . a hero to ennoble the pages of a humble tale."[31]

Catherine lived to see Sir Thomas More and Queen Anne Boleyn beheaded, and died on October 17, 1537. She was buried at St. Nicholas Church, Fyfield. Her lovely manor house, now a private home, still stands across the yew-tree walk. As noted by Ms. Moorhen, it is indeed strange that two of Lady Catherine's four husbands were involved in efforts to depose Tudor monarchs. That she believed her husband "Perkin Warbeck" was Richard of York, there seems little doubt. She persuaded her other husbands of it and wore black to the end of her life.

---

31 Shelley, p. 4.

Lullaby on p. 26 adapted from Sir Walter Scott.

"This World, My Prison" quotation for p. 135 is drawn from Ann Wroe's *The Perfect Prince*.

Bernard Andre's scene with King Henry VII and the Pretender's wife, which was written at the king's behest, is given verbatim on pp. 170–71.

Select Bibliography

Bacon, Francis. *The History of the Reign of King Henry the Seventh*. Edited by F. J. Levy. Indianapolis, New York: Bobbs-Merrill Company, Inc., 1972.

Baldwin, David. *Elizabeth Woodville: Mother of the Princes in the Tower*. Stroud, Gloucestershire: Sutton, 2004.

———. *The Lost Prince: The Survival of Richard of York*. Stroud, Gloucestershire: Sutton, 2007.

Fields, Bertram. *Royal Blood: Richard III and the Mystery of the Princes*. New York: HarperCollins, 1998.

Gregory, Philippa. *The White Queen*. New York: Simon & Schuster, 2008.

Hammond, P. W., ed. *Richard III: Loyalty, Lordship and Law*. London: Richard III and Yorkist History Trust, 1986.

———. *Richard the Third*. New York: W.W. Norton, 2002.

Kleyn, D. M. *Richard of England*. Oxford: Kensal Press, 1990.

MacGibbon, David. *Elizabeth Woodville (1437–1492): Her Life and Times*. London: Arthur Barker, 1938.

Mackie, R. L. *King James IV of Scotland, A Brief Survey of His Life and Times*. Edinburgh: Oliver and Boyd, 1958.

Moorhen, Wendy. "Lady Katherine Gordon: A Genealogical Puzzle." THE RICARDIAN, vol. XI, no. 139, December 1997, pp. 191–213.

———. "Four Weddings and a Conspiracy: The Life, Times and Loves of Lady Catherine Gordon, Part 1." THE RICARDIAN, vol. XII, no. 156, March 2002, pp. 394–424.

———. "Four Weddings and a Conspiracy: The Life, Times and Loves of Lady Catherine Gordon, Part 2." THE RICARDIAN, vol. XII, no. 157, June 2002, pp. 446–78.

————. "Four Weddings and a Conspiracy: The Life, Times and Loves of Lady Catherine Gordon, Conclusion." THE RICARDIAN, vol. XII, no. 158, September 2002, pp. 494–525.

More, Thomas, and Horace Walpole. *Richard III: The Great Debate*. Edited by Paul Murray Kendall. London: Folio Society, 1965.

Pollard, Anthony James. *Richard III: And the Princes in the Tower*. Stroud, Gloucestershire: Sutton, 1991.

Shelley, Mary. *The Fortunes of Perkin Warbeck, A Romance,* 1830, reprinted by Kessinger Publishing.

Williamson, Audrey. *The Mystery of the Princes: An Investigation into a Supposed Murder*. Stroud, Gloucestershire: Sutton, 1981.

Worth, Sandra. *The Rose of York: Fall from Grace*. Yarnell, Arizona: End Table Books, 2007.

Wroe, Ann. *The Perfect Prince: The Mystery of Perkin Warbeck and His Quest for the Throne of England*. New York: Random House, 2003.